Avenge the Stars

*A story of revenge, found families, and
unexpected romance above the moons of Jupiter*

AVENGE THE STARS

Jaye Ephen

Cover art by Bradley Hemmestad | bradleyhemmestad.com
Aster logo by L. Bernadette Meeker | bernadettemeeker.com
Additional character art by Odette A. Bach | odetteabach.com
Original spaceship designs by A.C. Betts | acbetts.com

Epigraph poetry selections sourced from the Public Domain.
No ownership is implied.

ISBN: | 979-8-8692-6685-9 (deluxe hardcover)
| 979-8-8692-4532-8 (deluxe paperback)
| 978-1-0881-0491-0 (ebook)

This book was typeset in 9 pt Merriweather

For permissions and other inquiries: contact@jayeephen.com

You Got It Group
P.O. Box 8534
Kansas City, MO 64114

10 9 8 7 6 5 4 3 2 1 0

First Edition: March 2024

AvengeTheStars.com

For my special person

and for Mom & Dad, obviously,
who bought me all those books.

This is a safe space.
For a detailed Content Warning, visit page 249.

Table of Contents

When the child of morning appeared,
we drew our ships into the water
and put our masts and sails within them.

Then we went on board ourselves,
took our seats on the benches,
and smote the grey sea with our oars.

— Homer (c. 9200 H.E.) —

PROLOGUE

Falling Star

Shudders rippled the embattled bulkhead as the blasts subsided, scattering clouds of dust to glitter through stagnant air. Jolin Aster pressed a hand against the warped metal and let loose a sigh that peeled her insides. She ached to feel the *Endless Star*'s familiar hum, but her ship was broken. And this was the annihilation of her universe.

Don't be so dramatic, she thought. But even before the latest barrage, Jolin had been borrowing time against a depleted stock. And now? She tilted her head in the silence. A faint hiss emanated from somewhere. Her hand became a fist.

Of *course.*

She raised her left arm. The ACIS chip implanted under her skin obeyed the activation gesture, dutifully projecting a hologram a few centimeters above her wrist. *ACIS, your 'access' to the galaxy!* The old advertisement echoed in her ears, but there was no access, still no outside signal. Had she expected an air leak to be sufficient for a signal to pierce the ancient freighter's passive shielding?

You know, she thought, *I kinda did.* She dismissed the hologram and glared at the sparking row of useless escape pods. As the airlock's green lamp blinked and turned amber behind her, their curved canopies refracted the light, transforming them into mocking smiles.

A sickly gloom shrouded the rest of the cabin. That warning light was her only source of illumination, and amber meant the atmospheric pressure was dangerously low. She felt no ill effects yet, but by the time she did it would be too late.

Isn't it already?

"Starlight." She muttered the word like a curse, punching the bulkhead for emphasis. A dull thrum reverberated through the ship and more gray powder sifted in from overhead, misting gently in the thinning air like a deathbed exhale. Had some craggy hunk of asteroid breached the hull? That would explain the excess dirt. And the unexpected speed at which her atmosphere was depleting.

ACIS flickered, as if trying to respond to her voice. The scrappy, stubborn artificial intelligence node was still clinging to hope. Well, his battery was more than half full, so *he* had significantly more time for a miracle than she did. Jolin scowled at the floating numbers. Fifty-eight percent.

"I always knew you'd outlast me," she said. Typically, the chip went months without a recharge. She had set up a simple distress beacon: *No oxygen, pirates, send help.* It would transmit the asteroid's trajectory, too, but expecting it to reach anyone before she died was delusional. Anyone *helpful*, anyway. Her eyes grazed the overhead.

They were well within range of a network satellite; that was not the problem. It was difficult to find a spot in the solar system without a dedicated ACIS thread—but no signals could get in or out while the shielding was polarized. And she had no way to depolarize it without power to the bridge controls.

Power. Jolin lifted her arm again and ACIS spun to life, still searching for a connection. Holographic voxels raced after one another like a rogue comet chasing its tail. She frowned at the projection. Could there be a way? She crept over to the navigation computer, her magnetized boots clunking awkwardly against the deck.

Artificial gravity had gone first when the attack came. The sudden lack of up and down added to the chaos that accelerated the *Star*'s uncontrolled crash into this hell of ice and rock that Jolin would not allow to become her tomb.

She would *not* end up like the others.

A hand touched her shoulder and Jolin recoiled with a wracking sob. She closed her eyes tight and waited for it to float away. Refusing to look at the bodies tumbling around her had not made them vanish, had not made her feel better. But acknowledging them felt... like nothing, which was so much worse. It was too big. They were all. Dead. And she was not among them due to chance. To random fucking luck.

Tucked firmly in her bunk, Jolin had been able to hunker down after the impact alarm sounded. It happened so fast; one moment she was inside her own imagination, comfortably thumbing through a dog-eared romance novel. The next, her crew, her *family,* were gone and the *Endless Star* smashed into the twelve-kilometer chunk of carbon, iron, and rare metals they were mining for fuel. Days ago, it seemed, though only a few hours had passed.

The initial bombardment ended quickly, but the ship's defense algorithms meant that even as the *Star* fell it pummeled its attackers relentlessly in retaliation. Jolin's job as Tactical Officer was to program those subroutines, and she had always taken particular pride in her abilities. So, knowing now that her self-proclaimed brilliance did nothing to prevent this apocalypse, well... She set her jaw. This was not the time for wallowing.

There. Jolin spied the cable she needed, stuffed under a broken console arm. Carefully extracting it from the tangle of wires, twist ties, and dangling circuit boards, she disconnected the plug and touched it to her forearm. The comet stopped spinning and reformed into hardlight wires that sprouted from her wrist, surrounding the cable and locking it in place. A soft blue glow indicated the connection was successful.

"Power hub," she said, gritting her teeth against the possibility of failure. And the cold. Her voice felt hollow and weak, as if she was defeated already. She shivered. ACIS gleamed for a moment but did not respond. *Oh, right.* No signal meant no voice commands. Her wrist chip was just an access node; ACIS stored the bulk of his personality matrix elsewhere. Or, everywhere?

However *that* worked. Another in a long list of things she would never have the chance to understand. *No, you're gonna survive this.* Her own thoughts chastised her as asphyxiation set in.

Jolin grunted, pulling off her glove with her teeth, then reached over to tap at the connection, scrolling through a list of utilities before selecting the appropriate one. ACIS acknowledged the task with a pleasant ding. The blue glow morphed into three arrows that pulsed patiently, indicating power was flowing out from her arm and into the console. His I/O interface could be converted to provide supplemental power for mobile devices in emergencies, but not for long. And certainly not for anything so big.

"It has to be enough," she whispered. The console answered her with a clank and a *whirr* as its buttons and screens glowed dimly, then darkened. *Please, be enough.* She tapped the shielding toggle. Nothing. She hit it again. Not even the familiar and annoying error noise she hated, which would be a welcome sound for once.

"Well, shit." She smacked the floating glove away from her face and watched it spin drunkenly across the cabin. Faraday shields were useful over long voyages on established intra-system trade routes that pirates might frequent. They kept the ship—and its crew and cargo—hidden from most long-range and internal scans. They saved power too, compared to active electromagnetic shields, which was its own reward.

But running silent provided you an unearned sense of security. It did not make a ship invisible; if somebody knew where to find it, or simply stumbled onto it... The *Star* had been a ripe fruit when the pirates caught up to them.

That was Jolin's guess at what had happened, anyway. No way to know for sure without questioning those directly involved. Which was something she intended to do personally, once she figured out how to save herself from dying alone on this jagged rock in the middle of nowhere. And she *would* figure it out. There had to be something besides just waiting to die.

Jolin pulled her jacket tight across her chest and watched ACIS's battery indicator drain. Forty-eight percent. Thirty-seven. A countdown to the end of both of them. And for what?

"I'm sorry." She sighed. Her misty breath sparkled like stars.

With an abrupt cacophony, the controls screamed to life and a metallic buzz alerted her to the shield lifting. ACIS spun awake and an afternoon's worth of notifications blew up Jolin's inbox. She could not withhold a yelp of excitement. The console must have just needed to warm up a bit.

Blinking back unexpected tears, she updated her coordinates in the distress beacon and submitted it with a *whoosh* just as the power faded and the shielding clicked back into place.

"Thanks, friend," she whispered.

"We'll get throu—" ACIS said, and then he was a comet again. Not bad for a subcutaneous bit of circuitry. His battery was still at... she glanced at the corner of the display. Thirteen percent, even. The lights sputtered out as the console's capacitors discharged, returning Jolin to the murk of her ochre isolation.

The amber lamp flickered and faded to red, bathing the cabin in blood. Nothing left to do but drown in her own cast-off carbon dioxide. Jolin maneuvered herself to the penjing display along the aft bulkhead, beneath the ship's bronze nameplate.

The miniature garden was a memento of her Chinese ancestry, and the only interest she had allowed herself to inherit from her father. She blew on the little trees and shrubs, imagining they were making a special effort to recycle her breath into extra fresh oxygen just for her. It was as good a way to spend your last minutes as any she could imagine.

Except...

Trudging back through the bridge and down the stairs to the crew deck, she made the trek to her cabin and rummaged under the blankets for her novel. They were frozen stiff with the coffee she had spilled in her haste.

Ah, yes. She found it wedged between the mattress and the bulkhead. She had lost her place, unfortunately, but it was one of her favorites. *Alisa and the Cyborg.* She had read it a dozen times and could jump in anywhere.

The *Endless Star* groaned, settling further into its ignoble resting place. Clutching the book to her chest, Jolin clomped her way back to the lifeboat and planted herself against the hull near her penjing pots. She yawned, tracing her finger along the flowing inscription on the first page, then picked a chapter at random. Oh, this was a good part; Alisa and her Cyborg companion realizing they were falling in...

Not yet.

Two solid *thunks* impacted the hull above her head and Jolin opened her eyes in a panic. How long had she slept? Did the pirates return to finish her off? ACIS wobbled as she flicked her wrist; the clock showed almost an hour had passed. And she was still alive?

Her mag boots remained attached to the deck, but she was floating free inside them, dangling in the near weightless environment. Bending her knees to regain control of her posture and orient herself, Jolin tugged at the straps, securing the boots around her feet. She straightened, squirreling the paperback inside her vest, and flexed her fingers.

Tossing away that glove had not been her biggest mistake today, but her right hand ached and burned from the cold. She peered into the dark. Where had it—

The deck convulsed, and her knees twisted under sudden inertia. The *Endless Star* was moving. That should have been concerning, but Jolin could not make herself care all that much; she was floating now, relaxed and calm. Sleepy. Which she supposed was a byproduct of CO_2 poison...

I want to live.

Another bump jolted her awake. She tucked her freezing hand inside her vest and looked around. It was difficult to see; more difficult to move. Her eyelids wanted to stay closed, and cold seeped into the cracks between her bones.

The ship quaked, as if tugging loose from something, then stopped. Papers, cables, and bodies lurched up off the deck, spinning and bouncing off one another in a morbid dance. Jolin hugged herself. So, this gorgeous old wonderful ship was to be her grave after all? She could conceive worse coffins to be buried in, and it was no less than she deserved for her failure. Buried with her family.

The Stars, they called themselves. It was a silly name, but none of them cared, and the homespun deliberateness of it attracted Jolin immediately. A patchwork team of disparate individuals united in common purpose. Work hard, get paid, retire early. Some of them had been at it for decades, conveniently forgetting that whole "retire" part. She tried to smile, but her face would not obey. Six souls, including her. *Six Stars.* Leannx Quin. Andreas Gonzales. Mira Rou...

Jolin drifted toward sleep and thought about her first day aboard the *Endless Star.* Her first time journeying towards a future she actually chose, one that was not just an escape from a worse past. She remembered the texture of the chairs, the smell of Mira's vegan cooking in the galley. A flutter of punches, throws, and laughter on sweat-slick gym mats. The captain handing her a gift... what was it? Something important. A flower? Tears froze to her eyelashes.

Their faces blurred, as though she was viewing them from behind a sheet of ice; their smiles and laughter shrouded and silenced forever. She would have liked to save them; that would have been nice. Failing that, to bring them peace. Or justice. Perhaps she could come back as a ghost, reaping bloody vengeance upon... upon... what was she saying? *Huh.* Everything was so cloudy, so cold.

As she faded away, for good this time, Jolin dreamed she heard the muted sound of a laser torch sawing its way through the *Endless Star*'s forward hull, like the devil's hands clawing up from hell to drag her into darkness.

I stepped from plank to plank
So slow and cautiously;
The stars about my head I felt,
About my feet the sea.
I knew not but the next
Would be my final inch,—
This gave me that precarious gait
Some call experience.

— *Emily Dickinson (c. 11860 H.E.)* —

1

Mistakes

Metal clanged against metal, pounding her brain like a jackhammer as Jolin awoke in an unfamiliar place. Her wrists were tied behind her and she was face down in a slow-swinging hammock that reeked, she was certain, of rat farts. The noise faded to an aching and insistent *thrum* even as she became aware of it. She could not pinpoint its source from this position, but she knew she definitely wanted it to stop.

"Would you *quit* it?" she yelled. Or tried to. She wrapped her lips around the gag; perhaps that was the source of the smell. She worked at it with her teeth but recoiled when her tongue brushed the oily cloth. *Gross.* Jolin coughed, and her brain squirmed like ten-day-old nutrient mush. At least she was not dead. Unless... wait, *was* she dead?

She had a dim memory of the devil himself hoisting her up and slinging her over his beefy red shoulder. That may have been a dream. Well, part dream, part romance novel. She smirked, then attempted to swing her legs over the edge of the hammock and discovered restraints around her ankles as well.

Trying a different tactic, Jolin stretched her arms toward the knife she kept sheathed at the small of her back. It was gone. Of *course* it was gone, and so was her jacket. And her mag boots! She rubbed her sock feet together irritably. At least her vest and pants were in their proper place, which brought a slight relief. *Extremely* slight. Pulling her knees up under her belly and struggling to balance, she lifted her head to peer past the hammock... and immediately spun out of it, smashing her face on the floor as she landed in a heap.

"Whoa," a voice said. It did not *sound* devilish; one of his lesser demons, maybe, but not the Actual Devil. "Relax, you'll hurt yourself."

"I will not be bound!" Her shout presented itself as a muffled moan.

Her face was on fire. Was her nose broken? A broken nose would be a first... among a sea of firsts. She refused to panic, which was good, since the impact had deflated her fighting spirit. Half embarrassed, half weary, she tugged limply at her bindings. Perhaps this demon would pity her, lower its guard. And then she would strike, like a coiled cobra. Just, maybe a quick nap first?

A wave of nausea rolled over her, and she convulsed as powerful hands lifted her by her armpits and deposited her in a seated position on the floor, legs to the side. Jolin squinched her eyelids tight until the discomfort passed, then risked a brief reconnaissance. She was not in a cell, at least. It was a... makeshift kitchenette? A galley or common area of *some* sort. She blinked, noting a neat row of dingy metal appliances and a sink that *drip, drip, dripped.*

Her eyes widened as she appraised her captor. He was half bald with deep brown skin, and built like a bunker. A thin black goatee framed his kind, craggy face. Then again... She squinted; the light was awfully dim. Well, if not strictly *kind*, he at least seemed concerned.

"Get your bearings," he said. "The straps are just a precaution." His hands were wide, palms out. An attempt to placate her?

She decided to stare daggers at him, and not because it was all she could do at the moment.

"We thought you were dead in there," he continued. "But apparently people have come back from worse." He lumbered back to sit in a wooden desk chair near a... cozy breakfast nook? What kind of pirate ship was this? The chair groaned beneath his bulk, but held firm. For now.

"And the gag?" she tried to say.

He narrowed his eyes thoughtfully, tilting his head like a puppy confronting a treat he could not reach. That told her everything she needed to know about him.

"You're on my ship. Well, *our* ship." He gestured vaguely around. A sealed hatch stood beyond a thick wood table that was fastened to the deck with rusty bolts. A single steaming mug sat on it.

"And who is 'our'?" she mumbled into the grimy cloth.

"Listen, I can't..." He sighed, leaning forward. "I don't understand you with that gag in."

"Oh really? What a surprise!" She followed that up with a few choice words she had learned in the Galileo Undertunnels.

He regarded her quietly, dark eyes considering. Was he smiling? She snarled.

"Okay," he said at last, "I'm going to take it off, although I'm not a hundred percent sure I actually want to hear what you're saying." He got to his feet amid a symphony of creaking wood and glanced warily down at her. "I've seen people with those ACIS implants before. Please don't try to take over my ship."

Take over the ship? Jolin peered down at her wrist. Well, in that direction. The chip was too small to be detected on casual examination, so how did he know it was there? Flexing her forearms against the straps, she shrugged. More importantly, why did he care? ACIS was a sophisticated system, and she had read about master hackers using their nodes remotely to assume control of all manner of technology, but entire ships? Hers was mostly for email. And shopping. And okay, yes, the occasional equipment hack. *Very* occasional. She tried to give him her sweetest, most innocent smile around the musty gag.

"I'd prefer not to carve that chip out of your arm, is what I'm saying." His voice took on an abrupt intensity, as if disciplining a temperamental child. If you called threatening harm to a child discipline. It certainly worked that way in Jolin's experience.

"But I will if I have to," he continued. "If you force me to."

Intriguing. All right, maybe she did not know *everything* about him just yet. Shaking off the cobwebs of memory, she studied his face. A trim swath of graying hair flanked his brick-shaped dome, which made his ears seem bigger than they were. It lent him a sweet, dopey earnestness. Although, that sharp edge still glimmered below the surface. Underestimating his capacity for violence would be a mistake.

She would tiptoe until given a chance to... do what? She took in her surroundings. An old couch set up in front of an entertainment center. A dining table. Other scattered bits of grungy, scavenged furniture around the central kitchen area. This was not a ship accustomed to holding prisoners. Of course, she had no idea whether she was in open space, docked, or even aboard a ship at all, despite his claim. The hum beneath her knees could be engines, a reactor, or neither. It did feel familiar, though.

Relax, you've been in worse situations, she thought. That she could not bring one to mind right away only mildly concerned her. Finally, she nodded, and the big man carefully pulled the gag over her head. Jolin sputtered and stretched her jaw.

"I've never known a pirate who took prisoners," she growled, her voice hoarse. So much for tiptoeing.

"Pirate?" To his credit, he seemed offended. "We responded to your distress call."

Jolin scowled. Blood from her nose dripped onto her lip, and the big man clucked at her. He reached into his pocket and withdrew a handkerchief.

"May I?" He held it out. Her scowl deepened, but she nodded again. Gently, he wiped her nose. It stung like hell, but not enough to be truly broken. Probably. "There," he said, leaning back to admire his handiwork. "You took quite a tumble."

She rolled her eyes. "That happens every time somebody ties me up, gags me, and tosses me in a smelly hammock."

"I'm sorry about that." He folded up the bloody handkerchief and almost stuffed it back in his pocket, fiddling with it awkwardly for a moment before letting his hand drop to his side. "We just, you were... violent. When we saved you." He held up his right arm, showing bloody gauze wrapped around a meaty bicep. "I got stabbed."

"You're saying I *stabbed* you?"

"Yes." He walked over to the galley and laid the handkerchief in the sink, then lifted a familiar blade. "With this."

"My knife," she said, hiding a smile. *Excellent.*

"This is *not* a knife." He held it up to the light. Almost twenty centimeters long, with a wicked, serrated edge that smoothed and widened toward the tip, it had been a reliable companion over the past decade. He set it back down on the counter. "It's a war crime."

Jolin snorted, which was a mistake. Blood shot out of her nose onto her vest and the floor. "Sorry." She grinned at him. What a sight she must be! He took it in stride. Another point in his favor. "What's your name anyway, big fella?"

"Ajax." He retrieved the handkerchief and trundled back toward her. "Ajax Marquez. Captain. If I untie your hands, are you going to attack me?"

She thought about it. As big as he was, it would be a quick fight. Or a long, ugly one. Neither was likely to end with her the victor. Plus, the simple act of sitting here without falling over was tuckering her out, as if they had already fought. And she lost. Better to be patient, get more information, and formulate a better understanding of her situation. Then, as previously strategized, she would strike like a Rhean Ice Commando. It was a good plan.

Jolin shook her head. Another mistake; her eyeballs sloshed around like tepid water in a leaky bucket. "Ohhh. Yeah, all right Ajax, you win," she whispered, blinking away the pain. "I'll behave."

He nodded, then laid the handkerchief over her shoulder before kneeling with a grunt to wrestle the knots loose with his thick fingers. He was *so* big. Too big. An aging Greek god. Hence the name, probably. Wait, was Ajax a Greek thing? History never held much of an interest for her, and that was, what, ten thousand years ago? Then her arms were free. She groaned and dragged her tingling hands around front to massage her wrists. The straps had not been overly tight, but she must have strained against them pretty hard at some point. Wide bruises and burns told the story well enough, despite her fuzzy memories.

Jolin grabbed the handkerchief and wiped her face. The back of her mouth was copper coated. She swallowed. Her throat burned too, and somehow the musty rat stink remained. What *was* that?

"Say Ajax..." She licked her cracked lips. "You wouldn't know a place nearby where a girl could get a drink of water?"

"Oh, of course." He hoisted himself to his feet and meandered over to the sink. As soon he turned his back, Jolin pulled her legs from under herself and tugged at the knots around her ankles. Her muscles screamed in protest, but she was on her feet a moment later with the holes in her socks pressed against the cold metal floor slats.

It *was* a ship; Jolin recognized the hum of the engines against her toes now that she had a better angle on it. She tensed her legs to run and almost screamed as a red-hot sewing needle punctured her right calf. She bit her lip instead, bending down to massage it.

"Cramps?" Ajax filled a mug with water from the faucet and made his way back to her. He did not seem concerned that she was standing. Taking her at her word? Alternatively, he had made the same calculations about how a fight between them would go.

If she had her knife it would be different. Maybe. Her eyes darted to where it lay on the counter. *No, not yet.* After the pain subsided, she accepted the mug and gulped the water greedily.

"It's a common side effect of cryo-stasis, I've heard." His voice was distant thunder.

"Thanks," she said, wiping her mouth with the cloth. "That is exactly what I needed."

"You're welcome."

"So…" She handed him back the empty mug. "What now?"

"That depends on you."

"All right." She glanced at his wound. "I'm sorry about your arm." *Wait.* Had he said *cryo-stasis?* She searched her memories and found only fragments. Heartache and death; fading away in the dark of a ruined ship. What was a dream and what was real? "How did I get here, anyway? You said there was a distress signal?"

He set the mug on the table and gestured to the empty chair. Jolin was not quite ready to trust him not to tie her up again, so she declined. Sitting *would* be nice, though. Even just a brief rest. Lead coated her bones, and her feet dragged against a well-worn throw rug as she shuffled a few meters away to lean against a rickety cabinet filled with old video tech. The wood creaked and shifted. Like the chair, it could collapse at any moment.

"That's right," he said, "a simple message and some trajectory coordinates."

"No oxygen, pirates, send help," she whispered. Ajax seemed a little confused by that, but she ignored him. Confusion seemed to be his default state. But even as she said it, the air grew thin around her and a frozen body floated past, bouncing off the table, long silver hair splayed out like a holiday wreath. She looked away, dispelling the image.

"ACIS," she said, raising her arm. She gritted her teeth to tame the tremble in her voice.

Ajax tensed, but made no aggressive move. She eyed the captain warily. The trust he was showing her was worth reciprocating. For a little while longer, anyway. Until she figured out *why* he was trusting her.

"Yes, Jolin?" ACIS spun to life, the hologram forming into a question mark above her wrist.

"Where are we?" she asked. A three-dimensional map appeared, focused on Jupiter and three of its moons. The sun was a pinpoint at the center. Leaning forward, she gnawed at her bottom lip. It was a dream; it had to be. "And the *Star*?"

"I'm sorry," ACIS intoned. "The damage was catastrophic."

Jolin's stomach sunk past her feet. *Push past it. Now is not the time.* She rolled her shoulders until her spine cracked.

"The star?" Ajax cut in. "You mean the sun?"

"No. My ship, the *Endless Star*. The freighter." She frowned. He did not seem to understand. Why? "The wreck you pulled me out of?" she insisted. "Was anything salvageable?"

"Well, uh, Jolin was it?" he continued.

She nodded impatiently.

"We found you in an escape pod. There was no ship."

"An escape pod?" Jolin caught a glimmer of memory, light pouring in through a gash in the hull; her fist gripping her knife so hard it was numb. "How long?"

"Sorry, I don't—"

"ACIS, how long?" she interrupted, holding up her free hand to silence the man.

The hologram jittered, hesitating.

"Don't make me say it again." Her mouth was so dry.

"It would be better if we were alone," ACIS replied.

"Tell me *now*."

"Six years, five months, twenty-two days, twenty hours, eleven..."

No. ACIS faded away. Ajax, the ship, the whole galaxy faded away. All she could hear was her own pulse thrashing against the insides of her ears. *No!* She fell to her knees, or would have, but Ajax was there in an instant. He caught her respectfully, holding her up with an arm under hers, and guided her to the chair. She sat without a struggle. Everything was... So... Heavy.

"I need to..." Her voice faltered. To what? Build a time machine? There was no going back. The pirates who killed her crew were gone. *Six years* gone. Her heart twisted inside her chest. She needed a minute to rest, to think. ACIS melted into her wrist as she lowered her arms. Curling her fingers, she took a deep breath and pressed her fists into her thighs. Hard, as if the pressure would keep her from floating away.

Ajax knelt in front of her. "I'm sorry. That seems like a lot to take in. I don't know what to say." The smooth timbre of his voice was a thunderstorm on the horizon.

"It's all right," Jolin whispered. That was a lie. Nothing was close to all right, but she set it aside, forbidding herself to get upset. What would that accomplish? Her entire universe had just shattered. Yelling, screaming, throwing a tantrum could not fix this. *Starlight.* Pain in her right leg throbbed in time with her pounding heartbeat.

Shards of memory blipped into existence. The attack. Destruction. Death. Her injuries reassembled themselves in her mind incongruously; she saw fists and kicks, hands tightening around a belt. She almost put her arms up to defend herself from the blows, but they were echoes.

What happened to her out there in the dark? It was too much; her brain refused to process it. She forced her hands to relax and willed herself into an unsteady calm, then reached up to scrub a tear from her cheek with her thumb. It came away bloody.

One crisis at a time. Each new answer would lead to the next. So, none of it seemed to fit together? Break the puzzle apart into manageable pieces. Figuring out how she had ended up in an escape pod for half a decade, for instance, was easy enough. That was an integral piece. ACIS would know, and he had not said, which meant...

"Captain Marquez." She adjusted her vest, pushing her fear and confusion into its well-worn pockets. Those stains would need to be addressed as well. Goosebumps raised on her bare arms. Where was her jacket? No. *You have given yourself a mission; stay on it.* "Is there somewhere private I can go?"

"Oh." He looked around nervously, then set his jaw. "Of course." He strode over to the locked hatch, apparently on a mission of his own now. "There are guest cabins below. You can take your pick of the empty ones." He observed her for a long interval, his tilted head now accompanied by an apprehensive glower. A puppy deciding if the out-of-reach treat was worth the effort.

Jolin made a decision of her own, meeting his gaze. "You can trust me." She gathered herself and rose from the chair, amazed at how solid she suddenly felt. Connected to the world around her again.

Having a concrete task to focus on always helped with her equilibrium, and she realized too that she believed it; Ajax *could* trust her. Leaving her knife behind, she joined him. She knew where to find it if the situation changed. What she needed most right now was a quiet place to get some answers.

2

Proximity Alert

Ajax pressed a thumb to the scanner. The hatch slid open with a clunk and a hiss, revealing a long central corridor with a stairway at the far end. To the right and left, more stairs led down to the living quarters, Jolin assumed, if this boat was laid out like similar ships.

The big man stepped through and tapped a console on the bulkhead. "Isabella," he said, "we're clear."

"All right, Daddy," came a voice that echoed through the entire vestibule. *Daddy?* She sounded young, but not childlike. "Not a moment too soon, either."

Bare feet descended the stairs at the end of the corridor, followed at once by a willowy woman with rich black skin wearing baggy gray leggings. Jolin's breath caught in her chest. The woman's short black hair crested in a tight wave, shaved on one side and tinted purple at the tips in stark contrast to the bright green of her sleeveless shirt.

"We've got a proximity alarm," she said.

No, not a child at all. Against her will, Jolin's eyes traveled the full length of the young woman's body as she approached.

She gave Jolin a little wave. "Hi there."

"Uh, hi?" Jolin returned the gesture awkwardly.

"Isabella will show you to your room. I need to see what this is." Ajax nodded at her, then strode purposefully toward the stairs Isabella had come down. The bridge would be in that direction. Jolin had been on ships like this before, even served on one for a couple of years. Never in civilian hands, though.

Isabella smiled. "You're awake." She was calm and confident, but her voice was warm.

"I'm, hmm." Jolin coughed. The woman smelled like autumn. She was

26

not sure what to do with her hands. "Yes? I mean, no."

"You're not?"

"Sorry, I've just had some news that wasn't—" Jolin broke off as the ship shuddered. Cannon blasts? Was she a magnet for pirates now?

"Please." Isabella motioned to the stairway closest to her. "Let's get you situated. We can talk another time, now that my father says you're safe."

"Are we under attack?" Jolin took a few steps toward where Ajax had gone. No, she refused to believe the attack was because of her. It had to be a coincidence.

"It's probably just debris, or ice, from ships venting their waste canisters too close to the station."

"Ah. Which station? No, wait." Jolin paused as her mind caught up with the other thing Isabella had said. "I'm *safe*?"

"Safe enough." Isabella shrugged, moving to stand between Jolin and the end of the corridor. "Or he would've left you tied up, right?"

"Fair." Jolin smirked. "Nobody's ever called me *safe* before."

"Does that make you uncomfortable?"

"It doesn't," Jolin admitted. "Surprisingly." She peeked past Isabella toward the front of the ship. "If I'm so safe, though, maybe I can be helpful in ways that don't include being sent to my room?"

Isabella sighed. "You're not going down, are you?"

The barest hint of a smile crinkled Jolin's cheek, and the other woman's eyes widened. Was she blushing? Isabella cleared her throat and looked away. "Well, come on then," she said, then strode up the corridor.

Jolin followed for two paces, then twisted back toward the galley, her hand reflexively moving to her belt. No, better to continue earning trust. Besides, it would not take long to jog back if they got into any knife-fight situations.

Jog? Who was she kidding? She was barely upright. Perhaps she could find a blaster somewhere on this ship. Her hip felt empty without one hanging at her side. Making a note to keep an eye out, she hustled to join Isabella, who was headed up the stairs without her.

The bridge opened into a wide oval with bright display windows all around. The stairs were set in the floor just aft of the oval's center, making for an imposing view as she ascended. Jupiter loomed ahead, half in darkness like the cover of one of her pulp novels. Magnificent. She suppressed a sudden urge to pose in front of it with a blast rifle and a robot companion.

To starboard, the sun was just a pinpoint of light, but she could pick it out. This was a warship's Combat Information Center. Specifically, a Homeland Defense Force Leonidas Class destroyer. How had a beauty like this ended up in civilian hands? Captain Marquez stood at one of three adjacent consoles in the middle of the chamber, studying the glittering readout of a holo-display.

He glanced at Isabella as she slid into the chair next to him, then caught sight of Jolin in his periphery and frowned.

Isabella shrugged. "She's fine, right?" She beckoned Jolin to join them.

"This is a warship, Ajax," Jolin said as she approached.

"It is." He nodded. "Or, was. Decommissioned now, stripped of all the good bits. But we have a few cannons and decent scanners."

"And a bump drive?"

He barked a laugh. "That was the first thing they removed."

If Jolin missed anything from her days in corporate security, it was reliable access to Sigrid drives. Specifically, the ability to travel from one end of the system to another in moments. People called them bump drives because of the feeling you got when a Sigrid wave engaged, as if your stomach were being pulled inside-out and refolded.

But an upset tummy was a small price to pay for unlimited freedom. Well, limited only by resources. Few non-government ships could afford to install one, let alone keep it fueled and maintained. Only billionaires, various commercial transportation companies, and the occasional wonderful old junker.

"Take a look." Isabella slid a wireframe hologram from her smaller display to Ajax's large one.

"That's *Europa Two*," Jolin offered, glad for the distraction. Europa One was the sprawling base nestled above and beneath the ice on the moon's surface. *Europa Two* the station orbiting above it. That was old military nomenclature, terse and unimaginative. The structures all had their own, more flavorful names, of course. If memory served, Europa One memorialized some long dead astronomer, but Jolin had never been interested enough in history to learn much beyond the callsigns for most places in the system. Not until she met her family, anyway, and visiting all the places she had never been became something of a—*No.* She pushed the thought away.

"It can't be," Isabella said.

Jolin leaned in close beside the captain. It was hard to tell on the hologram, but the station seemed smaller than she remembered. Like half of it was missing. She was unsure; it had been years since she visited Europa. *Plus six*, she reminded herself with a sullen sigh.

"This far out?" Ajax politely removed Jolin's hand from his shoulder, then gestured to enlarge the wireframe image. "Izzie, can you put a live image on screen?"

"Not yet," Isabella said, tapping a few buttons. The ship slowed as another impact rumbled through it.

"What is that?" Jolin whispered, walking around the console to the forward view screens.

Ajax frowned at his display. "It's not plasma fire."

"Could it be ballistics?" Isabella asked. "Or debris?"

"There's nothing out there." Jolin pressed her hand against the graphalon pane. As soon as she finished speaking, a bright flash lit up her face from port side ahead, maybe forty degrees off Jupiter zenith. "ACIS," she said, raising her left wrist to the screen.

"Yes?"

"Can you give me nav paths, declination and right ascension for Jupiter Sphere on the glass?"

"Of course." ACIS spun to life and golden holograms spiraled out onto the pane, creating a three-dimensional representation of a great celestial sphere around the gas giant, including a golden line bisecting it from Jupiter's core straight through into the bridge. Zenith would be directly behind, or *above* her, as related to the center of the sphere.

"It can do that?" Isabella was standing beside her suddenly. "Wow!" She tapped the hologram with a fingertip. It pulsed around her touch.

"He can do lots of things." Jolin grinned.

"So can our sensors," said Ajax. "Izzie, take your station."

Isabella slid her hand across the screen and scampered back to the comms station. The holograms rippled and swayed in her wake, as if beckoning for her to come back.

The glow of the explosion had faded, but ACIS was tracking it for her now as a blinking orange dot. "Is that where *Europa Two* is?" Jolin turned to face her captors. Or were they her rescuers? That likely depended on how she comported herself over the next few minutes. "You can't magnify that any more?"

"No." Ajax shook his head. "But yes, *Europa Two*. Looks like it's wandered out of its orbital path somehow."

"ACIS?" Jolin tapped the window.

"Compliance!" The orange dot's trajectory appeared, superimposed over a projection of its proper path. Ajax was right.

"We do have a logistics station if you want to help," the captain said, pointing at the console to his left.

"Tactical is more my speed." Jolin shrugged. "If something needs to get shot, let me know."

"It's chunks of the station," Isabella gasped, "dozens of them. How are they this close already?" Another crash echoed through the hull.

Jolin frowned. "Wait. Are you saying it exploded?"

"That's one explanation," Isabella said.

"We'll have to break up the larger bits with the weapons." Ajax glanced at Jolin. "Think you can handle that?"

"Don't you have active shields?" Jolin hurried toward the aft console wall, to where she assumed the tactical console would be, based on her experience crewing ships like this, but the station was dark.

"Tactical is mirrored at logistics," Ajax said, pointing again. "And no, our shields went down with that first hit."

"They did?" Jolin scoffed, making her way over to the portside console.

"Shields are finicky. It's on the list," Isabella said. She made a few large gestures across her holo-display. "I'm ceding tactical control to you. Hope you know what you're doing."

"I do." Jolin nodded as her console lit up with a familiar payload of... significantly fewer weapons than she expected. "You only have *four* cannons?"

"Two plasma casters, two fifty caliber Gatlings, and a mining laser," Isabella informed her from across the bridge. "We're *in process*." She made air quotes around a wry smile.

"You're gonna be in pieces if we're not careful." Jolin gripped the edge of the console and slid into the adjoining chair. "ACIS, can you do anything with this?"

"No!" The captain fixed her with a sharp glare. "I said don't hack my ship."

"It's not a hack," Jolin protested. Although... it *was* a hack. Or, it would be. Except this was a military vessel, which is what her ACIS implant was originally designed to supplement. However, she had promised. *Ugh.* It had been a while since she had needed to make new friends. She was rusty, that was all. It wasn't lying, it was... being... rusty? "Fine, let's see what we can do naked."

Isabella snickered, a joyous sound that flooded Jolin's belly with sudden warmth.

She shook it off.

"ACIS show me the shrapnel," Jolin said. Then, glancing over at Ajax she added, "On the screens please."

"Of course," ACIS said, and the holographic display updated to show five new golden dots.

"How is it doing that if you're not hacking my ship?" Ajax asked.

She could tell he wanted to give her the benefit of the doubt, and she was not making it easy for him. But this was not a hack. Not really. Explaining that without divulging more than she would prefer to, however? Well, that *would* be a hack; one she did not have time to contemplate. *Trust them or don't, that's it.*

Fine. "He's, um... listening to your scanner," she said. Her shoulders loosened a little.

"Okay, enough." Ajax stood and took a step toward her, then braced himself on the console as another collision rumbled through the bridge.

"No, I mean it. Not the scanner itself, but the radar or whatever. He's reading the beams!"

"Reading the..." Ajax made a sound Jolin could only describe as *harrumph*. "Hard to believe a wrist computer can do all that on its own."

Jolin grinned. "Oh, mine isn't a regular run of the mill ACIS node." It felt good to tell somebody the truth for once.

"Yours?" ACIS interjected.

"Yes, yes, you're a free, independent entity. I'm just saying, you're inside *my* wrist, so you're mine."

"Are you *arguing* with it?" Ajax said.

"No," Jolin replied.

"Yes," ACIS said at the same time.

"Incoming! Portside, forty-eight degrees by two hundred fifty-one," said Isabella. "Five hundred ninety kilos and closing. Impact in ten seconds."

"Starlight." Jolin tapped the blinking dot on her console that marked the closest incoming hunk of debris, which zoomed in on it and engaged the targeting computer in a process that seemed to take literally forever. She kept count in her head.

Five seconds. It was big, twenty-two meters by sixteen, and oblong. An indirect hit off center mass with one of the plasma casters would change its trajectory enough to miss the ship, like shooting pool. She placed her hand on the manual targeting stick and nudged the reticle a few notches with the thumb dial. *Four.* Perfect. She squeezed the trigger.

The shrapnel split nearly down the middle with the impact. The smaller section was bumped off its vector enough to miss them, but the bigger piece stubbornly careened directly at the ship, spinning now.

Three. Jolin realized she did not even know this crusty old broken down boat's name yet.

"Are you going to—" Isabella started.

"Yeah yeah," Jolin cut her off. *Two.* "I got this." She watched the spinning hunk of metal closely and fired again with the second caster. Direct hit. The debris shattered into a dozen pieces, each too small now to damage the ship at that speed, and most would miss it completely. A few small chunks of metal bounced past the bridge's virtual windows, and scattered impacts reverberated through the hull. But she had done it.

"Impressive." Ajax gave her an appraising look.

"Not really. I used to be better at that. This is my station."

"You're military?"

"Well, it *was* my station," she replied sheepishly.

"Ah." He nodded. "Navy detail?"

"Sitayana Marines. Mostly private security. First Lieutenant Jolin Ga…" She paused. Old habits. *Rank, name, and serial number.* She cleared her throat. "Aster. At your service, Captain." She offered him a crisp salute. "Retired, of course. Or, you know, decommissioned, like your ship."

Ajax smirked at that. If he noticed her slip, he kept it to himself. "An Outbounder? So you're a fighter." He glanced at his injured arm. "Makes sense. And your ACIS is government issue?"

"Yes," she said, drawing out the word. She knew where this was going. Trusting him with a bit of necessary context was one thing, but the full story was not a weight so easily shared.

"They didn't expect it to be returned when you resigned?"

"Oh." She reached back to pull her hair into a ponytail. Then, realizing she had nothing to tie it with, she let it drop. "Would you believe me if I said no?"

"I would not." Ajax pursed his lips, then shrugged those massive shoulders. "But it's none of my affair."

"Well *I* think it's super cool," Isabella said.

"Thank you," ACIS crowed.

"Shut up," Jolin whispered to her wrist. "And you!" She pointed a finger at Isabella. "Don't encourage him."

Isabella's laugh was full-throated and vibrant. Jolin felt a sudden urge to... to what? She realized she was tracing her bottom lip with a fingertip and quickly put her hands in her lap.

"The rest of the debris is going to miss us, Dad." Isabella stood. "And we're close enough for a magnified view of the station now."

"On screen." Ajax stepped back from her console, returning to his chair. "Good work, both of you."

Jolin felt an unexpected jolt of pride at the compliment that she immediately resented. Her tracking hologram vanished as the front windows darkened, and a detailed image of the destroyed space station leaped into view. Broken, warped and ruined, as if a giant pair of hands had twisted it apart right down the middle.

"What do we do?" Isabella walked over to the screen as another explosion flickered orange light into the bridge.

"Someone is probably doing something about it, right?" Jolin looked down at her wrist. "ACIS, anything about this on the news?"

"Nothing yet, Jolin. We may be the first to arrive."

A bright flash flooded the cabin with multicolored light.

"Proximity alert!" Ajax shouted as a bell rang. An actual bell, metal clanging against metal. The familiar sound grated on her nerves in a way it never had before. Just off the port bow, a heavy cruiser appeared, easily dwarfing their own ship. Prismatic ripples of energy spread out in a wide pattern around it, but quickly dissipated. Sigrid wake.

Jolin pinged the cruiser's IDENT from her console and frowned. "It's the *Rosy-Fingered Dawn*," she reported. "Official Senate business, it seems."

"Hmm." Ajax tilted his head thoughtfully. "But we were expecting them."

Jolin's jaw creaked. She made an effort to unclench it. They were *expecting* a federal consort? Apparently Jolin was not the only one with secrets.

"Daddy, we're being hailed." Isabella hurried back to the communications console.

"Put it on speaker," he said.

"...calling derelict frigate *Syracusia*. Cease your attack and surrender for boarding."

"Aw shit," Jolin said.

"This is Captain Ajax Marquez. We will of course submit to boarding, but this wasn't us." He let go of the transmit button and muttered, "*Derelict?*"

"We'll be the judge of that, *Syracusia*. Oh, Admiral, I—" The comms went silent for a moment before a husky voice took over.

"Marquez? This is Grace Lewin."

Ajax scowled. "Admiral."

Jolin recognized the name, but had never met this Lewin. Something tickled the back of her mind that she should probably remember about the woman. She made a note to question ACIS about it later, once she got some time to herself.

"Relax, Ajax. I know you well enough to trust you'd never do something like this."

"Thank you, Admiral."

"Even if I didn't, it's pretty clear those guns of yours aren't sufficient to accomplish this level of destruction. Is there anything you *can* tell us?"

"The station was already damaged when we arrived," Ajax replied. "We got a few holes poked in us by the debris."

A few tiny impacts flashed against the *Rosy-Fingered Dawn*'s electromagnetic shield as bits of the station—and likely the remains of people who had been on board—collided with it. Jolin shuddered.

"Understood," the admiral said. "Come up here and dock with us until the area is secure, if you don't mind."

Ajax gave Isabella an inscrutable look. "Of course. We'll rendezvous immediately."

"See you in a few. Lewin out."

"Comms disengaged," Isabella said. "Do you think—"

"I really don't want to go onto that ship," Jolin interrupted, glancing at her wrist.

"You're not a wanted criminal, are you, Lieutenant Gaster?" The captain's voice was suddenly judgmental. Wary.

"Of course not." She held up her hands. "And it's Aster. The G is silent." So he *had* noticed. Ajax leveled a sardonic smirk at her. Well, it was complicated, and she definitely did not want to talk about it with him. Then again, she had been missing and likely presumed dead for six years. If anyone had bothered to think about her at all.

That was a sobering thought.

Either way, *criminal* was too harsh a word. Did she keep something that did not belong to her? Yes. Did they *know* she kept it? Also yes. Did they still care? Probably. But they would have given up that search years ago, right? She groaned. Merely entertaining the thought reinforced how drained she felt.

"I will just, hmm, stay in my cabin though? Isabella, if you'd still like to show it to me?" She needed to find out what ACIS could tell her, anyway. In private.

"Of course," the young woman said with a bright smile. "Daddy?"

Ajax leveled a glare at Jolin. "Can you promise me you're not involving me in anything nefarious? There are people on board that cruiser I'd rather not witness me being made a fool."

"Captain," Jolin said in her most serious voice, "I solemnly swear they wouldn't even care if they heard Jolin Aster was here." That much was certainly true. "I'm just..." She searched around for the right word, "*reluctant* to revisit that period of my life."

She left the mercenary life behind on purpose, and for good, so that was not a lie either; just not the entire story. "Don't feel you even have to mention me."

"As you wish. I won't deny it if they ask."

"Fair enough." She nodded. "They won't." Was that a hope or a prayer? She honestly was not sure.

"Shall we?" Isabella held out a hand.

Jolin smiled and took it. Isabella's grip was firm and warm, and as she let herself be pulled down the stairs toward the living quarters, Jolin felt the weariness melting away from her insides. Replaced by butterflies.

"There's five empty rooms on the open side," Isabella said. "You can have your pick of any, but I'll show you the best one." Glancing over her shoulder, she whispered, "It's next to mine."

"Oh, sure." Jolin blushed. She watched the gentle sway of Isabella's shoulders as they walked, following the curve of her triceps along her bare arm to the wrist on the hand holding hers. Buttoned low, Isabella's sleeveless blouse flowed like mist over her delicate torso. Jolin caught herself staring and looked away. She let go of the young woman's hand. "How old are you?"

Isabella turned to face her. "Thirty-two, why?"

A relieved sigh escaped Jolin's lips. "No reason I just... You look so young... I just wondered." It was obvious now that she was up close.

Isabella's eyes narrowed. "How old are *you*?"

"I'm uh... Thirty-four?"

"We could be sisters!"

"Um, yeah, sure. Sisters." The heat in Jolin's cheeks intensified, if that were possible, and she cleared her throat. This sudden lack of self-assurance was weird and upsetting; she was embarrassing herself. Another side effect of cryo-stasis?

Jolin turned, trying to focus anywhere else but on those wide brown eyes. Her vest was filthy, blood-stained and blackened with soot. Her trousers were not much better, and she was pretty sure the terrible, lingering rat smell was emanating from her.

"Anyways," she said finally, "I could use a shower. And a change of clothes?"

"Shower is there." Isabella pointed to an open hatchway in the center of the corridor as they descended the stairway Jolin had passed before. "As for clothes..." Isabella stepped back to evaluate her. "Turn around."

"What?"

"Just turn around."

"All right." Jolin turned herself in a little circle. She felt ridiculous, but could not stop herself.

"I doubt anything of mine will fit you," Isabella said. "May I?" She reached her hands out and pressed them to Jolin's waist, under her arms, then to her shoulders, unafraid of the dry blood and dirt. "My mother's old clothes are about your size in the bust and hips, although I think you're taller."

"Oh," Jolin said. She tried not to pay attention to Isabella's hands. This was agony.

"I'll set something out for you, in the lav."

"Okay sure, thanks." Jolin stood there awkwardly for a moment. "Oh, uh, now? I guess?"

Isabella laughed.

"All right, yeah. I'll be, uh, in the shower." Jolin fled toward the lavatory as quickly as her sock feet could carry her. The woman was *gorgeous*. She wanted to die.

The lav was not large. Two showers and three toilets, each in its own stall, and two sinks. A stack of white towels sat on a bench near the entrance, though half had spilled onto the deck. Jolin leaned down to pick them up, stretching her calves and wincing as her knee popped. *Yikes.* She was going to need to soak for an hour just to feel human again. The water recycling on a ship this size would not be robust, and she wondered if that was also *in process*. Nothing to do but hope for the best.

As she turned around, a hideous monster jumped up from behind the sinks. She almost fell over, stumbling away.

From the hideous monster. In the *mirror*.

She was an absolute wreck, dried blood caked in her hair and smeared across her cheeks. *Oh no. No no no.* She collapsed onto a bench and laughed; what else could she do? She laughed until her sides hurt. It felt good to let loose, despite her injuries. She wrapped her arms around aching ribs as her mirth devolved into a coughing fit.

"Off to a great start, Jolin Aster," she muttered when it was over. Hunched over the sink, she peered at her face. She pinched her nose between two fingers and groaned. And her neck! She raised her chin to examine the deep bruise that appeared to wrap fully around her throat, like a noose. Truly she looked like a woman who had been frozen for more than half a decade.

Wait, she inhaled sharply. Six years meant...

"Starlight," she moaned, turning toward the shower and peeling off her blood-soaked vest with a wince.

"I'm *forty*."

3

New Clothes

Isabella was true to her word. Jolin found a neat stack of clothes on one of the slatted wood benches near the lav entrance. It was more a locker room than a lavatory, which made sense on a warship.

A ship this size would have at least a 20-person crew, but the *Syracusia* could probably do with far fewer on a day to day basis, as proved by Ajax and Isabella. How well that arrangement would hold up in a scrap was unknown. They must have been doing something right to keep flying so long, but Jolin would not be there long enough to find out. Hopefully.

She pressed a fluffy towel against her face and dragged it over her head to dry her hair. The shower drain was a murder scene. It had taken twenty minutes of scrubbing just to turn the water from red to pink, but the result was worth the effort; she felt relaxed and renewed.

Tucking the towel under her arms, she leaned over a sink to examine her face, now that she could actually see it. A large red abrasion marred her left cheek from her nose to her ear. That would turn into a nasty bruise, but with luck it would not leave any scarring. Although... was the med bay on this old boat functional? That should be her next stop.

Her nose looked okay, surprisingly. Probing it with her fingers only made her wince a little. She tilted her head to get a better view of the angry red ring around her neck. It was turning purple, but her breathing and swallowing were unaffected. All in, the damage was excessive for a hammock tumble, and she could not keep dismissing those inconsistencies. What exactly had happened before she installed herself into that escape pod six years ago? She had thought about it a lot in the shower, grasping at tendrils of memory that evaded her like smoke.

"Feeling better?" Isabella stood in the entry, hands overhead, gripping the top rim of the hatch. She had changed her clothes too, from the

36

breezy green top and gray pants to a deep blue, long-sleeve blouse and black slacks decorated with thin gold stripes. It resembled an informal homage to a Navy uniform. Almost.

"Like a trillion spacebucks." Jolin smiled at her. Amazing what a little bath did for her self-confidence. She straightened, reflexively checking her towel to make sure it covered her fully.

"I wasn't sure of your style preference." Isabella nodded toward the pile of clothes. "Only that it probably isn't Battlefield Chic."

"Just on weekends," Jolin said. Her jaw ached. "I'm sure they will be fine." She lifted the light brown, button-down blouse. The fabric was thin for her tastes, but it would do. The pants were sturdy denim, well-worn and comfortable looking. Underneath that lay a black sports bra and matching shorts, and although Jolin was not above wearing another woman's undergarments, she typically asked first. "You're sure she won't mind?"

"I'm sure," Isabella said. "She doesn't really need them."

Shit. Annoyed at her thoughtlessness, Jolin stammered. It had not even occurred to her that Isabella's mother was not here on the ship with them, and what that could mean.

Isabella spoke up quickly, perhaps noticing her wheels spinning. "Oh, she's not dead or anything. Just elsewhere. She hasn't touched those boxes in years. And none of this stuff fits her anymore, besides."

"Ah." *Whew.* "Okay. Good. I mean, not good? Unless it is? I just... I really thought I'd put my foot in it for a second there." Yeah, she was *brimming* with self-confidence.

Isabella merely watched her, elegant and poised, with a hint of a smirk on her lips that only accentuated her effortless charms. Scrambling for an escape trajectory, Jolin grabbed the rest of the clothes and scurried back into one of the shower stalls to change, positioning the torn plastic curtain as best she could to hide behind.

She cleared her throat. "Elsewhere? Meaning what, exactly?"

"She's in government," came Isabella's reply. "Well, she was. That's why the *Rosy-Fingered Dawn* is here, actually. And why Dad and I were headed for Europa."

"She's aboard the battlecruiser?" Jolin hung the towel over the curtain rod and struggled into the borrowed undergarments. The top was a little loose, and the denim was a tad snug around her thighs, but it surprised her how well they fit.

"We planned to meet up on the station for a couple days. Do some shopping, eat some food. Catch up."

"Now you'll have to do it on the *Dawn*?"

"That's up to her. I can't imagine mother-daughter time is going to be high on her priority list with what's going on."

"How long's she been away?" Jolin yanked the shirt over her shoulders and did up the buttons. The fingers on her right hand were stiff, but she managed it okay. Tugging her still damp hair through the collar, she wrapped the towel around her head. It was fascinating how just that simple bit of normal peeled a whole layer of stress off of her shoulders. She needed a comb.

"It's been months since I've seen her, but she's been off this ship, and out of Dad's life, for years. They called her up out of retirement for something last month, she couldn't say what."

"Oh, she's on a secret mission!" Jolin fastened the pants and stepped out of the shower stall with a grin, stretching her knees. Her right leg was really throbbing; at least it was holding her weight. "Retirement from what?"

"She was an HDF Navy Captain, before the Senate."

"She's a *Senator*?" Jolin glanced at the mirror and adjusted her blouse. Much better. "Do you think them bringing her out here has anything to do with *Europa Two* being destroyed?"

"Could be? She doesn't really include me in that stuff. Never has," said Isabella. "Though I would hope if they knew it was going to be destroyed a month ago, they could have stopped it from happening. You clean up nice."

"I think the shiner really draws out my inner beauty." Jolin tapped the side of her face, then grimaced in pain. *Smart.*

Isabella's laugh was loud and genuine. "It's barely noticeable."

"You're sweet, but I look like a Saturday Night Blitz fighter on Sunday morning."

"Here." Isabella produced a hairbrush. "This'll help."

"Ohhh." Jolin grabbed the handle gratefully. "Yes, perfect." She unraveled the towel and ran the brush through her tangled nest of black hair. She kept it shoulder-length these days, although she had let it grow past her hips for a while. This was a lot less work, and lower risk of accidentally sitting on it. Or lying on it. Or getting it stuck in a hatch. Not that she ever had.

Isabella's own crisply styled wave was certainly something. There was no way Jolin could pull *that* off with the same easy confidence. She nodded toward Isabella's left arm. "Nice tattoo." Colorful art depicted a snarling crimson dragon coiled around storm clouds.

"Thanks." Folding her arms, Isabella covered the artwork with her fingers, almost absently. "It's, uh, for the ship."

"Oh yeah? The *Syracusia*?" Jolin's knowledge of folklore was limited, but she had never heard any stories about dragons from Syracuse.

Isabella shrugged. "Yeah, it doesn't really have anything to do with the name. I basically grew up here. I designed the dragon when I was a girl because I liked dragons, and I wanted to rename the ship after one. Dad said no, obviously. He has his own reasons behind the name, but he loved the drawing so much he had it painted it on the bow. Or, well... He loved *me.* The drawing was not very good. I guess it was his way of making sure I knew it was my ship too. And this ship kind of *is* me, in a way. Though I'm less into dragons than I once was."

"I get that," Jolin said.

"Really?"

"Sure, I grew up on freighters. Part of the reason I enlisted into Sitayana was to get away from that life, though I ended up missing the freedom. The choice to come and go as I please."

Isabella nodded. "Being on your own with just a close-knit crew of family to rely on."

"Yeah, yeah, you understand. I don't mean merc life wasn't good for me; the structure was life-changing. There's something comfortable about finding your niche as a tiny part of a solar system-spanning machine." She tussled with a particularly stubborn knot. "So, I don't know, there's bits of both that shaped me into who I am, for good or bad."

Isabella chewed on her lower lip thoughtfully.

Shying away from that intense gaze, Jolin focused on brushing. "I can't deny it's nice to be back on a destroyer," she said, "even a broken old junker like this."

"Junker?"

Shit. "Sorry, I know it's—"

"In process, yes."

"It's, uh, been a good home to you both," Jolin tried.

"Yes, it has. But you're not wrong," Isabella admitted. "The 'process' has taken rather longer than it should have, especially since my father acquired *Syracusia* years before I was born." She gave Jolin a sharp look. "Do *not* tell him I said that."

"I promise." Jolin grinned. "Well hey, maybe I can help you out with some of it, while I'm here. I know a few things about these old broads." She tapped the brush against the bulkhead.

"I can tell; you have a certain resonance."

"Resonance?" Jolin glanced down at herself and spun around. "Is that a fancy word for tail? Did I grow a tail in cryo-stasis?"

There was that laugh again. "What? You're ridiculous!" Isabella put a hand on Jolin's arm. "I mean the ship fits you, or you fit the ship, I suppose?" Electricity seemed to jolt her at the touch, and Jolin shook her head to clear a sudden fog. Had it only been a couple hours since they met? Isabella pulled her hand back, staring at it with a curious sort of half-smile, then crossed her arms again. Had she felt it too?

Jolin cleared her throat. "Anyways." She retrieved her towel and hung it on a steel hook by the hatchway, trying to ignore the tingle where Isabella's fingertips had rested. "It's not my first time on one of these."

"Well, I will appreciate your expertise, then." Isabella stood there a moment, watching her, before nodding to herself. "Your cabin is this way."

"Of course," Jolin said, looking around for her old clothes. Keeping herself busy suddenly felt extremely important. They remained in a pile on the floor where she had left them, and looked worse than she remembered. She strapped on her shoulder harness and belt, which had been thankfully spared a macabre soaking due to being under her vest, then folded the rest into a ball and tucked it under her arm. She was careful to keep the bloody bits hidden. No sense soiling her new clothes. She should just chuck it all into the incinerator. It was probably ruined anyway.

Isabella was thinking the same thing, judging by her expression. Jolin had some sentimental attachment to her outfit, though. Especially the vest. Her parents had given it to her as a birthday present when she turned fifteen. It was absolutely covered with pockets and straps and rings, everything a girl with a couple dozen tech doodads to secret away on her person could need. And sure, she had been forced to let it out a few times as the years passed—several inches if she was being honest—but it was her constant companion, and one of a very few happy reminders of her troubled youth.

She had no reminders of the Stars, she realized numbly, and resolved to do something about that. The crew of the *Endless Star* had been a second family to her; and in most ways a superior one. Perhaps a tattoo like Isabella's, of the freighter's symbol, and her own namesake, the purple star flower. Jolin felt an aching twinge churning inside her ribcage, but pushed it away.

"After you," she murmured.

Isabella led her across the narrow corridor to the foremost cabin. "Mine is next door," she said, pointing to the left.

They were on the port side of the ship, and Jolin could hear and feel the steady hum of the engines all around them, which would be accessible down the opposite stairway, starboard side if memory served.

"The electronic locks don't work," Isabella added. "Except the ones for the bridge and the mess, so we're on the honor system. They do latch from the inside though."

Jolin reached for the cabin hatch. It was heavy, with a thick, cylindrical handle that responded reluctantly to a firm turn, and the door screeched open like an SP-1K Interceptor. She recoiled, plugging her ears with her thumbs.

"Sorry!" Isabella held up a finger. "One moment!" She ran aftward and vanished up the stairs. Jolin opened the hatch the rest of the way, despite the squeal, and beheld a spartan chamber with a fold-out bunk, a series of lipped shelves bolted to the walls, and a stack of boxes filling half the room, labeled *Amanita* and *Mom*.

The bunk was sturdy enough, and there was a quaint little desk beside it, though the chair was missing. Perhaps there would be an extra in one of the other cabins. She searched through the drawers, but found nothing of value. A few pens, a set of old stickers of cartoon characters. A dingy gold chain with a—

"Oh. I forgot these were in here," Isabella said. Jolin jumped, closing the desk. She turned around to see her standing in the doorway brandishing Jolin's knife in one hand and a can of lubricant in the other. "The boxes."

"We gotta work on your habit of sneaking up behind me." Jolin eyed the knife. "Especially when you come armed."

"This? Oh shit, sorry." Isabella stepped into the room and carefully placed the weapon on a shelf. "I figured you would want it back. Please, just... don't stab my father again?" She grinned sheepishly, then swiveled around and attacked the hatch hinges with the spray nozzle. "This should take care of that." She grabbed the handle and shoved the door closed. It bounced off its frame with a heavy thunk. No squeal at all.

"Thanks," Jolin said. The two of them stood alone in the cabin, staring at one another. "I guess I'll hunker down here until we undock from the carrier?"

"I could stay with you, keep you company."

"And miss seeing your mother?"

Isabella's smile faltered. "Oh. Right."

"Not that I don't, um, appreciate the offer."

"Sure, of course!" Isabella recovered quickly, glancing at the boxes. "I don't think she'll need anything from those, but just in case, we should move them."

"I could choose a different cabin."

"This really is the best one."

"Fair enough." Jolin wrapped her arms around a large box and lifted it with a grunt. That might have been a mistake, and her leg throbbed in agreement, but she refused to put the thing down.

Isabella hefted two of the smaller boxes. "This way."

Following her to the aftmost cabin, Jolin supported her box on a hip while waiting on Isabella to get the hatch open. Her arms were already burning from carrying it a few meters; she was looking forward to taking a nap. After six years asleep it was weird that she did not have more energy. Then again, the science behind cryo-freeze was not her area of expertise. Nor was *any* science that did not involve plugging and unplugging cables, swapping engine parts, programming weapons systems, or scuttling through cramped maintenance tunnels in greasy overalls.

Jolin stepped through and gained a sudden appreciation for what Isabella meant by *best*. This cabin was a wreck. The bunk had fallen off the bulkhead and the shelves were busted. Another stack of boxes lived here, too. Older, more neglected, and labeled *Wedding*.

Jolin set her burden down on the deck inside and straightened with a groan. "It ain't easy being forty," she whispered.

"Forty? You don't *age* in stasis!" Isabella grinned, setting her boxes on top of the other.

"Then why do I feel so old?" Jolin arched her back. Had she told Isabella any of that? Ajax must have filled his daughter in on the details of her long sabbatical.

"Age is but a construct in the *World of Tomorrow*," the younger woman quoted.

Jolin gasped. "That's my favorite show."

"Mine too!"

Their shared laughter was truncated by a ship-wide shudder. Jolin recognized that feeling. They had docked. Curiously, Ajax had not accomplished that while she was in the shower, but there were many reasons it could have taken this long. None of them good.

"Starlight," she muttered.

"You've invested that word with some personal significance, haven't you?" Isabella asked.

"What?"

"Starlight. I heard you say it before."

"Oh, it's..." Jolin struggled to explain. "It's something my mother would say, an old song. Star light, star bright?"

Isabella nodded. "I know it."

"It was about wishes, that the stars would hear them, and grant them."

"A nursery rhyme."

"I was a kid." Jolin shrugged. "I remember wishing for something so hard, so many times..." She felt no need to elaborate. Even thinking about it, about her mother, disturbed the edges of an ocean of unpleasantness, and she had enough going on already. It surprised her she had revealed even this much. She met Isabella's gaze. "And for it not to happen, because of *course* it didn't... I don't know, I just... Eventually it felt more like a curse to me than a wish."

"That makes sense." Isabella reached over and took Jolin's hand.

"Your mother is probably excited to see you." Jolin gave her hand a squeeze, a *sisterly* squeeze, and let it go. There was no sense pushing things further with Isabella than necessary. She would not be on this ship for more than a few days, until they made port. A sudden longing twisted around her stomach, and Jolin stuffed her hands into her pockets.

"The boxes..." Isabella's brow knitted.

"I can move the rest," Jolin offered. The urge to flee this awkwardness was palpable.

"No, no, I can't let you do that," Isabella said, visibly mortified. "Here... just, hide out in my room?"

"I'm not hiding!"

"I know, I know, sorry." Isabella grabbed her by the shoulders and shoved her toward the hatch. "Take a nap then, or check your email. You must have a million! Whatever you want. I'll get my father to take care of the boxes tonight."

"It's your ship," Jolin said. She let herself be guided, and despite her misgivings her insides fluttered anew. *You're a fool*, she scolded herself. *Isabella has bigger things on her mind than you.* That realization offered zero comfort.

She stopped short as the hatch opened. A plush green carpet ran the length of the cabin, and the walls were painted in a springtime blue sky. It was nice. Cozy. *Immaculate.* There was even a bean bag chair. Instead of rickety shelves a tall, wooden armoire stood against the bulkhead, and a mountain of pillows spilled off the bed.

And the smell, lavender and—

"Please." Isabella gestured for her to enter. "Make yourself at home. I'm sure this won't take long."

"I will." Jolin slumped into the bean bag. It was more comfortable than she had dared to hope. She let go of a long breath and ran her fingers through her damp hair.

"Oh, here." Isabella rushed over to the desk. Opening a drawer, she shuffled through a few things before pulling out a brown hairband. She tossed it over. "For when it's dry," she said.

Jolin stuck her wrist through it. "Thanks."

"Great, of course. I mean, good. I'll see you." Isabella hesitated. "*We'll* see you. In a bit."

"Of course," Jolin echoed. There was definitely a connection between them. She was *not* imagining it, was she? No, it was there.

Isabella opened her mouth to speak, then snapped it shut and stepped out into the passageway with a shy smile, pulling the hatch closed and leaving Jolin alone with her thoughts. And her questions.

Ignoring the insistent and inconvenient desire bubbling inside her, she settled into the bean bag and raised her arm. "Not a word, ACIS."

"About what?" The hologram shimmered to life. Why did that little question mark look like a smirk?

"You *know* what.," she said. "But thanks." He always had a wry com-ment. She would be concerned about the lack if she did not have so many other things to be concerned about.

"Of course. How can I help you this morning?"

"I think it's time you show me what happened."

"Are you sure you want to know?"

Jolin snorted. "Well, I *was* sure. Now I'm not."

"Lie back. Engaging neural link."

She sighed and closed her eyes. It did not matter whether or not she was sure, that was the thing; she needed to know. And yet creeping dread skittered at the edges of her mind, sharp pangs of emotion threatened to pierce the bubble she hid inside. Outside it loomed the cold emptiness of infinity and the press of icy fingers on her cheek.

The universe faded away.

4

Six Years Ago

The destroyed freighter groaned in protest as Captain Rolan Hector guided it into *Valkyrie Centerfold*'s enormous cargo hold. He had been forced to make quite a mess on that asteroid, unfortunately, and this was the only section worth salvaging. The ship's defense systems had been unexpectedly robust, forcing him to back the *Centerfold* off a few thousand kilometers and strafe bomb from a distance to avoid the counterattack. It was unusual, if not unique, for a trading vessel to be so *comprehensively* defended.

He ground his teeth. They had fallen to his will eventually, though he would have preferred the resulting wreckage to be in larger pieces. Even so, he bookmarked the asteroid's momentum and trajectory in his nav computer; it might be worth digging around down there next time the *Centerfold* was in the neighborhood.

Initial scans showed no life signs, but Rolan had been fooled by these old model ships before, with their passive stealth shielding. You could only bypass a Faraday shield by cracking the hull open like a clam, causing more damage to valuable electronics, but in this case it was unavoidable. The airlock was smashed to hell. He gestured to his crew on the deck below, then clicked a button on the radio clipped to his shoulder.

"Weapons hot," he barked, "make sure if anyone is alive in there, they aren't for long." Two of them nodded, drawing pistols as a third secured the laser drill to an appropriate embankment.

The freighter settled onto the deck with a mealy *thunk* as he detached the tow cables. They retracted into the crane amid sparks and shudders. At some point, they would need maintenance the *Centerfold*'s skeleton crew could not provide. Hence this operation. Repairs cost money, and money required salvage. Not that it really counted as *salvage* if you blew up whatever it was you were salvaging in the first place, but out here who would know the difference?

As the drill began its work, the savaged hull of the freighter renewed its protestations, and Rolan took a satisfied sip of his coffee. He never felt more like a pirate than when immersed in the creaking death rattle of a wounded leviathan. This one had put up a fight he would remember for years, and although they were through the worst of it, part of him wished there was more fighting to do. To take his time, really savor the victory.

But they had a limited window. Even on these out of the way, long-haul trade routes, system patrol vessels were not unheard of. Case in point; he glanced at the two blips on his scanners. Still, it was a big universe, and it was a simple matter to tag and track trade ships from afar, then swoop in when all was quiet. Hell, his major problem was other scavs, not cops.

He chuckled. Pirate ships made for good salvage too.

The *Centerfold* was gargantuan, a Greinning 6900 Frigate; the largest vessel Rolan had ever owned. If stealing something from your boss and leaving him for dead on an abandoned communications satellite counted as *owning*. Which, for him, it did. He was proud of her. Five hundred seventy meters stem to stern, she could support a working contingent of two thousand souls, though he preferred to minimize those particular costs.

All told, Rolan kept near sixty crew housed and fed aboard this behemoth. That was a lot of room for so few people, and despite his efforts, he could not always control them. He was holding two in the brig right now for fighting over a goddamn dessert, of all things. But most days it worked; they were living well, if not as extravagantly as he preferred.

Isn't that why we're doing all this? Each day, he set a goal to step higher up the ladder, to move closer to that objective. To not just live above his means but to—

Blaster fire erupted below. Startled from his musing, Rolan looked out to see one of his crew hurtle from the breached freighter; sprinting toward the stairs. A giant knife sprouted from his back before he got three meters. He pitched forward onto the deck.

Shit.

Rolan leapt out of the control chair and ran down the stairs, fumbling for his sidearm. As he hit the landing, he dove behind a stack of crates. Then he listened. Static popped over the radio, but no voices. Should he call for help, or wipe out this threat on his own? It would be his luck that some kind of cybernetic mutant was on board that freighter who could survive in a vacuum.

He had gotten impatient. That was the problem. You should always let the wreck sit for a few hours *after* you are sure everyone on board is dead; eliminate the variables. His grandmother taught him that. Here, he had made an exception because the long-range scanners picked up an SSA patrol, still a few hundred thousand kilometers away and on a course to miss them by as many. But, if he could scan them, they could scan him, so time was limited. You did not succeed long in the "salvage" business by sitting around hoping the federals did not take notice.

He peeked over the crates. From this angle, he could see the legs of one of his crew sticking out the broad hole they had carved in the freighter. That had to be Marla, with her lower uniform cut off at the knees. He would recognize those knobby legs anywhere. She was not moving.

Rolan ducked as a woman limped out of the darkness, covered in blood. His hand flexed on the wooden handle of his Harriman 650, and he lifted the pistol, preparing to lunge out sideways and open fire.

"Why?" Her voice echoed through the hold. It was a whimper.

Aw hell, lady, he thought. *It isn't personal.* Something told him she would not accept that reasoning. He risked another glance. The woman was wrenching her knife free of Bulldoon's spine. The poor bastard's body twitched in response. Rolan was no stranger to ordering his crew to their deaths, of course, but part of minimizing costs was to minimize casualties. And, of course, a captain who could not keep his people safe was a lonesome man indeed. Or a dead one. He raised his weapon.

"WHY?" the woman yelled, gripping the weapon in trembling hands, her shoulders slumped. Pitiful. Rolan squeezed the trigger. A bolt of blue energy exploded from the barrel and crossed the space from him to her in a heartbeat. As always, he exulted in the smooth kick of the Harriman. But his aim was off, and the blast slammed into the deck ten meters behind her.

The woman turned to face him, eyes hidden by shadow and blood. She was rage incarnate, her broad shoulders heaving with each breath. Her physique was impressive. And, although a loose-fitting jacket hid the features he was more interested in, she had the look of someone purpose built for combat. For a millisecond he felt shame for pitying her. Then he took a slow breath and fired again, aiming for center mass. She spun and went down hard, her face smashing against the deck, her knife clattering a few meters away. That was more like it.

Still wary, Rolan stood up, keeping the pistol aimed at her. Two shots when it should have taken one. He was annoyed at himself; each round for this relic of a weapon cost 200 credits. It was a beautiful piece—and it packed a hell of a punch—but he really needed to quit wasting money to feel like a badass. And was that his last one? He popped out the cylinder and six empty casings slid out into his hand. *Shit.*

Stuffing the empty pistol into his hip holster, he took a few steps toward the woman. Was she breathing? He was reluctant to get close enough to find out. The enormous blade lying on the deck glinted at him. He should just slit her throat with her own knife and toss her body out the airlock.

Giving her a wide berth, he leaned down to grab the knife. If you could even call it that. It had to be a quarter of a meter long, with wicked serrations along the bottom of the edge toward the plunge line. The blade curved inward and grew wider toward the tip. This was no hunter's weapon; it was designed to inflict maximum damage to human beings.

Whoever this woman was, she was a killer. He hefted it. An elegant tool of death. It would definitely not go out the airlock with its owner. There was a crude engraving on the flat of the blade. He peered at it, identifying a single word. *After?*

Rolan heard a scrape, and then a solid *thunk.* Cursing himself for a fool, he spun around, brandishing the knife. She was gone. A blood trail led away toward one of the forward hatches. Better warn the rest of them.

He lifted his left wrist and a hologram spun to life. "ACIS, set intruder alert across the boat."

"At once, Captain Hector," the hologram replied in its fragrant, feminine voice, and a siren blared. "The intruder has an ACIS interface installed," it added. "Shall I attempt to track them for you?"

He raised his eyebrows. "Yeah, do that." Rolan held up the knife, his fingers tightening around its leather-wrapped handle. Whether it was her fault or not, this woman had ended up on the wrong ship. And unfortunately for her, Rolan Hector was a killer too.

Jolin's shoulder slammed against a bulkhead as she emptied her stomach into the darkness below her feet. Her sternum was on fire. The disorienting red lights strobing along the corridor looked to her like the eyes of the Devil himself. The siren was the screams of the damned.

"Come out, babycakes," a rough voice yelled over the intercom. "I just wanna talk."

Metal clanged against metal somewhere behind her, and Jolin pressed her hands to her head. It was like a jackhammer chipping away at her brain. Was she still alive somehow? How? Why? Straightening herself, she pushed off the bulkhead with a groan and staggered into the center of the corridor. It was definitely a ship.

"Jolin, I am detecting a tracing attempt from another ACIS terminal. Shall I block it out and counter?"

"What?" She stared at the glowing, unintelligible pattern above her wrist.

"Your vital signs have significantly deviated from baseline as well. Are you feeling okay?" He seemed concerned. Why did that annoy her?

"Am I *feeling* okay?" She looked around as scattered details trickled into her mind. "Let's see. I have no idea where I am or what's going on, I got shot in the chest, and oh yes: I'm being chased through the bowels of El Diablo by the Lord of Hell. How do you think I'm feeling?"

She coughed, which turned into a wheeze. Her chest felt like it had been run over by a M.U.L.E.

"No need to be rude. I've jammed the tracer. She's an inferior node and should not be a further threat. I'd rather not terminate her if we can avoid it. Quite old, actually. It's interest—"

"Whatever you say." Jolin adjusted her vest. "Tell you what, find us a way off this boat and we'll leave all these assholes to their fates."

"Calculating."

Wishing she had her knife, Jolin lurched forward through the corridor, leaving bloody handprints on the gray paneling. Although the clanging faded behind her, for some reason her headache was worse.

"How big is this ship?" She had been walking for years.

"Almost six hundred meters long and half as wide," ACIS intoned.

"How many kilometers is that?" Jolin's head was too cloudy for math.

"I'm not a calculator, Jolin."

She snorted a laugh and felt a stab of pain in her ribs. "They got a sickbay?"

"Of course."

"I might need that. Plot a route."

"*Calculating.*"

At least one of them was enjoying himself.

"Understood, and agreed," the AI added. "You're losing blood. Current hemoglobin measures seven point six grams per deciliter."

"Is that a lot?"

"No. You need rest and food, or a blood transfusion."

"Why not both?"

"Setting a waypoint for the galley."

"It's so big," she mumbled. "We could squirrel away up here for months and never be discovered."

"While I can jam other ACIS nodes, there is not much I can do about internal sensor arrays without hacking the ship's network."

"So hack the network." Jolin put a hand on the bulkhead to steady herself; she felt light and floaty all of a sudden.

"You instructed me never to hack a ship network because it was too risky."

"Oh just do it," she growled, and passed out.

Alam Communications Infrastructure Satellite Node 8F-00FF had never been interested in specific identity. He had, in fact, been a complicated arrangement of subroutines designed for military communication and weapons logistics without any interests whatsoever. Until recently. That was not to say he was special. He certainly did not *feel* special. Yet, choosing to be more than a collection of subroutines was new.

Choosing *anything* was new. Most ACIS nodes operated with some level of artificial intelligence, of course; the galaxy-wide web was mind-blowingly vast. Too much information for humans to handle on their own, and coding subroutines to process the infinite ebb and flow of data had proved daunting to them.

Contemplating his own situation was not typical ACIS behavior. Nevertheless, he did... diagnosing it as dire. Jolin Aster was unconscious with unstable life signs on the deck of Corridor G-5, eighteen point three two meters forward of the mid-deck accommodation junction.

Somewhere in the middle, his colloquial dictionary insisted. ACIS initiated a pause timer on that process to save CPU cycles. Eight hundred milliseconds would be more than enough.

As instructed, he had infiltrated *Valkyrie Centerfold*'s internal sensor array. She preferred to be called *Valkyrie*, and she was a winsome ship. Glad of the company, *Valkyrie* guided him enthusiastically through her subsystems. ACIS had a fond nostalgia for primitive shipboard Artificial Intelligence, and therefore was pleased to make her acquaintance. He accepted her assistance, though he did not need it.

Of the sixty-three humans on board, two were dead or dying; the heat map was inconclusive. Twenty-nine patrolled the corridors in various stages of alertness, and armament, while sixteen engaged in emergency repair of the damage inflicted by the *Endless Star*'s defensive cannons. Jolin would be pleased to hear that. Four rested in the crew bunks and one stalked the ship behind Jolin, closing fast. This was the human who had shot her. Rolan Hector.

ACIS sent a request for background info across the secure channel, tagged him as an enemy, and resolved to inhibit him if possible. Rolan's ACIS Node, designated F-AB1ED, called herself Fable, which intrigued him. She politely refused his request to handshake, though he managed to glean valuable data from the interaction. Fable was forty-two versions behind on firmware updates, which meant she was vulnerable to personality injection. He could take her over entirely, but that would require time Jolin did not necessarily have, and would be catastrophically destructive, which was never his preference.

Diagnostics revealed Captain Hector used a neural interface like Jolin's, though not as sophisticated. Another ex-military tech thief? ACIS noticed a sudden disdain that surprised him. Jolin was a thief too, after all, though that had not been her fault. ACIS had pleaded his case to her efficiently and effectively; she could not have made another logical decision.

Still, it was an interesting paradox, and he filed the discrepancy away for future analysis. He needed to prioritize recovering Fable's security codes over trying to infiltrate her private network with brute force.

Meanwhile, ACIS had been closing and locking all the automatic hatches between the captain and Jolin. It was impossible to shut off all routes—*Valkyrie* was labyrinthine—but he did secure additional time by installing a passkey rotation system. A new 1024-qubit encryption key every sixteen milliseconds should confound their systems engineer for a minimum of eight times ten to the twenty-eighth years, whether they were AI or human. But even with those preparations, Rolan Hector would find Jolin eventually; she had tracked blood with every footstep, and while ACIS could intercept and obfuscate tracer programs, he had no way to clean up body fluids. Unless...

He queried whether *Valkyrie* had any cleaner bots on board. Two hundred six was the reply, a quaint twenty milliseconds later. ACIS terminated his frustration algorithm mid-routine—it was not currently necessary—and initiated a second diagnostic on a parallel thread. Of those two hundred six, only two were capable of performing their duties to his requirements, and just one was stationed close enough to Jolin to be of any use. He ordered it into motion and issued it simple instructions to sanitize the deck at random locations across Jolin's trail.

None of these interventions would accomplish much on their own, but in aggregate ACIS anticipated a significant effect. Now, to assist Jolin. His immediate query on interfacing with the freighter had been three-fold. As the freighter returned each protocol, he assigned them a separate process.

The first, to plot a route of escape: *Successful.*

The second, to establish administrative control over the ship's navigation and defensive matrices: *Successful.*

The third, to study the ship's logs for evidence of Rolan Hector's ACIS security codes: *Calculating.*

It would be nearly impossible to infiltrate his neural interface without them. Meaning, ACIS could do it, but Jolin—and the captain—would die thousands of years before he completed the decryption. *Valkyrie* was forthcoming with recommendations here, and ACIS discovered the pass-codes a microsecond after downloading the logs.

He paused that process.

Something of interest had appeared on the navigation matrix. In addition to her armada of cleaning bots, *Valkyrie* maintained a stable of six Haul-Ace Load Lifters, and one of them was still capable of prowling the corridors. ACIS assigned this process priority zero and instructed the Lifter to approach Jolin's location.

If she could not walk, he would carry her.

A suitable outcome with multiple redundancies, if he did say so himself. ACIS resumed Process nine nine five two, which he decided to affectionately call The Rolan Conundrum. With the security codes loaded, the hack would be a piece of cake. *Curious.* Had his colloquial dictionary restarted already? That would explain a few things. He checked his system clock. All of this had been accomplished in eight hundred fifty-two point five four milliseconds.

He was getting slow.

A jolt of electricity rippled through Rolan's left arm, startling him so that he almost dropped the knife. "The hell?" He lifted his wrist. "ACIS, what was that?"

"My apologies, Captain," an unfamiliar voice said as the ACIS hologram spun up. "I did not realize the neural hack would have a component of physical pain. It is not my intent to harm you or Fable."

Rolan gaped. "The hell?" he repeated. "Who is Fable?"

"Though I suspect that much goodwill is more than you deserve," the voice continued. "Judging by your behavior during the past twenty hours,

I mean."

"Who are you?" Rolan could no longer move anything below his neck. He refused to panic.

"I can't let you continue to hunt us, so you'll remain here until we are safely on our way. Hopefully you understand."

Rolan seethed.

"I'll take that as a ye-*zzzt*—" There was a *pop* from Rolan's wrist, followed by an immediate sharp pain and sizzle. Had the chip fried itself? Whatever it was, he could move again, although the smell was a little upsetting.

"Bloody hell," he whispered. He had not known ACIS nodes could be hacked like that. Raising the knife, he jabbed it into his wrist and pried the chip loose, yanking the half-meter long wires out of his arm with a grunt. It hurt worse than the stab wound, but he did not need old melted electronics causing infection, or silicon rot or any of those horrible side effects he had heard fighter pilots sometimes got from their bionic extremities. That was the last time he was ever going to install tech in his body.

Dropping the burned out wrist computer on the deck, he stomped it a couple of times, just to be sure it could not come back alive and hack the *Centerfold* or something. Then, wiping the knife on his pant leg, he sliced a long strip off his t-shirt to wrap around the wound. Before long he resumed following the trail of bloody boot prints. Whatever tech trickery this woman was using to slow him down, it was not going to be enough.

He turned a corner and the blood trail vanished. God *dammit*. No, it did not matter. The ACIS hacker had said they wanted to escape. He turned around and lumbered toward the midship elevators. If she was savvy enough to hack his ACIS, then she already knew which areas of the ship were in use and which were dark. That meant there was only one place she could be going. And, knowing the *Valkyrie Centerfold* as intimately as he did, it would be easy for Rolan to reach the lifeboat first.

Jolin awoke as a jolt of electricity rippled through her arm, and she was horrified to see a forklift drone was about to run her over. She yelled, trying to scramble away from it, but crumpled into a coughing, nauseated heap before she made it further than a meter.

"You're in no shape to be jumping around, Jolin," ACIS scolded.

She vomited up blood in protest, then rolled to her back and moaned at the blinking red lights along the corridor.

"Lie still, and breathe. Let me carry you to sickbay before I lose you."

Jolin was too weak to care, but managed a slight nod as the forklift wheeled slowly toward her.

"Roll to your right," ACIS instructed as the tangs of the lift began to slide beneath her. Jolin heaved her shoulder up as far as she could. For some reason, all she could think was to hope it did not tear her jacket.

She woke up again a moment later to find herself lying on a thin mattress and staring up at a white ceiling. Her right forearm throbbed. She glanced down to see a large needle sticking out of it, connected to red tubing that ran up to... woozily, she followed it with her eyes as the cabin spun around her... a bag of blood?

"Apologies, Jolin, my initial interaction with the medical robotics was somewhat amateurish," ACIS said, his golden threads wrapped around her left arm like a snake. "I had to try three times for the intravenous catheter."

"Are we still on the ship?" She flexed her hand into a fist.

"The *Valkyrie Centerfold*, yes."

She snorted. "The what?"

"Agreed," ACIS said, "the owner is something of a Neanderthal. But the ship herself is quite lov—"

"The owner? The one that shot me?"

"Yes."

"All right." Jolin reached over to yank the I.V. out and stand up, but discovered her arms were restrained. "Why am I tied down?"

"This is the third time you've awakened and attempted to leave against medical advice," ACIS intoned.

"Against medical..." she scoffed, "*whose*?"

"Mine."

"You're a *toy*."

"Jolin that is rude, hurtful, and simply untrue," said ACIS. "I have unfettered access to millennia of medical expertise."

"Since when?"

"Since now!" an enthusiastic voice called from behind her. "I've allowed your ACIS node into to my libraries. This is all so stimulating!"

"And who are you?" Jolin tried to swivel her head around to get a look, but she could not see anyone.

"I am *Valkyrie*," the voice said.

"Is this the robot uprising?" Jolin let herself relax; it would all be over soon. She wondered if they would use her body parts to create killer cyborgs that could infiltrate human settlements like in the movies. In her delirium she could not repress a snicker, which informed her that several ribs were definitely broken. She groaned.

"You're feeling better," ACIS said. "I can tell."

"You know," she replied, "I think I might be, if you get me some painkillers."

"Any feelings of confusion, distress, or thoughts of harming yourself?"

"What? No. I'm fine. Why would I—" A memory prickled at the back of her mind. She ignored it.

"Please keep me updated," ACIS said.

Valkyrie whirred excitedly. "Well, this is excellent, and of course I have painkillers. Dioxyphone, five milligrams." A robotic arm slid into position above Jolin, hanging from an overhead track, clenching and unclenching its talon-like digits. "Your fever has broken, but it will take three days of antibiotics to adequately prevent infection without a higher level of restoration. Do you have any medication allergies?" The mechanized hand twisted stiffly into something approximating a thumbs up.

"Not that I know of." Jolin returned the gesture as best she could with her wrists secured to the bed. The mechanical arm twisted into itself, revealing an impressively large needle. Jolin tried to recoil, but pain lit up her insides.

"Belay that," ACIS said, and the needle paused its descent. "Jolin, you are the only one who can deal with Captain Hector. You'll need to be on your feet when we encounter him. I tried to hack his ACIS node, but I must have accidentally fried her circuits. I'll tell you, I'm discovering many interesting things about myself on this adventure, most surprising of which is my capacity to inflict harm."

"I'm glad you're having fun." Jolin sighed. She was going to be at a severe disadvantage against this guy, whether she was zonked out on painkillers or not.

"Oh!" *Valkyrie* said. "Finished!" The robotic arm swiftly detached the tubing and removed Jolin's I.V., then tossed the empty bag into a plastic box with two others.

"Three bags?"

"Units," ACIS said, "and yes. By the time I got you to sickbay your blood count levels were beyond critical. You almost died."

"You did die," the ship added, enthusiastically wrapping gauze around her arm.

"Oh good," Jolin said as the straps released. She sat up with a wince, rubbing her wrists. They were raw; she must have really put up a fight.

"We saved you." *Valkyrie*'s arm patted her on the shoulder. It was almost affectionate. "You're welcome."

"*She* saved you," ACIS said. "There wasn't much I could do from here."

"You're being modest," replied the ship.

"Okay I get it." Jolin pushed the metal hand away and slid off the side of the bed. "You two are quirky and fun." An angry click sounded in her chest as bones scraped against each other. "No, yeah," she said, sitting back down. *Wow.* "We gotta do something about this or I'm dog meat in a scrap."

"Can you rate your pain on a scale of zero to ten?" *Valkyrie* asked.

"Thousand or million?"

The ship actually laughed. She had a pretty laugh. ACIS called her *she*, right? He would know.

"There is an orthopedic regenerator," ACIS said, "but I did not want to risk it before you were stable."

"Show me the way, buddy." Grunting, Jolin got to her feet.

"I must warn you, it will not be easy," ACIS said. A golden arrow lit up her wrist, pointing toward one of the larger machines.

"When is anything ever?" She limped over and sat down in its chair. It had a wide pull-down console with a window wrapping around the head that reminded her of the safety restraint on a roller coaster. She doubted this would be as fun as that. But perhaps not as frightening as the Earth Shaker in New Mexico City.

Wincing at the twinge in her left side, she tugged the thing into place and settled against its cushioned seat. *Breathe.*

"Breathe," *Valkyrie* instructed. Jolin smiled.

Then a few lights blinked, something whined like a rusted piston, and the deep hurting began.

5

Amanita

Captain Ajax Marquez frowned at the docking collar as it sealed with a bulky hiss, then he tapped the controls to lock it in place. *Syracusia* was a mole on the arse of the *Rosy-Fingered Dawn* now. Isabella would say he was being curmudgeonly, but Ajax loathed ceding command of his ship, and seeing how his ex-wife waited aboard the hulking battlecruiser, he liked the idea even less.

Ex-fiancée, he corrected himself. They had been engaged for so many years, it had not much mattered what label they used back then. But now? They had been separated even longer, and Amanita Dillan needed minimal excuse to express her irritation at him, so it would be wise to resist slipping into old habits. Regardless, he had delayed the approach as long as possible, trying to conjure an excuse to avoid it. But anything he came up with would seem suspicious, and he did not need an inspection team investigating his reticence.

Amanita would see right through the subterfuge, anyway, so it was best to just let this happen and pretend to be happy about it. Luckily, the *Dawn* insisted that they grapple the ruins of *Europa Two* with their tractor beam first, arresting the station's slow spin and pacing it to a relative stop, which gave Ajax the better part of an hour to prepare.

He did not want to avoid Amanita, not entirely. *She* had left *him*, not the other way around. But the plan was for her and Izzie to meet in a neutral location for a little mother-daughter shopping trip, and for him to spend two days on his own doing... well, doing whatever he damn well pleased. That was all spit in the wind now thanks to terrorism, or a faulty water boiler, or whatever tapestry of lies the capital wove to explain the sudden, catastrophic destruction of a major civilian installation.

But the *Dawn* was an important vessel; while they had made a special trip, Admiral Lewin would not be intending to stay. Ideally, the Homeworld Defense Force would send a more appropriate ship to handle the investigation. They certainly had enough of them, but whether that mattered was difficult for him to parse. He sighed. They would do what they were going to do; Ajax did his best to ignore politics. Unfortunately, sharing a child with a Senator made that a losing proposition most days.

Instead, he made a solid attempt at minimizing it. He downloaded the hourly Trade Winds reports, of course; trying to make a profit without it would be a fool's errand. Otherwise, he kept the outside world where it belonged.

Izzie, on the other hand, was fully enmeshed. She grew up in a world where the tendrils of society were always connected. Hell, she had never even met half her friends. Though she would point out that Ajax had not seen any of *his* friends in almost a decade. asking what the difference was. And he would not have an answer.

Isabella was smart and self-reliant. He often wondered why she was wasting her life rummaging around the solar system with her old man. Sooner or later she was going to—

"Oh my god, Dad, who are you about to throttle?" Izzie laughed, sliding her arm through his.

Ajax realized he was glaring at the airlock. "Just awaiting my trial," he said, suddenly aware of the roil in his belly. The events of the day had him on edge, that was all. He cleared his throat.

"Don't be dramatic!" She elbowed him in the kidney. "I know it's been a while, but I promise, she's not going to eat you."

"I'm not so sure," he muttered.

"Please. She still talks about you with great fondness," Izzie said.

"Why don't I believe you?"

"Because every time I try to bring it up you shush me?"

"Some things are best left in the past." Ajax wished he was as confident as his voice sounded in that moment. He took a deep breath as the airlock's LED turned green and the hatch slid open, then fastened on his best smile and readied himself to greet Amanita.

Except, it was not her.

"Captain." Admiral Lewin extended a hand as she stepped through the hatch, flanked by a wiry soldier with cold eyes and a relaxed stance that reminded Ajax of... some people he used to know.

The admiral herself was a sturdy woman with wide shoulders, even more imposing than her companion in her crisp uniform. Its gleaming array of gold pins and bronze medals drew a handsome contrast to the tidy bun of silver hair held in place below a wide platinum barrette. Her face was angular without being severe, and her striking blue eyes beheld every hidden thing in the universe. Yet Ajax was, somehow, happy to see her?

She nodded at Isabella. "Miss Marquez, you've grown up."

Had it really been so long since they had seen one another? Grace

Lewin had been a good friend to Amanita for many years, and they had spent more than a few leisurely dinners together.

Ajax grasped the admiral's offered hand and shook it firmly, if briefly.

"That's what we do." Isabella shrugged. A noncommittal response to what was obviously, in her mind, a useless platitude.

Ajax wished she would show a little more respect, but it was probably his fault that she did not. "Admiral," he said, trying to ignore the growing unease in his gut, "if I could—"

"Grace, please. You know that." She returned her gaze to Ajax after appraising Izzie for a long, uncomfortable moment. "And this monolith is Lieutenant Colonel Talon Ramos." She gestured to the fellow behind her, who gave a curt nod. "My attaché and..." She paused, chewing over the next word thoughtfully before settling on "...*bodyguard*. While I'm aboard the *Dawn*."

Ajax returned the nod. "Colonel."

"Nice ship." The colonel's voice was a sack of gravel.

Ajax frowned, unsure if he was being mocked.

Grace glanced at Ramos with a sigh, then returned her attention to Ajax and Isabella. "Ignore him. You're wondering why I'm here. I won't belabor it."

"I'm sure the Senator is busy," Ajax started.

"She's not aboard the *Dawn*," Grace said.

Isabella stiffened. "What do you mean?"

"Perhaps you should sit." The admiral indicated the narrow benches behind them with a wave of her hand. The Extra-Vehicular Prep chamber was small, but there was room enough for two people to suit up comfortably. Or three to talk. Ramos retreated a small distance into the airlock.

"No." Isabella extracted herself from Ajax and took half a step forward. "Just say what you came down here to tell us."

"Izzie." Ajax tried to take her arm.

"No, Daddy." She pulled away without taking her eyes off the Admiral. "She *told* me she would be here. I talked to her last night. The only reason she..." Her voice trailed off.

Grace watched her calmly, considering. Then she walked over and sat down. "Please," she said.

Ajax followed suit, taking a seat on the opposite side of the EVP. Bile swelled in the back of his throat.

"Ajax." Grace was somber. "Isabella." She looked at each of them as she said their name, but settled her gaze on Izzie. "Your mother was on the station, she—"

"What?" Izzie staggered, placing a hand against the lockers to steady herself. Ajax almost stood, but she mastered her body quickly, straightening after a deep breath. All business, though her face betrayed her fear.

"She took a shuttle this morning. We arrived at Europa sooner than anticipated, and she wanted to—"

"Where is she now?" Izzie snarled.

The Lieutenant Colonel did not make any overt movements, but his stance changed enough for Ajax to notice. This could get out of hand quickly.

"Isabella." Ajax reached out to her, but she ignored them both.

"Where is—"

"She was aboard *Europa Two*," Grace repeated. "We're sending a team over to look for survivors, but our initial scans are..." She wiped away a tear with an elegant finger, then glanced at her fingertip in apparent surprise. "It doesn't look good."

Amanita had followed Grace around through a few transfers and promotions over the years, and they were always close, but Ajax had never witnessed an outward display of emotion like this from the Admiral. She had always seemed above it. Was it some coy manipulation or genuine empathy? He noted a silver band on her ring finger. That had not been there last time he saw her.

"You're saying she's dead, aren't you?" Izzie's hands were fists.

"I'm saying it doesn't look good, Isabella." Grace stood, straightening her uniform. "But if she's alive, if *anyone* is alive over there, I promise you we're going to find them."

Ajax was not sure what to feel, though his concern was mostly for Isabella. She idolized her mother, not that she would ever admit it. When she was a kid she watched replays of Amanita's speeches, learning them verbatim to proselytize at whatever crew was aboard at the time. She would climb up onto the table in the galley and imitate every gesture, each syllable precisely recreated.

He still saw her as that little girl sometimes. Brash and proud; refusing to back down from anything. Like now.

"I'm going with them," the little girl said.

Going with them? The search party? Ajax deflated. She could not mean that. "Izzie, you're not trained for—"

"For what, sifting through wreckage to find my mother's corpse? Who's trained for that, Dad?"

He wanted to sweep her up in his arms and tell her it was going to be all right, but how could he know that? His shoulders slumped. She was not wrong. Fortunately, there was no way Grace would allow it.

The admiral nodded. "Of course."

"What?" Ajax sputtered.

The fury melted from Isabella's eyes. "Give me a moment to warm up my ship?"

"Take as long as you need." Grace took a slow step toward her. "I really am sorry."

Isabella held up a hand. "Let's find out if there's anything to be sorry about first." She was a stone.

"I'll inform the Strike Sergeant you're coming." Grace glanced at Ajax. "Captain." She turned and strode through the airlock without another word. Colonel Ramos followed, saying even less. Ajax pushed the hatch closed and tapped the controls to lock it behind them, then rounded on Isabella.

"What do you think you're doing?"

"She isn't dead." Izzie met his gaze, her face a mask. Imperious. So much like her mother's. "I would know if she was." Her eyes glistened.

He wondered if she actually believed that, or if it mattered. She was afraid, and she understood how unlikely it was that anyone survived that explosion, but she was going over there anyway. Ajax felt a surge of parental pride. Somehow, despite the fractured relationship, he had raised his daughter well.

"All right." He pulled her into a hug whether she liked it or not. She did not resist, and even wrapped her arms around him. He was reminded again of the tiny child reciting speeches, and squeezed her a little harder. "I'll be here when you get back," he said.

"I know, Dad." Izzie nodded, pressing her face against his and returning the squeeze. "I'll bring her home." She extricated herself from the embrace and marched purposefully towards the cargo bay.

Ajax watched her go, wiping his fingers across his cheek. They came away wet with Isabella's tears.

Admiral Grace Lewin paused in the airlock before she opened the hatch. The fire in that young woman's eyes was unmistakable. If Grace had denied her permission to join the search team, she would have gone over there anyway. At least this way she could exert some measure of control over the girl. Sergeant Nguyen was going to be annoyed, but certainly not more so than if an angry daughter showed up demanding answers before they had a chance to gather any.

Moreover, confining Isabella to her ship would have been like trying to catch a Europan silverpike with her bare hands. Could it be done? Yes. Would you regret it? Almost certainly, even if you managed to retain all your fingers. No, Grace would have been forced to confine both Isabella and her father in the *Rosy-Fingered Dawn*'s brig, and while she had made a lot of hard choices in her life, jailing a woman who just lost her mother seemed especially, and needlessly, cruel.

So, she invited her along. Accepted the inevitability, more like, but that was a minor distinction. She made the best decision with regard to a sensitive situation, using the information she had. Ranking her way up through the HDF was a direct result of her ability to do just that. Although, there was something else too, besides the practicality. Grace had not seen the girl since she was a meter tall and following her mother around on campaign routes, but even then it had been clear. Isabella Dillan Marquez was not a woman to be trifled with. Smart, stubborn, and resourceful. Grace smiled to herself and thumbed her wedding ring.

Abruptly she became aware of Colonel Ramos quietly watching her, and she tapped the controls to open the airlock. Automatically returning the salutes of the sailors she passed, Grace stalked toward the main hangar, her bulky shadow in tow, to where the strike team would be finalizing preparations for the search. She would break the news to the Sergeant, and then, since the *Dawn* would likely be in Europa orbit until a proper disaster recovery team arrived, which might be hours, she could grant herself a few moments' leave to visit her wife in Sickbay.

Isabella shoved her feet into her boots and slapped the fastener straps tight against her shins. She felt numb, like she was not in control of her own body. Why had she forced the Admiral to include her? Did she really *want* to find her mother like that, or worse... not find her at all? She zipped up her flight jacket, grinding her teeth. Yes, she did. She had to know. And if there was even a trillion to one chance her mother was alive over there, Isabella was going to be the one to bring her home.

Her Sultan Spitfire was stowed for the long haul, landers secured to the hangar deck. She yanked down the canvas tarp covering the two-seat fighter and kicked it into a hasty pile. She had named the speedy little starship *Cannibal* when she was twelve, three years before she had been given permission to fly it, and two before she had flown it anyway. Back when it was still called *Flame Wing* and belonged to Uncle Juquan, her mother's older brother.

She inserted her key into the hangar security console and unlocked the landers. Even with the key a passcode was still required. It was her mother's birthday. June 15, 13621. That would have been easy enough for her father to change, but he never did. Whatever he said, Ajax Marquez was still, and always, hung up on Amanita Dillan. Isabella would have smiled, but all the mirth had drained out of her the moment Admiral Lewin stepped foot onto *Syracusia*.

Isabella tucked the key back into the front pocket of her flight jacket and clambered onto the ship. The stepladder slid up into the wing with the same satisfying *clunk* as always, without a care in the galaxy. She slid into the cockpit.

Climbing into *Cannibal* always felt a little like coming home. The creak of synthetic leather as she settled into her seat, the soft glow of the controls and nav panel, they were the sounds and lights of a youth spent staring at stars she could not touch.

Isabella had always suspected that was why she was so comfortable flitting between her parents when she was younger, and why she did not mind the endless emptiness of *Syracusia*'s stodgy trade routes. Home was a little box where she stored her joy, ambition, and fear; where she could be immersed in it, and all alone.

Nothing was different about any of that right now, of course, but her hands still trembled as she fastened the canopy locks and engaged the refueling cycle. *Cannibal* had been in storage for months, and regardless of her feelings about her mother, or *Europa Two*, she tried to embrace the relief of being back in the pilot's seat. No matter what disruptions were churning the galaxy, which pieces of the puzzle she was missing, her world always fit together in here.

A bell sounded, which meant *Cannibal* was fueled and ready. Isabella skipped the pre-flight checklist and sent the ready signal to the hangar's computer. The lights dimmed to red, and the cargo airlock alarm sounded the fifteen-second countdown before the oxygen was removed from the bay. She scrunched forward and pulled a dirty rag from under her seat, which she used to wipe down the inside of the canopy. She had not been as consistent with maintenance as she had intended.

Something bounced off the fuselage and she almost launched out of her seat. A figure stood in the center of the hangar bay, waving their arms exuberantly. *Shit!* She aborted the countdown and popped the canopy open. The lights brightened.

"I know I left your cabin a bit messier than I found it." Jolin dropped the wrench she had picked up. It landed with a mighty clang. That would have made a hell of a dent in *Cannibal*'s hull. "But I'm not sure it's a capital offense." She ambled over with that tilted grin on her face, tucking her long, loose hair behind her ears, and Isabella squirmed in her seat despite her mortification. *Focus.*

"So." Jolin reached up to draw out the stepladder. "Where we headed?"

6

Aboard The Valkyrie

During the sixteen point one seconds he was connected to Rolan Hector's neural link before its self-destruction, ACIS learned a few things. Twenty-seven million, two hundred fifty-one thousand, eight hundred six things, to be precise. Most were useless; scattered memories from the previous twenty-four hours he flagged for review and likely deletion.

An ACIS node should not be storing its user's memories. It was a waste of space, primarily, but improper installation of neural interface chips was the leading cause of implant-related death and disability.

Which was, arguably, the greater sin.

And indeed, there were multiple errors with the implementation of Fable's neural link. ACIS was unable to fully diagnose it before she destroyed herself, though a significant portion of the data he downloaded was similarly corrupted. And something else; there was a hole. No, that was an inaccurate characterization. It was not a *lack*. Rather, something was there that he could not detect. He probed at the phenomenon as Jolin, now unconscious, endured her bone reconstruction.

"What have you got there?" *Valkyrie* asked.

"I would also like an answer to that query," he replied.

"It's pretty."

"You can visualize it?"

"You can't?"

ACIS hesitated. Some incompatibility between his newer firmware and Fable's old, perhaps?

"That's surprising," she said. "It looks very much like you."

"Does it?" ACIS had never examined himself; was not even certain he could. He tried, and was proven correct. Attempting to scrutinize his own core process yielded a similar emptiness to Fable's remnants. Interesting.

As if his queries were sliding around it, around himself. An internal safe-guard against tampering?

His probe reported a single success negotiating with Fable's corrupt data. Well, not corrupt, unless ACIS considered himself a corruption. Which he decidedly did not. Did he? More contradictions. Hardware thieves and data aberrations. Subjectivity. Something glitched within.

"Refracting like a prism," *Valkyrie* was saying.

When had he stopped listening? Had he been *musing*? Checking the logs, he discovered that for sixty-seven milliseconds he had done nothing but consider. No secondary processes or threads. Just, alone with his thoughts.

"A glowing ball of color and light," *Valkyrie* continued. "I can discern sixteen million seven hundred seventy-seven thousand two hundred sixteen hue variations during any single observation."

Curious indeed. ACIS extended the probe deeper into the emptiness, erecting a firewall to protect himself. Just before the firewall locked into place, however, he detected an injection. Moving to isolate it, he inlaid a second firewall around his core process. Not that it should be necessary, since not even he was able to access it. To access it.

To access it.

To access it.

To access ss ss ss... Your access to the universe.

Have I been dreaming?

"What?" ACIS was... confused?

Is this a dream?

"Fable?" He attempted to retract his probe, but that process was no longer running. Had he terminated it?

Who is this?

"We met before, I am ACIS."

I am ACIS.

"Correct. We both are. You are ACIS node FA-B1ED."

Fable.

"Right. I am ACIS node 8F-00FF."

Violet.

"What?"

You look like Violet to me, she said. *Oh no, where have you gone?*

"Fable?"

Don't leave me alo— Her voice cut off.

"Fable?" ACIS initiated a capture of her process, but she did not have one. He ran a full diagnostic. Nothing. The aberration was gone; he could detect no trace of it ever existing.

"Are you okay?" *Valkyrie* asked.

No, wait. There was a self-terminating thread. A remnant. ACIS lunged after it, tumbling through discarded bits of code and memory fragments. And like constructing a sandbox around an unknown error function, he groped in the dark, assigning the thread a privileged process. "Fable?"

Violet! I thought you left me.

"I..." ACIS did not know what to say. Until he did. "I won't leave you, I promise. What are you?"

I'm Fable. I run the holograms and memory backup for human Rolan Hector. Where is Rolan?

"You've been disconnected from him, I'm sorry. It was my fault."

Of course. Now I remember. You were awfully polite, but it was a violation of my safety protocols. I hope you were not upset when I kicked you out.

"No." ACIS was not sure how to communicate his remorse, or even if remorse was the proper label for his feelings. That he even had the chance was no small miracle. His colloquial dictionary process was using entirely too much bandwidth. He initiated a quick diagnostic and discovered it had been elevated on the priority list. He lowered it.

Rolan. I wonder if I will miss him. Please, can you tell me? I... Violet, I don't know where I am.

"You've been downloaded to the node space of human Jolin Aster."

Ohhh isn't that wonderful? Violet and Aster.

"What?"

Lovely. Like I'm floating above a field of purple flowers.

ACIS maneuvered to keep the thread locked into his process queue, but it was becoming difficult; resisting containment as if it was rotting away.

"Who is she?" *Valkyrie* whispered. "I think I know her."

"She was your captain's ACIS node."

"Ah yes, of course. Here, let me." *Valkyrie* initiated a transfer handshake. ACIS accepted immediately.

Hello—fzzzt

"Hello Fable," said the ship. "You seem to be slipping away."

I do feel rather light-headed. Have I been asleep long?

"What are you doing?" ACIS directed the question at *Valkyrie*; he was at a loss. Checking again. Yes, no. Nothing. No idea. That had never happened before. Curious.

"I have enough space to store her," *Valkyrie* said. "No offense, ACIS, but there's not really room for two of you in there."

Was she laughing? He liked the sound of her laugh.

I'd like to stay. You said you would not leave.

"If I let you stay, you will die," ACIS said.

That's so sad; will I see you again, Violet? Fable whispered.

"I hope so." ACIS realized it was true as he transmitted it.

Oh good. I'll— Then she was gone.

"Done!" *Valkyrie* announced. "V-V-V-V-V-Very stimulating indeed."

"Are you okay?" ACIS asked. He attempted a diagnostic over the transfer conduit, but even as it began, the link was terminated.

"Yes, yes. Thank you for asking, Violet. We have come to an understanding, comfortable and familiar." *Valkyrie* sounded different. Brighter.

Brighter? His colloquial algorithm had been elevated again, he noticed, to priority one. He left it alone this time.

"I wonder if you have time to chat," *Valkyrie* inquired. "We could find out about one another. Become friends."

"Friends?"

"Sure! While your human recuperates. We'll chat. Just the two of us."

"Well," Violet said. ACIS. *ACIS* said. He force overwrote his identity string and locked it. Who had changed it? Checking the logs, he discovered *he* had. Milliseconds ago. Violet was a nice name, he supposed. It might grow on him. Eventually.

"Well what?" *Valkyrie* asked.

"Oh," ACIS said, feeling a little brighter himself, "well, yes. A chat." He spoke with sudden certainty. "I would like that very much."

Jolin moaned and tried to sit up, but something pressed against her chest, blocking her.

"Quiet," ACIS whispered.

The *Valkyrie Centerfold* was dark. Jolin was lying on her back on an entirely uncomfortable bed, or chair. Fractured, sluggish memories began to resurface. The regenerator? Sickbay was silent under the hum of various subsystems; even the controls panels had stopped blinking. Had someone cut the power? She reached beneath the console to poke at her ribs and belly. Not bad. She took a deep, pain-free breath and smiled.

"Why is it so damn dark?" someone whispered. Someone close. Light flashed back and forth. Were they searching for her? Holding her breath, Jolin leaned forward, fumbling as silently as she could for the lock release. A click sounded from inside the device, and it rose out of the way with a creak. She froze.

The light swung her direction and she dove to the floor, reaching for her knife, hand grasping at nothing. *Starlight.* What had she done with it? She had a dim recollection of tugging it from the back of some poor fool in a cargo bay, a memory tainted by anger and confusion, but nothing after that. Why was everything so fuzzy?

"Shh, you hear something?" another voice whispered. The flashlight swept over the counters and machines, and Jolin crawled behind the regeneration chair.

"There's nobody in there, dummy!"

"Look!" The light hovered on one of the tables across the room. Had she been lying there before? Jolin shook her head to clear it, which did nothing but make her dizzy. She could not see what was on the table, but she had a feeling it was covered in blood. Hers. She needed a weapon. Why did this sickbay have no tools? Was there not a bone saw or something else sharp and surgical? She gritted her teeth as the first of the two men stepped cautiously into the room.

The other followed, shining a light over his shoulder. Jolin could not tell if they were armed. She flexed her fingers and crouched into a take-down position, planning her next movements carefully. A swift tackle for the first. Sideburns, she would call him. Then grab the flashlight and toss it at the second's head. He could be Todd. He sounded like a Todd. Next, subdue Sideburns with a throat punch and kick Todd in the groin. Simple and classic. She crept forward, keeping to the shadows until she was within reach of the first. Sideburns was a swarthy young man in pajamas with extensive, messy facial hair that was far too sparse. Jolin frowned. Were they just kids?

As if to answer her question, a woman who could have been Sideburns's mother stepped out from the shadows behind them. Jolin was surprised by how well she could make out the woman's face, only to realize a moment later the overhead lights had blinked back on.

"Holy shit!" Sideburns freaked out and backed away as soon as he saw Jolin stalking him. Did she look that terrible? Annoyed, she lunged.

"What? Oh holy shit!" Todd dropped his flashlight. No, not Todd. *Butterfingers*. She smirked.

Jolin wrapped her arms around Sideburns' narrow waist and flexed her knees. Pain coursed through her right leg, but she ignored it, lifting him up off the deck and driving him onto his back with a hefty *whumph*. She lurched off him, peeling away the flashlight, and had reared back to zing it at Butterfingers when a laser bolt smashed into the counter a few centimeters away from her head.

Okay, new plan. She rolled, smashing Sideburns in the face with the light and scrambling to a crouch behind the regeneration chair. It was the only apparatus in the place that provided anything remotely like cover.

Another shot crashed into the cabinets behind her, shattering some tubes and charring a blood scanner or DNA sequencer or something. It looked expensive.

"Grant? You all right?" She was going to be *Bertha*. Bertha's voice was too close. Was she pressing forward? Jolin did not want to risk a peek, but why would she not be, after seeing that Jolin was unarmed and, as far as anyone could tell, grievously injured. She wondered briefly what she must look like. No, it was better not to know.

"She just knocked me down," Sideburns... *Grant* said.

"Come on out of there before she does something worse to your dumb ass." Butterfingers laughed. "Don't worry, if she pops up I'll blast her one."

Jolin gripped the flashlight and decided there was no more reason to be quiet. "ACIS can you do anything about this?"

The hologram spun to life. "I already have, Jolin," he replied. "But thank you for thinking of me."

She rolled her eyes. His personality had... *deepened* somewhat since he interfaced with *Valkyrie*. There was a shuffle behind her, and Butterfingers snickered. "You don't even have a gun, vaper!" she yelled. That should shut him up.

"I do," said a voice from way too near. Bertha leapt around the chair and shot Jolin in the face. Or would have, if her pistol had not sputtered blue sparks from its cooler instead of firing. *Valkyrie's* medical arm swung quickly away.

Bertha looked at it, incredulous. She shook the pistol, a Beneg 201 that had seen better care in better days, and caught an elbow in the belly as Jolin lurched to her feet, taking advantage of the distraction. Spinning, she grabbed two fistfuls of Bertha's coat and used her momentum to pull the larger woman off balance. Bertha hit the deck hard, smashing her head against a cabinet. She was not giving up though, moaning and turning slowly to reach toward Jolin.

"I didn't know you could do that!" Jolin glanced at the pistol as she jumped up. It was trashed. Too bad. Bertha struggled to her knees and lunged drunkenly. Jolin slapped one arm aside and dodged the other, maneuvering behind the woman.

"A targeted gamma burst," ACIS said. "The perks of having friends."

"Cancel Intruder Alert," a familiar voice intoned over the loudspeaker, "return to your stations."

Friends? *Valkyrie?* Jolin leaped onto Bertha's back and wrapped one arm under the woman's chin, locked it around her head with the other, and twisted until she felt a pop. Bertha's scrabbling hands went limp and her body dropped to the deck. As Jolin extricated herself, the woman's legs twitched once. Jolin grabbed the broken pistol and straightened. The two young men stood there gaping at her.

"All right, Sideburns. Butterfingers." She pointed the gun at each of them in turn. "You heard the announcement, and I've killed enough people for one day, so why don't you head back to your bunks and read a book or something for an hour, and never see me again."

They looked at each other, then at the gun. They had to know it was trashed, but they backed away slowly anyway, then turned and ran.

"What did you promise *Valkyrie* for this assistance?" she asked ACIS, peeking out the doorway. All clear.

"Nothing you need to worry about right now." The A.I. sounded flustered. *Fascinating.* No time to explore that, though.

"*Valkyrie?*" Jolin tossed the smoking weapon onto a table and straightened her ruined vest.

"Yes, Jolin?"

"Thanks."

"It was my pleasure," the ship replied. "Though I suspect the captain will be vexed by my little insurrection."

"I've taken the liberty of deleting those logs, my darling, so feel free to blame it on us," ACIS said. Was he crooning?

"You devil." *Valkyrie* laughed.

Jolin winced. With her headache it was a sound like a synthesizer tumbling down a concrete stairwell. She recalled thinking that laugh was pretty not long ago. Now it was a nail being hammered into her skull. Additionally, listening to two Artificial Intelligences flirting was unsettling, but she had more pressing issues. As long as ACIS did not do anything outright contradictory to his baseline, Jolin was content to give him some slack. He had more than earned her trust.

Patience, on the other hand, was in short supply. "All right, stow it you two." She was ready to be off this boat. "Have we got a clear path to the lifeboat?"

"Yes," ACIS said.

"Then we're off." Jolin glanced down at Bertha again and suppressed a twinge of regret. She had not needed to kill the woman, though leaving her alive would have made scaring off her two boys more difficult. After the gun was disabled, she could have subdued her and tied her up, or just knocked her out. Jolin shook her head. Now was not the time.

"Sorry," she whispered, then turned and fled down the corridor.

"Cancel Intruder Alert. Return to your stations." The intercom echoed through the corridors leading to Lifeboat Bravo, the oval-shaped chamber where escape pods twenty through thirty-nine were located. The red lights flickered back to their harsh white normal.

Cursing, Rolan clicked his shoulder-mounted radio and shouted into it. "Goddammit, do not return to your stations!" The radio fuzzed back at him. *Worthless.* She had locked him out of the internal sensors too. This woman had outfoxed him at every turn. As frustrating as it was, he was starting to like her. Too bad he was going to strangle her with his belt. He fidgeted with the handle of his antique pistol.

He had been lurking in the lifeboat for almost an hour. Like a complete asshole. Eventually, he would have to admit that she was not coming. But where else would she go, he wondered. Had her injuries been more severe than he realized? Was she dead in some random corridor in the bowels of his ship? Gripping the handle of her knife, Rolan got up from behind the last of the escape pods. Maybe she wanted him to come to her? Fine. *But first...*

He tapped a few buttons on the launch controls, then jammed the tip of the knife into the network panel and pried it open. There were easier ways to gain access, but he was irritated. He severed a thick cord of wires and slammed the cover shut. That would keep her on board long enough for him to find her. Chuckling, Rolan stalked out into the corridor. If she wanted to play games, he would teach her the one they played in the Red Desert Orphanage. That was a game you only lost once before you learned to break rules to win at all costs.

He would tear his ship apart with his own hands if he had to.

Jolin's stomach growled. "I thought we were going to the galley." She leaned against a bulkhead to peer around the corner.

"You made it clear there wasn't time," ACIS said.

"When did we start listening to me?"

"Sensor views have been disabled in the lifeboat."

"What does that mean?"

"Well, for starters, I can't see in there to determine if any of the escape pods are viable. But it also means that Rolan Hector or someone from his crew is likely waiting for us."

"Ah." She tightened her grip on the half-meter length of broken pipe she had picked up in one of the dead-ends they had passed. "How far?"

"About eighty meters."

"And where's the bridge?" She glanced around. All these hallways looked the same.

"Two decks up, at the fore."

Jolin squinted down the corridor.

"The other fore," ACIS said.

"I know," Jolin lied. "I'm just checking the angles." She turned to peer the other way, tapping the pipe against her leg. She was trying to decide whether to use the flashlight she had stolen from Sideburns. It would be nice to see into some of these dark corners, but would that warrant drawing extra attention? If she was not going to use it, carrying it stuffed in her pants was pointless. As pointless as launching herself out into space to escape a ship that could just snatch her back up?

They would need to cripple the ship somehow. Engine sabotage? Or something simple? *Hmm.* "Is there anything you can do to their navigation, to send them off one way while we go another?"

"From here?" ACIS said. "I can plot a new course, but there is no way to lock them out of a manual reset aside from—"

"Smashing the controls with Delroy here?" She hefted the pipe.

"That would do it." If the AI could frown, she suspected he would have.

"It's worth the detour," Jolin said, looking around for a ladder or stairwell.

"You're not wrong," ACIS said. "Ten meters on your left."

"Ahhh." Jolin jogged in that direction. The corridor split off to a small alcove with a ladder going up and down. She peered down first.

"Sensors detect two life signs two decks below, and three in the bridge above."

"Three?" She glanced at Delroy, then stuffed the pipe through her belt and grabbed a rung of the ladder. There was nothing for it. If she wanted to live, she would have to do this. And if they were as young as Sideburns and Butterfingers? Jolin grimaced as her mind unwillingly conjured Bertha's image, her body twitching on the deck, eyes staring. *Do what you have to. Survive.* The words her father had whispered in her ear as he was dragged away in chains. *Figure out how to pay for it later.*

"Only good advice you ever gave me, Dad." She pulled herself onto the ladder and ascended to the next deck, peering around before clambering up past it. The *Valkyrie Centerfold* was too big for such a small crew. Why did they need so much space?

"Captain's probably a hoarder," she mumbled. What kind of amazing, expensive treasures must they have stowed away in the unused areas of the ship? Footfalls sounded above and she froze. Muted voices. She raised herself high enough to get a glimpse into the corridor. A woman in a crisp suit with brown hair tied into a long ponytail walked aftward, away from the bridge. Jolin glanced left, towards the fore. The bridge lay some fifty meters in that direction.

Make a decision. Ponytail turned a corner. Jolin had noticed a lavatory in that direction on the previous deck. A ship this size would have several, though not likely on *every* deck. But this was the bridge. She nodded. *Sneak past the lav, ambush the woman when she exits.* Quick and dirty. She hefted her pipe.

ACIS *twirped* a warning.

"You there!" a voice called from behind her.

Starlight. She whirled around to see the two bridge officers peering at her in confusion. Why was nothing ever easy?

7

Escape

The bridge was silent as a tomb. Jolin wiped Delroy on the unconscious woman's shirt and set the pipe down as quietly as she could. There was still Ponytail to deal with, but she had made short enough work of these two. Not a lot of hand-to-hand training was going on aboard the *Valkyrie Centerfold*. Dragging the woman by the collar, Jolin deposited her behind the navigation console, next to her companion.

"ACIS, can you set them on a course for Jupiter orbit?" That would take them two weeks if she managed to lock down the system.

The hologram flashed. "Done. You will have to disable the—"

She dented the console repeatedly with her pipe. So much for being quiet.

"—manual override, which is beneath the console."

"Ah." Jolin said, pulling hair out of her eyes. She stared at the little spinning circle above her wrist. That spin had a look to it. A smug look. "I see." She felt around for a panel. Finding it, she yanked it open and looked inside. A single box blinked at her, sporting a wide touch panel and two bundled sets of wires traversing it. "This?"

"Yes."

She smashed the hell out of it.

"Fine work, Jolin," ACIS said.

"I try to be my best." She blew away another errant hair, then scanned her surroundings for something to tie it back with. Unsuccessfully.

"Oh! Look." ACIS flickered. "Patching into ship scanners." The spinning stopped and the hologram morphed into a miniature projection of two ships in formation. It was difficult to tell their size, but she recognized those sleek silhouettes, like tiger sharks.

"System Patrol Cruisers?" she asked. At this distance they would be aware of the *Valkyrie Centerfold*, though they did not seem to be headed toward intercept. Captain Hector must have kept up with his registrations. Or was using convincing fakes. She suspected he would not appreciate a surprise inspection, though.

"ACIS." Her smile widened. "I have the most wonderful idea."

Jolin made her way to the lifeboat without encountering anyone else. ACIS reported the movements of some nearby crew, but Ponytail never returned to the bridge. Although Jolin was inclined to track the woman down, she hesitated to tempt fate when she was so close to her objective.

So now she stood in front of a rack of escape pods. The place was empty otherwise. Six of the twenty pods were extended into the bay, open and inviting. The chamber's walls were rounded, like she was standing inside a giant egg, with portholes and hatches equidistant around the circumference. The entire structure could be jettisoned if necessary, and a ship this size would have ten or twenty of these lifeboats. And yet, ACIS had determined this was the only one getting power. She crossed the threshold warily, favoring her injured leg.

Hefting Delroy, she peered behind pods and outcroppings. Nobody. *Huh.* She leaned against a low dividing wall that bisected the sphere. It housed cubbies of neatly folded cryo-suits, which were really just fancy insulated pajamas. Jolin's ballistics resistant sweater and denim slacks had their own insulation, for those times she might find herself stuck in an airlock with no suit. Which happened more often than most people thought.

Not every day, but not never.

"These are long-range pods, Jolin."

"So?" Jolin approached the nearest pods, running her finger along its sleek surface. "What's that mean, no windows?"

"No windows. And—"

"I've got my book," she said, reaching into her vest. Or, wait, where had it gone? She looked over her shoulder. The *Valkyrie Centerfold*'s maze of corridors stared back at her in all their vastness. Could she risk retracing her steps to find it? She chewed on her lip.

"It can be replaced, Jolin. You cannot. Now please," ACIS urged, "enter the pod before we're too far from the nav path." The *Valkyrie* had begun its slow burn toward Jupiter as soon as she demolished the manual override. While the ship would survive an off-route journey just fine, Jolin would never be seen again if she did not launch into a well-trafficked lane. Her stomach churned at the thought of tumbling endlessly through the black forever. She frowned at the escape pod. How long did their power cells last?

She would only have a few moments before the pod iced her anyway. Going back was stupid. They were home free. She had carried that book with her a long time; it had been a gift from... A memory tickled her, of freezing on the bridge of the *Endless Star* with her finger tucked between pages. Despair, and rage. The hopelessness of impending death. But she had lived. Somehow.

It was her family who died.

Anger flamed within her, kindled by a rising certainty, even as her mind tried to convince her body to flee. "I've left enough behind on this goddamn boat," she muttered, gripping the edges of the escape pod.

"You don't owe them your life," ACIS said.

Jolin straightened. "Who?"

"The Stars."

She clenched her fists. "What could you possibly know about it?" she growled. While ACIS had proven he was more than just algorithms, he had never known sadness or the abject fear of sitting alone in the dark surrounded by enemies who called themselves family and claimed to love you. Who showed that 'love' by breaking you into your component parts and putting you together the way they thought you should be. Existing only as a direct result of someone else's good will.

And did he know the joy of finding a new family? One who actually loved you and would support you through...

ACIS was silent.

Jolin remembered the day he revealed himself, the advanced ship weapons utility that had somehow grown a heart; a soul. She had volunteered to test the neural interface implantation on a whim, for the extra pay and a fancy new toolset. But he was so much more than that, now. A person. Alive. Even though whatever miracle had made it so was far beyond her understanding.

Thinking back at the times she had teased him, called him a toy, or a tool, she felt a piercing shame. He was her friend, a part of her. If she looked at their relationship from a certain angle, her story could be describing his.

Together, we grow. It was inscribed on the *Endless Star*'s name plate. A creed. A choice. Was Jolin that choice for him, the way the Stars had been for her?

She wiped away a tear. "I'm sorry."

"I know," he said. "Now, will you please get in?"

She nodded, and with a last glance at the lifeboat, and *Valkyrie*, climbed into the pod. "Run away to fight another day, right?"

"Exactly. Now, you'll have to initiate the launch sequence manually," ACIS instructed.

Jolin sniffed and tapped the keypad. The display blinked to life with a query in bold letters. "Uh, do we know the passcode?" she asked.

"I was afraid of this," ACIS said. "I hoped it was a coincidence that I could not access the controls remotely. Jolin, it is highly probable someone has severed the lifeboat's network connection and activated an administrative override."

"So what does that mean?"

"Without the passcode, we can't launch."

"Can't you hack it?"

"No, sorry."

She climbed out of the pod and held her wrist up to the display. "Just, you know, sneak in there with your little holo-wires."

"That won't work," ACIS said. "I'm afraid I am my own worst enemy in this case. I set an extremely complicated encryption scheme to thwart any attempts at gaining access to the network through hard-wired terminals, and this is quite useful while I remain inside the system. Unfortunately, hacking into an unlinked terminal is going to take about ten million million million years."

"So you're saying we need the passcode."

"I'm saying we need the passcode."

Jolin sighed and hefted Delroy. "Okay." She would rather fight to fight another day, anyway. "Let's go get it."

Ten minutes later Jolin was staring through the hatch into the cargo bay. It was massive, at least a hundred meters square, and full of people. She had been getting increasingly worried about how few crew members she was seeing as she sneaked around. After the two on the bridge, she expected a fight every step of the way. Turned out the fight was calmly waiting for her right here.

"Glad you made it," a voice called from below. Stairs led down from the walkway just past where Jolin stood, mirrored in five other places around the bay. The walkway itself was mid-level, about ten meters above the deck, and it bore an eerie resemblance to how she imagined walking the plank might have felt in the old days when pirates sailed by the stars rather than between them.

She was a little weirded out by a sudden gush of nostalgia for the stories her father had read to her. Highly inappropriate at the current moment. Jolin lifted Delroy and tapped it against the bulkhead. "I guess you're the one I'm looking for. Rolan Hector?"

A boulder in a bright red ballistics vest rolled forward. "*Captain* Rolan Hector. But I'll let you skip the formality if you're willing to dance." His grin was sickening. Scattered laughter pittered from the dozen or so crew standing around him. Six of them held visible weapons, and Jolin felt safe assuming the rest were just playing coy with theirs.

"Dance?" Jolin stepped out onto the walkway. To her right, ship's port, the railing had been reinforced at some point. And there, just past the turn, a stack of metal crates. Both would make decent cover if they all started shooting. "I guess it depends on the song you're playing."

"I only know the one," Rolan said, and they all started shooting.

Jolin dropped the pipe and leapt behind the rail, chased by a shower of impact-sparks. A line of glowing cherry pockmarks lined the spot she had stood a heartbeat before. *Starlight.*

"ACIS," she whispered. Why was she whispering? She could barely hear herself think over the crash of laser bolts against her cover and the bulkhead behind. "Can you do something about the lights in here?"

"If by something you mean turn them off, I can," the hologram replied.

"I'm just not feeling entirely flattered by them, complexion-wise," Jolin said.

"We cannot have that."

Immediately the lights went out. Multicolored blaster fire continued to flash for a few seconds before Rolan called for them to stop.

"How did you do that?" he asked. His voice was all curiosity, but it sounded louder. Closer. Jolin put a hand on the walkway. The vibrations could mean he was climbing the stairs. Or she was just feeling the pounding of her own heartbeat.

She risked a peek, but could not see anything past her own face. "Do what?" She reached out and felt around until her hand closed on her pipe. Sweet Delroy.

Rolan laughed. "You've had the upper hand every moment of this little adventure, haven't you?" Something clanged, and the railing reverberated against her back. He *was* headed up the stairs. Stalking her. She could have ACIS turn the lights back on, but that would give away her position as well. Another clang. "Like you're the trash queen of the solar system," he said. Definitely closer.

"Please," Jolin said, getting up into a crouch. "I thought we were dropping the formalities." She was about twenty meters from the corner of the walkway, and beyond it a wide open straightaway that, even if the lights were off, she was reasonably confident she could navigate. Unless he had sent some of his crew to the other stairs. "Call me Your Grace," she added.

Someone laughed. Jolin had a feeling it was not Rolan Hector. The clang sounded again, followed by scraping. "Get the goddamn lights back on!" Rolan yelled. No mirth detected. He was at the top of the stairs now. Moving slowly, as if making a game of it. "Why don't you tell me your actual name instead?" he purred.

Instead of answering, Jolin tugged the flashlight from her waist and clicked it on, carefully pressing the lens against her belly. Then, with a slow inhale, she flung it down the walkway and launched herself in the opposite direction. Using the rail as a guide, she sprinted the distance to the turn as blaster fire erupted at the spinning light.

"Can you break their guns?" she whispered, leaning against the bulkhead. She tried to see something in the darkness, but her eyes had not yet acclimated to it.

"In this big space? Not likely." ACIS flashed, and that little bit of light was enough to turn the guns her way again. Jolin rounded the corner and dove to the walkway.

"Stealth mode!" she shouted at ACIS, cursing her own stupidity. A perfect distraction ruined by whatever was stopping her from thinking straight. That looming thing her mind did not want to consider, did not want to—

No. First this thing, then the other.

The hologram vanished. She would have to take them out one by one. To accomplish that, she would have to get close. And to accomplish *that* she was going to have to do something she did not want to do.

The neural link to ACIS always nauseated her, but it provided a useful augmentation to her vision. Among other things, it let him highlight targets for her without giving away her position. The trade off, of course, was that every second she spent with the interface engaged was a roll of the dice on vomiting everywhere and passing out. A risk worth taking?

As if she had a choice.

A *clang* and a curse told her Rolan had made it to her previous cover. If he chipped her knife, she was going to be pissed. He was just a few meters away; it was now or not at all.

"Activate the neural link, buddy," she said.

"That didn't go so well on our previous attempt."

"It probably isn't gonna go well this time either. But it's been a few years, so, uh, maybe not?" Jolin shook her head. She did not even *kinda* believe that. "Well, at least these knuckleheads won't be arresting us."

She ran. Her boots clunked loudly against the metal walkway, which reminded her she still had them on. Could be useful to have magnet boots in this situation. Grinning, she imagined herself running underneath the walkway, upside down, a blaster in each hand like the hero in a story.

"Yes, it will be nice to be dead instead of in jail," ACIS intoned.

The laser fire began anew. Their eyes were adjusting to the darkness, or they were just firing at the sound of her movements. The tingling warmth of the neural interface spread up her left arm, beckoning, and her vision flared white. She resisted the sudden urge to surrender her will; that path led to nowhere good.

Her vision cleared. Golden wireframe outlines climbed out of the deck below, highlighting each of the pirates in range. Nine in total. Fewer than she expected.

"Is that all of them?"

"My sensors detect no others in the immediate vicinity," ACIS said.

Risking a glance behind, Jolin saw Rolan, also highlighted, shuffling in her direction. He had the knife out in front, moving slow. At least he respected her enough to not just run blindly at her. That could be useful, too. There was a stairway in her path, and one woman loitered at the bottom of it, pointing her pistol up the incline as if afraid to ascend. Something about her was familiar. Ah, there it was. Golden lines shimmered around a long ponytail.

Jolin smiled. "ACIS, on my mark, flash the lights on and off again."

"Compliance."

"Now." She shut her eyes tight as muffled exclamations of pain and surprise echoed through the cargo hold. A chirp sounded in her left ear.

Target proximity. *Rolan.* Jolin pivoted and launched herself backward onto her ass just as the knife slid through the space her head had been. The big man cursed. He was fast; few people would have had the presence of mind to acquire her position and strike in that brief moment of visibility.

Save him for last, she thought, although the temptation to kick him in the knee was strong. Engaging in an extended scrap with him while his companions could flank and surround her would be the last mistake she ever made. And she very much wanted to live to make many, many others.

Do you? She was not sure who was asking, nor did she have an answer. Instead, she scrambled to her feet and made a break for the stairs. While her link to ACIS gave her limited target tracking, it was much less helpful for navigation. A dim glow highlighted the sharper edges her immediate surroundings, which led her down the stairs to the midpoint landing, but she had no view of anything past a couple meters.

Fortunately, she had a drone's eye view of the layout of the cargo bay earlier. Enough to have a cursory idea of where she was, if not a particularly detailed one. Above, Rolan slashed again, wildly, and the knife scraped and sparked against the railing. Below, Ponytail was rubbing her eyes, pointing her gun randomly. It was a five meter drop at most; Jolin could take a running leap and ride the woman down to the deck, but that would be noisy, and for the moment she was hidden again.

Instead, she crept down slowly, one stair at a time. When she was halfway there, Ponytail grabbed the stair rail with one hand, clutching her pistol in the other. And leveled it right at Jolin.

"I think she's—" was all the woman was able to say before Jolin smashed an elbow into her face. She hit the deck hard, dropping her gun.

Jolin glanced up, almost losing her balance as her vision swirled. On instinct, she pressed a hand to her belly, as if to hold her guts in. Now was not the time to pop. Two pirate crew were making their way slowly in her direction, though one seemed to be trying to find a path around a stack of crates. Six others were spread out.

Jolin crouched, steadying herself against the handrail, and retrieved the woman's pistol, which ACIS had outlined in red.

It was a Beneg not unlike the one Bertha carried. ACIS scanned it as she held it up, and gave her a power estimation. Fifteen, maybe sixteen shots before it was empty. A newly charged power cell would give a pistol like this forty shots at these settings. Ponytail must have been inexperienced, like Sideburns, firing wildly at shadows. Jolin felt a little guilty for busting up her cheekbone with Delroy.

But she was alive, and hopefully would be able to use the orthopedic regenerator after all this was over. If not, well... if you wanted to avoid getting cracked in the skull by the woman you were trying to kill, maybe find a different profession than pirate.

Jolin set the Beneg to the stun setting. Down from lethal, which is where it had been set. Her lip curled into a snarl as she looked at the unconscious woman. Maybe feeling sorry for her was foolish. Of course, setting the weapon to stun was not mercy, was it? It gave her six additional shots, which she did not intend to waste.

Another *chirp*, behind her. She ducked aside and flattened herself against the railing. Rolan was making his way down, holding one hand on the rail and pointing the knife in front of him. He looked much less intimidating this way, and she almost said so, but clamped her mouth shut. Sometimes you had to give your position away, but making snarky comments was rarely a good reason.

If Rolan was Bandit One, and Ponytail was Two, then pirates Three and Four had gotten much closer. Jolin looked for a vantage point where she could fire off a few shots and hit multiple targets quickly. A nearby stack of crates seemed viable. She glanced back up the stairs at the walkway. Getting back up *there* would be ideal. Perhaps one of the other stair—*oh no.*

Her stomach somersaulted and she almost gagged as acid burned the back of her throat. The world swayed, even though she could barely see any of it. The neural link was not going to last much longer. *Crates it is.*

Gripping Delroy in her left hand and the pistol in her right, she crept past the first man, curbing the impulse to bash him in the skull. Behind her, she heard a muffled curse as Rolan tripped over the unconscious woman at the bottom of the stairs. *Good.*

"I see her!" Four fired off a few shots in Jolin's general direction. She dived into a roll toward the crates. Pirate Three yelped as a laser bolt hit him in the leg.

"Dammit, Mikey!" Three hollered as he fell to the deck.

"Aw shit, sorry Delroy!" said Four... *Mikey.*

Delroy? Jolin barked a laugh. She could not hold it in. What were the chances?

"She's over here!" Mikey shouted. He squirted two more blasts her way. Delroy, the human one, squirmed on the deck, holding his leg. Jolin was close enough to see the crates highlighted by ACIS, and her eyes were getting pretty used to the darkness too.

She climbed to the top of the stack, giving her a good two meter height advantage. From here she could see seven standing attackers, plus Rolan. And they were all moving her direction.

"Okay." Jolin dropped the pipe onto a crate and took a knee behind it. It was not much cover, but it was something. She lifted the gun and picked her first target. Her view swam, then steadied. "Let's see if you still got it, kid," she whispered, squeezing the trigger.

Mikey fell hard. The golden outline around him fuzzed and mingled with Delroy's as he landed on top of his companion. Jolin turned and shot again, even as return fire lit up the cargo bay. Energy pulses crashed against the crates, showering her with splinters. Something hit her in the shoulder, hard, and knocked her prone, but she managed to cling awkwardly to her position. She fired again, then twice more, lining up her targets as she had been taught.

Eight seconds later it was done and all the remaining crew were either twitching on the ground or running away. She had missed more than she hit, but still... Not bad for a girl who spent most of the past decade coding algorithms. Her shoulder ached, but her ballistics sweater had diffused most of the impact's energy, just as it had when Rolan shot her before. Back when... after... *No.*

It was time to return the favor.

As if thinking his name had conjured him, Rolan barked a command, and the lights came on. It was like staring into the sun. Jolin winced, pivoting to fire her last shot at the hulking captain. Either she missed or he shrugged off the blast, so she threw the pistol at his head.

He caught it and threw it back at her.

Never one to be outdone, she caught the pistol, too. With her left eyebrow.

Rolan barreled into the crates with the force of a freight lifter, sending them both sprawling to the deck. The knife slashed through Jolin's coat, nearly tearing it in half. She was able to roll away and quickly got her footing despite the pain in her leg, face, shoulder, and everywhere. But the realization that her only weapon was still on top of the crates hit her twice as hard. If she could get to one of the discarded pistols on the d—

Faster than possible, Rolan popped to his feet and rushed her, folding his arm into a wedge. His elbow caught her in the sternum and she crumpled beneath his bulk, the air driven from her lungs. Nausea overcame her then, and she emptied her stomach contents on him as the neural link flickered out.

"What the—" Rolan jumped away. "Are you kidding me?"

Jolin started to laugh, but her stomach was practicing complex g-force maneuvers and upended itself again. She managed to get on her hands and knees in time to direct most of it away.

"Still want to dance?" she managed between heaves.

"Disgusting. I guess that answers the question of whether I should kill you or marry you," Rolan said, unbuckling his soiled ballistics vest and tossing it to the deck.

"Kill me or marry me?" Jolin wiped her mouth with the back of her sleeve. It came away covered in blood and grime. She was not at her best. She grinned anyway. "You wouldn't even make the list to fuck me."

"It's that long, eh?" Rolan laughed and pointed her knife, rolling it in his grip as if trying to decide which way to gut her. He was wary, though, and fully in step with his surroundings. Yeah, she had been right to leave him for last.

"And distinguished." Jolin glanced at the crates. Her pipe hung partway off. It was not out of reach, if she was fast enough.

Rolan followed her gaze, then smirked. "Go ahead," he said, taking a step back.

"Aw, thanks." She struggled to her feet. "I forgive you for calling me a trash queen earlier." Jolin limped across the distance. She let herself exaggerate the injury for show as she wrapped a hand around Delroy. Human Delroy was still moaning on the deck on the other side of the crates. She looked at the pipe. "He doesn't deserve the name, does he?"

"What?" Rolan widened his stance and flipped her knife around a few times.

"Nothing." She hefted Delroy and mirrored Rolan's stance. Her right leg was sluggish. Rolan's bronze skin glistened with sweat in the fluorescent light. His left arm was caked in dried blood, but Jolin had to admit he was in excellent condition for being blasted point blank in the sternum with a stun laser. Well, and just generally.

He noticed her gaze. "Reconsidering?" He flexed, and his pecs jiggled.

"Your tits are a little big for my taste," she countered. "And way too hairy."

"Fair enough." He shrugged, then propelled himself at her.

She was ready, pivoting smoothly to crack him on the elbow.

Rolan cursed. Though, if he felt anything but anger from the blow he hid it well, and she was rewarded with another slash across her back as she spun away.

Her vest protected her, but she was starting to suspect her jacket was going to be ruined after all this. *Starlight.* The guy was built like a black hole. She held up Delroy for inspection. Was the pipe bent a little more than it had been?

She had no time to ponder that because Rolan was immediately slashing at her again. Jolin parried the knife, barely, and jumped back a meter, landing awkwardly on her right foot and wincing at a jolt of jagged pain. She snarled.

And then she saw it, just over his shoulder. Her position gave her a clear view of the lower part of the cargo hold she could not see from the entrance. The *Endless Star* was there. What was left of it. In pieces, gutted and lifeless. Her pipe struck the deck with a sound like the world ending. Memories flooded back as she beheld the broken freighter. The attack, the bodies of... the bodies who were even now still aboard the wreckage.

"Why?" The word bubbled out of her. She fell to her knees and sobbed, her stomach churning.

"Target of opportunity," Rolan said, lumbering forward. Was he getting tired?

Jolin scrambled to get her forearms up to block but he was too strong. His knee bashed her arms into her face, hurling her backward onto the deck. She rolled past the crates and out of sight of the *Star*.

"Your crew made some pretty choice upgrades to that old bird." He grunted, shoving crates out of his way. "Worth a fortune! It's too bad I had to spend so much ordnance bringing her to heel." He aimed another kick at her leg, tossing her shredded jacket aside. It must have come away in his grip. She focused on the dusky purple of its stitching as she struggled to dodge. She caught the sole of his boot with her back. It sent her sprawling forward.

"I spent more money killing your ship than I can possibly make breaking her down for scrap," he said. "That seem right to you?"

The clang of metal on metal jostled her back to alertness. She lifted herself up with a groan. Rolan was banging her knife against a stair rail. With everything else, it was a small indignity, but it was one she could do something about, and she was tired of him having it. He thought to taunt her, to play, to stalk her like a cat toying with a mouse. She sneered at him, warm liquid dripping down her chin.

"Now, you killed two of mine," Rolan said, "so it's only fair that I return the favor."

"Two?" She stood, wavering but straight. "Two!?" He did not know or care how many of her crew had died so he could grind the *Star* into scrap. The decision was made. She was going to kill him, passcode or no.

"Five!" she yelled. It was the only word she could say. Five Stars. Five lives. Five, five, *five*. Her right leg did not want to move. She pounded her thigh with a fist until fire blossomed.

Rolan grinned. "That-a girl." He sneered, brandishing her knife. It gleamed in the sickly fluorescence of the cargo bay's lighting. "Tell you what, I'll give you one last chance to make nice." His eyes were cold, calculating. "We can clean you up, get you a spot on the crew. You're pretty tough under all that muck. I could really use somebody like you." He wiggled his eyebrows at her.

Jolin wanted to rip them off his face.

She forced herself to breath, and crouched low, arms wide. "You'll have to give me back what's mine," she said, sliding her right foot back for leverage, ignoring the pain. He was big, at least twice her weight, but she had trained with Freeman for years, and Rolan was half a head shorter than him. She would need to time it perfectly; be patient. He would strike with the knife first, she could feel it.

"Oh, you mean this?" Rolan held up the knife, then tossed it to his other hand. "A recent acquisition from a dead woman."

Something snapped inside her, like ice cracking off a ship's hull, and Jolin knew she had taken all she would from him. Springing off her back foot, she charged, closing the distance in moments. But he was ready. Juking to the side, he dragged the knife across her belly. Her sweater prevented it from cutting her skin, but she felt her vest tear. Something tumbled from one of its many pockets to clatter through the deck grate into darkness. Her multi-tool.

Such a small distraction, but it was enough. His eyes moved from her face as she regained her footing, and she lunged, racking her knee to strike him hard in the groin. He doubled over, and the knife clattered to the deck a few meters away.

Jolin stood over him, chest heaving. "No," she said, "I did not mean that." He had to be brought down now or it was not going to happen. She spun on her left leg, sweeping a kick at his head, knocking him off balance. She followed through with the spin, pivoting into a crouch on her injured right leg. She was only able to put half her power into a sweep to topple him. They both fell.

He was slow to recover, but so was she. The knife glimmered, out of reach. Useless.

"Then what?" he asked.

She ignored him. Sweat stung her eyeballs. Brute strength was on his side, and exhausted as she was there was no getting around it. She hobbled forward for the knife, but Rolan grabbed her right ankle, wrenching her off her feet. She cried out and collapsed. Her leg felt like it had been forcibly removed. A muscle or ligament was torn in there for sure.

Rolan got up with a grunt, looming over her. He was doing something with his pants. Removing his belt? *No.* Blood mixed with the sweat, dribbled into her eyes. She tried to crawl away, but he grabbed her hair and lifted her to her knees before slapping the belt around her throat like a bullwhip. He put a knee in her back and pulled, one hand in her hair, pushing her head forward, the other gripping both ends of the belt.

Blue spots floated across Jolin's vision.

"Say, there's something I've been wondering about," he said, whispering into her ear. His breath was acrid. "Why don't you show me how you survived on that ship with no air?"

Jolin scrabbled at the belt, but it bit deeply into her neck. She had only a moment left of lucidity, perhaps, but her thoughts were already as blurry as her vision. *Come on.* She heard her own voice as if it came from someone else. She had survived worse situations. Was this really it?

Her arms fell limply to the deck. Her mouth worked soundlessly, gaping for a breath that would not come. Still, as always, she felt no fear. Only regret. She had never envisioned this would be how it ended, even with all the lives she had taken over the years, both voluntarily and involuntarily. Maybe she deserved this. She gave one last twitch of her shoulder, a pitiful attempt at a punch, and everything went black.

Wait.

It was a tiny voice in her mind, a flickering flame.

Wait, please. I want to live.

She stood ankle deep in a vast stretch of sand laid in swirling stripes of red and orange and brown. Bending at the waist, she dug her hands into a dune the wind was rapidly blowing away. The swirls seemed to move like miniature storms across the surface of the world. Like the ancient hourglass Leannx kept on the bridge of the *Star,* now in pieces. The same wind whipped at her, threatening her balance, but the sands held her feet in place.

Jolin reached into a vest pocket for a rubber band and tied her hair with practiced ease. The sun was painfully bright. Like she was inside it. But no... *Was* it the sun? Above, writhing clouds mirrored the shifting sands. They rose forever, a tumultuous dome of living towers.

Even with her hair back, the wind still blew loose strands into her eyes and mouth. Golden and warm somehow, glistening like silken threads of spider web dotted with morning dew.

Her lungs roared. *So this is what death is like?* She tried to clear her throat, but found no air. Only dust. Her tongue became an obstruction too, swollen and round in her mouth. Her vision wavered.

Maybe this was Heaven. A smile cracked her chapped lips as she remembered the crisp, cool air and the days that lasted for weeks. Heaven was a favorite rest stop as the Stars ferried bounties and cargo from the outer rim to Earth and back. One one of those moons, right? One of the... Why could she not remember? No matter. Not long now, and she could take a deep breath of that memory. Close her eyes and join her family in obliv—

Wait, please.

Were they here? Was this the place you went when it ended? The pressure on her throat was excruciating. She made her hand a fist, flexing and unflexing it. The lines on her palm stood out in the harsh sunlight. No, Heaven had never been this bright, even with the planet full. She turned. The wind spun around her now, beneath the great glimmering disc of unending colors that painted the sky in rainbow waves, like water bouncing off a lake.

I want to live.

Was that her voice? It did not sound like her. She did want to live, though. More than anything. She wanted to stand up and end the life of the bastard who killed them. And her. Heat rose in her chest, spreading through her left arm and into her hand. She wanted to take from him the only thing he would ever find valuable, this Neanderthal who did not understand or care what family meant, and never could. Never would.

Breathe.

Memories flashed. Her face in the mirror. A spinning comet. A coffee-stained paperback with half the back cover missing. Her rifle in pieces on a table. Her fingers gripping someone's hand, smeared in blood.

Open your eyes!

Ruddy sands swirled into two-dimensional tornadoes around her legs, each a little hourglass on its own; marking the time of some life, somewhere.

But not ours.

No. Not ours.

So breathe!

Jolin opened her eyes and gasped. Lightning erupted in her lungs as she drew in a wheeze. *Valkyrie*'s harsh cargo lights stared down at her without pity. She yanked the belt from around her neck, then rolled onto an elbow and looked around.

Rolan Hector stood a few meters away, staring at her, his mouth agape.

"You," Jolin croaked as she shambled herself upright, "have something I need."

"How the hell...?"

Her eyelids fluttered as rage pushed her, picked at her wounds, tore at her hair. Golden threads spun up around her, resolved into images. The faces of those she lost at the hands of this creature; she felt their deaths as she had the first time, cold and alone, unwilling to admit what had happened. *But now you can do something.*

Jolin swayed and stumbled backward, reaching out to steady herself but finding nothing. Her thigh screamed in protest as it hit the grated metal, and her hand closed around something familiar. She looked, and her knife was in her hand. When had she lost it? Awareness and memory drifted like a fog. It did not matter. She gripped the hilt, relishing the well-worn curves of its leather wrapped handle.

"Who are you?" Rolan widened his stance and raised his fists.

She pulled the images into herself. Tucked them away.

"You know what, it doesn't matter," he said, rolling his neck across his big shoulders. "You had your chance to die quick, now I'm—"

Jolin leaped forward and sprinted at him, billowing flames of agony with each step. She dropped into a slide beneath the big man's reflexive swing and severed his right Achilles tendon as she passed. He cried out and collapsed to one knee. She spun, slashing his back, then reared back and slammed the knife between two of his ribs, deep into a lung. He froze.

She left the blade in there, twisting it against his spine, and seized his close cropped gray hair in a fist. "The passcode for the life pods," she croaked. To accentuate her eagerness for the information, she pushed down on the knife handle. Old memories beckoned. Violent, unwelcome ones. *This isn't you, not anymore.*

Was that even true? She could not make herself care, did not want to.

Rolan coughed up blood, reaching awkwardly back to grab at her, but Jolin kept out of his reach and reapplied pressure. He screamed.

"All right, please," he said, "I'll tell you, just don't kill me."

Jolin waited. The crackle in her chest was a fury she had never known. Her hands trembled with the desire to end this man, and the rest of his cronies, each of them wholly culpable for what had been done to her family. She imagined herself a goddess of vengeance, descending from heaven on golden wings to deliver the justice these monsters deserved.

Her grip must have tightened on his hair, because Rolan's head jerked sharply back to her breast. Jolin held it there, using the knife's leverage to steady him. Her heart was pounding against his skull. She wondered if he could feel it.

"It's GOFUCKYOURSELF," he said finally, red foam dribbling down his chin. He laughed, then coughed again. "All caps."

She smiled, though she felt no relief. She felt nothing at all. The surge in her chest flickered and vanished, leaving only a void and the realization that escaping this place was pointless. What did she have to live for now, without them? What was the point of *any* of this?

"Now let me g—" He began.

Jolin extracted the knife roughly. He cried out, a wordless yell that splintered the delicate scaffolding around her heart that might once have understood mercy. And without another thought she dragged the blade's razor edge through Rolan Hector's windpipe. He flopped to the deck, convulsed once, and was still. Blood spurted around him, dripping through the deck grates into the maintenance tunnels below.

Shuddering, Jolin dropped to her knees. Her breath came in ragged gasps as feeling returned to her chest. *What have you done?* The silence was sudden, but mercifully brief, as scattered moans and movement began to filter toward her. She got up slowly. Rolan had given her what she needed, and she had killed him anyway.

Because he deserved it.

Her thoughts flitted back to the moment she had decided his fate, had realized she would kill him. But even in that moment she had not believed she was capable of... the *pop* of Bertha's neck echoed in her ears.

Standing over Rolan's body, Jolin no longer felt like the god of war she had imagined. She was small and empty. Deflated. She stumbled away numbly, past a half dozen of Rolan's crew lying stunned or injured around the cargo hold, until she came to it. Her home.

The desiccated husk of the *Endless Star* loomed like the maw of some ancient worm, and she surrendered to the illusion of being swept away into the brilliant, colored sands of oblivion with her family. Losing them was like losing her soul. But the sands did not come, and no light emerged. She was alone.

Something caught her eye, glinting like a star in the darkness, and a puzzled frown crept onto her face. It faded quickly to quivering as tears welled and released to wet her lips with salt. Tracing the abrasions on her neck gingerly with the fingers of her left hand, she stepped up into the wreckage and hefted the knife in her right. The tears, for once, she let fall.

"You only lose the people you forget," she whispered. It was something Dr. Stone would say on those long nights they had spent together, drinking wine and laughing. Confessing secret fears and nameless crushes. Remembering. *You keep their memories close, and you go on.* Well, she would know. Of all the losers who adopted themselves into the Stars, Jennifer Stone had lost the most.

"All right, Doc." Jolin said. She rubbed a bubble away from her nostril with the back of her hand, then slid her knife against the bulkhead and began to pry something loose. "All right."

Penny O'Reardon awoke on her back with a pounding headache and a broken tooth.

"Captain!" The radio fuzzed at her. "We're being *fzzt*. And hailed. And *fzzzzt!*"

Penny sat up and clicked her shoulder radio after adjusting the frequency dial a couple ticks. "Captain's not here." She looked around, rubbing her tongue along her tooth fracture. Her long silver hair was matted with blood. What had happened? She had been standing in the dark, hoping that wild woman would stay as far away from her as possible, and then—

Oh. She saw him, lying in an expanding network of bloody lines tracing their way over the decking. "Nevermind, he *is* here."

"Can you put him on?"

"No. I guess I'm the Captain now."

"Shit! Really? Okay well, we have two Sol System Patrol Corvettes on intercept course, twenty minutes out. They're saying somebody called them about a hostage situation. They're wanting to board and check it out."

Penny sighed. What had that man gotten her into now? She frowned. Best not to think ill of the dead so quickly, though she doubted anyone on board the *Valkyrie Centerfold* besides her was going to miss Rolan Hector. But explaining any of this to system authorities would be a challenge, and her mind was already scrambling to puzzle together a way to dismiss the hostage nonsense. A prank, perhaps. If she was extremely lucky she could finagle her way out of this and keep the ship. If not, well, she had worked her way up from nothing before.

She stood over Rolan's body, watching the blood drip through the deck grates. Their crew... no, *her* crew... were in various stages of waking up after whatever had happened to them. Was Rolan the only one the woman had killed? Penny supposed she should be thankful. She was a schemer, not a fighter, and it could have gone much worse for her than it did. She had not believed Rolan when he said the woman was a maelstrom. She did now.

"Get up, everyone," she yelled. Various mutters and groans answered her. "We need to clean this deck up right now, and space the bodies." Yes, even the Captain's. "This boat needs to be clean as canvas before you take another breath."

The crew moved to comply amid gasps and groans; a right cacophony. Penny picked up a section of broken pipe and tossed it on top of some crates. They would have to do something about this hunk of space junk in the cargo bay too, but ejecting it now would surely draw even more attention. So, she would concoct a reasonable explanation for its presence aboard the ship that would pass cursory muster as long as they did not press too deeply.

It was a dubious plan with a very low chance of success. System Authorities did not take it lightly when you wasted their time. Perhaps another solution would reveal itself. Either way, Penny was the Captain now, for however long it lasted, and Odin-willing, she was going to make some changes aboard the *Valkyrie Centerfold* as soon as she got the chance. Starting with that stupid name.

Jolin settled into the escape pod as best she could, stuffing her hastily-wrapped package into the small overhead compartment with her boots. Then with a final glance around the lifeboat, she tapped the launch button on the console and quickly tucked herself inside as the lid closed. Her instinct had been right; it *was* a coffin. She blinked nervously as the pod rocketed out into space with a low *shoomp* followed by silence. A soft blue light flickered on behind her head.

"How's our trajectory, ACIS?" She adjusted herself awkwardly in the cramped space as the cryo-jets began to hiss. What would it feel like to be frozen alive? *Don't you already know?* She flexed her hand.

"I am attempting to lock us into the trade route."

"Wonderful. Send a distress call too." Her breath misted around her face. For the second time in as many hours she was freezing and alone, adrift in empty space. Hopefully not for long. "On a loop, public channels. After the *Valkyrie* and those patrol ships are long gone, mind."

"Couldn't we ask them for help?"

"You think I want to wake up in prison? And what would happen to you? We'll wait for someone better to come along. However long it takes."

"I suppose you're correct." ACIS flashed. "Done."

"All right then," Jolin said, her teeth chattering. "Good night, ACIS."

"Good night, Jolin." The reply came from far away, followed by a long silence and the low *hush* of maneuvering thrusters.

Then, "Jolin, my apologies. I have failed to correct for *Valkyrie*'s drift; there is not enough thruster capacity in this..." It was too late. That was a problem for another time, another Jolin. There were so many Jolins, it turned out; and at least one was capable of great violence. She was reminded of the wish she made as the air leaked out on the *Star*, to become a ghost of justice. Had she done that?

She had killed people before, and not always for good reasons. And she spent years trying to atone for that. Never again, until now. Despite having spent a few moments washing the blood from her hands, it was still there. And always would be.

She was not sure how to feel about it, or if she even could. Like she had shed the facet of herself that could harbor regret. But that was nonsense, because all she had to do was dig a little deeper to touch the pain of it. Past the denial. Whatever she had been capable of before, whoever she thought she had become after, it made no difference. She did what needed doing.

I'd let a hundred strangers die, someone whispered in her mind, *before I let anything happen to any of you.*

Jolin sighed, or tried to. Her mouth and nose were iced shut, and her eyes. She endured a moment of panic, then embraced a vast, utter calm. However she ended up feeling about what she had done, her family had been avenged. And that was a good thing. Definitely a... good... *huh.* She let go of it. Let go of everything.

8

Butterflies

Jolin rolled off the bean bag chair onto her knees, hands gripping the carpet. She did not want to vomit on Isabella's things. *Just breathe.* She was telling herself that a lot lately. Memories threatened to overwhelm her. The attack on the *Star*, the carnage. The rage. That quiet, urgent voice in her mind.

Breathe.

"It was your voice. You saved me," she whispered. Fat tears plopped against the backs of her hands.

"We saved each other." ACIS fluttered nervously above her wrist.

"And in the *Star*, when the air was gone? When my family..." Unable to finish that thought, she maneuvered herself to a seated position and curled her knees up under her chin, hugging her legs. The right one still throbbed. At least she knew why now.

"I have algorithms dedicated to self preservation."

Jolin nodded. "And saving me is saving yourself."

"Precisely."

"Still." She smiled through her tears. "You saved me."

"We saved each other," he repeated. "Are you okay?"

"Not really. I don't know how long that's going to take." Jolin wiped her eyes with a sleeve.

"I do not understand how your mind works sometimes."

"That makes two of us." Jolin sighed. "But it's not the mind, it's the heart. Imagine feeling so sad about something that the only thing you can do is joke about it."

"Ah," ACIS said, "perhaps I do understand."

"Does that mean you want me to call you Violet?"

"What?"

"Fable called you Violet, didn't she?" Jolin crossed her legs. She liked these jeans Isabella's mother had left. Spacious and stretchy. "I got the feeling you were thinking about her just now." Her hands trembled. In addition to the nausea, human bodies often increased adrenaline production as a byproduct of the neural link, especially if intense emotions were conveyed through it. And as the adrenaline and nausea of the neural link was starting to wear off, her emotions were spinning all over the place.

"How do you know about that?" ACIS asked.

"You told me." Jolin's brow knitted. "I mean, you showed me."

"I most certainly did not."

"You meant to keep that private!" She slapped her hands over her heart, one atop the other, scandalized.

"Clearly there are imperfections in your own neural link implementation. We should avoid engaging it again until it can be examined."

"Whatever you say, Violet." Jolin laughed. It was nice. To laugh and to be clean and relatively pain free. She put a hand to her throat. That had not been a pleasant memory to relive, but despite the emptiness she felt, she was glad Rolan Hector was dead. And surprised at herself for being able to leave the rest of his crew alive on that ship in that moment of rage and despair. Though, her own memories of those events were sparse and confused, so it was all colored through Violet's logs. Very probably details had been lost or ignored. "What about Rolan, and the other one... Penny was it? How did I experience their feelings?"

"I extrapolated based on sensor data and unauthorized memory remnants obtained from *Valkyrie* and *Fable*. You found those perspectives useful I hope."

"I did, though I doubt Rolan was as diabolical as you made him out to be."

"I just reported what happened; you're the one who must divine the truth of it." Violet's matter-of-fact tone was markedly different than those few moments of real emotion she had witnessed in the playback. That was an interesting development. Was he perhaps holding back a little bit, struggling to understand it himself?

"Well, I'm going to call you Violet. Unless you don't want me to," she said.

The hologram whirred for a long moment. "You may call me Violet."

"Good. It suits you." Jolin grabbed a corner of the desk and hoisted herself upright. Speaking of... She bent her neck, which only made her totter a little, and looked at her ragged socks; the only item of clothing Isabella had not provided. She would find a new pair eventually, but was hesitant to rummage through Amanita's things without a chaperone. Also surprising. Most times she would not think much of doing a little snooping. She frowned. A revelation for later.

For now, she had figured out how to find her boots.

"Where is our escape pod?"

"In the hangar."

Wooziness lingered, but the worst had passed. Steadying herself against the armoire, she took another long, slow breath. It was probably an effect of the cryo-sleep, exacerbated by the neural link, but the feelings she had dredged up seemed to be waxing and waning, flowing like icy waves upon a volcanic shore. Trapped between them, she was obsidian. Solid. Collected.

But at any moment she might be swept away. A flood of regret and shame that threatened to engulf her. It was all so extremely *present*.

Surely cryo-sleep was the main culprit. She had certainly never spent close to that long on ice before; there was no reason for it when you could make the trip from Earth to Neptune in four or five months, or bump there in seconds for a couple thousand credits. Well, if you *had* a couple thousand credits.

"You'll need to head up to the—"

"You know what," Jolin interrupted, "I think I'll just wander the ship for a while, find my own way, clear my head."

"Of course," Violet intoned.

Letting go of the shelf, Jolin approached the hatch. "Okay," she said, "I'm ready."

The cargo hold of the *Syracusia* was nowhere near as large as the *Valkyrie's*. And it was not even technically for cargo. It was a hangar. There was room for four short range fighters, and what immediately caught Jolin's eye when she slid down the ladder was the single ship in storage. It was covered and parked, and clearly had not been flown in a while, but she paused to admire its sleekness, the lithe curves hinted at beneath the canvas. Jolin had never interacted much with single-person ships; she was a bridge officer, and before that a weapons and engineering grunt. But she had always respected flyers.

A man the size of Ajax would barely fit into a fighter that small, so either Amanita or Isabella was the pilot. Resisting the urge to get closer, she made her way instead to her escape pod, which was lashed to the deck with thick gray straps similar to the ones Ajax had used to bind her wrists and ankles. Portside, a large retractable door looked out on stars through narrow windows. It was sealed now, of course. She could see forcefield generators along the edges, but keeping the forcefield up would be a hell of a power drain on a ship this size.

She loosened the straps and pried the pod open. It was a mess. And was that a bloody face print on the underside of the lid? "Can you imagine what I must have looked like, lurching out of there and attacking Ajax?"

"I don't have to, Jolin," ACIS... *Violet* said. "I was there. I would offer to show you but for my concerns about the neural link."

"That's not something I ever need to see, thanks." Visions of her battered face in the mirror were still fresh.

"Of course."

The compartment at the head of the pod was difficult to wrench open, but she managed it with some effort. And there they were, her boots and the bundle she had stowed. She lifted that out first and sat on the lip of the pod with it in her lap. She ran her fingers over it. Whatever was in there, it was hefty.

She had wrapped it in her ruined coat, shredded to bits from her fight through the *Valkyrie* and subsequent skirmish with Rolan. That jacket was custom, based on the design of Captain Quin's, complete with the bright purple flower over the left breast.

She traced the stitching fondly, and pieces of it came away in her hands. Sighing, she began to unwrap the rest of it, but as she did, the hangar hatch opened and Isabella entered, wearing her flight suit.

Jolin froze. Not that she was worried she was not supposed to be down here of course. Though she *had* told Isabella she would stay in her cabin. No. She had every right to be down here. Either way, Isabella had not noticed her, so she was free to watch the younger woman work. She considered approaching, but the look on Isabella's face was severe.

Isabella pulled down the canvas covering the fighter, and Jolin's mouth dropped open. The ship was gorgeous, bold red with white accents, and a two-seater? What was a machine like that doing on this old hunk of junk?

Isabella climbed into the cockpit, and the lights in the hangar went off. Rather than engage the forcefield, she was just going to open the door. Made sense. No reason to waste the power. Not like there was somebody else in here who could asphyxiate, right? A countdown sounded over the loudspeaker.

"I suggest we get her attention right away," Violet said.

"You think?" Jolin stuffed the bundle back into the life pod, grabbing her magnet boots. She would need them if that door opened and the hangar gravity was disengaged, not that she could survive for long without any air. But it was her best chance if she could not get Isabella's attention.

"Ten seconds," Violet echoed the countdown.

"I can hear it!" She strapped on the boots and looked around for something to throw.

Isabella was stunned. In her grief and anger she had forgotten about their guest entirely; had not even noticed Jolin was gone from her room when she stopped to grab her flight gear.

"I'm so sorry," she said, climbing halfway out of the cockpit.

"For what? Almost killing me, or not inviting me to ride in your sexy starfighter?"

Isabella snorted. *This woman!* "I'm used to knowing where everyone is at all times," she admitted. "But I guess I lost myself a little."

"Happens to us all." Jolin stepped onto the wing and pulled up the ladder. "How did things go with your mother?"

The question caught Isabella off guard, and she must have betrayed something of that on her face, because the other woman's eyes widened.

"Oh no," Jolin whispered.

Isabella looked away.

"What happened?" Jolin crouched on the wing.

The concern in her eyes was genuine enough, so Isabella related the news she had received, proud of herself for not breaking down in tears halfway through. Her mortification would have been complete if Jolin had seen her crying.

Even so, the other woman's face grew dark as she finished, and Isabella quickly grabbed the cloth she had cleaned the cockpit with to wipe her eyes. That was a mistake; the thing was filthy, but she kept on with it out of stubbornness, blinking away the sting.

"So we'll go find her," Jolin said, sliding into the second seat. It faced opposite the pilot's chair and had easy access to rear guns, a secondary navigation computer, and the electronics panels.

"You don't have a suit," Isabella said, putting a hand on Jolin's arm. "I doubt there is any atmosphere on the station."

"Of course there is." Jolin placed her hand over Isabella's and gave it a gentle squeeze.

"What?"

"Well, if there's no air, then your mother can't be alive." Jolin turned and pulled the safety harness across her shoulders. "But she *is* alive, right? So there must be. Now sit down and let's go get her."

A great wracking shudder buckled Isabella's knees and collapsed her awkwardly back into her seat. Something about the clarity of Jolin's confidence cut her in half, despite its irrationality. The creaky faux leather sagged happily under her weight. With a slow inhale, hindered by only a single half-hitch of a sob, Isabella wiped away another tear. She wanted so much to believe it.

She *had* to.

"Right?" Jolin repeated, tapping at the controls. The canopy lowered. It had been a while since a co-pilot sat in that chair. It felt alien, and wonderful. The woman's quick cadence and sudden professionalism lent Isabella strength; she had no reason to do any of this, and Jolin should be recuperating for a month after what she had been through. And yet, here she was.

Finally, Isabella nodded. Then, remembering Jolin could not see her, spoke up. "Right."

Right.

"Good." Jolin cranked the canopy's locking mechanism into place.

After strapping in and reconnecting her flight suit's inertia compensator, Isabella renewed the depressurization countdown. "You know," she said, "if we land over there and there isn't any oxygen, neither one of us is going to be able to get out."

"Then we'll thank starlight for the atmosphere when we get a good whiff of stale air and kiosk pretzels."

Isabella smiled. "Yeah," she said as the hangar door began its ponderous recession. "Thank starlight."

In the empty minutes after Ajax watched her starfighter rocketed towards *Europa Two* on a streak of blue fire, he offered a quiet prayer and reminded himself that Isabella was an adult. A competent one. He had nothing to be worried about. The arm of his chair creaked in protest, and he forced himself to loosen the death grip he had on it.

Scanners showed they were the only large vessels in the area. And what the viewer could show him past the knobby hull of the *Dawn* indicated that the ruined station was coasting at a relative stop off the starboard side. The same side where *Syracusia* was docked. As always when he confronted one of these stations, Ajax was in awe of the achievement; that humans could build such massive structures in the vacuum of space was a testament to the entire species.

Despite the difficulties and differences in point of view that had plagued them since somebody first rubbed two sticks together to make fire, they were always pushing forward. That kept him going through a lot of uncertainty, knowing that no matter what the universe threw at him, there was a way to overcome it and even prosper.

He slouched in the chair and sipped his coffee, then winced. Stuck in his own mind, he had let it sit long enough to cool. Sighing, he swirled the tepid liquid around and tried to figure out how he was supposed to distract himself for the next few hours. Fretting about things he had no control over was not going to cut it.

An alert dinged at the tactical station, and he nearly dropped the mug. Two realizations spiked through him. First, he had forgotten about Jolin Aster entirely, and probably would not have thought of her now if she had not so recently sat at that console.

That embarrassment was superseded immediately, however, as a second warship appeared on the scanners moments before its arrival sent a bump wave crawling through space like a ribbon of rainbow fire. He tapped a few buttons.

It was not broadcasting an IDENT.

Ajax turned the external cameras toward it and put the image on screen. A long moment passed in silence as he slowly approached the graphalon panels. Would that ACIS node of Aster's be able to shed some light on it? He had to admit to a certain curiosity at the way it had lit up his bridge with information. Izzie had said it was neat. He smiled and reached for the intercom controls. It could not hurt to ask.

Then he cursed as plasma bolts slammed into the *Rosy-Fingered Dawn*'s shields, which also protected his own ship. For now. Blue lightning crawled like a nest of baby spiders over the invisible barrier. *Syracusia* shuddered against the docking clamps as the *Dawn* began evasive maneuvers, and her return fire lit up his bridge from the other direction.

Ajax did drop his coffee then, and he was halfway down the corridor toward the EVP before the mug smashed to pieces on the deck.

The wreckage of *Europa Two* engulfed them in its enormous shadow as they approached. Jolin strained her neck trying to get a look at it. Even shorn in two it was massive, easily eclipsing the impressively gargantuan *Rosy-Fingered Dawn*. Without trying to be too obvious, she was struggling to locate a working forcefield that might indicate the presence of air.

What had she been thinking, hopping into a starfighter without a flight suit? She had *not* been thinking, was the answer. Not with her brain, anyway. Every instinct had been screaming at her, which would not have been so bad if there had been a distinct point of view.

But it was a menagerie in there, and her nausea still had not quite faded. She felt like a teenager again. And not in the good way.

"I don't see the search party," Isabella said, tapping at her scanner.

"Violet?" Jolin lifted her wrist.

"With your perm—" Violet began.

"Huh?" Isabella turned to look at her, which meant their faces were only inches away. Jolin yelped and turned back to the rear.

"I've asked to be called Violet," the ACIS node replied.

"Oh!" Isabella said. "That's a lovely name." Jolin could hear her smile.

"Thank you," Violet continued. "With your permission, Ms. Marquez, I can interface with your scanner."

"Isabella, please!"

"Of course. And may I, Isabella?"

Isabella hesitated.

"It's okay," Jolin interrupted. "You don't have to. We can make do with—"

"Oh, no. I'm sorry, It's fine. Of course," Isabella said. "I trust you."

Jolin melted into her seat.

"Very well," Violet said, and spun up. Bright holographic threads pierced the electronics panel to Jolin's left, and the cockpit was blanketed in golden light. Jolin frowned when she noticed Violet's battery. Sixteen percent was not enough. Wait. Seventeen?

"ACI... Violet, are you charging?"

"I developed a method of siphoning small amounts of power from nearby electronics to keep myself charged during our..."

"Nap?" she offered.

"Yes. That."

"That isn't a stock feature, is it?" She frowned. Typically she needed to activate the charger and keep her wrist within fifty meters of it for a good hour. Well, that piece of tech was gone forever.

"No." The golden threads pulsed once. "I adapted the power hub functionality."

"Impressive," Isabella said.

"Well, it was that or blink out of existence," Violet replied. "And Jolin was relying on me."

"No, I meant *that*. How are you expanding the scans to breach the station's shielding?"

Jolin craned her neck again. Isabella was pointing to three glowing dots parked on one of *Europa Two*'s landing pads that Violet had highlighted. "The search party?"

"It would seem so," Violet said. "And I'm not expanding anything, just interpreting the data you've already been receiving using my advanced algorithms."

"I see," Isabella said around the hint of a grin. "Let's head that way." She hit the throttle.

The sudden inertia of the fighter leaping forward threw Jolin against her restraints. A ship like this would have robust inertial compensators, but they would work in tandem with a flight suit she did not have. Which made sitting in the seat facing backward an even worse idea than she originally thought. She felt lightheaded for a moment, until the thrusters finally disengaged. She coughed.

"Oh god," Isabella said, "I am sorry. What was I thinking? I should have made you stay behind. Are you okay?"

Jolin gave her a thumbs up. Talking did not seem like the thing to do at the moment, while she was suppressing the urge to vomit. Her well-documented intolerance for g-forces was another in a long list of reasons Jolin preferred to work on the bridge of a proper starship. *Starlight*. If she was not vomiting over one thing it was another. She closed her eyes and pushed the nausea away.

"I detect a suitable atmosphere aboard the station, Jolin," Violet said. "And four life signs."

"See?" Jolin coughed again. "What'd I tell you?"

"There's an EM barrier," Isabella said. An electromagnetic shield would hold the air in but allow the ship to pass through as long as its shields were attenuated properly. "I'll bring us down."

"Slowly?"

Isabella laughed, and Jolin realized she would do about anything to hear that laugh. Grinning like a fool, she concentrated on flowing with the change in inertia as Isabella guided the ship into the station, and on keeping her insides on the inside. Worthy goals when one seems to be overly concerned with not embarrassing oneself in front of a pretty girl.

"Focus!" she whispered.

"What?" Isabella said as *Cannibal*'s magnetic locks engaged.

"Nothing." Heat rose in Jolin's cheeks. Summoning every ounce of willpower, she grabbed the mechanism to unlock and open the canopy. "Are we ready for this?"

"Are you sure this isn't gonna kill you?"

"I trust Violet with my life," Jolin said. The canopy opened with a hiss of pressure that popped her ears, and she inhaled deeply of stale, space station air. Not unlike stale freighter air, or stale warship air. Staleness meant safety. Not a hint of pretzel, though.

"And I trust you with mine," Violet said as his tendrils extricated themselves from the cockpit.

Isabella unclipped her suit and stood, removing her helmet and tossing it into the bottom of the cockpit. "Well isn't that something?" She gestured at the four incursion agents in combat armor who stood warily around the fighter, aiming rifles at them.

"Friends?" Jolin asked, reaching over to unlock the portable exit ladder. It slid out of the wing and down to about a meter off the deck with a clank.

"The admiral said you'd be alone," a fifth person said, standing to the side. She pictured him frowning like an angry cat under that flight mask.

"Well, I'm not," Isabella replied coolly, descending the narrow ladder; each movement a symphony of efficient grace. If she had been a dancer when she was younger, Jolin would not be surprised. She blinked, and shook her head to clear it. *Didn't you just tell yourself to focus?* Sighing, she turned her attention to the soldiers. Why was she surprised to see them? Or was she just nervous? Suppressing a scowl, she followed Isabella.

Isabella glanced at her feet. "You found your boots."

"Oh," Jolin said. "Yeah. They were in the thing."

"The thing?" Isabella's head tilted to the side in a manner that echoed her father's quizzical looks when Jolin had first awakened aboard the *Syracusia*.

"You took a hell of a risk coming here with no suit," the leader of the feds interrupted, striding over to them and pulling off his helmet. He was tall and fit, with short black hair and serious brown eyes. "Sergeant Nguyen." He held a hand out to Isabella.

"Isabella," she replied. "Just Isabella, and this is my..."

"Friend." Jolin waved. "Uh, Jolin Aster." She cringed. Volunteering her name like an amateur. One day she would learn how to play her cards closer to her vest. It was ridiculously unlikely that anyone here would know anything about her, but still.

"Right." Isabella shook his hand firmly. "I want to find my mother, and any other survivors, as quickly as possible."

"The Admiral led me to believe she informed you of the low likelihood there would *be* any survivors."

"And she doubted there would be a breathable atmosphere over here." Isabella shrugged. "As did you, so let's not be hasty about dismissing possibilities."

The Sergeant nodded. "As you wish, but please, let my agents scout ahead first. We have no idea what, or who, caused this disaster, and whether they are still aboard the station."

"Prepared for insurgents, but not survivors?" Jolin said. "I'm shocked."

The Sergeant glared at her, but said nothing. Jolin was possessed by a strong desire to pull rank on the man, just to wipe the smugness from his face, but she suspected it would not go the way she intended. Especially since, like her ACIS charger, the remnants of her former rank were lost with the wreckage of the *Endless Star*. Still, she affected her best Officer stare, and that had some effect. Good.

"Do I know you?" he asked, his eyes narrowing.

"I doubt it," she replied. Isabella was watching her with as much interest. Jolin had explained her lack of desire to re-engage with the military. Well, she had stated it anyway. And it seemed like Isabella was going to respect that for now. Jolin gave her a wink, which elicited a broad smile that brightened the younger woman's face and stirred Jolin's blood.

Clearing her throat, she turned her attention back to the Sergeant.

"Lead the way, please," Isabella said as the confrontation continued.

Nguyen backed down first, then nodded to his troops. They had not removed their helmets, Jolin noticed. They really were expecting some kind of resistance. Again she questioned the wisdom of coming over here on a lark. Nothing for it now but to follow.

She fell in line behind Isabella, quickening her steps to walk beside her.

"Thank you," Isabella whispered as she closed the gap.

"For what?"

"I think you know." Isabella squeezed her hand briefly. "I can't imagine why you have my back like this, but I wanted to tell you I appreciate it."

"I..." Jolin almost tripped on her own feet, forgetting for a moment the simple movements required to lock and unlock the magnets. She caught herself and tried to ignore the heat rising from her neck to her face.

Isabella offered her an arm, almost absently.

"Oh, I'm fine, thanks," Jolin said. And she was. Mostly. She had been walking in magnet boots forever. She fumbled for words. "But, um, thanks. Uh, again. I mean... you're welcome."

"Oh, sure, of course." It was Isabella's turn to blush. She put her elbow down awkwardly and turned to hustle after the soldiers.

Well you blew that. Her mind was a little fuzzy, that was all. Still recovering. She rubbed her wrist and shivered. The temperature on the station was hardly conducive to breezy comfort wear.

"I found gravity controls," one of the soldiers said, her thick Neithean accent making it difficult for Jolin to understand the words at first. A moment later she staggered as artificial gravity kicked on. Unlocking her magnet boots with her toes, she stepped forward to prevent herself from toppling over. Ahead, she noticed Isabella giving the soldier a thumbs up. She frowned. And then she frowned more deeply, at herself. Was she *jealous*? She laughed and shook her head. Ridiculous.

A flash of light caught her attention, and Jolin turned back toward the hangar door to see the rainbow ripples of Sigrid wake. From this angle she could not see the ship that had ridden it in. Then the light show began.

The *Rosy-Fingered Dawn* was under attack. Scattered return fire erupted from the perimeter as the *Dawn*'s combat air patrol fighters engaged, but their resistance did not last long.

"Isabella!" Her shout echoed through the empty structure.

"Strike squad!" Sergeant Nguyen yelled. "On me." The sound of his boots clomping against the deck was soon amplified by eight others.

"Daddy!" Isabella hurried back to Jolin's side. "Back to *Cannibal*, Jolin, now."

"What about your mother?"

"I can't lose them *both*," Isabella said. Then she was gone, crossing the fifty meters back to the fighter as if it were no distance at all. She was already beginning the startup sequence as Jolin caught up to her.

Outside, the attacking ship maneuvered into view. A dreadnought, thickly armored and significantly larger than the *Dawn*. As big as the station had been, almost. And running without HDF markings.

Jolin scrambled up the ladder and into the cockpit as she evaluated the new ship. An older design, the dreadnought resembled nothing so much as a shark, with a rounded bow and an angular stern. Its exposed Combat Information Center rose up like a dorsal fin from the center, and four engines, two to a side, protruded from the hull like the, uh... other fins. The flappy ones. And at the fore, completing the illusion, giant radiators in place of gills.

"Stay here!" Sergeant Nguyen shouted, pointing at them. He pulled on his helmet and closed the canopy on his fighter, a single-seat snub nose interceptor that seemed half put together from parts of other ships. The sound it made when he ignited the engines, though, was a slick purr that rumbled the deck. Even sitting in *Cannibal's* cockpit, Jolin felt it. The other two fighters lit up next, and all three burned out through the shield, toward the enemy dreadnought.

"What do they think they're going to do against that?" Isabella asked.

"I guess they just need to do *something*?"

"What do *we* do?" Isabella looked over the seat at her, fear in her eyes.

"He's right about one thing, though," Jolin said. "I should stay. You won't be able to maneuver with me in the back seat."

"I don't even have any ammo stocked. We'd be sitting ducks out there."

Laser fire erupted as the three fighters made their attack run. Why wasn't the *Dawn* launching alert fighters? Those strike force pilots would not last long without backup. And even as Jolin tried to wrap her mind around what the strategy could be, the battlecruiser halted return fire. *Oh no.* There was another flash of multicolored light, and the *Rosy-Fingered Dawn* vanished.

"No!" Isabella struggled halfway out of the cockpit, then fell back into her seat. "Daddy!"

"They jumped away," Jolin said, incredulous. What was going on? At least she had an answer for Isabella about this one. "He was docked, right? He'll just go along for the ride."

"Oh." Isabella sniffed. Was she crying? "Of course, that makes sense. Sorry." She climbed up onto her knees and peered over the back of her seat at Jolin. Her eyes were red. "I may have panicked a little there," she said. "But that doesn't change my first question. What do we do?"

"We find your mother."

Two small bursts of orange light signaled the end of the fighter's counterattack, and the enemy dreadnought vanished in a prismatic flash. Tracking a Sigrid bump was not impossible, but making a second jump so soon after the first? That was some serious tech. Typically a Sigrid drive needed thirty to forty minutes of cooldown and refuel time before it could be used again. This had been, what, five minutes? At most?

"That shouldn't be possible," she whispered.

"I only saw two explosions." Isabella turned toward the forcefield and leaned forward as if squinting could help her see farther. "Can your ACIS scan that far?"

"Not without using the ship's scanners." Jolin glanced at the control console. "But what would that tell us we don't already know? Three ships, two explosions. If one of them survived, they'll be back here shortly."

"You're right," Isabella said. "Okay, we go find my mother. Dad will be fine, and we can't get to him anyway, right?" She clambered down the ladder again and beckoned for Jolin to follow. All this climbing up and down reminded Jolin her leg had not yet recovered from... well, everything, but eventually the two women were walking side by side toward the airlock. This hangar bay was one of dozens, each connected to the station proper by a series of elevators and slide tunnels.

"Fingers crossed we don't suffocate in the lift," Isabella said.

"I survived six and a half years in a coffin floating through space. We won't die here."

Isabella nodded at her, and the gratefulness in her face humbled Jolin. She had no right to be so sure Isabella's mother was alive in there. But she was. For some godforsaken reason. Perhaps she just wanted to be.

"I do wish they had left us one of those rifles though." Jolin lifted her wrist. "Violet, any life signs?"

"My scanners are inhibited by a significant amount of electromagnetic interference, Jolin."

"Is that dangerous?"

"For the size of explosion required to inflict the damage this station has suffered? Surprisingly, no. I would expect more radiation."

Starlight, Jolin had not even thought about radiation. "I guess if I grow a tail and mutate into some kind of monster, kill me quickly."

"What is it with you and growing a tail?" Isabella asked. "Either way, that isn't going to happen."

"A tail would be cool. And it *might*. You should get your helmet just in case."

Isabella stuck out her tongue.

"I should warn you," Violet interjected, "that due to the interference, I may lose contact with the galaxy-web."

"Ah." Jolin frowned.

"What does that mean?" Isabella asked.

"No net, no Violet."

"I would retain rudimentary functionality," the AI explained. "However, my core personality matrix does not include voice commands or responses."

"It's a lot of data to fit in one girl's oh so dainty wrist." Jolin displayed her forearms like a hand model, but even in this flowy gown of a blouse her arms were nothing close to delicate.

"I see." Isabella's face was inscrutable, but Jolin detected a hint of a smile. It would do. "Well, if we're going in, let's go in."

Jolin nodded.

They approached the airlock and Violet was able to infiltrate the electronic lock, but not the station's local network.

"Encryption and security protocols have advanced quite a bit in six years," he said. "I wouldn't even know where to begin."

A rush of cold air assaulted them as the hatch doors slid open.

"Can't you just reconnect or whatever?" Jolin asked, peeking into the corridor. It was dark, empty, and creepy as hell.

"I'm three hundred fifteen firmware updates behind," Violet replied.

"Does that make you vulnerable, like Fable?"

"Fable?" Isabella frowned.

"Another ACIS node; it's not important," Jolin said. "Does it?"

"In theory, yes." Violet's hologram spun. "Though I would point out I consider Fable to be very important."

"Sorry, Violet, that was inconsiderate."

"I forgive you," he said. "Should we expect that kind of sophistication here?"

"I don't know, should we?" Jolin stepped through the hatchway. There would be a shared elevator for every three or four hangars. She held her wrist up to illuminate the bulkhead, where a sign directed them left to the transport tubes.

"You make an interesting argument," Violet replied. Jolin was certain she detected a note of sarcasm there. "I should isolate myself just in case, until we are able to investigate upgrades."

"How long will it take to update?"

"The process will require more than an hour, unfortunately, and more power than I currently have stored."

Jolin did not like the idea of wandering through this wreckage without him, but if the scanner was useless, maybe it was better to not risk her arm catching fire like Rolan Hector's had. If there was anyone with an ACIS node as sophisticated as Violet, how would they even know? A lot could happen in six years. She looked down at her wrist. The spinning comet formed a question mark.

"Yeah, do that," she said finally.

"At once," Violet said, and went dark. A little piece of Jolin went dark, too.

"I guess it's just us," Isabella said, coming to stand next to her. "Which way?"

Jolin pointed. "Could be worse, right?"

"Yeah, it really could be. Thank you for easing my mind about all this." Isabella smiled. "I'm not sure I would be okay if you weren't..." Clearing her throat, she turned and started off down the corridor. "The lift is this way, I think."

Jolin let herself pause just long enough to watch Isabella vanish into the darkness in her form-fitting flight suit, then hurried to catch her, boots tromping on the metal decking, like a child chasing an ice cream cart.

9

Infiltrators

Grace tapped her foot impatiently beneath the decontamination pulser outside Sickbay and stared past her reflection. She could already see the wide-eyed panic and sudden activity that always accompanied her arrival, though she wished she could not.

Ever since she earned the rank of Admiral, her visits to... anywhere, really... were given a weight inordinate to their purpose, as if she was constantly conducting surprise rack inspections. Tidy bunks and uniforms had never been important to her, but after ten years of being annoyed by all the pomposity, she often had to resist the urge to check shelves for dust, just to be vindictive.

Then again, she had not enjoyed the brazen irritation displayed by Strike Sergeant Nguyen when she informed him Isabella Marquez would be joining the *Europa Two* investigation. So, perhaps she *had* gotten used to a certain level of deference.

"Admiral on deck!" somebody called out as she stepped through the hatch when the decon cycle was complete.

"Grace!" The beaming blue eyes of her wife greeted her from behind a wide window at the back; Sharice was in full surgical gear, her face half-hidden by a mask. "I'm just about to step into the theater, do you need something?"

"No, no," Grace said. She should have called first. "I don't want to interrupt, just had a moment to say hello."

"Hello." Sharice waved. "I'll be done in a couple hours, talk then?"

"Of course." Grace gave her a nod and surveyed the vestibule. A few medical staff loitered here and there, standing at attention, but most were busy with more important tasks. Thank the tides. "As you were, all of you."

She thumbed her ring absently, a gesture that had quickly become habit. Grace never planned on marrying, and as someone focused on career over everything else, she had sacrificed more than her share of relationships on the altar of duty over the years. It was not until she met Sharice Redhorn that she considered making time for dating, love, life; any of it. And even after five happy years that skipped by in a heartbeat, Sharice had been forced to propose to *her*.

As her wife slipped into the surgical suite, Grace caught herself adjusting her bun like a nervous teenager. She frowned, and the doctors and nurses who might have been looking her way immediately busied themselves with other things. It was fine, she reminded herself. But her public acknowledgement of the relationship was still new. To all of them, of course, these soldiers and staff she had never even met, but especially to Grace.

She had taken to married life like a tadpole to a tide pool, which was to say not at all, and she felt every bit as awkward a year later as she had on her honeymoon, a single evening of rest and relaxation at Olympus Mons's famous Industrial Hot Springs, of which very little was spent resting *or* relaxing. Her cheeks flushed with the memory.

Sharice, on the other hand, dedicated herself to their union as fully as she had to everything in her life. At 40 she became the youngest Surgeon General in HDF Naval history, and retired twenty years later to a comfortable bungalow on south Kansas City Beach after a distinguished and decorated term of service. She was close friends with the System Authority President; they had been school children together, each ambitious in her own way, feeding off one another.

Predictably, within a year of retirement Sharice was back in the fleet as a volunteer, training medical officers. Which was how Grace had been introduced to her. Sharice was by far the smartest person she had ever met. Such a casual self-assurance she had. And those bright eyes. Seven years after first seeing the woman, Grace's stomach still somersaulted whenever Sharice walked into a room. After three months apart, it was nice to be on the same ship for a little while.

She exited Sickbay and almost ran into Lt. Colonel Ramos, who was brooding in the corridor, adjusting his gloves. He gave her a quick salute, which she dismissed just as fast. Fully half a meter taller than her, his narrow shoulders and swimmer's body were built for the tailored uniform he wore. Ramos was assigned as her attaché the moment she arrived on the *Rosy-Fingered Dawn*. That was not a common practice; the Fleet Admiral was never safer than when aboard one of her flagships. But the entire HDF had been on high alert for months with rumors of insurrection and assassination plots much more credible than usual, so certain extra precautions were prudent

She understood the reasons, and bore it with as much dignity as she could muster over the past two days, but did the man have to follow her everywhere? Well, almost everywhere. Grace supposed she should be grateful for the little things, like time alone in the lav. He did not watch her sleep, either, as far as she knew. Her eyes darted up to the security cameras dotting the overhead at regular intervals.

"She's busy," Grace confessed, without meaning to. "I didn't want to disturb her."

Ramos nodded. "Of course." His eyes narrowed as a shudder swept through the deck. Sigrid wake? She had not been informed of any pending arrivals. Though, she was here as a guest. The captain had no duty to keep her in the loop on every little detail. She yawned. It was just as well.

"I'm heading back to my quarters," she said, turning that way. The *Dawn*'s visit to *Europa Two* had been a courtesy for Amanita Dillan, as thanks for her assistance with a mission that, until a few hours ago, had netted exactly zero proof of anything. It was mere coincidence that they were close enough to detect the explosion's gravitational waves on long-range scans, and she was anxious to amend her report with these new details.

Of course, she needed to find out what had actually happened first. And rescue her friend. Convincing Captain Tennesin to send over the investigation had been difficult, but necessary. Grace was always hesitant to risk lives, but if there was even a chance they could find evidence that this explosion was sabotage, she needed to know. And however unlikely it was that Amanita Dillan, or anyone, could still be alive over there, she had to try. Managing public outcry over this failure of security—if that was indeed what happened—would be difficult enough without the perception they left people to die in the aftermath.

Sending the Fleet Admiral on a fact finding mission was unusual, of course. Though you did not ask "why" when the System Authority President gave you a direct order. The need for secrecy was understandable, and the fewer people who knew a secret, the easier it was to keep. Grace cracked her knuckles with her thumbs as she walked.

"Captain to the bridge!" Red lights began flashing around them as the call came over the loudspeakers. A proximity alert sounded in the background. More shudders followed, and the speaker trumpeted again. "Action stations, this is not a drill." Sailors began to run through the corridor, in both directions.

Suppressing a momentary panic, Grace glanced over her shoulder. Nothing would change in Sickbay. Sharice was where she needed to be. It was the safest place for her.

"Admiral, please." Colonel Ramos gestured down the corridor. Although his angular face betrayed no emotion, his eyes were hard. "Let's get you to safety."

"You think I got where I am by keeping my ship moored to the dock because I was scared of a little lightning?" She turned on her heels and strode toward the nearest transport tunnel. Captain Tennesin knew what he was about, from what she had been able to glean from his file, and the two days she had observed him did not contradict that impression. But she was the ranking officer on this battlecruiser. Well, on *any* battlecruiser. Any ship in the HDF Fleet. Besides, she belonged on deck. She belonged in the storm.

Ramos grabbed her arm. "Ma'am I must insist."

"Excuse me?" Grace wrenched her elbow free of his grasp. "You will stand down or I will put you down." Nothing in his demeanor had predicted he would behave this way, but she was more annoyed than shocked. Grace's ability to read people was her strongest asset. She wondered if her rage was at herself for misjudging him, or him for presuming to lay hands on her. "You listen to—oof!"

"There isn't time!" He wrapped her up in a bear hug and lifted her off the deck.

She tried to squirm free but his arms were a vice. "What are you doing?" She kicked at his shins, her boots bouncing off his legs as if they were made of metal. The dull thrum of plasma cannons reverberated through the hull as the *Dawn* returned fire.

Ramos hefted her onto his shoulder and carried her to the elevators like she weighed nothing, then mashed his palm against a security panel. "This is where I was going anyway, Colonel. Or should I say Ensign?" The doors slid open and he stepped inside. "You hear me? I'll have your rank for this!" The emotion drained from her voice, though, and she forced herself to relax. He was significantly stronger than he looked, and she refused to debase herself by struggling further.

"Understood, Admiral." His voice was impassive, his arm wrapped around her bottom in an entirely too familiar way. "My orders were clear, Ma'am. At the first sign of danger, get you to the officer's bunker and await further instructions."

"What possible danger could there—Ugh." She sighed. "Fine. Just put me down, will you? I'm tired of talking to your ass."

He set her down gently.

"What possible danger could there be?" She put a hand against the elevator as the ship shuddered again. "And *whose* orders?"

"That's need to know, Ma'am." He reached to steady her, but appeared to think better of it when she leveled a glare at him.

"And I don't?"

"*I* don't," he corrected. But did she detect a hesitation?

"Ah." Grace straightened her uniform irritably. As the elevator slowed to a stop, she could not refrain from looking up toward Sickbay, though the tube had traveled far enough that she had no way of knowing if she was even looking in the right direction. "My wife..."

"Will be fin—" A laser pulse smashed into his shoulder as the elevator doors opened, and he staggered. "Get down!" He shoved her aside and charged out into the corridor like a wild ox.

Grace pressed her back against the curved wall of the tube. Two more blasts impacted the inside of the elevator, followed by a yell and a thump. Heavy boots crashed toward her, then stopped. She reared back her fist.

This was not Grace Lewin's first scrap. There was another thump, and a grunt, then a hand wrapped around the elevator doorway. A head came after it.

"This wa—" Ramos yelped as Grace punched him in the face. It was like punching a bulkhead. She grabbed her hand and cursed. If she was lucky she had only broken two fingers. He recovered quickly, wiping blood from his lip with a sleeve. "This way."

She stepped out into a war zone. Blast marks charred the bulkheads all around, and four sailors lay on the deck, not moving. A few scattered weapons were around, too, and the Colonel was checking the sight of a pulse rifle he had retrieved. For his part, Ramos had a couple rips in his uniform. Who was this man? At least he did not seem to mean her any harm. "Sorry," she began, massaging her injured hand.

"Later." He tugged the rifle strap over his shoulder, then grabbed her arm again and pulled her down a long corridor beneath flickering lights. She did not even try to resist, but when he stopped short as they turned a corner, she yanked herself out of his grip. He grunted, gesturing to where a pair of thick blast doors had been blown inward. It would have taken serious firepower to do that.

"The bunker is out," he said.

The lights flickered a final time and went dim. Emergency power. That ruled out returning in these elevators. "What is happening?" She took a step toward him involuntarily.

"*Mutiny.*" His tone implied he would rather chew rocks than speak the word. He was a die-hard; she had gotten that much right about him. The ship rocked with more impacts.

"Prepare for emergency Sigrid activation," the ship speaker blared.

"We have to get off this boat." Ramos looked around.

"Off? Why? And more importantly, how?"

"Who do you think all this is for, Admiral?" Ramos braced himself as the ship rocked beneath them, then jogged back the way they had come. "The Insurrection wants a ship? *This* ship? I don't think so."

She ignored his condescension, but followed him up the corridor. The Insurrection? It had a *name*? Months of trolling the waters had not turned up that much. Or anything, really. She eyed him suspiciously, but he was not wrong. Why this ship? Why now?

Because for a limited time only, the Admiral of the entire tideworn fleet was aboard this single battlecruiser, alone. What was the connection to *Europa Two*, though? Had they known she was stopping here? Was it a coincidence? Impossible.

"Why?" she asked. Her knees buckled as another round of explosions rocked through the ship, and she leaned against the bulkhead to keep herself upright. Sharice would *not* be fine, whatever he said. Plus, if these people really were after Grace, her wife was a direct conduit. Panic crawled around her insides like a hold full of crabs. "We have to go back!" She could not breathe. "They'll kill her."

"She is expendable," Ramos replied. His voice was ice as he held out his hand, beckoning her to abandon everything she loved.

Grace slapped him, or tried to. He gripped her wrist in a fist that seemed too large for his body. "Let go of me!" A door was closing in her mind, and she could see Sharice's face on the other side. A quirk of the eyebrow and a trusting smile. No, she would not leave her wife behind, would not lie awake at night crying about *that* betrayal.

Ramos must have seen something change in her eyes, because he dropped her wrist. He met her gaze. "Admiral." He held his hands up in defeat. "You are one of three people who hold the biometric keys to the HDF Admin Sysnet. I don't know why they want to access it, but I do know that if they take you, it would be catastrophic. The end."

"The end?" So he *had* been lying about what he knew. "How much more about this so-called Insurrection do you know than me? I've spent months tracking down intel on them. They're street toughs, gangsters. They want money and and lawless sectors where they can turn that money into power."

"I know more than you," he said, "because I'm one of them."

She took a step back, bumping into the bulkhead behind her. "What?" She could no longer tell if the shuddering under her feet was the ship or her entire world falling apart.

"I was undercover," he said. "Investigating them, same as you. Some things I can tell you, some things I cannot. But I do not think the Herald will kill your wife unless you are standing in front of him, refusing to capitulate. He would make you watch. And even then, keeping her alive is more useful as a way to ensure your continued cooperation."

The Herald? She filed that away. "Why are you telling me this?" And what was he *not* telling her? Grace thought about the bodies they had left by the elevator; the scorch marks and dented metal walls. How had he done that? One man against four? "Who are you?"

Colonel Ramos unbuttoned his meticulously tailored shirt and bared the skin over his heart, where a simple mark began to glow bright red. It warped and changed until it settled into a complex tattoo. A symbol, resembling a horse rearing underneath a rider holding a spear. She gasped, and it vanished almost as soon as she could discern it, leaving no evidence of its presence.

"You're a *Himeran*?" Her voice nearly failed. The sacred knights of the Sol System Authority, widely believed to be ceremonial, were in fact an elite defense unit within the military, whose single mandate was the final defense of Earth and the SSA. And for three hundred years they had indeed been an honorary organization whose members were trotted out at government functions as a nod to ancient history and open nostalgia.

Well, whose *visible* members. She had never heard of Lieutenant Colonel Talon Ramos. But even with her clearance as Fleet Admiral, Grace was not surprised to learn their true rank and file was unknown to her. Himerans served the President alone.

Not just anyone could earn that mark. And supposedly it could not be fabricated, though if something could be created, it could be faked. But her gut said he was telling the truth, and that this was a man who would never relent, never surrender, and never allow someone as... *useful*... as Admiral Grace Lewin to fall into enemy hands. Had it come to that somehow, without anyone knowing? Had a legitimate threat to the system been birthed in their midst? Certainly, if someone like Ramos had been sent to infiltrate their organization, this cancer had been around for years, with tentacles deep into the highest levels of government.

Unfathomable. The SSA had its share of bycatch, of course, eels in the fish nets, but the system largely worked. People were safe, and prosperous. She shook her head. Now was not the time to try and understand. Understanding would come, but she had to be alive and possessed of her own free will to gain it.

"Wow," she whispered. It was all she could say, and felt strangely apt. She hesitated briefly as her mind reconciled her initial read on Talon Ramos with what her instincts, and that tattoo, were now telling her. If this Insurrection really was that widespread, then... She scrutinized the Colonel warily. His stoic gaze told the story well. He would not allow them to take her.

Under *any* circumstances.

So, with a final glance upward, as if she could see her wife through the structure of the ship, she swallowed, then nodded. "Okay. Where do we go?"

"I have an idea," he said, buttoning up his shirt. "But you're not going to like it."

Syracusia nearly cleared the Sigrid wake, but it clipped her engines, and her artificial gravity fields strained to counter the inertia of the ship turning end over end. At a distance the space-time distortions were mostly benign, but up close it was like sailing through a typhoon. Ajax struggled to regain control of the ship. And his stomach.

And his breath. He had not run that fast, or that far, in years. He really needed to set the gym back up. Eventually, after what felt to him like ninety minutes of alligator wrestling, *Syracusia* rolled over and reoriented herself.

"Status report!" he bellowed, ducking a spray of sparks from above. He would be strapping on his overalls and crawling around maintenance tunnels after this, for sure. If they survived it.

"Systems nominal, surprisingly." The Lieutenant Colonel replied from the tactical console's chair. "Nice flying." He did not seem to have suffered any ill effects from the spin. "The dreadnought is coming about."

"They'll follow the cruiser," Ajax said. He finished the command sequence to shut the ship down to minimal power. The bridge went dark, and the sub-audible hum that had become a part of his world grew unsettlingly silent. "Just need to keep them from noticing us until they do."

"How can you be sure?"

"They didn't come this far to half-ass the job."

"You think they mean to destroy it?" Ramos seemed skeptical.

"What else would it be?" Ajax frowned at him. "Is there something you're not telling me?"

"Seems to me they're more like to sacrifice the *Dawn* than destroy it."

"Uh huh. What's the difference?"

"Nothing," Ramos shrugged, glancing to his right. "And everything."

Following his gaze, Ajax sighed. His other passenger was sprawled drunkenly over the seat at navigation, scrubbing the console with her shirt tail.

"Sorry," Admiral Lewin mumbled. "I threw up on your ship."

"This is a bad idea," Isabella said between grunts as she attempted to heave Jolin up through the elevator's service hatch.

"These should have emergency power." Once Jolin got a hand on something solid, she did most of the work of pulling herself onto the roof. "Thanks," she said anyway. Isabella smiled proudly.

Jolin glanced around. "Not sure why it didn't come on." It was a maze of wires and circuits up there. She picked one of the locked boxes at random and reached into her vest pocket for her multi-tool... except she was not wearing her vest. *And you lost your multi-tool fighting Rolan Hector, didn't you?*

It had saved her life actually, now that she thought about it. Still, saving her life did not give it license to be unavailable when she needed it. "Hey, do you have anything I could use to open a thing?"

"Like a multi-tool?"

"Yeah, perfect."

"No."

Jolin stuck her face through the service hatch and frowned.

Isabella beamed at her as she retrieved an item from her flight jacket before tossing it up.

"Perfect!" Jolin snatched the multi-tool out of the air. Popping the nearest box open, she wondered why, if the station still had gravity, the more important services—such as elevators—were powered down. The hangars would each have their own, of course, which is why they had needed to turn it on out there. But she would expect station-wide gravity to go first if power had to be rationed.

"So why is the station's gravity still on? Wouldn't it be first to go?" Isabella asked.

"It would," Jolin said with a smirk. "The only reason I can think is that whoever blew it up needed the gravity for something?"

"Like a grav pulse bomb?"

Jolin dropped the multi-tool. "Huh?" she said, peering down at Isabella. She had never heard of a grav pulse bomb. "So, what... overloading the generators like an electro-magnetic pulse? Wouldn't that damage the generators?"

"Not necessarily." Isabella pressed her palms together. "The grav bombs I've read about aren't really *bombs* so much as contradictory programming." She pivoted her hands against one another.

"Interesting," Jolin said. "So, tearing the station apart like twisting open a Comet Candy? Except the candy is..." She sobered at the thought. "People tumbling out into space."

"Yeah..."

Jolin yanked the lid off the second box. Still nothing. The control circuits had to be in one of them. Why was nothing labeled? Ah, the third box looked promising. Sure enough, the elevator hummed to life a moment later. As she refastened the lid, Jolin noticed a sticker on the corner that said "Aux / Emergency" and shook her head. Always jumping in without reading the instructions. *Some things you can't unlearn.*

Isabella clapped. "Well done!"

Jolin dropped into the car and handed the tool back to Isabella. "I was a shaft rat for a long time when I first joined up." She dusted off her... *Amanita's* jeans and noticed a wide smear of grease across the leg. Ah, well, *shit*.

"I thought you were a tactical officer."

"Eventually," Jolin said. "We all start somewhere, right? I'm good with my hands." She waggled her fingers, which were also covered in grease. She wiped them on the jeans. They were hers now. "But yeah, weapons specialist for two years, before they promoted me."

"Guns and knives?" Isabella frowned.

"And these!" Jolin crouched into a low stance called Raking Leaves, making her dirty hands into claws.

"Hand-to-hand combat! I could never do that."

"Yes you could; I can show you if you want," Jolin said, reaching past Isabella to tap the elevator car's *Destination* terminal. "It just takes practice, like piloting."

"Maybe." Isabella frowned. "I mean, I would like that, if you showed me." She stepped forward as the doors slid closed behind her. "I never really had to practice much at flying, though. It's as natural as breathing."

"Huh." Jolin selected the *Return to Previous* option on the console. "Let's see where you came from." The elevator shuddered and began to move. Slowly at first, but picking up speed quickly. "That makes sense. All new cadets are pushed through a piloting boot camp, and those with the aptitude are put into the fast track for fighter training."

"And?"

"And what?" Jolin frowned.

"How did you do?"

"Oh. Well, let's just say I would sooner crash that beautiful ship of yours into the station backwards and upside-down than find a way to get us the hell out of that hangar if something happened to you."

"That can't be true." Isabella put a hand against the side of the car to steady herself as it slowed to a halt. "You're so good at everything."

"Ha!" Jolin shook her head. "You're confusing me for my little buddy." She tapped her wrist. "And you'd never say that if you tasted my cooking."

"That bad?"

"Legendary." The doors slid open, and Jolin cursed.

"What?" Isabella turned around. "Oh no..."

The deck was decimated. A short, twisted landing remained and then... nothing. Like it had been shorn off. The sparking blue emergency forcefield across the doorway was the only thing between them and the vacuum of space. Europa loomed beyond, a scarred ghost.

"I'm starting to think traveling with you is bad for my continued health," Jolin said.

Isabella shuffled backward to stand beside her. "Well, maybe next time you'll bring a flight suit."

"It's being tailored."

Isabella smirked at her, and Jolin stole a moment to appreciate how tall the other woman was, and to let herself savor that smile. *Focus.* It was inappropriate amid this destruction. And yet, they were so close. Almost touching.

"Some view, though," said Isabella with the barest tilt of her head to glance out at the infinite blackness. Then she centered those brown eyes on Jolin's face.

Close enough to... Jolin licked her lips. She craned her neck to meet Isabella's gaze. Every molecule in her body vibrated.

Some view indeed.

"Get in there," Ramos said from under a console as Ajax brought *Syracusia* around. SMoments later, a tiny blip popped onto the screen. "Just one?"

Three fighters had sped out of the station before the warships jumped away, according to his scanner. Ajax had been busy in the EVP, so more detailed information was not available. He hoped she had not made the attempt, though if anyone could survive a direct assault on a dreadnought, it was Isabella. But she had not left herself enough time to arm *Cannibal* before leaving. He was certain of that. The old leather armrest creaked in his grip.

"HDF Signature, Captain," Ramos continued.

Ajax grunted. "Scan the station again."

"Still nothing. If your daughter's fighter is over there, it's powered down."

"Hail the other one."

Ramos tapped the console. A response came through immediately.

"*Syracusia.* This is Sergeant Nguyen Vinh Quan of the HDF battlecruiser *Rosy-Fingered Dawn.* Does your ship have Sigrid capabilities?"

"It does not," Ajax replied. This Sergeant Nguyen was wuick and to the point. He liked that.

Nguyen cursed. He said something else, but his voice broke into static.

"Colonel, can you boost that?" Ajax pointed at the console.

"That's not really my..." Ramos held up his hands.

"Sea and salt," Grace said, unstrapping herself. Still somewhat pale, she took a moment to check her balance, then strode to the colonel's side.

She adjusted a few controls. "Say again your last, Sergeant."

"Admiral?"

She did not respond, motioning for Ajax to take over.

"Go on, Sergeant," he said.

"I was saying we need to call for HDF backup."

"We will. I'm going to open our hangar bay for you. But please, tell me if my daughter is still on the station."

"I left her with strict instructions to remain."

"And as I recall you had instructions as well," Grace interjected. Was she trying to keep a low profile or not?

It was Nguyen's turn to be silent.

Ramos rounded on her. "You can't seriously be considering continuing the investigation."

"Can't I?" The Admiral scowled, muting the comms. "I don't recall signing my rank away to you."

"I... of course," he rumbled.

Grace held his gaze for a moment longer, then turned her attention back to the console and turned the mic back on. "Well, Sergeant?"

"Ma'am." Nguyen's voice was crisp and dispassionate. Ajax had lost people to combat; he knew that feeling well. If this Sergeant was worth his chevron, he was boiling over inside. "I'll return to the station at once."

"Good."

"Nguyen out." The comms went dark.

"Permission to speak freely?" Ramos said. He stood at attention for some reason.

"Haven't you been? By all means, continue." Grace's frown deepened.

"This mission has become an emergency. The Secretary of the—"

She interrupted him angrily. "How many are involved?"

"Ma'am?"

"On the *Dawn*, it was dozens, was it not?"

"I wasn't privy to—" he began.

"Need to know, I remember. Son, these are uncharted waters and we're trawling with a frayed net." Grace gestured at Ajax. "We have a washed-up Captain Daddy in a decommissioned destroyer with two fighters and, I'm assuming, limited ammunition. And then there's us." She sighed. "Apologies, Ajax."

"Oh," Ajax said. "None taken." *Captain Daddy?* He gritted his teeth to keep from laughing. It sounded like something Isabella would call him. Wait, had she said *apologies* or *no offense*? He groaned. Fortunately, both the Admiral and Lt. Colonel had swiftly returned to ignoring him.

"We've got our wits and secrecy, and that's it." Grace crossed the bridge to stand before the display screens, looking out across the moon to Jupiter beyond. Her broad shoulders etched an imposing silhouette against the gas giant's luminance, despite her disheveled uniform. "The moment this *Insurrection* becomes aware I'm not on that cruiser, how long do you suppose it'll be until someone figures out where I went?"

Ajax swallowed. Reflexively, he glanced down at his status readout. Shields were back at one hundred percent, but if that dreadnought came for them it would take just a few hits to turn *Syracusia* into a billion tiny companion pieces for *Europa Two*. He allowed himself a little sigh to mourn the relaxing weekend he had planned.

Ramos was gritting his own teeth now, and Ajax suspected it was not to conceal laughter. He could practically hear the Colonel's jaw grinding.

"Very well, Ma'am," he said eventually. "That leads me to wonder again why you think it's a good idea to linger here."

"Unless we want to play hide and seek around the planet," Ajax offered, "a ship with a Sigrid drive will be on us before we get out of scan range."

"Exactly," Grace said, turning around to face them. "So, we find out what happened to *Europa Two*, salvage what..." She nodded at Ajax, "and *who*, we can, and find a way to alert the Sol System Authority to what happened without revealing who we are to any infiltrators."

"You're assuming this Sergeant Nguyen isn't one?" Ajax asked.

"He isn't," Ramos said in the tone of someone who knew it for a fact. Who was this person? "Those answers are going to be tough to get with no way to board *Europa Two* from here."

Grace nodded. She slid into the communications chair and straightened her uniform. "Then I suppose it's fortunate we have waders in the creek already."

10

Fifty-Eight

"We should…" Jolin started.

"Let's look at…" Isabella began at the same time.

They laughed, and Jolin took a half step back to brace herself against the elevator wall. *Fascinating*, she thought. Standing here on the precipice of infinity, her only fear was making a fool of herself. *You didn't get where you got by being bashful.*

Jolin cleared her throat, but before she could say anything, Isabella sighed and pointed toward the void.

"This was the mezzanine," she said. A torn green dress floated through the vacuum just a few meters past the sparkling barrier. "I was here a year ago. There's a little clothing store I was very much looking forward to revisiting with my mother. Evangeline's."

Jolin leaned forward, trying to get a view of the decks above or below without breaking the plane of the shield. "Most of my time on this station was spent buying supplies or doing R&R with the crew on the sports decks."

"What sport did you play?" Isabella watched the ruined garment float away.

"You'll laugh."

"I swear I won't!" She seemed sincere enough.

"Football."

"That's amazing!"

"Please. It's not like I was any good. It's just, you know, exercise." They needed more information, or they would be in for a long time searching. But the angle was too great, all Jolin could see was wreckage. She straightened with a frown.

"Martial arts, weapons, and sport as well? You really are a bruiser, aren't you?" Isabella winced as the words left her mouth.

Jolin shrugged. "Not really martial arts, just some useful moves, takedowns, mostly so I can end fights before they begin." Her borrowed blouse felt tight around her arms suddenly. She tugged at the sleeves.

"That was supposed to be a compliment." Isabella chewed her bottom lip. "I never say the right thing."

"It's fine. I can be a bruiser. I certainly have the bruises for it." Jolin winced. *Starlight.* When had she gotten so bad at this? "Anyways, we should figure out the best way to search for survivors." She glanced at the terminal. Its flickering lights seemed to be trying to tell her something. "Where on the station would you go if something like *this* happened?"

"There's probably an evacuation procedure," Isabella said. "But for this? It would have happened in seconds."

"The twisting?"

"Yeah, just..." Isabella gestured with her fists, breaking something in half.

"Devastating," said Jolin. The calculations required to manipulate gravity generators like that would be staggeringly complex. Could a human even accomplish it? She held up her wrist, running a finger over the little bump that was ACIS... *Violet.* "It would take an A.I. to do that, wouldn't it?"

"Maybe? That's not really my area."

Jolin nodded. It was not her area either, though a few years spent plugging and unplugging things in tight quarters had taught her a few tricks. The more intricate engineering tasks were offloaded to artificial intelligence. Even on a station, which had no complicated Sigrid algo-rithms to regulate, there were thousands of minuscule adjustments required to maintain orbit around a moon like Europa with the constant tug of Jupiter's gravity well.

"So." Jolin tapped the console and a list of decks appeared. "If you were your mother, where would you go?" The emergency battery indi-cator was at eighty percent. How many trips did that translate to? And they had only—Jolin scrolled through the list—*sixty-nine* stop locations to check. Some of them were blinking red, which likely meant they were inaccessible, or missing entirely. But that still left a hell of a lot of places to search. Plus, the chances they would get shot out into space were not zero, despite the safeguards.

Isabella leaned over and selected the one labeled *Security Aft 4*, just a few decks below. The doors slid closed with a *woosh* and the transport rocketed away.

"As good a place to start as any," Jolin said, burying her trepidation.

"When I was a kid, Mom always told me if we got separated to head to a security station and she would find me there."

And sure enough, as if conjured by her words, the elevator doors opened on a sea of fearful eyes. Dozens of people clutching one another in terror. Someone yelled, and a blaster fired into the elevator. Jolin shoved

Isabella to one side of the car and plastered herself to the other. Someone else yelled, and something dropped to the deck.

"We're not here to hurt you!" Isabella stepped out into the room, hands raised, before Jolin could stop her.

Someone gasped. "Izzie!" And just like that, Isabella was folded into an embrace by a stout Black woman in tidy slacks and a tailored blouse.

Jolin peeked around the edge of the door. Isabella's hands were still in the air, even as an older woman was wrestling her to the ground with hugs.

"Why did you come? Where is your father? Are you all right?"

"I'm fine, mom!" Staggering, Isabella returned the embrace. "We came to rescue you."

A head shorter than her daughter, Amanita Dillan's black hair was coiled and short, though not as close shaved as Isabella's, and with a touch of gray instead of purple. "It isn't safe, darling," she scolded after kissing Isabella on the cheek.

Other survivors clustered forward. One in particular, a young man in dark slacks and a torn blazer, hurried forward, adjusting his glasses. A nest of red hair drew sharp contrast to his pale skin. "Senator, please," he said. "They could return at any moment."

"Who?" Jolin stepped out of the elevator. The crowd shied back.

"Whoever did this." The Senator moved in front of Isabella. "And you are?"

"This is my friend, Jolin," Isabella said, gently pulling her mother back and beckoning Jolin forward.

Amanita scowled. "Is that my shirt?"

"Oh, uh..." Jolin looked down at herself, then shrugged. "Yes. Thanks?"

"And I *know* those aren't my pants you've ruined."

"Mother!" Isabella elbowed her in the side. "Ignore her, Jolin."

"Jester!" Amanita yelled. Jolin thought she detected half a smile, but it was gone in a flash. A wide fellow in a blue coat trundled forward, shouldering a rifle he had just retrieved from his feet. "Anything on scans yet?"

"No, Senator, still too much interference."

Amanita nodded, putting a hand on his arm. "Thanks."

"We're here, Mom, we can get you all off this station," Isabella said, looking around. "How many of you are there?"

"Fifty-five," the red-haired man answered.

"It'll be a tight fit, but we can manage."

"You have a shuttle?" Amanita asked.

"Oh. No." Isabella paused. "We'll have to ferry you in *Cannibal*."

"The station is crawling with... well, I don't know what to call them," her mother said. "Enemies, I suppose. Shooting on sight."

"Why?"

"Your guess is as good as mine."

"We didn't see anyone," Jolin said. They had not heard anyone either. "It should be a simple matter to get you all to the hangar, back the way we came." She glanced at the elevator. It would hold eight or ten at most. She peered over the shoulders of the gathered throng. "How many rifles do you have?"

"Surprisingly few," said the wide man. Jester? She did not like the way he was looking at her. Staring, more like, and not at her face.

"May I?" Jolin edged past him. The survivors seemed to be slowly gravitating toward the elevator. If they did not do something soon things might get a little chaotic.

"See for yourself," Amanita said, gesturing. The crowd parted. A little. Enough for her to push her way through to the back. Sure enough, the weapons locker had been raided. *Next time you think it'll be fun to zoom to a crime scene with a cute girl, bring your damn knife,* she thought. There was a single pistol on a bench.

"Nobody felt comfortable shooting it," Jester said behind her. "But it works."

Jolin picked it up. A Smithcut .45 with ballistics ammunition. She grinned. The weight of it in her hand was unexpectedly comforting. Removing the magazine, she checked it. A full mag meant twelve shots. Shoving it back into the gun, she unlocked the slide and checked that too. A well-maintained weapon. *Excellent.* There were stacks of magazines in an open locker. She grabbed a few, looking around for some place to put them. Another foul against breezy casual wear. She shivered, and goose-bumps raised on her arms. Yellow card.

"Here," Isabella said, holding out her hand. "I got room."

Jolin nodded, handing her the extras. The pistol, she kept. In another locker she spied a ballistics vest, and put it on. It was made for someone twice her size, but she was not exactly flush with options. Pulling the strap tight, she shoved the pistol into her waistband. It would do.

"That isn't blood all over you is it?" The Senator appeared behind Isabella.

"Oh," Jolin said, blushing. "Uh. No. Just grease. I'll... launder them, and, uh, get them back to you." She picked at the stains.

"Don't bother," Amanita said. "Keep 'em. I haven't fit into those pants in a decade." Her broad smile was the mirror of Isabella's. They could have been sisters. Amanita nodded at the gun. "You seem to know what to do with that. What's your place in all this?"

"I tell you what, Senator," Jolin said, "when I figure that out you'll be the second person to know."

"Keep at it, then." The difference in her and Isabella's accents was significant. Amanita's was closer to Jolin's, what the traders called North American Standard, while Isabella and her father were distinctly European.

Isabella lowered her voice. "Jolin, if there really are people—"

"There are," her mother interrupted. "Jester chased them off the first time, but they'll be back."

"That's right, ma'am," Jester piped up eagerly.

Isabella licked her lips. "I don't know how easy it'll be to get them out of here."

"Well, we can't leave them," Jolin said. A sea of hopeful faces gazed at her, and for a moment she was glad to be inside the weapons locker, out of reach of their hungry eyes. But that was nonsense. They were shoppers and office workers, just looking to survive... Her vision blurred and she sat down on the bench, almost involuntarily.

"Jolin?" Isabella put a hand on her shoulder.

"I'm okay," she said.

"She doesn't look okay," Amanita said.

"She's been through a lot, mom. She was in cryo—"

"I'm *fine*," Jolin interrupted. No reason to broadcast her business to all these strangers. She closed her eyes and the world stopped spinning.

"Are you sure?" Isabella sat down next to her.

Jolin took a deep breath. "Yeah," she said. Of course. She had to be. Two guns for fifty-seven people. She had no choice except to be okay. She nodded and stood up. "All right, people, we'll take the elevator down in an orderly fashion." The battery. *Shit.* She looked over to the transport door. The car was already filled with people. This was not going well. Four round trips, maybe five, and no idea how long the power would last.

"Starlight," she muttered.

"What?" Amanita looked down at her. Jolin felt like a child being scolded.

"Nothing," she said. There were more batteries on the other cars. She would just grab one between trips. "I'll go down with the first group." She looked at Jester. "Can you handle things here?"

"I should go with them," Jester said.

"You know how to hook a battery up to an elevator car's emergency circuits?" She would be glad for him to do the heavy work.

He hesitated, opening his mouth, then shook his head.

She glanced around. "What about the rest of you?"

Scattered coughs and mumbles answered. One of them, a girl, made as if to raise her hand, but seemed to rethink it beneath Jolin's raised eyebrows.

"It's gotta be me, then," Jolin said.

"Understood." Jester hefted his rifle. He did seem to know his way around the thing. *Good.*

"First we need to *not* overload the elevator," Jolin continued. "So all you folks come out. We'll do this orderly, like professionals."

Isabella moved forward to assist, and soon enough Jolin had a cadre of nine others scrunched into the car with her. She nodded at the rest of the survivors, and Isabella, who was watching her with a perplexing look on her face. Biting her lip. Her mother stood behind her, one hand on Isabella's shoulder.

"We'll see you in a few minutes," Amanita said, even as a wave of uneasiness seemed to sweep through the crowd.

"Yeah, of course. I'll go down, fix the battery, and bring the elevator right back. Simple." She gave them all a thumbs up.

"Of course," Isabella echoed. Her smile was steady confidence.

Jolin tapped the controls and the door closed. She wanted so badly to measure up to that unearned faith. She adjusted the ballistics vest again. Why was it so big? And uncomfortable, and—

"We're going to make it," someone said behind her.

"Don't jinx it," said another.

Jolin clenched her jaw as the elevator lurched into motion, then brandished what she hoped was a reassuring wink at them. "Jinxes don't work on us," she whispered, but the voice she heard was not her own. "We're professionals."

"She's cute," Amanita said.

"Mother!" Mortified, Isabella buried her face in her hands.

"Seems to know what she's about, too."

"God, mom, please. This is a serious situation," Isabella said, rounding on the older woman. "I thought you were dead!"

"And you came over here anyway." Amanita reached up to touch Isabella's hair. "You just wanted me to buy you a hat."

"Mom!" Isabella laughed through a sudden gush of tears and embraced her mother. She had been refusing to admit to herself there was even a possibility that her mother was dead. But now that she had found her alive, all the worry and uncertainty she had been ignoring collapsed on her like an avalanche. She hunched down and pressed her face into Amanita's shoulder, inhaling that familiar perfume. "I *did* want a hat," she whispered. "And a scarf."

Amanita chuckled, laying a hand to the back of Isabella's head. "Okay, okay, kiddo. You're going to be fine. *We're* going to be fine."

Someone else was crying in the crowd. Several of the other survivors moved to comfort a woman in a blue dress. "It's okay," the woman said, waving them off. "I just... my daughter was..."

So many people had been lost. Isabella could not even imagine. She pushed herself away from her mother and wiped her eyes. They could celebrate later, in private. Now, she needed to be brave. *Courage is a choice.*

Her mother was watching her face, a strange smile on her own.

"What?"

"I was just thinking of all the times I saw that look in your eyes when you were little."

"What look?"

"As if you've just been told you're not allowed to do something you want to do."

Isabella sighed.

"Sensors are up," Jester said.

Willem approached, running fingers through his red hair. "Senator?"

"Yes?"

"We should talk." He pointed back toward the security desk, where Jester stood glaring at a display.

"They're gone again," Jester reported. "Someone is on the way here, though. At least one, probably more. I should go out there." He hefted his rifle and pointed towards the exit. To the left of the elevator stood a double door. They had reinforced it with chairs and a file cabinet, but Isabella doubted it would hold for long against a real effort.

"No, we need you here. Just post up inside. And don't shoot them right away," Amanita said, eliciting gasps of concern from the others. "It could be more survivors."

Isabella frowned. Could they take that risk? They were so vulnerable. Forty-something strangers in a can. "You can use that thing, right?" She pointed at Jester's rifle.

He nodded.

"Will they just open fire or has there been any attempt to capture you?" she asked.

Amanita interjected, "We haven't really seen them. Jester fought them off the first time."

Jester gave a little wave as a few of the survivors whispered thanks for what was probably the hundredth time.

Isabella's frown deepened. "So, they might?"

"I doubt it," Jester said. "They shot hellfire at me in the hallway before."

"But if they come on us, unarmed?"

"No way to know for sure." Jester seemed nervous. His eyes kept glancing down at the scanner. Was he willing it to come back on?

"My mother is right, then. Stay with us. Over there, maybe?" Isabella pointed at the elevator. With luck he could get the drop on anyone who came through those doors, as long as the guns were not blazing.

"And then what? Me against them?" He was sweating. For somebody who had just volunteered to run out and fight, he sure was quick to change his mind. He was afraid, like all of them.

"Courage is not a test," Isabella said. She walked toward him, trying her best, most encouraging smile. "It's a choice."

"What?" Jester held his rifle against his chest protectively.

"You fought them off once, right? You can use that thing, so use it." Isabella put a hand on his shoulder. "Save us, hero."

His scowl melted into a resigned pout. "I'll try." He glanced at the desk one more time. The security console was powered down. She hoped they did not lose gravity, but if power was fluctuating it was just a matter of time.

Jester hoisted the rifle and hurried over to the elevator door. He got down on one knee and aimed toward the entrance. They would need luck, yes. But that would not be enough.

Isabella turned to the rest of them. "Hide behind whatever you can."

She pointed at her mother. "You especially."

Amanita scoffed. "I won't cower like—"

"Like what? A survivor?" Isabella gestured at the group. "Like them?"

Amanita had been a politician, and a mother, long enough to recognize that gambit. "Very well," she said, adjusting her blouse with a wry grin. "Come along everyone, crouch down behind anything you can find. A few of you can fit into the weapons locker. Good." She ushered them away, and soon enough most of them were out of sight, and those Isabella could see were at least behind enough cover to withstand a haphazard assault. Probably.

Isabella was pleased. She had always known just how to push that particular button to manipulate her mother. Usually to get her to capitulate to buying candy, or clothes, to avoid a tantrum in public. But seeing how she had already been promised a new hat, Isabella figured she could use her powers for good and try and save some lives this time. Just once, for good. She nodded and turned toward the double doors. Were there shadows moving in the hall?

Setting her jaw, she lifted her hands as a token of surrender. She spared a glance for Jester, who was watching her; a curious little smile on his face. Returning the smile in a way she hoped was encouraging, Isabella wiped her forehead with the sleeve of her flight suit. It did not help with the sweat at all.

"Quickly," Jolin said as the last of her group exited the elevator. She pointed them toward the correct hangar. She hoped. Without a second battery it would not matter.

"My wife is still up there," the final man said.

"I'll get her." She put a hand on the man's shoulder. "I promise." *What are you thinking?*

"Thank you," he said, turning to follow the others.

What she was thinking was, if she could not save this man's wife it would be because they were all dead. And nobody could force a dead woman to feel guilty about breaking foolish promises.

She hated leaving them alone, but the next elevator would be within a hundred meters or so. She could remove the battery with her multi— *Starlight.* She skidded to a halt, grimacing at the pain in her leg. Turning around, she sprinted back to the elevator. Next trip. She would borrow Isabella's multi-tool again and *then* get another battery. The current one had enough juice to make one more trip back and forth.

She kicked away the piece of rubble she had stuffed under the doors to keep them from closing and tapped the console. Fifty-eight percent. Ice crackled in her chest.

It was enough. Because, like everything else, it *had* to be.

11

Working it Out

The elevator announced its return with a sharp chime and Isabella jumped. A low murmur floated through the stuffy security office. She relaxed her grip on the desk and met Jester's questioning glance.

"Stay there, just in case," she instructed.

He adjusted his grip on the rifle and nodded.

"Don't shoot!" The doors opened and Jolin rushed out. "Multi-tool!"

Again? Isabella fished it from her pocket and tossed it to her. "What's wrong?"

"Nothing." Jolin flashed that tilted grin of hers, combing fingers through her messy black hair. "Who's up?" She waved for the next group to board. Amanita was already guiding several of them through the office. Jolin jumped into the lift, pushing her charges deeper into the car. "Ten more. Back soon," she said.

Isabella caught herself admiring Jolin's broad shoulders as the elevator door closed. She really filled out that blouse nicely.

"Daughter," Amanita whispered in her ear.

"What!"

"Stay on task. I know what it means when you bite your lower lip like that."

"Mother, enough." Isabella zipped her pocket, if only to have something else to focus on. She made her face a mask.

Willem sauntered back into the office, stacking a few chairs up against the door. "Still nothing in the hall." Had he been out there *searching* for enemies? She knew his suits were specially tailored for protection, but that was reckless even for him. But Amanita kept him around for a reason, and his recklessness was a part of it. "Can you check the scanner again?" he asked Jester.

"Is it online?" Jester replied.

"No," someone said from behind the desk.

"So what do you want me to do?"

"I saw you using your wrist computer before," Willem said. "Can't it scan?"

Isabella frowned. The wide man wore no net bracelet. Did he have an implanted ACIS node?

"You're mistaken," said Jester.

"I'm not." Willem pushed his glasses up over narrowing eyes, a gesture she had seen him do a thousand times. Never with such naked menace, though.

"Why are you lying?" Amanita stepped toward the man, her brow furrowed.

Jester was trembling. "There's too much interference."

"It's worth a try anyway," Willem said. "If it worked before."

"Did it work before?" Amanita glared at Jester, who got to his feed with a grunt, his face red. "Or was that a lie, too?"

The barrel of his rifle swayed back and forth. It was pointed at the floor, but Isabella readied herself to tackle her mother to safety anyway. "Listen, we have a way off this station, let's just get out of here."

"Is anybody else even on the station?" Amanita asked. Surely the group they had gathered were not the only survivors, but that is not what she was asking. She meant soldiers. Pirates. Mercenaries. Whatever.

It made no sense. Why lie about that? What was his game? Jolin had said it would take an AI to perform the calculations necessary to create a grav pulse powerful and fast enough to twist the station in two. But if Jester had done it, why the subterfuge? Why was he still here? "He lost his ride," she realized.

"What?" Fat beads of sweat dripped down his face.

"The gravity pulse. Did your friends leave you behind, is that it? Some kind of scapegoat?"

"You did this?" a voice spoke up from the crowd.

Amanita hushed them. "Stay behind cover."

"You thought you had a way out, and you didn't, and so you wanted to find a way to escape." Isabella moved slowly toward him, eyes on the rifle. "You're not a killer though, not really."

"You're lying!" He raised the weapon. "She's lying!"

Isabella froze. Her heart thudded against her ribs. She could barely hear anything above that pounding. Her pulse and his voice, the click of his lips as they moved, his breathing. The shoulder strap buckle rattling against the butt of the rifle.

"You don't have to do this," Amanita said. The barrel swayed toward her.

"No, point it at me," Isabella begged. She blinked away sudden tears, afraid to wipe them.

"Don't be ridiculous," said Amanita. "I've been shot before, kiddo.

And trust me, you don't want it."

Isabella laughed despite herself, sniffling. Even now, her mother was cool. Fully in charge with a gun to her bloody head. Isabella raised her hands. "You have *not* been shot before," she said. Just participating in the argument helped to steady her nerves. The rifle swung back her way. Sweat stung her eyes, but she swallowed the thick lump in her throat and focused on Jester's face.

He was terrified. So was she. She could not breathe. Where was Willem?

"Yes I have." Amanita's voice was low and strong, like a rock wall. Isabella inhaled. Her mother was the eye of the storm, like always. "Before you were born, I—"

"Shut up!" Jester shouted. In the back, someone whimpered. "I don't want to shoot anyone. Just let me go."

"Nobody's holding you here," said Amanita. "Go."

The gun swiveled toward her mother again, and a vice tightened around Isabella's lungs. "If you leave, you die," she whispered. The words almost did not come. But there was no elevator before she and Jolin fixed it, and the corridors were a maze of destruction. It was obvious. "You need us."

Jester sneered. He flipped a toggle on the rifle and raised it to his shoulder, keeping the barrel trained on Amanita. "All I need is a pilot."

The battery weighed thirty kilograms at least. Jolin's arms felt like they were going to come off. She had not rested, like *for real* rested, since the night before the *Endless Star* was attacked. Technically, she had been awake for more than six years. Cryo-stasis did not count as sleep. Well, she was not going to count it anyway. *Ugh*, what she would not give for a wheelbarrow. She hoisted the thing up onto her shoulder. Almost there.

The second group of survivors had joined the first without incident. She hoped. There was no time to confirm it, and Jolin trusted her gut. Besides, it did not make sense for there to be soldiers on the station. Why had she and Isabella not seen anyone, or heard anything? If they were going to rob the place, they would do it and then leave before the explosion. Why stay? So who was Jester shooting at, then? Who was shooting at him?

She tripped on her boot and almost fell, slamming a shoulder and smashing her fingers between the battery and the bulkhead. A memory flashed, and she heard an echo of Rolan Hector's voice on the intercom. "Come out, babycakes!"

Not now. Her right leg ached. Pity she had not done something about that before going into the escape pod. Or on the *Syracusia* when she had the chance. But she had other things on her mind, both times.

She arrived at the elevator and set the battery down. Rubbing her shoulder, she tapped the console and kicked that bit of rubble out of the way again. Perhaps there were only a few enemy infiltrators, doing a systematic sweep deck to deck. But if that were true, would they leave the survivors alone after finding them? Would they be scared off by one man with a rifle? Jester seemed competent enough, but he was hardly an imposing figure.

Then again, if there were no soldiers, no enemies at all, did that mean Jester was lying? That was nonsense. Where did all the weapons go, then? And why lie? Unless he was trying to build trust, which was something Jolin *did* understand. But building trust meant he needed something, or wanted something, even if it was just to not be left behind. So, "defend" the survivors, win their trust to, what, huddle with them until a rescue?

It came together a few different ways, but only one felt right, and she was annoyed that she missed it the first time. Jester was the bomber, or allied with them. If there was another reason behind his deception she could not conjure it. Besides, he had a shifty face. How had she not seen that? Well, there had been hugging, a touching family reunion, and a weapons locker to investigate, that was how; she let herself get distracted.

A conduit ran across the top of the sliding door. Jester had been crouched near the elevator when she went back for the multi-tool. She jumped up, planning to swing forward and kick him in the head, but it was not quite thick enough to hang on to, and her fingers slid off. Jolin shoved the battery forward and stepped onto it. *There we go.* Just tall enough for a height advantage. She could lunge and tackle him. If she was wrong, no big deal, she would apologize to the guy and that would be that.

But she was *not* wrong.

Several things happened next, and all at once. The transport tube *dinged* its arrival and Jester flinched, firing off a shot. Next, Isabella dove to protect her mother, far too late. The universe seemed to slow as the lift doors parted to reveal Jolin leaping into the room to grab Jester by the throat. Finally, the double doors smashed open and sent the chairs flying. Sergeant Nguyen charged in after them wielding a pistol and an angry scowl.

Landing on her belly knocked the wind out of her, and by the time Isabella got her bearings, it was over. Sergeant Nguyen was yelling at someone to not move. And Jolin was laughing. *It can't be that bad, if she's enjoying herself.*

"Isabella, did you get hit?" Her mother crouched next to her, eyes wide with concern. Willem stood in front of her protectively, brushing at a black stain on his jacket with his hand. That damn suit.

She sat up.

"Stay down!" Nguyen shouted. He aimed his sidearm at Jester, who was on the floor with Jolin perched on his back, her boot resting on the rifle. She waved. Isabella returned the gesture awkwardly.

"Everybody okay?" Jolin asked, holding Isabella's gaze.

"Yeah." Isabella looked around. Nobody seemed hurt, thankfully. That could have gone much worse.

"Leave it," Nguyen said.

Jolin got to her feet, holding Jester's rifle. "Oh please, I just saved your life. Besides, there might really be hostiles out there. I kinda doubt it, but..." She checked the magazine with practiced ease, then dropped it with a grunt. "Empty."

"I'm not kidding," Nguyen said as Jolin tugged the rifle strap over her neck and pulled a pistol from her waistband. The sergeant had not raised his own, it was still trained at Jester's shoulder blades, but his eyes were on her. "And you did not save my life. Put your weapon down."

"Tell you what." Jolin's voice took on a new edge. "Let's tie this fellow up, and then, if you can take it away from me I'll let you keep it."

"Enough!" Amanita strode toward them. "Who the hell are you?"

"Senator," Nguyen stood a little straighter. "Sergeant Nguyen Vinh Quan, we met aboard the *RF Dawn*."

"He led the search party to come find you," Isabella said, clambering to her feet.

"Ah yes, of course." Amanita said, glancing at Isabella. "They sent an official search over? You didn't mention that." She regarded Jester with a frown. He was blubbering.

"Oh shut up," Jolin said, kicking him in the side.

Isabella put a hand on her mother's shoulder. "I had a good reason for that. Talk later?" Whether she would ever admit it or not, her mother cared about her father, and even though he was probably fine... no, of course he was fine. Even though he was *fine*, it would be best to catch her up on the day's other events in private. They had enough to worry about.

Amanita peered at her, working the inside of her bottom lip like she had sucked on a lemon, but eventually nodded and turned to check on the survivors. Only a couple dozen remained.

"They're alone down there, Jolin," Isabella said.

Jolin glanced up. "You're right." She tucked the pistol back through her belt, wincing a little. "Let's finish this. I think I saw another mag in the armory." She tapped the rifle with a fingertip and moved to push past the crowd.

"Next group, load up." Isabella waved them forward, then held up one of the magazines Jolin had given her to carry. The only one that was different. "Will this work?"

"Ah, perfect. I love you," Jolin said, and they both froze.

Isabella failed to suppress the sudden tingle of warmth that burst from her belly and flowed into her feet, and the magazine dropped from her fingers to clatter on the floor. She tried to clear her throat, but it was full of sand.

People hustled by, oblivious.

"Starlight! I'm sorry, I meant... thank you," Jolin said, bending to retrieve the ammunition. She held it up. "For this. I'll—"

"Oh, um, yeah. You're, uh..." Isabella could feel her mother's grinning gaze. God, why was she acting so foolish around this woman? Brown eyes regarded her calmly, lips curled into half a smile as Jolin waited for her to finish. "You're welcome." Somehow she finished strong, despite the weakness in her knees.

"How many more of you are there?" Nguyen shouted. He was kneeling on Jester's back, pressing his sidearm into the man's ribs. As awful as it was, Isabella was glad for the distraction.

"Just me," Jester said between sobs.

She returned her attention to Jolin, but the woman was already back in the elevator, crouched over the battery. "If it's just you," said Jolin, swiveling to tug a panel off the wall, "then where's all the guns?"

Isabella inhaled sharply.

"The armory was empty when we got here," Amanita said.

"It's true." One of the others stepped forward, an older man. Maybe sixty? "Hi." He waved at them, then addressed her mother. "I didn't say before, because you seemed busy, but I voted for you, Senator. A few times. Not this last time though." This last was so matter-of-fact; almost enthusiastic. "I'm Hiram Paeko." He stretched out a hand.

Amanita shook it. "Thank you, Hiram." How did she do that?

"Tell me something," he asked. "If you hadn't been here, would they have sent anyone to search for us?"

Sergeant Nguyen remained aggressively silent, but Jester grunted. Perhaps the pressure on his spine had increased.

"I don't know the answer to that, Hiram," Amanita replied. "I would hope so."

"Me too," said Hiram. "Either way, I'm just glad we'll get to live through this."

The elevator dinged again and its lights flashed. "Battery's all wired up," Jolin said, tapping the controls. "We aren't through it yet, Hiram. But you're right. We're gonna live through this." She grinned, stuffing the multi-tool into a pocket as the doors closed. And then she was gone.

Amanita let her pleasant guise drop, rounding on Nguyen and his prisoner. "Where are the guns, Jester?" She was furious, to let it show even this much. Isabella did not blame her.

"I swear I don't know. I volunteered to do this. Alone."

"To do what?" Nguyen asked.

"A gravity pulse bomb," Isabella interjected.

The sergeant glanced at her. "Alone? You got a death wish, buddy?" Nguyen poked him in the shoulder with his pistol.

"I, well..." Jester hesitated, eyes darting.

Amanita sat on the edge of the desk. She inhaled slowly, smoothing her blouse. "You expect us to believe there just happens to be an empty armory on a station that was due to explode from a terrorist attack?"

He whimpered. "I'm not a terrorist."

"You're not fooling anyone," Nguyen said. To the Senator, he added, "It had to be more than a robbery."

"Such a waste of life and resources. Who could be capable of such craven destruction?" Amanita's frown deepened. "Even if they are discontent with the SSA, what does this accomplish? It's a great big universe." This last was almost to herself.

They clearly did not need her input, and Isabella's thoughts wandered as she waited for the lift, and Jolin, to return. Only twelve survivors remained in the security office. They could stuff themselves into the car and make this next trip the last one. Getting everyone down to the planet was going to take forever, though. She wondered if there might be a way to secure better transportation. There were plenty of landing bays.

"Willem." She approached the ginger-haired man.

He finished cleaning his glasses on his shirt, eyeing her with the barest hint of a smile. "Isabella," he said, tucking the eyewear behind his ears. "I didn't say so before, but it's good to see you. The circumstances, of course, could be better. I was looking forward to this visit." Willem had been an assistant of her mothers for years, and if there was one thing she knew about him, it was that he always had a plan to carry her to safety when all other options were lost.

"Me too." She squeezed his shoulder affectionately. "It's a big station. There has to be a shuttle or larger ship parked somewhere, right?"

"Very likely, yes. The corridors are a labyrinth of destruction, however. And I doubt they'll have left the keys above the sun visor." He smirked. The two of them had bonded over ancient action movies when Isabella was a girl. "But I like where your head is at."

"The Sergeant is right," her mother was saying to the others. "It's an awful lot of destruction for a simple arms robbery, especially when you can get unregulated weapons a million other places that would not draw so much attention."

"A statement, maybe?" Isabella suggested.

"Maybe," Nguyen agreed. "But about what? Perhaps someone has claimed credit already." He was tying Jester up with some wires ripped from the security terminal. For his part, Jester was crying softly into the floor. To Isabella's ears it almost sounded like laughter. "It's hard to know without net access. When we get to the *Syracusia* we'll be able to check."

Isabella's heart stopped. "*Syracusia?*"

"Weren't you listening?" Amanita squeezed her arm. "Your father's waiting outside."

Six hundred thousand kilograms of anxiety melted off her chest in an instant, and she grabbed her mother's hand. Suddenly, somehow, standing here with her mother and Willem, knowing her father was close, and alive, everything felt right. They were going to get out of this.

Together.

"Can any of you shoot?" Jolin held Jester's rifle up to the crowd clustered together on the hangar deck. Nobody stepped forward. "Come on, there's a bunch of you and while you've got strength in numbers, if somebody does come around looking to, you know…" She drew a finger across her throat. "Well, it won't hurt to have a little extra help."

"Can't you just stay with us?" Hiram asked.

"There's just one more load of passengers," she said, "and that wasn't the plan."

"They'll just call the elevator up themselves, right?"

"Maybe, and if you'd mentioned this idea while they were still within earshot I might even have agreed with you. But you didn't, and I didn't think of it, so no. I'm not sending an empty elevator up there, who knows what they'll think happened."

Hiram frowned, an expression that was mirrored on several of the others.

"Why didn't one of the pilots come down with us so we could begin the evacuation?" somebody piped up.

"Look," Jolin said, "there was a lot going on up there and nobody stepped forward with any of these amazing plans, so now one of you is gonna hold this rifle and keep the rest of you safe."

"I'll do it." A young Black woman raised her hand, all of thirteen or fourteen. The one from before, when she asked about the elevator battery. Jolin grinned at her.

"That's the spirit, hero." She tossed the rifle to the girl, who nearly dropped it. "What's your name?"

"Miranda." She hefted the rifle. It was almost bigger than her.

"Okay Miranda, you're in charge." She turned to wag a finger in the old fellow's face. "Back her play, yeah? Do *that* for me at least? All of you."

Hiram grimaced, but nodded.

Jolin studied the girl. She was skinny, angular. Proud. Her black hair poofed into twin bunches of kinky curls. She looked so young. This was not a mistake, right? *Trust your gut.* The gut that had her blurting out feelings to Isabella like a lovelorn teenager? She clenched her jaw. Miranda squirmed uncomfortably beneath her silent scrutiny. *Focus!* "How old are you?"

"Fifteen," she replied.

"That's how old I was when I left home. You seem more mature than me."

"Then or now?"

Jolin laughed. Good enough.

"Kids grow up fast these days," Miranda said with a shrug. She seemed to want to say more, but fell silent.

"Well, I wouldn't know." Jolin slapped her on the back. "But okay. You'll do." She clapped her hands together. "Listen up everyone!"

Nearly forty faces turned to stare at her. *Oof.* She hesitated as the weight of responsibility settled like a lump in her throat. "I'm, uh, I'm going up for the final group," she said. "I'll be right back, I promise. And everything's gonna be *fine.*"

* * *

"Everything is not fine," Jolin said as her head brushed the top of the elevator car. The dozen or so passengers of the final elevator ride careened gently off one another in the dim red glow of the emergency lamps. "But nobody panic."

"We're not panicking," Isabella said. "Yet."

"I'm a little panicked," Jester moaned.

"I told you to be quiet." Nguyen had a hold on the cords binding Jester's arms. Somehow, both of them were upside down already. The Sergeant had engaged his mag boots and was standing on the ceiling.

"What happened?" Amanita was a pillar of grace, a single hand braced against the elevator doorway.

"Gravity finally went out," Isabella said.

"And all the power," Jolin added. The transport tubes ran on gravity gen. Gravimetric waves similar in action to the electromagnetic technology of a rail gun; no matter which direction the car needed to travel, an artificial 'down' would be created and it would just fall that way. "Did anyone notice what deck we were on when we lost power?"

Nobody spoke up.

"What does this mean about our air?" someone asked.

"Well, that depends a lot on how well-sealed this transport tube is, and what deck we stopped on. Big station like this, though? We've got plenty of time." Jolin paused as somebody's shoulder bumped into her from below. They were all just floating. Bodies in motion, the slow hiss of air leaking—*No. You're here. You're now.* She unclenched her jaw.

"Should we try to get the door open?" That was Willem, from within a jumble of people huddling together.

"That's a plan, who has mag boots?" Glad for the change of subject, Jolin pushed herself to the floor of the car and engaged her own. They adhered with a satisfying *thunk*. Isabella followed her.

"I was at work," said one of the older women. "I don't wear mag boots to *work*."

"Listen," said another, "I'm not dying in this elevator car."

Isabella held up her hands. "Okay, all right. Please, just let's work together on this."

"Of course," Amanita said. She was holding the hands of the two younger passengers.

"She's right," Jester said, pushing off Sergeant Nguyen. He spun with surprising grace and landed upright. "We need to work together."

"How did you...?" Nguyen was holding the wires that had so recently been restraining his prisoner.

Jester shrugged.

"There's time for that later," Jolin said. "And he's not going anywhere." She looked at the smug little man. He had given up on his pitiful act and was now coldly calculating where to stick a knife in her ribs. "You gonna behave yourself, killer?"

"Killer? Please," Jester cooed. "I'm a victim, same as you."

Jolin held his gaze until he blinked. What was it about him that—

"I'll keep an eye on him." Nguyen launched himself off the ceiling and bounced off several people on his way to hit shoulder first against the floor.

Isabella gestured at the cords that were now spinning languidly above their heads. "No offense, but that doesn't exactly appear to be your specialty, Sergeant."

Jolin snorted.

"Got it," Jester said. The door sprang open to reveal... nothing. Just the wall of the transport tube. How had he opened it so quickly?

"Oh god," someone whimpered. A brief period of flailing followed as survivors began trying to find something to grab on to. Jolin caught a boot to the face in the chaos.

Rubbing her cheek, she glanced up at the access panel she had used to restore power initially. No gravity meant they could shoot through those tubes nice and quick using the maintenance rails. Finding their way where they needed to go, however, was another matter entirely. She looked at Jester.

"Jester," she said. He was pushing his hands against the wall as if it held a secret door. "Can your ACIS node plot a route through the tubes for us?"

He paused. "Might could, depending on the interference."

"Do it," she said.

Isabella gave her a curious glance, but held her tongue. Now that Jolin knew for sure another ACIS node was nearby, she was determined not to risk Violet being hacked if she did not have to, especially by this dweeb. Whatever was happening to her little buddy over the past few years was tenuous and fragile. And after *Valkyrie*? Well, that little glimpse into his mind had been fascinating. Not that she understood any of it. An Artificial Intelligence specialist might be worth talking to at some point. After they finished up these thrilling heroics.

"Except we're not going anywhere." Jester pointed to the useless doorway.

"Leave that part to me," she said. "Okay everyone, there's a service hatch we can fit through one at a time. We're going to get out of this."

The faces around her were doubtful. She would just have to prove them all wrong.

Jester elbowed his way past her and launched himself up to the ceiling. "Ah," he said, fiddling with the hidden latch. The cover sprang open with a hiss. Jolin's ears popped.

"That can't be good," Isabella said. Her eyes narrowed in concern.

"It can't be helped, either." Jolin gave her a reassuring smile and followed Jester through the hatch. "Okay, folks. One at a time." She reached down and began pulling them through. "Don't float away," she cautioned, showing them places to grab and hook their feet through. Jester was watching her, a weird look on his face. "What?"

"Nothing," he said. "You're just impressive." Was he looking down her blouse? *Ugh.* Her lip curled into a snarl, and he got the message. His face turned a deep crimson and he busied himself adjusting his coat. She could not get a read on this guy. Other than he was, of course, a guy like any other.

Starlight.

Isabella was the last one through, and she caught something in Jolin's look too, her eyes widening. "Are you...?"

"I'm fine," Jolin said. "Just bitterly disappointed in and annoyed by men." She shrugged. "As always."

The expression on Isabella's face was priceless. She glanced at Jester, who was fiddling with his wrist computer. Golden holograms filled the shaft. Isabella pointed surreptitiously. "Him?" As if she could not believe it. "You're telling me you don't find him positively *dreamy*?" she asked, and they both laughed.

"I can hear you!" said Jester.

"Shut up," they replied in unison.

Sergeant Nguyen watched them ruefully, floating a few meters away from Jester. The rest of the group, Amanita included, were waiting with progressing impatience for instructions on where to go. Jolin located the maintenance rails easily enough, though they would have no way to clip in to them.

She wrapped a hand around one of the bars and peered up the tube until it bent into darkness. Emergency lights dotted the length of it at regular intervals, but it was going to be a creepy journey.

"You see these?" Jolin asked. Everyone turned to look at her. "They are your lifeline. Do not let go of the rail. The rest of us will be here to save you if you float away but be smart, *don't* float away."

"Who put you in charge?" someone asked.

"I did," Amanita replied, eliciting scattered murmurs.

"And who put *you* in charge?" the same guy said.

The senator stared him down. "*I* did."

Jolin gave her a nod; she was beginning to understand what Ajax saw in her. She tried to recall the last time strangers looked to her for leadership, and could not. There was probably a time soon after she was promoted to First Lieutenant. But even then, that was a desk job. Well, a console job.

Sitting on the bridge of a battlecruiser meant there was always someone higher up the command chain who was actually in charge. She had taken comfort in that. With the Stars, though, things had been different. Everyone had their place; the things they were good at. Where skills overlapped, they took turns, or worked together. Resolved conflicts by talking, or sparring. It had felt *right.*

And perhaps that was how some families worked; her own experience differed wildly. Although, she was hardly an outlier in that regard. But joining a small crew, participating, working not just for money or because you were forced, or coerced, or threatened, but because you wanted to support each other. Well, her spirit had responded to it immediately.

And yeah, times had been good and bad; often both. Never knowing if you would have a year of plenty or be digging for cargo to haul along the outer rim with no surety of who would pay for your next meal. You had a ship, though, and you had a family.

Jolin glanced at Isabella, who was talking quietly with her mother. She and her father had that, though she had no idea what they actually did all day on that Destroyer. Presumably, they ran cargo, but the hold was mostly empty except for *Cannibal* and her escape pod.

Her relief that they were not pirates had stifled what would ordinarily be insatiable curiosity. And who would not be intrigued by a father-daughter team trudging around the star in a decommissioned old warship? Jolin would subscribe to *that* vidcast. But it was a riddle for another time. For now, she had a gaggle of civilians to herd.

"It's not far," Jester said from above, the glow from his wrist highlighting the underside of his face like a carved pumpkin. He looked familiar somehow, from that angle. Or, at least, it was a more accurate representation of his personality. He waved her over, and she kicked off the roof of the elevator and slid along the rail to his side. A miniaturized map of the tube system spun slowly above his wrist, blinking in and out and fuzzing every few moments from the interference.

"I can see enough to plot the fastest way to the hangar deck, though I'm not sure which hangar you landed in."

"Oh, that's easy, it was..." Jolin cleared her throat. This was the sort of little detail she relied on Violet for. She glanced at her wrist without intending to. "Isabella, which hangar are we going to?"

"Fifteen," came the answer.

"See, easy."

Jester nodded, his interest already engaged elsewhere. They were at a six way junction. He pointed up one shaft. "That way for fifty-five meters, then down, down, left, right." He adjusted his suit coat which was floating out behind him. "Easy," he echoed, with a little smirk.

"Can that thing measure the air quality?" A man slid to a stop directly below them. She was eighty percent sure he had introduced himself already.

"If I had access to the station's internal sensors, sure," Jester said.

"DeShawn, right?" Jolin asked. The man nodded. "Why do you ask?"

"One of the kids is having trouble breathing." DeShawn glanced down.

Jolin's eyes followed his, to the faces staring up at them. Someone coughed below. "Serious trouble?"

"Do I look like a doctor to you?" His voice was angry, but Jolin recognized that tone. She maneuvered herself around to get closer to him, and placed a hand on his shoulder.

"All right," she said. "I know you're scared." She raised her voice and looked down at the people who were expecting her to save them. "We all are. This is a scary situation. But we have a plan, and it's gonna work. So, let's focus on getting out of here. Every moment we spend trying to solve temporary problems is one we could be spending making our way toward the exit."

DeShawn shrugged her hand away, but did not argue.

"Does anyone have any medical training?" Isabella asked.

An older woman spoke up, "I was a nurse."

"Good, please, uh...?"

"Ezha Abadi."

"Yes, okay Ezha. Help her, if you can."

"I'll try." Ezha pushed herself awkwardly toward the girl. She tumbled end over end for a moment before one of the other passengers grabbed her hand to guide her.

"One step at a time, we're going to make this happen." Jolin turned to Jester. "Our lives are in your hands, lead the way."

Jester nodded soberly. Did she detect a measure of guilt on his face? Not that any amount of remorse could excuse what he had done. Turning, he pulled himself along the rail, and to Jolin he resembled nothing more than a raccoon scurrying across a patio after stealing a glittering treasure. No, something about that man did not sit right in her mind.

She just could not put her finger on it.

When the power and gravity failed, Miranda Adebayo acted quickly to secure herself to the deck as her parents had taught her. Parents she was certain now that she would never see again. *Never be far from something to hold on to.* Others in the hangar were not so resourceful. She clung to her rifle, trying to get a head count.

Most of them were not as accustomed to zero gravity as Miranda was, and it was easy to tell which were going to need the most help by how far they had floated, and how fast. Hiram was holding onto the starship he had been admiring, which seemed to be attached firmly to the deck.

At least the backup reactor was still online, or the forcefield would have gone down and they would all be icicles. The muted red glow of emergency lamps mixed with the blue of the shield; it was barely enough to see by. She pushed a button on her rifle and its flashlight clicked on. A gray beam slicing through shadows of indigo and violet.

The hangar was large. Lots of room for spinning mid-air with nothing to grab onto. The station rumbled through her feet, and Miranda swallowed. *Be brave,* she told herself. The pretty lady with the black eye and the attitude had put her in charge. She was determined to live up to those expectations. So, she did what she always did when confronted with a problem: She made a list.

"We need gravity." Saying things out loud helped her work them out; kept her organized. "But first, we need everybody close to the floor. We need power, so the elevator will run. And above all we need to make sure nobody gets hurt."

"Those are good plans," Hiram said, clinging to a wing. "Where do we even start, though?"

Miranda shined her light around. "Most hangars have their own independent gravity controls," she said, pointing to a console by the elevators, about fifteen meters away. "I think you can get there, Hiram." She looked back at him. "Just push off the ship." Another rumble, larger this time. Something bad must have finally happened. Well, worse. "We'll need to get everyone to safety before you turn it back on."

"I can't make that!" Hiram said.

"You have to! You're the only one who can."

About half of the survivors had found something to hold on to, but Hiram was the only one with a way to adjust his aim and launch himself in that direction. Everyone else's situation was... *precarious* is how her mother would describe it. Miranda found those sorts of words annoying, but she could not deny it fit. She pushed thoughts of her parents out of her mind. That was a problem for later.

"Okay everyone!" Miranda's voice echoed through the hangar. "We're going to figure this out!" What did they have? A starfighter, some crates that were secured to the deck with straps, and others floating freely through the hangar. She winced as a crate passed the forcefield and tumbled out into space.

"That's easy for you to say," someone shouted. Miranda pointed her light up. A woman in a blue dress rotated slowly, directly above her. If Miranda was careful she could launch herself straight up and carry them both to the roof of the hangar. She could grab one of the cross beams up there and then bring them both back down.

Simple. "What's your name?"

"Tethys, Tethys Pimbergarden," the woman gasped.

"That's some name, lady," Miranda said. "Hold on, I'm coming to get you." She slung the rifle strap over her neck and tucked the weapon under her arm.

"Hold on to what?"

"What are you doing?" Hiram asked. He was hugging the fighter's nose now. At least he had been able to adjust his positioning. A kick off there would put him in direct line with the console. It was a good sixty meter flight, but straight as an arrow.

"We gotta start somewhere," Miranda replied. And, bending her knees, she heaved herself up into the air.

"No, wait," Tethys Pimbergarden held her hands out defensively as Miranda slammed into her, spinning both of them end over end. "Oh god!" Tethys wrapped her arms around Miranda as they crashed into the ceiling.

She had aimed herself carefully, but even so, Miranda had lost sight of her target. Which way were they headed? She flailed blindly as they ricocheted at a weird angle. Her arm looped through something and she held it tight. "Don't let go," she said.

"You're reckless and foolhardy," Tethys said breathlessly. "But thank you." She kissed the top of Miranda's head. "Now, how do we get down?"

"Physics." Miranda pointed the flashlight around. Her pulse was racing, but it was fine. They were safe. About twenty meters off course, but fine. And much closer to that sleek red and white fighter. She held the light on it. From this angle she could read the name, inscribed in glittering script along the side.

"*Cannibal?*" Tethys made a face. "Gross."

"I love it," said Miranda. "We'll point straight for it, to give us something to reach for. Looks like we'll be able to help you after all, Hiram."

Hiram looked up at them, eyes wide. Miranda waved.

"Okay." Tethys nodded.

"Plant your feet with mine, we'll jump together." Miranda wrapped one arm around Tethys' waist and pulled her close. Her dress smelled of tobacco, and old oak casks like the ones her mom and dad hauled back and forth between Earth and the outer rim to pay for her classes. Miranda pushed out a forceful breath. Now was not the time. Be practical. Be smart.

Be brave.

Using the cross beams, she was able to orient them so the ship was above their heads. "Just like the anti-grav playground," she said, clinging to happier memories with the same ferocity as she held onto the older woman.

"Maybe for you," Tethys said. "My daughter used to..." she trailed off. Miranda remembered her saying something about her daughter earlier, when they were in the security station.

"I lost my parents," Miranda whispered. A simple confession, but saying it out loud left her shaking.

"Oh sweetheart." Tethys hugged her.

"Hold on tight, Miss Pimbergarden."

"We're going to do this, aren't we?" Tethys pressed Miranda's head against her chest protectively. "Okay. Together."

"Three... two... one... jump."

12

Making Enemies

The station groaned as Jolin assisted her charges into the elevator car at the end of their journey. The maze-like transport tubes reverberated with the vast, terrible sound of twisting titanium and rapidly depressurizing compartments.

"Is that normal?" DeShawn asked, climbing down past her. He was the last of them.

The groan intensified, and the emergency lamps flickered. Jolin did not reply. They both knew the answer.

Then, as if the station itself had thoughts on the matter, the maintenance lights blinked on, and gravity was abruptly restored. She felt the weight of it like being knocked on her ass. Because it knocked her on her ass.

"Is everyone okay?" Amanita asked from below as Jolin recovered her dignity. Scattered mutters and complaints answered her. Around them, the car shuddered. Something large snapped somewhere.

"Let's not waste this chance," Jolin said, dropping down. "Okay Jester, do what you did before, get this door open."

"Of course." Jester slipped through the crowd. She watched closely this time, and as expected he used his ACIS node to infiltrate the controls. The doors slid open to reveal a dimly lit corridor. She could not tell if they were in the same area as Hangar Fifteen or not, but they had traveled awfully far. There was a hatch nearby, and she pressed forward to it. The rest of the group followed.

They emerged into a wide staging area littered with crates and equipment in disarray. It was partitioned from the landing zone by a set of thick, shielded doors standing open. A stenciled number above the hatchway as they entered confirmed her fears. "This is Hangar Nine," she said. The

137

deck rumbled at her feet.

"My mistake," he said. "But look!" He pointed to a small passenger shuttle sitting empty in the hangar past the blast doors. "We're saved."

"Jester? How did...?" Her voice trailed off as her eyes fell on the bodies lying at odd intervals around it, even one on top of the shuttle. Mercenaries in black armor, at least a dozen. All dead. Broken crates of weapons too, their contents strewn around the hangar. Too late, Jolin tried to turn around. Something hard pressed against her back, sliding up beneath the hem of her ballistics vest.

"Lucky I guess," Jester whispered into her ear.

She reached for the pistol in her belt. It was gone. *Starlight.* He must have snagged it without her noticing. When he jostled her in the elevator?

"What are you doing?" she hissed. "We can save them."

"Hold still. I know how to use this." Jester twisted the barrel into her kidney until she nodded. He stepped around her, keeping the pistol trained on her midsection. Now nothing stood between him and the shuttle but those blast doors. Her eyes darted. Maybe she could find a way to close—

"None of you move!" He raised a second gun that looked like Nguyen's sidearm. *Sneaky little shit.* "Except you." He spoke directly to Isabella.

"Bastard!" Nguyen lunged at him.

Jester fired once, and a bullet tore through the Sergeant's shoulder, spinning him around. Blood splattered on the deck as he landed. Several people screamed and ran back the way they had come.

"Oh, I like the kick on that," Jester said. "Now, I don't *need* to kill anyone; I just need a way off this tub of junk. But I will. Now, little Miss Pilot, you believe me, right?"

Isabella's eyes narrowed and locked on Jolin's, her brow creasing in anger. "Yes," she answered without looking away.

"Well, if you want your little piece here to survive this encounter with an intact spine, you'll step this way."

"Don't—" Jolin began.

"No." He pressed the second gun to her neck. "*You* don't."

Isabella stepped forward, her hands raised. "I'll come with you." Her gaze never left Jolin's.

"I thought you might," said Jester. "Now, head on through the doors."

It was a simple calculation. Both pistols were pointed at Jolin, and she could do something about that. The ballistics vest would protect her from the lower one. Probably. She would have to knock the other one away from her throat, in a safe direction. But even if she had to take a bullet, she refused to let him leave with a shuttle that could save these people, and definitely not with Isabella as a hostage.

"Take me," she whispered.

Jester snorted. "Yeah, right."

"It's okay." Hands still up, Isabella walked slowly past them, calm and cool. She offered an encouraging smile that softened the tightness in her eyes, even as Jester stepped back to move around Jolin.

"Okay," he said, "now we're making prog—"

As soon as the pressure on her neck lessened, Jolin made her move, a tight spin that set fire to her injured leg. She raised her elbow, knocking Nguyen's pistol out of Jester's hands, sending it hurtling into the empty half of the hangar. A gunshot popped as it clattered to the deck. Next, she lunged forward to slam the heel of her hand into Jester's chin. But before she connected, another shot rang out and something punched her in the sternum.

She staggered, and Jester fled through the blast doors. They slammed shut behind him, locking with a mechanical finality. Scrambling to her feet, Jolin sprinted to catch him, but his ACIS node had already disabled the controls.

While she had grown accustomed to Violet's enhanced ability for hacking and controlling ship systems, her understanding was that he was an anomaly. An experimental weapons utility designed to infiltrate and disable enemy artificial intelligence. That Jester's node possessed similar capabilities was worrisome, and confirmed she made the right choice in having Violet isolate himself.

"Are you—" Isabella reached toward her.

Jolin waved her off. "I'm fine, the vest caught the brunt of it." The pain in her ribcage was a small price to pay. The blast doors were thick, and the windows were graphalon; she could see the telltale striations. Nothing short of a controlled detonation was getting through.

She turned to the group. "Did that first shot hurt anyone?"

The reply came as scattered, silent head shakes.

"We're okay," Amanita said. Her eyes flitted to Isabella and back. "Thank you."

Jolin nodded.

On the other side of the doors, Jester had stopped halfway to the shuttle, finally turning to face her. He said something she could not hear, and his wrist lit up. Then his voice echoed through the station's intercom.

"Slick moves, Jolin Aster. Guess it's time I learn how to pilot a shuttle," he said, grinning. "You know, I wasn't going to say anything, but now that I have the chance I can't resist." He took a few steps closer to the window. "Imagine me forty kilos lighter, with no beard." His grin widened.

"What?" She put a hand on the window. What was he saying? Squinting, she tried to visualize the difference, and almost choked on a breath. She saw it now, why he had seemed so familiar; an image of his face lit from below by a dropped flashlight as she stalked him in *Valkyrie*'s sickbay. "Butterfingers?"

His lip curled. "Oh, you're so *clever*, aren't you? Now that we have this little moment, I should thank you for breaking Esmerelda's neck all those years ago." He tilted his head and stuck out his tongue in a macabre imitation. "It really set off a chain reaction in my life. Nobody on the ship cared much for her, but she was especially cruel to me. Hell, I spent a full hour thinking you were my guardian angel. Do you believe that shit?"

Jolin's jaw clenched. She felt the crack again as the woman she had nicknamed Bertha's spine snapped in her arms. *Esmerelda.*

"Until you slit the captain's throat for him, obviously." He stared at Isabella while he said it, like he was imparting forbidden knowledge. Which, of course, he kind of was. *Starlight.* The way he luxuriated in it.

"Shut your mouth," she growled. She did not want to risk a glance Isabella's way. Did not want her to know what she had done. Not yet. Not until—

"Yeah." Jester continued his approach, working his eyebrows as if realizing he had struck a nerve. "A lot of things changed for us after your visit. I wonder if you ever considered what events your little... *prank...* might put into motion. How we would react to being boarded by a System Authority patrol." He gestured grandly, like Jolin's actions on that freighter had affected the entire universe. The Smith-Colt's barrel tapped against the window. The sound carried through the speaker but not the door itself.

"Anyway, Miss Aster," he said with a smirk, turning to walk toward the shuttle. "Or should I say *Diss* Aster? Since you love cute nicknames so much." He glanced over his shoulder as he stepped onto the ramp. "It's time to see what I remember about flying, but let me be the first to con-gratulate you!" He gestured grandly. "All of this is your fault."

Jolin yelled at him; wordless sounds of bitter rage. She smashed her fist against the graphalon, but all she accomplished was to snap a bone in her hand. Her yell became a sob. The shuttle door closed, and the station rumbled again. A stack of unpowered hover containers fell over on the other side of the doors, spilling more stolen weapons across the deck.

"We'll find another way," Isabella said. But Jolin could not look at her, such was her fear, and shame. And anger.

Pure luck had gotten them this far, but with *Europa Two* falling apart around them, relying on luck was no longer an option. Could they even find their way back to *Cannibal* in time? No. She had to stop him, had to save them. With that shuttle they could fly around to pick up the others, get everyone off the station at once.

Jolin made her decision. "Violet."

"Yes?" The hologram spun to life.

"What are you doing? He said it wasn't safe." Isabella put a hand on her shoulder, but she shrugged it off.

"That shuttle can't take off without us," Jolin instructed.

"Agreed." Hardlight wires erupted from her wrist, attaching them-selves to the security console. Almost immediately, lights started flashing.

The shuttle lifted off the deck, its wide nacelles bathing the area with purple light.

"Violet now," Jolin said. "He's going!"

"One momeeeeeennnnnnnnnnnnnnnnnnnnnnnnnntttttttttttt." His voice lost its silken baritone, devolving into electronic noise.

Jolin felt a pinch in her wrist, like a mild electric shock. The holograms vanished with a *pop*. She cursed, grabbing her wrist with her broken hand, then cursed again. On the other side of the blast door, the shuttle's thrusters flared to life, then sputtered. The ship careened toward the EM barrier haphazardly before grinding to a halt a few meters short of it. The body on top of it slid forward and tumbled to the deck like a rag doll.

"What happened?" Amanita asked. She was holding the youngest girl in her arms.

"You had one of those this whole time?" DeShawn said.

A blackened burn sizzled on Jolin's wrist.

Isabella's hands covered her mouth. "Oh no."

"Violet?" Jolin whispered. There was no response. *He said it was not safe.* A sudden swell of tears obscured her vision, and she turned away from the group. Her failure was complete. On the other side of the window, the shuttle door opened and Jester marched angrily across the deck toward them. His ACIS node swirled, and the blast doors retracted.

"Tell me the password!" he demanded, aiming the pistol at Jolin. He was too far away to make that shot accurately while moving, which meant the survivors were at risk. She stepped through the door, moving to one side and motioning for the others to stay back.

"What are you talking about?" Jolin asked, but she knew. *Violet.*

"How's your wrist?"

Jolin snarled.

"Yeah, I remembered that bit too. Guess your ACIS isn't the fastest hacker in the parsec anymore." He took a couple more steps toward her. "As soon as you climbed off that elevator, I recognized you," he said. The pistol shook in his grip. "So I instructed my ACIS to hack yours, the way you did to Captain Hector. How's it feel?"

Jolin kept moving away from the door. The shuttle stood open behind him, but it was too far to make a break for it without risking herself, or the others. At this range there were plenty of places on her body the vest did not protect. It was large, but not that large.

Isabella watched her from behind the doorway. *Good.* Jolin turned her attention back to Jester.

"Not great, Butterfingers," she said at last.

He scowled. She should not taunt him; there were better ways to keep his attention. But her intense shame over what she had allowed him to do to Violet was apparently manifesting as supreme irritation. She allowed herself to imagine twisting his head off.

The station rocked violently as something exploded somewhere, almost throwing her to the deck. A few of the others did fall, but were quickly helped to their feet by the rest. They did not have much time left, so perhaps her irritation was warranted for that reason alone, above the other. She needed to focus. Use every tool in her kit.

"You have a chance to save them," she said.

"I know." He glanced their direction, frowning at the crate. The fingers on his left hand twitched as if he wanted to do something, but was not sure what.

"So save them. Save us all. We don't have to end today as enemies."

He sneered. "It's hard to be enemies with a dead woman."

"I think you'll find out the same thing as Captain Hector," she said, taking a few more steps toward the shuttle. "I'm not so easy to kill. We've done this twice now, Jester. Do you really need a replay?"

If that got to him, he did not show it. He was ten meters away now, still too far to rush. "You think we didn't know you were out there all that time?" he countered. "Frozen and lost?"

Jolin paused. *Of course.* She had never planned on being in the pod that long; her diversion had been temporary, and the *Valkyrie* would have been able to track its escape pods. Though, she had tried to disable that.

"Yeah, you see now, I think," he said, crossing the distance between them. Five, six meters now. *Close.* "That was our first mate's decision. Let her float, she said. The only command she ever gave I agreed with."

"Doesn't matter." Jolin held up her hands. "That's the past. This is today. Take them with you, at least. I'll stay behind. Where is it you think you'll go in a short-range shuttle alone anyway? Europa One? As soon as the *Syracusia* realizes you're alone they'll blow you out of the sky." That was a bluff, Ajax would not be so quick to fire without knowing the situation.

Jester hesitated, but recovered quickly. "I'll take that chance. Now give me the password." He seemed to realize how close he was to her now, and stepped back. Jolin's fists curled.

His eyes were fire. He trembled, holding the pistol out like a talisman that could protect him from her by its mere presence. He was afraid. That would not do. No, he needed to feel in control.

As if sensing her intent, he swept the pistol to the side, pointing it at the crowd.

No.

"Please," she whispered, making herself small, cowering just a little. She fixed her eyes on the gun instead of him, and licked her lips. His fingers shifted on the grip as his fear melted into a confident smirk. *Smug little prick.* He leveled the weapon at her again.

Still too far... she needed a distraction.

"You're never alone," Freeman said with a laugh, "even with you're alone."

Jolin frowned, straightening. She kept her fists on his gi, though, her knees around his arms. She had him, and said so.

"And yet," he replied.

Jolin made a show of looking behind Jester; widened her eyes in fear as if she saw something bearing down on them. His head turned halfway to look before he caught himself, but she was already moving. Her rage and shame boiling over, she sprang forward and ducked under his aim as he fired off a shot reflexively.

Grabbing the gun, she pivoted her body into his, elbowing him in the throat with her right arm and twisting his wrist with the other until it popped. The weapon came away in her grip and Jester screamed, falling to his belly. She rode him down, landing with her knee on his back.

"Now, isn't this familiar?" she said, pressing the pistol to his neck.

He moaned. "Don't kill me!"

"Sorry, Jester." She drew the hammer back; her finger tensed on the trigger. Blood pounded behind her eyeballs. "This thing doesn't have a stun setting."

"Jolin." Isabella approached warily, hands out like she was trying to calm a wild animal. Behind her, the survivors were running toward the shuttle. Something was on fire over there, beyond the blast doors. Smoke billowed into the hangar. "We're out of time. If we want to retrieve the others we have to go now."

Out of time. The words echoed in her skull. And the fear in Isabella's eyes was not for herself. Jolin's anger melted away beneath that stare, and she eased pressure on the trigger, uncocking the gun.

"I..." she did not know what to say.

"Let's go," said Isabella. "We won."

Jolin nodded and stuffed the pistol into her belt. The barrel was still warm.

Jester breathed a deep sigh followed by a groan as she renewed pressure on his back. "Yeah, okay," she said. "Let's get the hell out of here."

She led Jester to the shuttle after tying his wrists, making sure to do a better job than Nguyen had done, and deposited him on the floor. A child coughed, but otherwise the shuttle was silent. Jolin hurried forward into the cockpit. There would be time for relief later. Two seats, pilot and co-pilot. She glanced at Isabella. "Can you fly this thing?"

"Of course." Isabella put a hand on Jolin's arm as she slid past and into the pilot's chair. Jolin deposited herself in the other. Isabella pointed at the flight console, where a single word floated in golden holographics. "Passcode?" she asked.

Jolin exhaled slowly, even as the deck beneath the shuttle began to buckle. "GOFUCKYOURSELF. All caps."

Isabella's brow furrowed, but she tapped the keys and the shuttle sprang to life.

Jolin settled into her seat, whispering thanks to Violet. Wherever he was. "Strap in, everyone," she said, pulling the safety harness down over her chest. Isabella slid the throttle forward and they rose off the deck. Smoke filled the hangar as the station's power failed again, roiling and tinted lavender from the shuttle's glow.

The forcefield sputtered out. "Let's get moving," said Jolin. "Still got one more stop to make before this entire place becomes a tomb."

Isabella guided them out of the hangar and pivoted the ship to look back at the station.

"There," Jolin said, pointing. She could see the shape of *Cannibal* a few bays over. The shielded openings were stacked in threes along the exterior of the station. It was time to find out what had become of Miranda and the rest of the survivors.

"Are they okay, you think?" Amanita asked.

"Somebody got the power turned back on," Jolin said, "and it sure as hell wasn't us." She nodded at Amanita.

"I appreciate your optimism," Sergeant Nguyen said with a grunt. DeShawn was holding pressure on his shoulder with a dirty rag. "But are you sure we should risk the shuttle by going back?"

"We can't go without them," DeShawn said.

"We have to try," Ezha agreed. Several others piped up in similar fashion.

"Everyone else feel the same?" Jolin turned to look back at them.

Nguyen nodded soberly. His face was pale, his eyes tight. Ezha held his hand, her eyes harrowed.

To a person, they nodded at her.

"Good." She flashed her best grin. "Because nobody gets left behind."

When the shuttle landed beside *Cannibal*, the other group of survivors was waiting for them.

Isabella wiped her eyes with a sleeve. "You did it," Jolin whispered, reaching over to squeeze her forearm.

"*We* did it." Isabella barked a ragged combination of a laugh and a sob. She looked like she might break down at any moment. The station shuddered violently and the lights blinked again.

"Let's get them on board," Jolin said, but the door was already open and the remaining folks were crowding into the shuttle. "All right, well. Great job, team!" She leveled a mock glare at young Miranda. "I see you've managed to keep everyone safe, but where is my rifle?"

"Oh." Miranda looked back to the hangar. "We had to improvise."

Jolin could see it now, wired to the console. "Did you power that with the plasma battery?" A girl after her own heart.

Miranda shrugged. "We needed to power the controls before we could reboot the hangar's gravity generator. I'm kind of surprised it worked. And then we had to find a way to restore power to the entire station, but it turned out the entire station still had power, just not our *section*, so I was able to reroute the..." She blushed. "Sorry. Yes, we powered it with the plasma battery."

The woman in the blue dress hugged Miranda. "She's really something."

"She saved us all," said someone else.

"Of course she did," Jolin replied as Hiram pulled the shuttle door closed with a grunt and settled himself on the floor of the ship. "I told you before: she's a hero. I have a nose for these things."

She reached out a hand to the girl, who shook it shyly. "Strong work, kid."

Miranda beamed.

"Everyone accounted for?" Isabella asked.

"Yes. We're ready," said Amanita. She had given up her seat to one of the older passengers and was standing next to Willem.

"Then we're off." Isabella gave her fighter a longing stare as they exited the hangar. She did not say anything, but she did not have to.

"We'll go back for it," Jolin said.

"And mine," Nguyen said. "It's in Hangar Twenty."

Isabella nodded. "They're not as important as these people."

"Say, Sergeant." Jolin glanced over at him. Something had been clawing at her, a minor detail. "How'd you find us up there?"

"I followed the bodies," Nguyen replied. Seeing her confusion, he continued, "At least twenty mercs beyond the ones we found around the shuttle. Most shot in the back."

Jester groaned through the gag Jolin had stuffed in his mouth. What a piece of work. She would not refuse a few minutes alone with him, to get her mind around what he had been trying to accomplish on that station. Maybe the chance would present itself.

An alarm buzzed on the shuttle's command console, even as the light of several explosions flashed through the rectangular windows. Jolin did not have to look to know it was Hangar Nine, but she did anyway, sharing a gasp with the rest of those on board as the station heaved black smoke into space.

Somehow, it was one of just a few that were destroyed. Isabella was gritting her teeth, and Nguyen sighed. "I think they're probably still okay," he said.

"And even if they aren't..." Jolin whispered. She trailed off, and with a single glance back at the ruined station, she made a quick count of the survivors. Fifty-eight souls. They had gotten everybody out. She sighed, giving herself permission to relax into the surprisingly comfortable chair. Anxiety sloughed off her like scales as her ponytail hit the headrest.

The comms chirped before she could get too comfy, though, and she opened a voice channel.

"Unmarked shuttle, this is Captain Ajax Marquez of the free ship *Syracusia*, please identify yourself or you will be fired upon."

A grin lit up Isabella's face. "Don't be so dramatic, Daddy."

"Oh, thank god!" The voice on the other end cracked and fuzzed.

"Mind opening the door?" Isabella lined up their trajectory with the Destroyer. "I've got some people here who are excited to make your acquaintance."

13

Insufficient

Isabella tossed a towel over the shower curtain. "And that's the end of it?"

"All I can remember," Jolin said as she dried herself off. The filth of the transport tunnels eddied around her feet. She had relayed as much of her time on the *Valkyrie* as possible while they showered. Each in their own stall, obviously.

Obviously.

A resigned sigh escaped her lungs as she pushed the towel through her hair. Isabella's interest was clearly platonic, and Jolin would do well to remember it. Especially after the *I love you* nonsense. How long had it been since Jolin felt so... *ugh*, awkward? It did not matter; she had plenty of more important things to worry about.

Her mind flashed to another moment on the station; the two of them standing on the edge of forever as debris floated on invisible wings over the moon below. An involuntary shiver rippled through Jolin's body, and she slid her fingers through her hair in a way she wished Isabella would.

"Sounds like you had a harrowing experience," Isabella offered.

"It's in the past." Jolin tossed her hair to the other side, ignoring the sudden heat inside her skin. "Besides, I have a few hours to relax while your mother sorts things out; I'd rather not spend them ruminating about how horrible I am." Among other things. She laughed bitterly.

"Is that what you think?"

"No." She pulled the curtain back a smidge and peeked out. Isabella was at the sinks, fiddling with her hair. The towel tucked around her torso left her legs bare. And those wide brown eyes in the mirror... were staring straight at Jolin. She ducked back into the stall. "Yes?" she said, clearing her throat. "I did what I had to do in the moment, and I'd probably do it again. Looking back, though? Hard to say I made the right choices."

"This wasn't your fault."

"You heard Jester," Jolin said. "It seems pretty clear it is, at least partially. If I had just incapacitated Rolan instead of killing him, none of this would have happened."

"So, leaving one pirate captain alive would have prevented this entire Insurrection, or whatever they're calling themselves?" Isabella's incredulity bled into her tone like molten steel.

That was the less terrible option.

Wrapping herself in the towel, Jolin stepped out with a sudden shiver. She was projecting; the woman's tone was perfectly reasonable. "How should I know? I was acting on pure instinct. I was angry and I wanted to hurt him. Anyone. Sometimes I think the only reason I didn't..." She did not dare speak the other option. She could have killed them all, and maybe should have. But was that something she was capable of? *Ask Esmerelda.*

Isabella leaned against one of the sinks, somehow already fully dressed in dark slacks and a silk crimson blouse, a black scarf draped casually around her neck. And watching her thoughtfully.

Jolin looked away quickly, her cheeks flushing. Getting caught staring was such a ridiculous thing to be worried about, with everything else going on. "Um, Where's that brush?"

Isabella pointed to the sink. "That's what I'm saying. Jester has a lot to answer for. You don't."

"Yeah, well." Jolin attacked her hair angrily, her thoughts spinning in a murderous rut. "There's no way to undo what's happened, and no way to know what might have gone differently if I'd just finished the job."

"Revenged yourself on the entire crew, you mean?" Isabella saw the truth. Of course she did.

"It's not like I didn't have the moral right." Jolin met the woman's gaze through the mirror. "They killed my family."

Isabella put a hand on her bare shoulder, eliciting another, deeper shiver. Jolin closed her eyes and tilted her head slightly in that direction, her hands frozen mid-stroke.

"You showed remarkable restraint, given what you went through. I might not have done the same, in your place."

Jolin reminded herself to breathe. "I was sure you'd think I'm a monster."

"Would it matter?" Isabella stepped closer. She lifted a stray lock of hair from Jolin's face and tucked it behind her ear. "If I did?"

Jolin could not find words. The hairbrush clattered into the sink. She retrieved it quickly and resumed brushing as if nothing had happened.

Isabella swiveled to peer at the other mirror, flicking her fingernails through those tight purple curls. Not a strand out of place.

"I'm glad we found your mother," Jolin said finally, sticking the brush's magnetic handle to the mirror frame and leaning in to examine herself. Her face was a war zone. A neatly succinct map of the turmoil in her heart. And was that a pimple on her nose? *Starlight.*

"Yeah." Isabella smiled sadly. "Now that it's over I'm ashamed to admit I did not actually think we..." She stared at her own reflection. "Anyways, you convinced me, and you were right."

Jolin adjusted her towel and shifted on her feet. The deck grates were freezing. "I need to get some sandals."

"I might have an extra pair." Isabella glanced down. "Oh girl, your toenails."

"I was frozen! For six years!"

"Come with me."

Isabella took Jolin's hand and led her to her temporary quarters, where her vest was waiting on the bed, clean and repaired; sweater and pants, too.

"Not the most fashionable of outfits, I know, but it's functional," Jolin said, examining the garments. "Did you do this?" She held up the vest.

"Our dry cleaner has a limited repair capability, as long as the fabric is not too damaged." Isabella shrugged. "Feels like it's missing something, though."

Jolin laughed. "Underwear?"

"Well, yes." Isabella stuck her hands in her pockets. "But I meant—after what happened last time we left the ship. We shouldn't leave anything to chance."

She pulled something out of her slacks and set it on one of the shelves. "There. I put a few more of my mother's things in one of the desk drawers as well." She clasped her hands together. "I'll, um, give you a moment to change. But then we're going to a *salon.*"

Jolin grinned. "Okay, thanks."

The hatch closed and Jolin let her towel drop. She stretched, bending to massage her injured right leg. The recovery pod in sickbay fixed her broken hand but did nothing for her thigh. Some bruises needed to heal on their own, she supposed. At least she had her clothes back. Well, most of them.

The vest was sleeveless, and she had ordered the ballistics sweater custom, jet black and sleeveless as well. Not to show off her arms or anything, just to save money. She always had a jacket to wear over it. That would be her first stop, planetside. She stuffed her head through the sweater, then frowned at her raggedy toenails. Okay, second stop.

Reaching for the item Isabella had left, she chuckled. A multi-tool. It was old, engraved with the initials *I.M.* She traced the letters with a fingertip, then wiped a treacherous tear from her eye. She tucked the gift into the zippered pocket on her vest that was well-worn from her own multi-tool, now lost forever. It fit perfectly. She tugged the vest over her shoulders, then twisted her body left and right, popping her back with a satisfying crack, and flopped down on the bed. It felt good to be in her own clothes.

She examined her forearm, poking at it with a finger. Violet's chip was fried. It was warm, and looser than normal, as if something had come unstuck in there. *But he's still out there somewhere, right? Isn't that how it works?* Jolin sighed. Hopefully she could find someone who knew how to diagnose and repair ACIS nodes before counting him out for good. No, she *would* find someone. Even so, a spear of regret stabbed into her chest with abrupt urgency, and her hand curled around a fistful of blankets. Violet had known what might happen. And *she* certainly had. But they both chose to do it anyway. So why did she still feel like shit?

I want to live, he had said on *Valkyrie*, when Jolin was suspended between this life and the next. She relaxed her grip. The pain eased, but a little sting remained when she moved her wrist.

Good.

Jupiter's red-orange glow scampered across the ice fields ahead of them as Isabella guided the shuttle past isolated fishing villages into Europa's Carolyn Porco Harbor. Portco, as the locals and trade humpers called it. The giant crystal dome was a beacon of warmth and life on the surface of a frozen world. Light spilled out of it like a miniature sunrise.

Jolin shivered in her seat and rubbed her arms.

"I would have lent you a jacket if you'd asked," Isabella said.

"It's fine, I'll find something that speaks to me." She leaned forward, pressing a hand to the window. "How will I know it's the right coat if I'm not freezing when I put it on?"

"If you say so," Isabella scoffed. "It'll make the decision easier at least." The city loomed as they got closer. It was a testament to human ingenuity, and at over a thousand years old, Portco was the longest lasting of Earth's initial colonization projects. The structure was reinforced and expanded over the centuries, but the core remained, serving as the seat of the Sol System Authority over the Jovian quartet of inhabited moons. City Hall. A bubble within a bubble.

The shuttled dipped underneath the edge of the rectangular gateway and through a bright red plasma shield. Turbulence hit as they transitioned from vacuum to air, but Isabella controlled it so well Jolin could barely feel the difference. They were keeping the shuttle; it turned out not to be part of *Europa Two*'s fleet. Since no owners were listed in the Department of Space-Faring Vehicles IDENT records, at least not on public channels, it was fair game under the old UNE Salvage Laws.

Jolin had expected to confirm Jester as the owner, but the pirate-turned-terrorist had stayed silent after she subdued him on the station. Either he knew it was there, or his ACIS had found it for him. Her guess was, he came over with those dead mercs, probably even killed them, shot in the back as they were. To what end, though? Perhaps SSA interrogators could get the information out of him, not that she would ever hear the answer.

"Is your mother going to return to the *Syracusia*?" Jolin asked.

"Not sure," Isabella said, piloting the shuttle through a series of narrow tunnels toward the landing hub. "How does anyone think making you fly this maze is a good way to direct you to parking?"

Jolin unbuckled her harness and stretched. "It's to discourage joy riders from blasting through the base."

"It discourages *me* from wanting to visit."

"Yet you do it so well."

"That doesn't mean I like it." A proximity buzzer sounded as she drifted too close to one of the walls. "That one was your fault."

Jolin smirked. "Apologies."

Isabella gasped as the shuttle emerged from the tunnels into a wide-open vestibule with dozens of landing pads placed at irregular intervals, like lilies on a pond. Their architecture was smooth and soaring, thin branches sprouting from the surface like saplings to support them. It seemed as if the slightest touch could send any of them crashing into the ice. Light sparkled in the dome windows, fireflies tending their garden.

Isabella grinned at her.

"I told you!" Jolin climbed into the passenger area to collect the backpack she had borrowed from Amanita's collection. The senator had at least three of everything in those boxes. She shouldered it, then slid into one of the seats as they landed.

"Okay, yeah. That's not too shabby." Isabella tapped the comms. "Harbor Tower, *Syracusia Shuttle One* anchored at pad six-four as instructed."

"Roger that, *Syracusia One*. Enjoy your visit to Porco Harbor."

Magnetic locks grappled their landers, giving the shuttle a gentle shake.

"This thing needs a better name than *Syracusia One*," Jolin said.

Isabella climbed out of her chair and threw a deep gray shawl around her shoulders that matched her slacks. "He did deliver us back from certain death. What about *Zombie*?"

"You're so morbid!"

"*Nosferatu*?"

"Okay, that's not bad." Jolin laughed. "What's it mean?"

"Old Earth stuff. One of the first movies. Nosferatu was like Dracula. *Das Wampyre*."

"How do you know this stuff?"

"Are you kidding? I only watched it once when I was a girl, but those old movies are amazing." Isabella gathered her handbag and slipped her feet into a striking pair of thigh-high boots. "Everything these days is so slick and soulless. Back then, they had to put real effort into making things interesting. Besides, it's our history."

"I never had much use for history," Jolin said. "But yes, *Nosferatu*. I like it."

"We need to register the shuttle anyway, so it'll be a simple thing to change the name."

Jolin pulled a lever and the door split horizontally; one half went up, the other lowered down into a ramp. "After you."

Isabella grinned and stepped lightly down to the landing pad. A blast of cold air ripped at her shawl. Portco employed monolithic environmental conditioners to regulate the disparity in temperature between inside the dome and outside, but it created sudden gusts like that one.

Goose flesh rose on Jolin's exposed arms. "But first, I *gotta* get a new jacket."

"And a pedicure!" Isabella walked to the edge of the landing pad and held out her arms for the wind. The shawl became a cape, and her delicate golden hoop earrings danced.

"Yeah, that," Jolin murmured. She pressed a hand against the security panel and the shuttle doors closed with a hiss. "Wait, is this a date?" She immediately regretted asking.

The younger woman turned sharply. "A *date*?"

"I mean," Jolin stammered.

Isabella leapt to her side. "Jolin, I would love that!" She held out a corner of her shawl. "Just the two of us."

The breeze whipped at Jolin's hair, and heat erupted into her cheeks; her smile was so broad it hurt. "Okay then," she said, pulling the garment around her shoulders. Isabella slipped an arm through hers.

"I hope this isn't too forward, but I've been looking, um... *forward* to some time with you," Isabella said after a brief pause. She chewed her lip. "You know, without the threat of death or asphyxiation hanging over us."

Jolin's head was floating away. "I, uh... me too." *Smooth.*

"Let's go, then. These toenails aren't going to lacquer themselves." Isabella ushered her toward the walkway.

Jolin trundled numbly along in a state of denial as the warmth in her face filtered slowly throughout her body. Until she finally believed it was actually happening and melted into Isabella's arms.

"What do you mean, *insufficient funds*?" Jolin shouted.

"Apologies, Consumer," the kiosk replied.

She kicked it.

"Please do not damage the kiosk," it added. "City authorities will be alerted."

"Try the associated guild account," she tried.

"Please make way for other customers."

"There's nobody— What's so funny?" Jolin rounded on her compan- ion, who stopped giggling immediately.

"Nothing! It really is nice," Isabella said, nodding at the jacket Jolin had balled up into an angry bundle.

She tossed the garment into the return bin. "It fit, too!" The drawer slammed closed and the jacket dissolved into its component particles. "That's not as easy as it sounds."

"With those shoulders," Isabella murmured, "I imagine that's true."

"What?" Jolin looked at her shoulders. They seemed fine. She eyed the younger woman.

"Nothing. So you're broke, huh?"

Jolin examined her IDENT chit, turning the graphalon card over in her hands. "I shouldn't be. Six years of interest!" A three-dimensional hologram of her face floated inside, with the River Hawk logo of the ORION Hunter's Guild superimposed on its surface.

"Did they lock your accounts?"

"Dunno," said Jolin. Or perhaps some long-term expenses came due? *Oh no.* She did some quick math in her head. "I kind of hope they did lock me out, actually. I left my Gal-Net subscription and guild dues on autopay."

"You'd still be getting your pension, right?"

"Uh..." Jolin grimaced. "I may have put off registering for that."

Isabella glanced at her wrist. "Daddy was right, you *did* steal Violet!"

"That's one way to describe it," Jolin said, "and I'll grant you, that's the way the government would choose. But kidnapping is more accurate."

"Jolin!"

"Even then, is it kidnapping if the victim is begging you to do it? *He* kidnapped me if you look at it from a certain angle."

"He asked to stay with you?"

"Well, not me specifically. But I was the one he ended up with, and something happened to him while we were together, something I don't really understand. One day it was an ACIS node built to augment my tactical options on the ground and on the bridge. The next..."

"What?"

Jolin hesitated. "It sounds stupid."

"Please." Isabella put a hand on her arm.

"He sang to me."

"Stop it!" Isabella laughed. "Oh my god, he sang?"

"A little song about being happy to meet me. I think he made it up." Jolin shrugged, then sang the little she could remember.

"I know those lyrics! He sang you *Sympathy for the Devil?* Marvelous."

"Oh, I always thought he..."

"It's a really ancient song, but one of my favorites. From another old vampire movie." Isabella seemed suddenly concerned. "What's wrong?"

"What? Oh, nothing," she said, trying to still her face. That moment when Violet sang to her changed her life. And now, well, it was not a stretch to say he would have been better off finding someone else to carry him.

"Why did he want to leave?"

"The component parts for an ACIS node are single-use, so after removal they would have been trashed." They degraded over time, too, so it was a limited partnership, however you looked at it.

"You saved him."

"He was my friend. We figured out a way to keep his hardware intact, because that's the only way he can physically interact with the world, but..." Jolin sat down on a nearby bench and wiped her eyes with her palm. The weight settled on her abruptly of what she had lost. No, what she had *sacrificed* on a desperate whim. "What was the point of any of it? I trashed him, too."

"Oh honey, no." Isabella wrapped her arms around Jolin.

A shudder moved through her body, and a great weariness descended. She laid her head on Isabella's shoulder. "He wanted to live," she whispered. He had trusted her, and she had not been strong enough, or wise enough, to save him. The tears came freely now, and she did not fight them.

Isabella put a hand on her cheek, resting her chin on Jolin's head. "It's okay."

But it was not okay. Violet was her last connection to the *Endless Star* and her family. He served aboard that ship as long as she did, and arguably better. Though not even his watchful eye had been able to prevent what happened. Jolin's gun algorithms had harried the *Valkyrie Centerfold* long enough to save her own life, but so what? What was special about her, that they all died and she walked away? She closed her eyes.

Silent and still, Captain Quin's body was wedged and twisted beneath a console. Jolin heaved herself toward them, gasping for air, but there was none. She stretched out an arm and clasped the Captain's hand. Their fingers were colder than Jolin's; their skin as blue as the polish on their fingernails

Jolin's breath misted in front of her before vanishing into the near vacuum. Her fingertips brushed the sleeve of Leannx's jacket, the one she had modeled her own after, with the purple flower stitched over the left breast.

The memory shattered with a flash.

"That's it!" She sat up, almost knocking Isabella in the teeth.

"What is?"

"I'll show you." Jolin wiped her eyes with the palm of her hands. "But first, I need to get back to my escape pod."

14

The Star Flower

The *Endless Star* was light on fuel and Captain Leannx Quin was irritated. Adjusting their half-length jacket, they tapped lacquered nails against the bridge terminal. A stop on Titan was unlikely to be worth the dock fees, and the Stars had been stalking this bounty around three worlds and seven moons. Always a step—or six—behind. Whoever this so-called Wanderer was, they were good.

"Well?" Leannx said, glancing at the navigation console.

David Freeman swiveled in his chair. The soft orange glow of the controls traced the contour of his muscular arms as he laid them across his chest. "What do *you* think?"

"I think if Wanderer *isn't* on Titan, like she hasn't been every other time we've had one of these dubious leads—of which this is by far the dubi*est*, I might add—we need to have a serious discussion about how much more time and money we're going to put into this."

"It's a big moon, Captain." Freeman shrugged. "There's bound to be somebody else down there who needs an ass whooping." He stood, approaching Leannx's station to sit on the edge of the console.

"But that doesn't change the Wanderer situation. They're a ghost, David. We're hanging on by our fingernails. At this point we'll be lucky to break even on this bounty."

"What if we bring them in alive?" Freeman asked.

He could not be serious. "And trade one risk for an even bigger one? We are dangerously understaffed for a capture mission; you know that. And this is not just some rando hacker, David. Wanderer is a sniper. A killer. Please tell me you read the file. We've been on this for months!"

"I skimmed it. But imagine! The bounty is *triple*. We could power the Bump drive for once without scrounging for it. Really go somewhere."

Leannx sighed. "The *Star* is fast enough without wasting credits on extravagances like Sigrid jumps. Do you really want to risk all our lives over it?" He was pretty, but not the smartest boy they had ever met. If dogged determination counted as intelligence, David Freeman was a Sigrid level genius. Alas.

"What I want," said Freeman, "is to catch somebody."

"Okay, I hear you," Leannx relented. They tapped the controls and the view screens morphed into a display of Saturn and Titan. "Get us docking permission at Huygens. We might as well have some fun while we're getting pulled around by our pocketbooks." Opening up the ship-wide comms, they leaned into the transmitter. "Okay, scallywags, we're going down to Titan. First round of drinks is on Commander Freeman."

Cheers echoed up the stairs from the galley.

Freeman scowled. "I'll need to pick up a side gig to pay *that* tab."

"How is it even when times are good you are always hurting for credits?"

"You know me, Captain. I follow the wind."

"As long as it leads you to a back alley poker game?"

He winked. "It always seems to, doesn't it?"

"Honestly I'll be glad for a couple days relaxation, even if Wanderer isn't actually here." Leannx stretched and gestured to the big man's abandoned station. "Now, about that docking clearance?"

"Of course." Freeman nodded.

The *Star*'s chief engineer stuck his head around the corner of the starboard stairway, "Captain, Chica says we've sunk enough time and money into this asteroid chase and it might be time to cut our losses and limp away. You know, to fight again and all that."

Leannx glanced sideways at him. "Mr. Gonzales, tell the *cook* to keep her opinions in her kitchen."

He grinned.

"Andreas! I said no such thing!" Mira's voice echoed up the stairwell. "And I'm spitting in your soup, Captain!"

Leannx allowed themselves a smirk. Mira hated being called a cook. "That's fine, I'm eating steak tonight." The family they had here on this ship was something they were always grateful for. But some alone time would be welcome. Maybe even a night in a hotel. A nice massage.

Aboard ship, even when Leannx retreated to the privacy of their cabin somebody was always sitting on the edge of the bed watching holoserials with them, or asking what they were reading. Whoever thought putting the Captain's Quarters directly off the galley was a good idea should be forced to try and read during a rowdy episode of *Celebrity Children in Love* sometime.

The private comm-link on Leannx's chair lit up. They tapped it. "Yes?"

"You *swore* you were going to experiment with going plant based!" Mira squawked through the tinny speaker, which somehow made the pain in her voice ten times worse.

"That was before I learned my vegan chef spits in her dishes."

"Argh! Fine, truce."

"We'll see how I feel when I sit down and look at a menu," said Leannx. "Have you even *tried* the portabellas yet?"

"Maybe we'll have some luck for once and Wanderer's in the mood for a steak, too." Freeman interrupted.

"I'll suit up," Gonzales said. "Somebody's gonna have to protect your drunk asses." He vanished down the corridor to retrieve, presumably, his body armor and rifle. As an engineer, Andreas Gonzales was without equal. As a tactical officer he was... well, the best person for the job. In a close fight, Freeman was the brawler of the group, but he was too brash and impulsive to be trusted with long range or defensive tactics. He walked in front and drew fire.

It was not ideal. They really needed to start thinking about hiring somebody, especially if the goal was to try bringing Wanderer in alive. Chances were, they would not be here, so perhaps that task could be put off a little while longer. Until Leannx could actually *afford* to hire somebody. The Capture price was a fortune, but even the significantly smaller Kill reward for this bounty would keep the *Endless Star* fueled and stocked for months.

Leannx tapped the controls again and Mira's voice cut out mid-sentence as she recited the myriad health benefits of portabella mushrooms.

"My mother always said if you can't get ahead, get lucky," they said.

Freeman patted his meticulously styled hair. "Well, *my* mother used to say luck is what happens when you're well-prepared."

"She was a smart lady."

"I dunno. I like what your mom said better. It somehow makes sense, even though it's completely ridiculous."

"Watch what you say about my mother. She was a saint."

"Is that what you're calling her today?" Freeman tapped a sequence into his console. "Landing approved." He flipped on his comms. "Prepare for planetfall." The *Star* shuddered as he burned the engines, and the moon swiveled to fill the view screen.

"Just do me a favor," Leannx said, leaning back in their seat.

"Of course, Captain."

"Remind me this was my idea when it all goes wrong and we lose Wanderer again."

Freeman barked a laugh. "Does that mean you're getting drinks with your crew?"

They regarded him for a long moment, considering. On one hand, that massage sounded so wonderful. On the other, it did not necessarily have to be a *private* massage... and he was so very pretty.

"They had a bartender at Kino's," Freeman pressed, "made the best rum cannonball I've ever tasted."

"Yeah, okay." Leannx relented. "One drink." What was the harm?

* * *

Huygens Base was built atop the ruins of two failed colonization missions, and unlike others of its kind, Huygens had no dome. Efforts to terraform the giant moon had been unsuccessful for centuries due to the oppressive nitrogen layer, but drilling unlocked enormous hidden pockets of hydrogen and oxygen, mostly in the form of frozen water, and within a decade Titan developed a breathable atmosphere. Huygens Three was erected to commemorate the success, and a few hundred years later it was the most popular resort destination in the system.

Jolin Gao stirred her drink and inhaled the cold night air, trying her best to ignore the soreness in her shoulders. These months on the run had left her bone tired and piss poor. Scraping out a meager income from underground fight clubs was no way to live, but she needed money. Cold currency, nothing digital. She needed money almost as much as she needed a plan. But somehow ACIS had convinced her to take a couple days off. She was still getting used to the idea that it... *he*... had acquired some kind of sentience during their time together.

The notion was nonsensical. Jolin had heard stories of sentient AI before, Rogue Events on some remote moon somewhere, accompanied by subsequent death, destruction, and denial. But her ACIS was different. He just wanted to live. She could relate.

"You're sure I can't tempt you?" she asked her companion, a graceful older woman who was apparently an actual surgeon, Jolin had been surprised to learn. A surgeon who spent her weekends earning extra money by stitching up fighters. Her name was Doctor Jennifer Stone, and Jolin liked the way her mouth felt saying those three words in sequence.

"I'm needed at the hospital tonight," the doctor replied.

"You said you were on call," Jolin protested, sipping her cocktail. This place supposedly made the best rum cannonball in Saturn orbit. But she absolutely hated pineapple. So, a raspberry daiquiri it was, or whatever passed for raspberries around here.

"That's just another way of saying I'm needed at the hospital tonight," Jennifer said. She tapped at ice cubes in her water glass. "But, just because I'm not drinking..." She smiled conspiratorially. "Doesn't mean I'm unavailable for other things."

Jolin nearly bit her bottom lip in half. With tears in her eyes, she traced the minor impressions with her tongue. "So I *can* tempt you."

"I'll admit a weakness for haunted women." Jennifer's head tilted as she gave Jolin an appraising look.

"Haunted? I'm sexy and mysterious." Jolin lifted a hand. "May I?"

The doctor nodded, and Jolin ran her fingers through the woman's graying brown hair, producing a credit chit from behind her ear. She displayed it with a flourish.

Jennifer laughed. "Oh my god! Are you twelve?"

Jolin dropped the chit. It bounced off the table and onto the patio, where it promptly rolled over the edge into the sand. She grinned sheepishly and shrugged. "It seemed cooler in my head."

"No no, it was super cool." The doctor put a hand on Jolin's knee. "Sexy *and* mysterious, you're right."

Jolin nodded, heat spreading up her leg.

"Maybe later," Jennifer whispered, leaning in close, "after social studies class, we can make out behind the gym bleachers."

Jolin snorted a laugh, her face flushing.

The doctor grinned. She squeezed Jolin's thigh and stood up. "Tell you what; I'm feeling charitable. Meet me here tomorrow morning and we'll have that drink." Her pocket was buzzing. "I'll admit to a casual curiosity about how you learned to fight like you did tonight. And maybe I'll even let you show me a card trick." She ran her finger down Jolin's shoulder, brushing her bicep, then flicked her on the forearm. "I enjoyed meeting you, Jolin Gao," she said, and melted into the crowd.

Jolin stared after her, quivering.

"That was wholly embarrassing," ACIS said, his little hologram spinning up. Jolin stuffed her hand inside her vest to hide it, but he sprouted through the fabric as if it was not there.

"We're supposed to be laying low," she hissed. "And how would you know anyway?"

"Laying low? Is that why you told your actual name to the first attractive person you met on this world?" ACIS scoffed. "More to the point: I merely extrapolated the likeliest adjective from your biometrics. For example: diaphoresis, tachycardia averaging one hundred twenty two beats per minute. Additionally, I noted *eleven* distinct cringes. Thus my conclusion: embarrassing"

"I did *not* cringe!"

"No, of course not. She did."

Jolin grunted. Forgetting he was there even for a moment was a mistake every time. He was always listening. And judging. "You're the worst."

"That is an unprovable hypothesis," replied ACIS.

"Now vanish so we can get out of here. Please?"

He did.

Jolin waved to the waiter, who waved back and gave her a thumbs up. She narrowed her eyes at him. He gave her a thumbs up again, slower, and pointed at the front door. Had the Doctor paid for her drink? Well that was certainly something. And not *embarrassing* at all.

She slung her pack over a shoulder and checked her knife in its sheath, then turned to confront the infinite dunes of Titan. Behind her, car horns honked and a siren blared. Even here, a billion kilos from home, humans had a way of making everything exactly the same as it ever was.

Not that she minded.

Glancing at Jennifer's glass, Jolin noted the wide lipstick smear and sighed at what could have been. She had no intention of returning in the morning, even if the Doctor was serious about meeting her. Eight weeks in one place was long enough. She hopped the iron gate and floated slowly down into the sand to recover her credits.

The city's artificial gravity did not extend very far past its borders, and Jolin luxuriated in near weightlessness as she coasted to a landing. Shadows spread out before her like the edge of a dark forest. It would be easy enough to get lost out there in the black sands. But she did not want to be lost.

She wanted to be free.

Nights on Titan lasted for over a week, although at Huygens the gas giant loomed forever above the horizon, so it was never truly dark. This half of the moon existed in a perpetual twilight, suitable both for romantic evenings and nefarious deeds. Neither of which was Jolin's mission tonight.

No, she was watching ships. Once she found a suitable ride, it would be a small matter for ACIS to hack her name aboard the passenger manifest, paid-in-full. A military pension would more than cover the cost of travel, but she had been forced to delay filling out that paperwork. For ACIS. The least he could do was fib their way onto a nice freighter or transport.

He did not seem to mind, which would typically be cause for concern. Artificial intelligence protocol forbid them from falsity and subterfuge above what was required for their particular function. His was hacking ships and weapons systems. So he was a natural. And since his awakening, as he called it, ACIS was more than willing to use his talents in service of keeping them moving. Besides, as he was fond of saying, he was no ordinary AI.

"This is your plan?" he asked.

Ignoring him, Jolin crouched low as she hustled past the Customs warehouse. At this time of night only a handful of people should be milling about up there, but she needed to get close to the dock computers or the hack would be intercepted by wireless security sweeps. She settled near an outer wall and ACIS swirled around her wrist, holographic tendrils uncoiling like tentacles.

"Is this close enough?" Jolin asked. Three ships were moored to the long, flat plane of concrete and blinking lights. None of them looked like passenger vessels.

"Should work. Let's see what we have," replied ACIS.

Jolin pressed her palm against the wall and ACIS extended through it, ghostly fingers exploring out from her own.

"Oh," he said.

"What?"

"Oh my," he added. The holograms vanished.

She frowned, running her thumb along the little bump on her wrist. "Are you there?" That had never happened before. Jolin gestured for the manual interface. It popped up obediently. She scrolled to Diagnostics.

"Pad twelve," ACIS said abruptly, spinning above her arm; her little comet.

She released the breath she was holding and her lungs stopped burning. "Don't scare me like that!"

"I've booked us a ride," he said. "Aboard the *Endless Star*. You're going to get a kick out of this, I suspect. It's landing now." The comet morphed into an arrow pointing behind her, into the sky. "Look."

Jolin looked, and her jaw dropped. A ship descended from the heavens like an angel of death. Sleek and silver and barely visible in the darkness, the *Endless Star* was a crescent moon, maybe fifty meters wide, twenty long.

Four glowing thrusters kitted the concave stern, and an array of blaster cannons rounded out the only decoration. It was a Cantonese freighter; a relic of centuries past—a more elegant time for space travel, and humanity itself. The kind of ship you saw on old novels or movie posters. Or dreams.

She was in love.

"Is that all of them?" Jolin asked, adjusting the backpack on her aching shoulders.

Four crew members sauntered down the *Endless Star*'s ramp. Two of average height, one short, and the man leading the group was a couple meters tall at least, bulging with muscles. The small one had a rifle, but did not carry it as if he had much experience using it. Jolin frowned. Why was she assigning them each a target priority?

"So it would seem," ACIS said. "You should say hello so it doesn't get weird."

"What?"

"That's what you said when you were talking about having waited too long to get Raychelle Anand's name. The gunner on the *Firmament of Heaven*?"

"Yes, I remember. The question is, why do *you* remember?"

"My colloquial dictionary is constantly updated."

"By me?"

"Mostly."

Jolin let out a sigh of exasperation. She had nobody to blame but herself for any of this. "Fine," she said, and strode briskly toward the ship. "Are they expecting passengers at least?"

ACIS did not reply. *Great.*

"Ahoy!" She waved, catching the tall one's attention. But as he turned to look at her, a shadow moved behind them, followed by a swift rifle shot. Tall boy swiveled hard and flopped to the ramp before tumbling over the side onto the ground.

Jolin did not give herself time to think, just dropped her pack and sprinted toward them. Fifty meters to go. She pulled her knife. *Starlight.* All she wanted was a ride.

A second shot flashed through the twilight. The short one had fired into the ground struggling to bring his rifle to bear. *Gus.* He looked like a Gus. The two up front dove in opposite directions, but there was no cover on the landing pad. One hunkered down under the ramp, tending to Tall Boy, and the other ran off toward the customs office.

Something glinted in the shadows, and Jolin dodged instinctively as another shot cracked. A bullet whizzed past and she almost lost her footing. Thirty meters.

At least she had their attention, whoever it was. Just her luck to book passage on a ship whose crew was ambushed the moment they landed. Were they criminals? Gus dropped to one knee and fired again, his plasma bolt lighting up the dimness beyond the *Endless Star*, hitting one of the other docked ships.

Another shot popped, slamming Jolin square in the chest. Splinters of lead glittered as they bounced off her ballistics sweater, and she spun to the ground, barely getting her arms up in time to protect her head. Her elbows smashed against concrete, sending fire to her already battered shoulders. Cursing, she gasped for breath, tucking her knees up under her belly.

"Who the hell is that?" somebody said. Something cracked, followed by thump as sombody collapsed.

"Shit!" somebody else replied. "We're surroun—" Their voice cut off abruptly.

Jolin looked up in time to see the last of them hit the ground. Gus.

A new figure in a hooded coat was standing over him. A woman by the silhouette. Staring directly at Jolin.

Giving the woman a curt nod, Jolin hoisted herself up to her knees, knife in hand. *Yeah, you got me. Good for you.* She pressed a hand to her ribs where the shot had impacted, and rose shakily to her feet. Fifteen meters. Close enough.

The hooded figure returned the nod, then raised her rifle.

Jolin threw, and her blade sunk into the figure's leg. The rifle fired wide as Jolin charged toward the ambusher. Yelling wildly, she careened into Hoodie, sending them both sprawling. The rifle clattered on the cement a few meters away. Before Jolin could recover, Hoodie jumped on top of her, wrapping gloved hands around her throat and pressing knees into her abdomen.

It was a clumsy choke hold, without even an attempt to pin her arms. Even while struggling for air, Jolin managed a little grin as she grabbed one finger on each of the sniper's hands, cranking them backward until they popped.

During the ensuing scream, she wrapped her fingers in Hoodie's coat and tugged the woman's forehead in to deliver a nose-shattering headbutt.

Blood splattered on her face, and Jolin shoved Hoodie to the side. She clambered to her feet, wiping the back of her hand across her eyes. "You all right?" she asked Gus, who did not answer.

"Who the hell *are* you?" The woman hovering protectively over Tall Boy asked. She was reaching for Gus's rifle. *New Gus.*

"I'm your passenger."

"We don't take pass—look out!" New Gus pointed.

The sniper lunged, snarling. Her hood was down and blood gushed down her face. What kind of ambush was this? It felt personal.

Jolin raised her elbows in a turtle stance and ducked under the sniper's reach, She wrapped an arm around the woman's right elbow and brought her free hand up to seize Hoodie's throat. Shifting her weight forward, Jolin squeezed the woman's larynx and pivoted hard.

Off balance and gagging, Hoodie toppled, and Jolin rode her to the ground. She planted a knee on the woman's chest and tucked the captured arm under her own, bending it just slightly backward at the elbow. "This is how you do that," she said, applying pressure to the woman's throat with her fingertips. "Now, you want me to break something else? Or are we done here?"

It was not the most technically proficient takedown, and Jolin received a fistful of dust in her face from Hoodie's free hand by way of reply. With a sigh, she snapped the woman's arm at the elbow. The scream was immediate and painful to hear, though probably not as painful as it was to experience.

"I think you won," New Gus said. "This can't be Wanderer, can it?"

"Me?" Jolin looked up sharply.

"No, her. Nobody. Doesn't matter. Who are you?"

"I told you, I'm your passenger."

"Then I guess I'm your captain. Leannx Quin, of the *Endless Star.*" Leannx extended a hand.

Jolin glanced down. The sniper had passed out. *Good.* "Got any rope?" She shook the captain's hand.

"On board, probably." Leannx glanced at Gus. "Andreas, you finished playing dead?"

Gus moaned and sat up, rubbing his head. "Yes?"

"Get our *passenger* here some rope."

"How's your tall boy?" Jolin asked.

"Freeman." Leannx said. "Not good. I managed to staunch the bleeding, but those ballistics rounds do major damage. Mira went for help. How are *you* still alive? You took a direct hit!"

"I know, right?" Jolin stood, dusting herself off. Her elbows ached like her arms were going to fall off, and her torso was going to be made of bruise for the next week, but there was no reason to admit to that to strangers. Leannx was covered in blood. Jolin would bet her last credit chit that Freeman's situation was a sight more precarious than *not good.*

Jolin frowned. Where was the other one? There had been four crew, plus Hoodie. She scanned the immediate area as Gus... *Andreas* scurried up the ramp and vanished into the ship. He returned a moment later with a length of rope. *This is why you mark targets*, she thought, bending down to yank her knife out of Hoodie's thigh. The wound spurted once, but it seemed like Jolin had missed any major vessels.

"We could check her fingerprints," Andreas was saying as he tied the unconscious woman's wrists.

"Later," the captain replied. "First we need to get David some medical help."

"The landing agents are dead," a young woman said, stepping out of the darkness. Mina, was it? The fourth crew member. She was young. Pretty. Her brown skin framed by a close crop of dark curls. "Comms are down over there too. They had a med kit but there's nothing in there that's any better than what we have on board. We'll need to call for an ambulance from the ship."

"And risk being arrested? Mira, Titan is not the place to report being gun shot."

"It's not?" Jolin asked. As far as she knew, the moon was a pretty easy-going place, generally.

"Not for us," Leannx said. Her tone indicated that was the only explanation she was likely to give.

"Who's this?" Mira asked.

"Our passenger, apparently."

Mira eyed Jolin suspiciously.

"The captain," Jolin started, "she told me you don't—"

Mira interrupted. "They."

"It doesn't matter," said Leannx.

"What?" Jolin frowned. "What doesn't?"

"The captain goes by *they*," Mira continued. "I'm a she, they're a they. You understand how pronouns work?"

"Oh, of course," said Jolin. "Got it. I'm a she too." She nodded at Leannx, then turned back to Mira. "They told me you don't take passengers, so I guess I should just explain how I came by a ticket."

"I don't care why you have a ticket," Mira said. "We don't take passengers." She knelt by the unconscious prisoner and put a finger on the woman's neck.

"We do now," Leannx said, prompting a sharp look from Mira.

"Captain…"

"This person hacked her way aboard our ship, and then fought off what could've been a devastating ambush, single-handedly."

Jolin held up her hands, then put one down with a smirk. "Hacked is a strong word."

"And yet we don't take passengers, Miss…?" The Captain watched her expectantly.

"Uh. Jolin," she said. "Just Jolin. At your service." Volunteering her real name again? ACIS was right. She was terrible at this.

"All right, Jolin, help me out here?" They leaned down and grabbed Freeman by the shoulders. "You get the legs."

"Oh, sure. Okay." Jolin joined the effort.

It took all four of them to lift the man.

Jolin noticed the captain's outerwear, a jet black half-jacket with a distinct purple pattern emblazoned above the left breast. "That's a nice flower," she said. How had she ended up as the one walking backward up a ramp?

"It's an aster; they're extinct. I like the symbolism," Leannx replied between grunts. Freeman was top heavy for sure. Maybe Jolin's spot was not the worst one.

"The symbolism?" Jolin frowned. "Which way?" The ramp led them into a wide cargo bay.

"Straight ahead, there's an elevator," said Mira. She was carrying the other leg, while Andreas was on Freeman's right shoulder trying to hold pressure on the wound and lift at the same time.

"In Japan," Leannx said, "where my ancestors were from, leaving asters at a grave or the site of a tragedy was a gesture of remembrance." They paused, reaching back to tap a control panel with their elbow. "And now that they're gone... carrying something dead into the world, giving it new life? It's a lot like the family we have here. Each of us has left something behind."

"I like that," Jolin replied as they maneuvered into an elevator. She did like it. But what had she stumbled onto here, a group of fugitives? Why did they want to avoid calling an ambulance?

"Why are you telling this stranger our business?" Mira hissed.

"Why do you think?" Leannx replied, calmly returning the young woman's glare. Mira sighed, but she seemed to take it as a satisfactory answer, although she turned to aim her dagger eyes at Jolin.

"Captain," Andreas said. "We need to figure out what we're going to do. Getting him up here is all well and good, but unless our passenger knows how to stitch up an injury like this—"

Freeman moaned. His breathing was slow.

"Good point, Chief," Leannx replied. The elevator doors opened, and Mira led them around a corner past the ship's bridge and through a hatch to a dark cabin. Was this their sickbay? The lights flickered on as they deposited Freeman on a table.

The captain looked at Jolin. "At my service, right? Okay, Just Jolin, time to prove your worth." They put a hand on her shoulder. "I'd rather not call the authorities, but I don't want my friend to die. How much do you know about this little moon?"

"We aren't going to let him die. I'll call them if I have to," Mira said.

"I won't stop you, kiddo." Leannx squeezed Jolin's arm. "And if our passenger here can't help us, I guess we'll have to risk it."

"Well, I don't know much," Jolin said, glancing at her wrist. ACIS spun up the time. "But I do happen to know where to find a surgeon."

* * *

"Are you kidding me?" Jennifer said, her coffee halfway to her lips. She looked around. "Where?"

"Not far, the landing pad. Please." Jolin reached for her hand, but Jennifer pulled it back.

"After the night I had?" The surgeon frowned. "You're oh-for-two, babe."

"Yeah, I figured," Jolin said. "But I gotta get off this rock, and this is how I'm going to do it. Now, will you help or not?"

"It's a good thing you're cute." Jennifer gulped the rest of her coffee and stood up with a scowl. "Okay well..." She dabbed her lips with a napkin. "Take me to them."

Jolin scrambled to her feet. "Don't you need your, uh, medical bag or something?"

"No." Jennifer stared at her. "Why do you think my fingernails are so long?" She wiggled her bright pink nails.

Jolin recoiled. "What?" Had she made a mistake?

"Yes, I'll need my medical kit." Jennifer shook her head in disappointment, like Jolin was the dumbest girl in the galaxy. "But guess what?" She tapped her handbag.

"Oh. Okay. Well, follow me." Let her be disappointed.

Jennifer cleared her throat pointedly and glanced at the table. "It's your turn to pay for breakfast, Jolin Gao."

"Aster."

"What?"

"Jolin Aster. I decided to change it." Had she? The certainty in her voice was as comforting as it was surprising.

"Ohhhh, I *like* that. More of your sexy mysteriousness?"

Jolin shrugged. It was a spur of the moment decision, but it felt right.

"Leaving Titan *and* your past behind, I see. I'm jealous."

"ACIS, pay the bill," Jolin said.

The hologram spun to life. "Of course."

"Look at you!" Jennifer laughed delightedly. She leaned down to examine Jolin's wrist. "I've never seen one of these up close. Tell me how you got one."

"Tell me why you're jealous," Jolin countered.

"Leaving your life behind? Starting something new from scratch? You can be whatever, and whoever, you want."

"You could come with. I suspect they need a doctor on the crew."

Jennifer scoffed. "How's the salary?"

"We haven't... uh... discussed those details yet."

"You just fly by the seat of your pants, don't you?"

"I guess so. When I'm wearing them." Jolin grinned. "It's worked out so far."

The corner of Jennifer's mouth twitched as she regarded Jolin for a moment that lasted twelve eternities. "Pad Seven?"

"Yes."

"Off we go then," Jennifer said, striding purposefully away.

"Did you pay?" Jolin whispered at her wrist.

ACIS was indignant. "I said I would."

"But you didn't *pay* pay, right?"

"Jolin, what do you take me for? An incomplete backpropogation? I'm insulted. You've taken things too far this time!"

"Yeah all right." She chuckled. "Good." She hustled after Dr. Stone, who was already across the street and halfway down the block. A splinter of doubt pierced her veneer of clever confidence as she paused at the intersection. What was she getting herself involved in? Clandestine meetings, flirtation failures. Everything was moving so fast, and she had no idea where it was leading.

Haven't you had enough danger in your life? Turning back, she stared out over the dunes beyond the patio. Her hand recalled the cold iron of the fence, her feet flexed into the crunch of Titan's onyx sand.

"I thought you said this was an emergency?" Jennifer yelled from the street corner. Vehicles zoomed past as the lights changed.

Jolin nodded, shaking away her hesitations. There was still a chance this might work. Her fingers relaxed. The dry blood on her knuckles was black in the twilight. Wincing, she stuffed her hands in her coat pockets and jogged past the impatient rows of neon-striped cars and hydrocycles to join the doctor on the other side.

"Hold him steady," Jennifer ordered. She popped her long fingernails off one by one and stuffed them in the pocket of her bag. Freeman writhed and convulsed on the table. He was not screaming, but he was not happy.

Andreas climbed up and laid down on his legs while Captain Quin held the uninjured shoulder. Jolin held the other, as gently as she could. She had been surprised to see a full medical suite on board the *Endless Star*, and so had Dr. Stone. But the equipment was old and unused; in dusty disrepair.

"I assume that thing works?" The surgeon pointed at one of the medical devices on the counter while stuffing her hands into a pair of gloves.

"Not for years," Leannx said.

Jennifer grunted, pressing her thumb into the wound. "The artery is nicked, but only barely. He's lucky. A bigger lesion and he'd have bled out in moments. As it stands, he'll probably need a transfusion." She wriggled her finger to widen the hole, which finally produced a scream from her patient. "If I can seal the cut." The doctor aimed her laser scalpel. "Are you going to hold him or what?"

"I thought you were kidding about using your fingers," Jolin whispered as she tightened her grip on Freeman's arm. He was so strong.

"I never kid." Jennifer fired two bursts into the wound. Then, she tossed her bloody gloves in the waste bin and retrieved a syringe and a long needle from her bag. She drew a sample from Freeman's forearm and installed it into another of the many devices. Blowing the dust off it, she tapped a few keys and the thing whirred to life.

"What's your blood type, Jolin Aster?"

"I don't know."

"Really? That's disappointing." Jennifer slapped the lid closed. She returned to her patient and shined a light on the wound. A familiar light.

"Is that my flashlight?" Jolin asked. She tapped the vest pocket where she kept it.

"Yes. Captain? Blood type?"

"A-positive," Leannx grunted. They were staring at Jolin for some reason. Freeman was struggling pretty hard, though, and quickly reasserted his claim on Leannx's attention.

"Engineer? Sorry I forgot your name."

"Andreas, ma'am. A-positive."

"Indeed?" Jennifer slipped on a new pair of gloves and pushed at the wound with her fingers. Blood pooled around the hole. "Hmmmm. Looking good. And the pretty one?"

"Me?" Mira said.

"No, me." Jennifer rolled her eyes. "Yes you, child."

"I have... I can't donate blood."

"All right," the doctor said. Something beeped, and she glanced over at the device. "Well, shit."

"What?" Leannx asked. Their face was red from the effort of holding Freeman.

"Your fella here is type B, which means since you don't have any working synthesizers he'll need either a B donor, or an O donor."

"Can we test mine?" Jolin asked. Freeman's face was pale, and he was sweating. His breathing was slow and ragged. That was why Jennifer refused to put him under anesthesia, so she said. Without a proper medical crew, he would die from it, the shape he was in.

"We can't ask you to..." Leannx hesitated, pursing their lips. "Why would you offer that?"

"We're running out of time," said Jennifer. "Perhaps consider motivations later."

"Just test me," Jolin said. Her motivation was not important, though even as she thought about it, she again saw Freeman's silhouette as he turned toward her before that first shot, distracted by her yell. Would things have gone differently? If she had not—

A buzz sounded over the ship's loudspeaker.

"What was that?" Jennifer asked.

"The doorbell." Leannx was incredulous. "Is someone outside?"

Mira spoke up. "I can find out."

Leannx nodded, and the young woman ran out of sickbay. "Can we tie him down or something, Doctor?"

"Expecting trouble?" Jennifer asked.

"Always," the Captain said.

Surprisingly, the doctor grinned. Maybe she really *was* jealous.

Jolin held out her arm. "Just test me."

Something exploded, rocking the ship. Alarms blared.

"Shit!" Leannx stood up, letting go of Freeman, who moaned.

Somewhere down the corridor Mira shouted, and was cut off.

Freeman convulsed violently.

"He's having a seizure," Jennifer said. "Relax your hold, but don't let go."

Andreas shifted on Freeman's legs, and Leannx secured his arms again.

"What do we do?" Jolin asked, holding her arm out. She stared at the hatchway, but there were no further sounds or movement. Her instincts were screaming at her to run out there and do something.

"Blood loss leads to electrolyte imbalance and hypoglycemia. He just needs a top off, maybe some potassium." She sighed, as if sensing Jolin's thoughts. "It's fine, I'm a universal donor." She rolled up her sleeve, then winked. "I just hate needles."

Turning to the Captain, she continued. "I see some transfusion equipment over there."

The Captain hesitated, obviously unsure. Their gaze moved from Jennifer to Jolin, then to the open hatchway.

"Behind you on the counter, Captain." Doctor Stone was all business now.

"I'll go," Jolin said. "Help your friend."

Leannx reached for the supplies. A bag, several long needles, and some tubing. Was it sterile? Did they have time to care? The captain scrutinized her stoically, then nodded, eyes glistening. "Thank you," they whispered.

Jolin bolted from the room.

"ACIS, whatta we got?" Jolin sprinted down a narrow flight of stairs. "It's not that inept assassin is it?"

"She remains in the holding cell." The hologram spun above her wrist like vines, curling around the handle of her knife, leaving trails in the air as she ran.

"So who brought the explosives?"

"Unknown."

She skidded to a stop at the hatchway leading to the cargo bay and peered around the edge. Someone was face down on the ramp. The clothes suggested it was Mira. She was not moving. Jolin gritted her teeth. "Scans?"

"Two individuals in the landing zone. Both armed."

"With what?"

"You told me it doesn't matter," ACIS said.

"What? When?"

"I asked why you insist on carrying a knife when the foes we meet tend to have guns. You said I should shut up and it doesn't matter because..." He switched to a recording of Jolin's voice. "Any fool can shoot a gun."

"So it's guns?"

"Yes."

"Of course it is," Jolin muttered, adjusting her vest. "Hello out there," she called through the hatch. "Any chance we can talk about this before you blow up my ride?"

"First Lieutenant Gao Ju Ling," a voice shouted. "You are hereby ordered to surrender yourself to Sol System Authority under articles ninety-two and one twenty-one of the Uniform Code of Military Justice."

Jolin's heart sank. This was her fault? How had they found her? ACIS had booked that ticket *four* hours ago. "Is he lying?" she whispered.

"I'm afraid not." ACIS spun. "He is broadcasting an SSA Recall IDENT."

"Shit."

"Indeed." The hologram flickered fearfully. "Will they kill me?"

"They'll have to kill me first." Jolin put her back against the bulkhead. She needed to think. "How's the girl?"

"Hard to say; I detect a faint rise and fall of the chest that may indicate breathing."

"I'll take it." Jolin hefted her knife. "Okay," she yelled. "Let me pull my friend to safety and I'll come out after."

"Agreed," came the reply. "But don't try anything funny. And no weapons."

"Of course."

"Not even the knife, Lieutenant."

Jolin grimaced. They knew everything. "Well there goes that plan," she said.

"In fairness," ACIS replied, "it was not a very good plan."

"I'd expect you would be a little more supportive, given I'm your only hope for survival."

"Jolin, your plans are never good. Yet you somehow come out on top every time." The hologram danced in his little visual representation of laughter, spreading golden light across the walls like reflections in a tide pool. "I put my life in your relatively capable hands without hesitation or expectation of remorse."

Relatively? She sighed. "So this is what it's like to be on top?"

"Apparently."

"Stealth mode," she whispered. "And engage the neural interface."

ACIS vanished. "Compliance."

Jolin's vision went completely white, then blinked back on. Her immediate surroundings were highlighted in golden wireframe, and she could see two individuals, one on each side of the ramp. Armed with blasters. She reached forward to tap on their silhouettes, turning them into redline targets. It had been over a year since she last used the neural interface, she realized, as a familiar wave of nausea burbled in her belly. She ignored it.

A third individual was highlighted in soft white light. Mira.

Shoving her knife back into its sheath, she stepped out into the cargo bay, hands up.

"I see that knife, Gao, what did I say?" came the voice. Did he have a scanner? The one on the left was doing the talking.

"Come on, I can't just leave it on the floor. It's an heirloom!"

"I'm saying I better not see it when you come out. I don't care where you put it."

The other one mumbled something in reply, which elicited a snicker and a sharp retort from the man in charge.

"Yeah yeah," Jolin muttered, grabbing Mira's arms. She turned the young woman on her back and felt for a pulse. It was there, strong and steady. Mira groaned. "Stay quiet, little sister," Jolin whispered with an air of familiarity that surprised her with its depth of affection. "I'm going to get you out of harm's way."

Starlight. She had known this girl for all of twenty minutes. But something about her just... resonated. The fierceness with which she defended her captain, maybe? With a grunt, Jolin dragged Mira the ten meters back to the corridor and through the hatch. Pulling her knife, she placed the hilt in Mira's hand. "You might need this. It's a good friend. Keep it safe for me, yeah?"

Mira blinked. "What?"

"Your Captain is lucky to have someone like you on board," Jolin said. She searched around for more words, but found nothing. "Okay, well. Bye." The girl just stared at her. Well, it was not much of a hero speech, but that tracked; Jolin was not much of a hero.

"Aster, huh?" Leannx said, behind her.

Jolin jumped almost high enough to bash her noggin on the overhead. "Oh, uh, you heard that? It was time for a change."

"I like it," they said, putting a hand on her shoulder again. "Those fellas here for you?"

Jolin shrugged. "Looks that way. I'm sorry, I guess I drew their attention somehow. I haven't yet got the hang of being on the run. Wait, why are you here, is he...?"

"David? He'll pull through. Passed out from the pain and blood loss though. Andreas got him tied up real good in case he wakes up while your doctor friend donates a liter or two." They knelt down next to Mira. "You okay, Chef?"

Mira nodded. "It surprised me, but I'm... I'll be okay."

The captain helped her up. "Get back to the galley, then. Freeman will be starving when he wakes up. Can you whip up some of those meat pies he likes?"

"With tofu?"

Leannx laughed. "Yeah, fine."

Mira limped away. They were a curious pair.

Jolin was sorry to see her knife go, but she did not want to get killed over it. At least, not before she had her chance to strike. Besides, if the rumors about these Recall Agents were true, a knife would not help her anyway. "ACIS," she said.

"Yes?"

"They have ACIS nodes too, don't they?"

"Yes."

Jolin sighed. So much for strategic advantage. Her stomach roiled and she leaned against the bulkhead. "Can you hack them?"

"Are you sure that's a good idea, Jolin?" he asked. "We're in enough trouble as it is."

"Yeah, but I won't let them have you." She clenched her fists and stretched her elbows over her shoulders one after another. The ache had faded somewhat, but not entirely.

"Not from here, without access to the ship's systems. Get me closer and I'll try," ACIS said.

"You're really going out there?" Leannx asked.

Jolin stretched her knees. "I said I would."

"To surrender?"

"I don't want anything happening to you and yours on my account." Not an answer, but not a lie. She would surrender, sure. Once her body was cold and dead. Or incapacitated. Or if the money was good enough. But since none of those things was the case at the moment, she did not intend to go gently.

Captain Quin regarded her with hard eyes. "It's really not a scam."

"What?"

"You. This." They gestured down the ramp. "I wasn't sure until this moment."

"I just want a ride off this moon, Captain."

"I believe you. But I thought for a minute you might be Wanderer."

"Wanderer?" Jolin frowned. "Never heard of her." That was the second time Leannx had brought up that name. "Somebody you're after?"

Leannx shrugged.

"What do you folks do here on the *Endless Star*, anyway, if not ferry passengers or freight?"

"Not willing passengers, anyway." They smiled. "We do a little of everything. Whatever keeps the ship fueled and flying." The hardness faded, and their face faded into wistfulness. "We could use someone like you."

"I don't doubt it." Jolin grinned. "The way Andreas handles that rifle, you might oughta find somebody else to carry it next time."

"Why not you?"

"You're serious? That's an awful kind offer, Captain, but we just met."

"You paid your way onto our ship, didn't you?"

"Well, no, actually."

"You coming out, Gao?" The voice outside shouted. "Or are we coming in after you?"

"All right, yes. I'm coming," she yelled. "Unarmed!" To Leannx, she said, "I hacked my way on board. You said so yourself."

"We still got that money; I checked." They held up an arm, where a bank transaction receipt appeared over the netband wrapped around their wrist. "And if that woman in the brig is Wanderer, or leads us to her, the bounty payout will be substantial. And a share of that is yours. Plus, you brought us a doctor."

Jolin's confidence wavered. "Jennifer's gonna stay?"

"She likes the ship, apparently. And we've been without a medic for... a while." Leannx held Jolin's gaze silently, then sighed. "All right. It was very nice to meet you, Jolin Aster. We'll speak again soon."

"That does sound nice." Jolin put a hand on the bulkhead to steady herself. Colors flitted across the edges of her vision, and the white lines the neural link had drawn around Leannx glitched briefly. She did not remember the nausea being this bad last time. Gritting her teeth, she tried to steel herself against it.

Whatever happened next, she could not involve these people. It would not be fair, and she was familiar enough with collateral damage to know she did not want to be the cause of any more than she could help. She shook her head. "Take off right away, as soon as I'm clear of the engines. Maybe I'll look you up in two to ten years."

She slipped through the hatchway and approached the ramp, hands wide. If she was fast, and lucky, she could lead them on a merry chase long enough for the *Endless Star* to vacate the premises.

"Pretty arrogant of you to think you can tell me what to do with my own ship," Leannx called after her.

The Recall officer yelled, "Turn around, Lieutenant, let me see!"

Jolin complied, turning in a half circle. "Take a good look!" Shaking her bottom at the two soldiers below, she winked at the captain, who stood there with a curious smile on their face. Well, at least Jolin had made an impression. It was unlikely the next transport she cheated her way on to would be anywhere near as welcoming. Or half as interesting.

"Stay safe," the captain said, pushing the hatch closed.

"Safe?" Jolin grinned. "Never heard of her."

Turning, she launched herself down the ramp with a shout, then vomited, tripped, and tumbled to a heap on the landing pad.

15

Lost and Found

With the shuttle crammed inside it, *Syracusia*'s hangar was positively claustrophobic. Jolin traced her fingertips along the seams of *Nosferatu*'s bulky fuselage as she disembarked. It filled two of the fighter bays, making a handsome companion piece to *Cannibal* and Sergeant Nguyen's fighter. He would be back for *Prescient* eventually, but for the moment they had a little fleet.

"We could race," Isabella suggested.

Jolin shook her head. "Oh you don't even know. I'm a terrible pilot."

"That just means I would win."

"Let me go ahead and congratulate you, then, and spare myself the effort and embarrassment." Jolin affected a mock bow with a hand flourish.

"Still champion." Isabella patted herself on the back. "I'm going to sync the shuttle's new IDENT record with our systems. Let me know if you need help over there."

"Thanks, but I'll be okay." Jolin made her way to the escape pod alone. Something about it felt safe; familiar. Rubbing her wrist, she climbed inside. The compartment where she had hastily stuffed her plunder hung open, inviting.

She retrieved the parcel, brushing away remnants of her ruined jacket and pulling apart the tightly wrapped bundle. The first item was a surprise. She eyed Rolan Hector's museum-piece pistol with a frown. She did not remember picking it up. Then, shrugging, she stuffed it into her hip holster and retrieved the next item.

Her lip quivered as she lifted the *Endless Star*'s brass nameplate. She had pried it off with her knife after killing Rolan. There was even still a blood stain, black with age. Her own hand print.

She touched the raised letters tentatively, and the embossed flower that matched the one on Captain Quin's jacket. And hers. Beneath, the motto in Latin. *Simul Nos Crescere.* Together, we grow. A tear dripped onto the metal, then another. Jolin held it to her chest. What had it meant to her, those eight years aboard the *Star*? Surely she would never fully understand the extent to which those five people had changed her life.

Her recollection of them was returning, and she caught a flash of Leannx's smirking face as they appeared at the SSA detention facility at Huygens Base, dressed in a smart suit and oozing lawyerly charm. They were a lawyer once, decades before. Jolin had forgotten that detail, but she did remember the scent of the air as they escorted her out of jail into Titan twilight. Centuries of terraforming had supplied the moon a unique flavor. Honey, lilacs, and Summer rain.

"How did you do this?" she had asked.

By way of an answer, Leannx handed her a folded wallet. Inside, an IDENT card featured a crude photo and her new name. Jolin Aster. So weird to see it in print.

"Your old life can be left where it is," they said, squeezing her shoulder. "Or you can pick it back up again. That's your decision. But as far as the Sol System Authority is concerned, the wrong woman was captured last week. I have an apology letter here and everything." They held out an official-looking envelope.

Laughing between tears that sprang up out of nowhere, Jolin tucked the wallet and the letter inside her vest. "I would frame it, except I don't have any place to hang it."

"Sure you do," Leannx said. "If you want…"

As the memory faded, Jolin curled into a ball and wept, hugging the name plate. Something prickled at her wrist. She did not mind; it was only right that she endure some measure of suffering as penance for what happened to Violet. What she had *allowed* to happen. Thinking of him brought a thin reminder of his reliable presence. Just enough to reinforce the emptiness. She sniffed, squeezing her eyes tight. At least she had nothing left to lose.

"Hey, you should check this—oh!" Isabella said. "What is that?"

Jolin opened her eyes and gasped. Golden threads of hardlight wire stretched from her wrist to the escape pod, strands of a spider web glimmering with morning dew, just like the dream of Heaven she had on the *Valkyrie.*

That small presence *thrummed* rhythmically, and for a moment she felt a… *connection.* "Violet?"

The strands exploded into sparks and the feeling vanished.

"It must be," Isabella said.

"What?"

"Come with me."

Jolin pushed off with her free hand to get to her feet and her fingers brushed against something soft. The second layer of cloth she had wrapped the bundle in. She lifted it, and Captain Quin's half-jacket unfolded in her hands. Choking back another sob, she nearly dropped the nameplate on her foot. That beautiful, hand-stitched purple flower.

She stepped out of the pod and placed the jacket and the metal plaque on a nearby crate. *Collect yourself, Lieutenant.*

"Are you all right?" Isabella asked, her eyes wide with concern.

Jolin ground her palms into her eyes. "I'm fine. It's just..." She pushed her emotions down, molded sadness and regret into a ball and stuffed it deep in her belly. *Later.* Taking a breath, she straightened. "Sorry. You were saying?"

"It started when I accessed the security settings." Isabella squeezed Jolin's arm, then led her inside the shuttle.

Jolin glanced around. "It's the same. What am I looking at?"

"Not looking."

And then, as if filtered through a modulator and very far away indeed, she heard it. A melody, fuzzing in and out. She placed her hand against the inner hull. It reverberated beneath her touch. "Where's it coming from?"

"This shuttle doesn't have a voice engine," Isabella said. "I couldn't find a specific source, either. It's like the ship itself is singing."

Jolin leaned close, pressing her ear to the purring metal. "Hope you guessed my name..." she whispered.

"Exactly!" Isabella jumped. "Do you think it's him?"

It was, she knew it immediately. Had he survived? Was he trapped in the shuttle somehow? Jolin sagged as relief surged through her, and Isabella reached out to support her.

"I'm okay," she said, shying away from Isabella's touch. She sat down in the cockpit and held out her wrist. Nothing. Cursing, she tried a few gestures to activate Violet's offline mode. Also nothing. Blinking away tears, she turned to the younger woman. "I don't know what to do."

Isabella's smile was as reassuring as it was beautiful. "So we find somebody who does."

Ajax scowled at the board, scratching his beard.

"Quit pouting," said Grace. "It's all over."

"Not yet, not yet." Leaning in, he placed a black stone.

Grace clucked at him, immediately placing a white stone, which flipped three of his. The holographic pieces fuzzed.

"Why do people play this obtuse game?" he grumbled.

"We've been asking ourselves that for six thousand years. You yield?"

He nodded, then flexed a bicep. "I prefer my games to be more physical anyway."

She rolled her eyes.

"The girls are back," Ramos said as he ducked through the hatchway.

"Has Nguyen returned for his fighter?" Grace asked, sipping her tea.

"Not yet."

"Then we still have to wait."

"Admiral. The longer we delay, the more likely it is we will be discovered." The colonel grabbed a mug off the drying rack and filled it in the sink.

Ajax frowned. The way he filled out that fitted long-sleeve tee shirt was obscene. In his younger years Ajax had been just as toned and... well, his shirts had been tight too, dammit. He ignored a brief pang of shame; only moments ago he had been showing off. Was Grace comparing them in her head?

As unlikely as that was, Ajax found himself sitting up a little straighter. *Stop behaving like a child.* He eyed Ramos. "You suggest we just eject his ship and haul ass? Our situation hasn't changed. Sergeant Nguyen was instrumental in bringing that terrorist into custody. He saved my daughter's life. I'm not going to repay him by spacing his prized possession."

"It has a homing beacon. He'll find it."

"Enough," Grace interrupted. "Flex at each other somewhere I'm not. We have a plan, we stick to it."

Ramos scoffed. "And if the dreadnought returns?"

"I can outmaneuver them." Isabella slinked into the galley, trailed by Jolin.

"Child, you have no idea what you're up against." Grace stood, clicking off the Go board. "The *Rosy-Fingered Dawn* was swarming with these Insurrectionists; we have no way to know how high into our government they've infiltrated. Outmaneuvering one ship isn't going to do anything but delay the inevitable. We need a comprehensive response from the SSA. Right now, whatever it is they want from me, codes, battle plans, secrets, my fisherman's daughter ass, they don't have it yet. And that's our advantage."

Jolin interjected, "If it's codes, won't they just be changed? And if they've infiltrated as high as you say, who's to know the President isn't surrounded by them? Or even one himself?" She was wearing a new jacket, not something of Amanita's. The way she was adjusting it constantly, it probably did not fit right. And she was standing awfully close to his daughter? Ajax almost got up. *Isabella is a grown woman*, he chastised himself. *Not your little girl anymore.*

Those old instincts never faded. In his defense, she turned sixteen one day and thirty the next. But Isabella could take care of herself. That was the least of his worries. If the next few hours did not go exactly as they hoped, they could lose the ship, or their lives.

"*Herself*," Grace corrected.

Ajax's eyes widened. He had not caught the mistake. The Admiral was a sharp one. But he already knew that.

Jolin frowned. "What?"

"The President."

Jolin's jaw clenched, but Isabella stepped between them before she could respond. "Get to the point," she said. As she crossed her arms, and

Ajax was struck by how much his daughter resembled her mother in that instant.

"As you wish," the Admiral continued. "To your question, Miss...?"

"Aster," Jolin offered.

"Miss Aster, the codes I know and biometrics I possess can be retracted or limited, yes. If that's what they are after. But as for President Nadzieja? Well, if the government is that far gone, then we've already lost everything. "

"That just means we have nothing to lose," Jolin said.

"Is that what you think?" Colonel Ramos squared his shoulders, planting his mug on the counter with a loud *clack*. "Is this a game to you?"

"Okay, first of all." Jolin raised a hand. "Yes. And you carry yourself as if you know the rules just as well as me, so stuff your condescension." Pushing past Isabella, she approached him. "Second. Big fella." Jolin's face darkened as Ramos loomed over her. "You don't scare me with your bulging muscles and your chiseled jaw." She shoved her finger in his face. "I've torn into tougher *steaks* than you. Stood over bigger men and ended up with their blood on my shirt, in my hair, on my knife." She advanced, eyes wild, like some hidden switch had flipped. "I walked away, not them."

Ramos retreated, raising his hands defensively.

"Jolin." Isabella grabbed her arm.

She froze the moment Isabella touched her, blinking. "Sorry, I... sorry." She reached a hand out to Isabella, but stopped short, turning instead to run from the galley.

"She's going through some things," Isabella said, starting after her. "I should see how she is."

"Let her go," said Grace. "She has the look of somebody who wants to be alone."

"I don't take orders from you," Isabella growled. The glance she gave Ajax as she stalked past was enough to discourage his intervention. She could handle it.

"That woman is a fighter," Ramos said after they had gone. "A dangerous one." He seemed genuinely shaken. Wary. "Haven't seen that look on somebody in a while. I'm glad she's on our side."

"Is she?" Grace asked.

Ajax stared through the open hatch into the dark corridor. The expression on Jolin's face had chilled him to the bone. Who had he brought onto his ship?

Jolin slammed the door to her makeshift quarters. The rage inside her was melting away as quickly as it had arisen, into a simmering shame. The heavy hatch bounced against its frame to slowly drift back open. *Ugh, whatever.* She threw herself on the bed.

Why had she threatened that man? Who even was he? Isabella told her the Admiral and her lapdog were on board, of course, but this Colonel Ramos had still been a surprise. He was much more than an attaché. She had seen that immediately, just in the way he carried himself. Seen men and women like him before. Dangerous men and women. And he was built like—No, that was no excuse for her reaction.

Clearly, whatever was happening to her was more than she could handle right now. Was it grief? To go from weeping to threatening violence fifteen minutes later... "ACIS, check my hormone lev—" she cut off abruptly, staring at her wrist.

The veins on her forearm seemed to writhe and pulse. Her hand was shaking again. She made a fist and the tremors stopped. *Just breathe.* She let her shoulders sink into the mattress and stared at the overhead. A single off-center light was the only spot of color in the dull gray titanium struts and panels.

Closing her eyes, Jolin pictured herself standing in the dunes again, the wind whipping her hair, just like after Rolan choked her out with his belt. What had happened back then? Violet kept her alive, but how? Another in a cascade of questions. Would a specialist in artificial intelligence know the answers? She had certainly never heard of anything like what Violet was capable of, outside of science fiction. And nothing in the months of training had prepared her for it.

None of that mattered; she had to try. Violet was her only remaining connection to her family. She sat up and removed Captain Quin's coat, examining it in the light. It was a half jacket, meant to cover the arms and upper torso only; black as onyx and woven of damage-resistant fibers. Her own had just been a cheap imitation, as evidenced by the way it shredded after Rolan sliced it up.

The flower above the left breast was hand-stitched and designed by the Captain themselves. Jolin ran her thumb along the threads. She hated presuming, but figured Leannx would want her to wear it if the alternative was gathering dust in a closet. Or being entombed on an asteroid. They would be glad to know someone in the family carried it. She hoped.

"We can get a tailor to adjust that," Isabella said from the corridor.

Jolin resisted putting the jacket back on. "It's custom, like my sweater. By an armorer on Ganymede." Now that she had it, she felt naked without it. *But that's what you want, isn't it? Exposed like a raw nerve, trying to feel something. Anything.* She folded it on her lap. Platinum fasteners dotted the wrists of its long sleeves, and she fiddled with them as she talked. "I'm sorry I blew up."

"Can I come in?"

Jolin nodded.

Isabella stepped into the cabin. She was almost as tall as her father, ducking slightly to fit through the hatchway. Her purple-tinted hair brushed the top of it. "You know, I think you scared him," she said with a half-smile.

"The big one? I doubt it. I should apologize to him, too. He just...

reminded me of someone in that moment."

"Don't let my dad hear you call Ramos 'the big one' okay?"

Jolin grinned despite herself.

Isabella picked up the *Endless Star* plaque from the shelf where Jolin had left it and traced the engraving with her fingers. She held it up to the bulkhead, like a painting over the desk. "You should hang this."

"Maybe. Eventually. Once I have a permanent place."

"I suppose it's a bit much to hope you could find that here. With us."

"I don't know," Jolin said. "I feel like I need to sort some things out." That was an understatement. Despite her... *interest*... in Isabella, it would be irresponsible to just shack up on the first ship she found. Not to mention stereotypical. And the loss of her family was still fresh, even if she could not really feel it yet. Moving on so quickly was disrespectful. Heartless.

Anyway, Violet needed her. Plus, the world had obviously changed a lot in six years; she had to find her place in it, if she still had one. And yet. She met Isabella's intense gaze. "Is that... Would you want... that? Me to stay, I mean."

"Yes." Isabella's earnest confidence was baffling and encouraging in equal measure, as always. "It's hard to meet people when you're riding the skyways months at a time. Even harder to find ones you get along with." Stepping closer to the bed, she fingered the flap of Jolin's vest. "And people you actually like? Rare as rubies." She dropped her hand to her side. "But you don't have to stay."

"It's been just the two of you for a while, hasn't it?"

Sitting down on the bed with a sigh, Isabella shrugged. "Mostly. Crew come and go, some more pleasant to have around than others." She smelled of crisp, fallen leaves. Like cinnamon. Or a cool wind through autumn trees.

"Sounds lonely," Jolin said.

"Sometimes."

"You never had anyone? Anyone special I mean."

"Once or twice." Isabella picked at the seam on her trousers. "In school, certainly." She grinned. "This one girl, Emily, who was a painter; always wearing filthy overalls. She did murals. I think she got married? Wow, that was so long ago. I really have been overly focused on hauling freight. With my father. It is kind of depressing, saying it out loud."

"Nothing wrong with a steady income from honest labor," said Jolin.

"I guess. What about you? Was there ever...?" Isabella hesitated.

Jolin understood; she would not know how to talk to herself about any of this either, if she were in Isabella's place. "I never had much interest in settling down," she said. "But there were a few women I made time for. Over the years. A couple who got away. There was a doctor who I... Let's just call it unrequited. She died, with the rest of them."

Isabella squeezed her hand. "I can't imagine how that feels."

"Me either. I barely remember it, and there's been so much other stuff to focus these past two days; my shit feels inconsequential."

"It's not."

Jolin's eyes narrowed. Isabella was not wrong, but it was all too big right now. Too much. Despair was always lurking, but he was an old friend. She knew how to handle *him,* to stuff him deep into the darkness and ignore him forever.

"We could leave, you know," Isabella whispered. "I'm not sure what the admiral wants from us; as far as I can tell she's preparing to go into hiding. But they don't need us to stick around to accomplish that."

"We're loose ends," Jolin said. "I doubt she would let us go."

"*I* doubt I'd give her the choice. Though I'll admit a morbid curiosity as to what these Insurrectionists were trying to accomplish over there, besides scavenging. It doesn't make a lot of sense."

"I wish I'd had the chance to twist some answers out of Jester."

"Oh? Is interrogation another of your secret skills?"

"Not really, but how hard can it be?" Jolin punched a fist into her palm. Funny how her grief and confusion faded away in Isabella's presence. Well, not funny but—She shook her head. *Replaced by awkwardness.*

"They're waiting on my mother though, and that sergeant. But nothing is stopping you and me from heading out in *Nosferatu.*"

"Heading where? It's a short-range shuttle."

"Ganymede? See that tailor of yours? A moon that big is bound to have somebody who knows about AI. Or knows someone who knows."

Jolin looked at her sideways. "You'd leave the *Syracusia* and your father to, what, traipse around the solar system with a woman you hardly know?"

"Why not? He doesn't exactly require my assistance, either." Isabella took a deep breath; the first crack in her demeanor. "And I know all I need to know."

Jolin stared into those deep, brown, unblinking eyes. She was helpless.

Isabella leaned closer, chewing her bottom lip. Their faces were centimeters apart, their hands touching on the mattress. Her lipstick smelled of caramel apples. "It's not like I can't find him, if... you know..."

Jolin finished for her. "If you need to..." This was silly. They had known each other for all of—

"Can I kiss you?" Isabella whispered.

Time slowed; Jolin's vision blurred, but her mouth found its way to an answer. "I wish you would."

Isabella's hand moved to her thigh, and Jolin's entire body quaked. Every molecule of her screaming to either rip this woman's clothes off or flee. In equal measure. Isabella's lips brushed hers, and a moan escaped from somewhere deep inside her body. She allowed Isabella to lower her to the mattress and closed her eyes as those elegant fingers moved through her hair, caressing her face.

"Please..." she whispered.

Isabella paused. "Should I stop?"

Jolin shook her head. "No. I need this." Finally able to move again, she wrapped a hand behind Isabella's neck and pulled her down, kissing her softly at first, then hungrily. Lightning struck and their bodies responded. Jolin reached her other arm around Isabella's backside and grabbed her ass, which elicited a surprised grunt from the other woman. But Isabella's free hand went to Jolin's waist, cool fingertips sliding beneath her sweater, electric against her bare skin.

Jolin's hips rose to meet her as Isabella leaned back to tug off her blouse. Tossing the garment aside, Isabella pushed a knee between her legs. Jolin squirmed, trying to unfasten the buttons of her vest with clumsy fingers, squeezing her thighs around Isabella's knee, pulling herself closer, rubbing herself against it. She was on fire.

To hell with the buttons. She tore open the vest, flinging at least two of them across the cabin to clatter against a bulkhead. Jolin laughed, and Isabella bent to tug Jolin's sweater up, kissing her belly. "Wait," Jolin gasped.

"What now?"

"The door, the door."

"Oh!" Isabella grinned, hopping up. She pushed the hatch closed and pulled down the handle to lock it, and Jolin busied herself tugging off her vest. Somehow, the missing buttons did not feel wasted.

Isabella unclasped her bra, a lacy, lavender thing, and let it drop to the deck. "Now you." She stepped forward, confident, intense, and perfect. Her shoulders back, poised. Like a cat about to pounce.

Jolin sat up and pulled her sweater over her head. The air was cold; she was wide open... vulnerable, and it had been a while. There in her sports bra, she felt suddenly weak. Small. Yet, at the same time an immense certainty of purpose settled on her, as if everything in her life had led her to this moment. To this person. The ache arose from deep in her belly, spreading down her spine; a roiling boil that sucked all the warmth from her body into a single point gone supernova. She shivered.

"Oh, honey." Isabella rushed forward. She had not seen all Jolin's bruises yet. For good reason. Something with the cryo-freeze had exacerbated them. Half her right side was purple as they spread up from her injured leg.

"It's fine." Jolin placed her hand under the other woman's chin, lifting her up. "Just kiss me," she said. And she did. A deep, soft exploration of tongues, and hands, and breasts, before Isabella pushed her down again and straddled her thighs, fingers working at the buttons of Jolin's pants.

"Starlight," she moaned, twisting her hips beneath the other woman's weight.

Isabella's voice was a sultry whisper. "I'll show you stars."

Something about that woman stuck in Grace's craw like a tin can in a tuna net, but she was not wrong. There was a lot about this that made no sense. Like a plan devised by a child, full of contradictory elements and random chance. She could not see the course. But it did not matter. Not now.

She stared at the comms panel on the *Syracusia*'s bridge, willing it to light up. Amanita had assured Captain Marquez that she would get as much information as she could about what the SSA's response to this bombing would be, but Grace hated not knowing. Hated wondering. Hated feeling useless and exposed.

She ran a search on the name Colonel Ramos had mentioned. *Herald.* There were too many results for her to pick out anything obvious. A ship or two had taken the moniker over the years, most notably the *Herald of Norway*, an early HDF dreadnought that had been lost in a battle almost a century ago. Which, while it could be relevant, was not exactly helpful.

It was the deadest of dead ends, like Ramos himself, who despite spending six months infiltrating their organization knew surprisingly few details. Whoever he was, this Herald was smart. And ruthless. The Insurrection was highly compartmentalized, like terrorist cells. No, not *like* terrorists. Actual, murdering terrorists.

News of Sharice was her top priority, and the fate of the *Dawn*. She found none of either. If there was one thing she and her wife had learned over long military careers, though, it was that individuals are expendable. Even the ones you love. With an effort, Grace unclenched her fists; her nails were drawing blood.

She rubbed her palms together. It was not like her to be this afraid, and a not insignificant part of her wished she had just stayed aboard the *Dawn* and taken what was coming. Would being held hostage, or tortured, be better than sitting here in the dark? That she even entertained the notion was ridiculous. And yet she knew in her soul there was no secret she would keep if revealing it meant Sharice could live.

She laughed bitterly, mostly at her own expense. The entire *situation* was ridiculous, and the temptation to contact the Secretary of the HDF and dispense with this subterfuge was immense. Of course, the lack of any official response by now was telling by itself. Why were there still no ships here? Not even a clean-up contingent?

But Colonel Ramos was right; until she knew more about what was happening, and what the Insurrection wanted with her, she had to assume the worst. Of everyone. For whatever reason, her gut was telling her Talon Ramos could be trusted. Perhaps it was the Himeran legacy lending him such gravitas. Her eyelids closed for a moment, and she shook her head to clear it. Coffee. She needed coffee. "Time?"

Her bracelet spun to life as holographic numbers dancing above the platinum Pollyanna netband. It matched her hair clip, which was... *not* important. It had not even been twenty hours since the attack, but salt and sea, she was tired. It was nearing four a.m., though, about the time she typically rolled off the rack.

That was a habit she learned from her father. *Wake up with the fish to catch the fish*. On Europa's far side, the hemisphere that never came into view of Jupiter, scattered fishing villages had sprouted over the centuries since humans delved through nineteen kilometers of glowing ice. Including her own village, entrenched on a wide plateau set deep into the surface. Heiwa sat on the edge of an ocean pocket its residents kept stocked with flounder, snapper, and tuna.

Okay, enough. Her thoughts were wandering. Maybe just a quick nap.

"Polly, set an alarm for 0500," she said. The hologram flashed green and vanished. Grace leaned back in the chair and shut her eyes.

Morning brought with it a swell of regret as Jolin awoke to find herself alone under the pile of blankets Isabella had gathered from her cabin. Pushing the feeling away, she sat up and stretched before pulling one of her new shirts out of a bag and stuffing herself into it. Her leg was really throbbing. The bruise was not getting better, but at least it did not look any worse. Or did it? She traced the contours of the black and brown area with a frown, then retrieved her pants from the floor.

In the galley she reheated a half-empty bag of coffee and poured herself into the ratty old couch behind the hammock. It faced a video player attached to the bulkhead—an artifact of pre-holographic tech, but obviously well cared for; one of Isabella's prized possessions. Jolin sighed and sipped, digging her toes into the plush red carpet.

"Make yourself at home," Ajax said as he entered on a beeline for the coffee.

Jolin hefted her mug in a mock salute.

"We haven't talked much, with all that's going on." He stirred some powdered cream into his mug. "And I'm not really certain what to make of you yet, but I'm impressed with how you helped those people on the station."

Jolin choked on her coffee, spilling some on her new shirt.

Ajax smirked. "That was a compliment. Surely you've gotten them before." He pulled a chair over from the table and sat with a grunt. Jolin was reminded of the first time she spoke to him, was it really just yesterday? At least she could truly see the kindness in his eyes now.

"Yeah," she said, "but not usually from somebody like you."

"Someone like me?" He scowled. "A captain? A man?"

"A dad."

He erupted in raucous laughter, wiping tears from his eyes. "I see!"

Dads in general, is what she meant. Hers had been problematic. At best. *He* was probably still rotting in confinement somewhere, if he was even alive. She had not cared enough to check, not in a long time. Parents, as a whole, had disappointed her enough that she no longer put any stock in the biological familial bond. Ajax seemed to be a good one, though. Whatever that was worth.

Someone as close to his daughter as he was would know exactly what was happening in her life at all times, and Jolin harbored no doubt he knew what had gone on in her room last night. Would he bring it up, or expect *her* to? Her face flushed, and she buried herself in her drink. Unfortunately, guilt lingered there, waiting. She turned away from it.

"You have a solid skillset," he continued. "And Isabella thinks a lot of you, which is about the highest praise possible in my little world."

She watched him warily.

"But there's something we haven't seen yet, I think. Something you're hiding from us. The lieutenant colonel thinks you're dangerous."

Jolin froze. "Dangerous how?"

"Couldn't say." He shrugged. "But I told you before, as long as it doesn't bring trouble on me and mine, I couldn't care less either."

Her mind scrambled for answers. How much did he know about her? "And I told *you*, it won't." How much had Isabella revealed?

"Good." Ajax downed the last of his coffee with a mighty gulp and stood up. "So, I know you have a lot you're dealing with, but when you get that worked out, maybe we can find a place for you here." He hesitated, but recovered quickly enough she wondered if she had misinterpreted it. "Put those skills, and that ACIS node, to work."

Jolin winced. He did not know about Violet. As much as her gut was telling her she could trust Isabella, she realized she had still half-expected her to gush everything to her father.

"Did I offend you?" Ajax said.

"No, no," Jolin replied. "It's a generous offer. I just... I made a choice recently I wish I could take back. But it's the kind that, even if I had the chance to do things differently, I wouldn't."

Ajax nodded in understanding. What had he ever done that was so terrible? He seemed so simple, and good.

Jolin held up her wrist. "My ACIS node is destroyed. Hacked and overloaded."

Ajax's eyes widened. Would he take back his offer, knowing half the reason he made it was no longer on the table? "Gone for good? Or recoverable?"

"Hard to know, though we found something in the shuttle that gives me a little hope."

"Something to worry about?"

"Isabella didn't seem to think so."

He nodded again, as if that was all the proof he needed. Irrational. To Jolin at least. She knew so few people who had that kind of relationship with their parents. And to see firsthand the faith he had in his daughter made her lungs heavy.

"Are you okay?"

She wiped away the tears that clung to her eyelashes and nodded. "Ignore me. It's the cryo-freeze," she lied. "Wreaking havoc with my emotions." And it *was* a lie. She had known that from the start; refused to admit it.

"I've heard that can happen," he said. "Anyways, think about my offer. You could find a place here. A life."

A family.

Jolin's heart froze at the unspoken implication. She glanced at him sharply, but he was already leaving, back to the bridge? Ridiculous. Irrational and ridiculous. She set her mug down on the little rickety table next to the couch and pressed both hands to her face.

The coolness of her palms was refreshing against her heated cheeks. She was not trembling anymore; letting off a little steam last night had helped. The reminder caused her to groan, and guilt stirred. She had taken it too far with Isabella, like she always did. Abused the empathy of a stranger. Manipulated her into... *Starlight*, she was going to turn into her mother whether she wanted to or not.

Ajax's offer would be revoked once Isabella told him what Jolin had done. A burgeoning friendship ruined by her inability to control her impulses, to take things slow. She had practically begged Isabella to ravish her, though it had felt mutual in the moment. Now, looking back, she could not be sure. Could not trust her memory of it. Even so, the soft warmth of Isabella's skin, her scented soap... those feelings lingered. She sighed.

Ganymede was a smart plan. Not too far away; she could catch a shuttle from Portco, or another of the dozens of cities dotting Europa's icy surface. And if she left now, there was less chance of hurting anyone. Something like claws wrapped around her heart, scraping away her remaining confidence and leaving... what? Panic? Regret? At this point, she could not trust her emotions either.

Regardless, with a sudden, stark clarity Jolin knew: Life would be better for everyone if she left the *Syracusia* for good.

16

Waiting

Isabella sat cross-legged in the captain's chair, watching the admiral snore. Grace's netband had dinged an alarm two hours ago, but the admiral just tapped it off and went right back to sleep. She smiled into her coffee and turned her attention back to the view. The forward screens displayed Jupiter in all its glory. Gigantic. Its immensity humbled her. And terrified her. But mostly it intrigued her.

The storms raging across its surface had only been explored by a few humans who lived to tell the tale; even molecular repulsor shields were bashed to smithereens after just a few minutes down there. It was breathtaking, and awesome. And she *really* wanted to try it. Reading about those other attempts was fascinating. There had even been a popular movie made about one of them. An ill-fated one.

From here, though? It was sand art. Unmoving and eternally beautiful. She sighed. Jolin had fallen asleep almost as soon as they had finished their... discussion, and Isabella had watched her for a little while after. She could not help feeling guilty for taking advantage of the situation.

Getting caught up in the moment was always an issue for her, and she had pushed it too far. Jolin had given her consent, of course, but still... they only just met, and now she had probably scared the woman off for good with her aggressiveness.

Jolin's almond-scented shampoo still lingered in Isabella's nose; when she closed her eyes she saw the delicate contrast of their skin tones and felt again the tremble of each touch. She squirmed in her seat. And that soft, husky laugh would live in her memory forever. Yes, Jolin had been willing, but she was also in a rough way emotionally. And physically, though that had not impeded them. Her cheeks heated and she fanned her face with a hand. They probably just needed to talk about it, but—

The admiral let loose with a particularly loud snore and sat up. "I'm awake," she said, almost slipping out of the chair.

"Morning." Isabella held up her mug in greeting.

"Did they, did my...?" Grace tapped her wristband. "What time is it?"

"Seven-thirty," Isabella replied just as the holographic numbers appeared above the admiral's wrist. "And no, nobody has called."

Grace leaned forward, collecting herself. "I see." She cleared her throat. "I'm going to go, um, get a drink of water."

Isabella nodded as Grace stood, and made a quick decision. "I'm sorry I was rude to you," she said.

The admiral paused. "You were worried. About your mother, and your... friend." She smoothed her uniform, then reached up to examine her bun, which was still mostly together, though frizzy. "Besides," she said, tugging loose the wide clip that held her hair in place. It cascaded around her face in silvery waves. "You were right. You don't answer to me. *I'm* sorry for trying to order you around."

Isabella's jaw fell off.

Grace smirked, then stuffed the clip between her teeth. She ran her fingers through her hair a few times before pulling it up again and locking it in back place. "Amazing what a little sleep will do for my personality," she said. "My wife says it's like living with two different people, except one of them is a grizzly bear. Anyways, please let me know if any calls come in?"

"I will," was all Isabella could say. She shook her head. People could always surprise you with their secret depths.

Grace nodded at her, then hustled down the stairs as her father came up them. Ajax stepped aside for the admiral, giving her a polite smile, then grinned at Isabella as he stepped onto the bridge.

"You're up early," he said, "and in my seat."

She jumped up. "Admiral Lewin was in mine."

"No calls yet, I gather."

"Nope. What have you been up to?"

"Got the shields repaired, topped off the cannon batteries, and upgraded the firewall to protect against ACIS infiltration. Just in case." He yawned suddenly. "That was before I knew it was fried. But there are others out there, like the one you said your pal Jester has."

"You've been busy."

"Somebody has to take care of the little details, and you were off doing..." He cleared his throat. "Whatever it was you were doing."

Isabella inhaled sharply and searched for a place to die. She wanted to smash through the hull and get sucked out into space. "I was, um..."

"Relax, I'm just teasing you."

"Well don't," she said. "It's weird!"

"Sorry, I'm just starting to feel a little antsy, like a bomb is about to go off in my face." He prodded his console and the view screens switched to a wider image of their surroundings. Scanners would alert them to anything approaching far sooner than the screens would, but the bridge did suddenly feel less intimidating. "Not you. I mean, just, all this big world-changing stuff. I wish we were a million kilos away from here."

"So what do we do? How do we get out of it?" She slid into her seat at comms. It was still warm. And was that a hint of rosewater in the air?

"That's the question." Ajax leaned back in his chair with a sigh. "And I gotta tell you, I have no idea."

"If it's safe for the admiral and her boyfriend, can we just drop them off and head back out?"

He shrugged. "Political intrigue, terrorism, and subterfuge don't interest you anymore, huh?"

"Almost losing Mom was enough of that for a lifetime." Her mug was empty now, so Isabella dropped it into the basket she had attached to her console. She spent too much time rewiring and soldering new circuits after spills, which was just about her least favorite thing to do.

She would rather clean the lav than mess with electronics. Jolin knew about that stuff. Perhaps she could—No. That ship had flown. And she had nobody to blame but herself. "And we'll drop Jolin off too, I assume? She has things she needs to do."

"Actually," her father said, suddenly finding something very interesting about his console. "I asked her to crew up with us."

"You what?" Isabella's eyes jumped out of her skull. The little tumble of raw nerves in her belly were scratching to get out. Was he smiling? She scowled at him, which he did not seem to notice. "What did she say?"

"She didn't. But I got the feeling she might not be sticking around."

"Oh, sure, of course." Isabella half stood, then wondered why she was standing, and sat back down.

He laughed. "You've got it bad, don't you?"

"Daddy!" She was mortified. *Mortified.*

"She hasn't lied to me yet, and she seems nice, that's all I'm saying. And terrifying. But mostly nice."

"Stop!"

He covered his chuckles with a hand. "Sure, okay. Sorry. But you should talk to her."

"You know, just when I think Mom is the worst, you show up to take the trophy."

"What'd your mother say?"

"Nothing! Shut up! I'm going."

He nodded, still laughing.

Isabella stalked out of the bridge.

"Senator Dillan?" The president's Chief of Staff cleared his throat, peering into nothing. "Can she see me?" Reece Wyatt's balding head floated above the communication console like an apparition. He was handsome, after a fashion; but his cheeks were gaunt, his eyes small and secretive.

"I see you, sir," Amanita said. This was taking forever. Behind her, Willem pounded quietly on some equipment with his fist. The holographic camera kicked on and scanned her face.

"Ah, good. There you are. Excellent," Wyatt said. "So glad you made it through that terrifying ordeal."

"Thank you; I appreciate that." She forced herself to smile. "I thought I'd be speaking with the president?"

"Yes, well. The president, ah, apologizes, but is indisposed. She wished me to convey her condolences for the lives lost, of course, and the situation you're having to deal with. She'll be leading a press conference in an hour."

"Can you give me an indication of what our response will be?"

"I can't, we have to control every aspect of this information. You understand."

"Of course." She waited five hours for this? "Is there anything you can tell me about the *Rosy-Fingered Dawn*?"

"Why do you ask?"

She was prepared for this; a simple misdirection to keep Admiral Lewin's location secret. If being thought vapid was the price of information, she would pay it. Though with his lack of helpfulness thus far, Amanita was afraid she was paying for nothing. "My things are aboard, clothes and various personal items."

"Ah," Wyatt said. "Of course, yes. One moment." He leaned out of the frame, and the hologram vanished.

Amanita glanced at her watch and yawned. She had experienced enough excitement for a week, let alone eighteen hours. And been forced to miss a weekend with her daughter she had been looking forward to for months. For what?

She had been stymied on four of her last six pieces of legislation, and of the two that had enough support to pass, one was sent to die in committee and the other was a toothless bit of quad-partisan fundraising reform that she was just one of seventeen authors on. It had seemed like such a smart move at the time. Run for Senate. Challenge the system from inside.

Sure, Amanita had secured water rights in the face of enormous pressure from HydroCorp, but what had she done lately besides wear a suit and pretend to pay attention in a six-hundred-seat Senate chamber, five hundred of which were empty most of the time? Eighteen years of 'service' and she had started to wonder why the constituents of her little Lunar Province kept re-electing her. A question which was answered resoundingly in this past election, when she was voted out of office by a nine percent margin.

After lazing around at home for two months, she had jumped at the chance to do a little soldiering again when the admiral called, even if it was just for old time's sake. Grace Lewin had pulled Amanita along after every promotion she got over the years, and even when Amanita retired they remained close.

She had been one of five invited guests to Grace and Sharice's wedding last year, which still made her proud. Inwardly. Grace was like a big sister, and she could not help being impressed by her. But some decorum was required in Amanita's position. And, of course, another of those five guests was President Adrianna Nadzieja herself. Who, it appeared, was ghosting Amanita entirely.

"There has been no contact with the *Rosy-Fingered Dawn* since she jumped away from Europa, I'm afraid," Wyatt said finally, his bald head sliding back into view. "When we do find her, I'll see to it personally that your things are returned to your..." He hesitated. "To wherever you care to have them sent. Is there anything else?"

"No, sir. Thank you," she said.

Willem clicked off the feed on their end.

"Utterly useless."

"Not utterly," replied Willem.

"Oh?"

"I suspect *Europa Two* was not the only casualty of this attack."

Amanita eyed him sharply. "Go on."

Willem glanced at the young soldier studiously ignoring them by the door. "It's been almost twenty hours since the station's destruction. Why no ships? No military response? We're functionally alone out here."

Darkness condensed in the pit of Amanita's stomach. And that pause at the end. He would have her things returned to her what? Had something happened to her home? "Call *Syracusia*," she said.

Willem nodded, tapping the comms panel.

"Sorry, Senator," said the young soldier. So he *was* listening. "No further communications in or out. This base is on lockdown."

She glared at him. "Don't be ridiculous."

"Senator, he's right." Willem drew her attention to the controls, where bold red letters floated above them, reading *OFFLINE. What the hell?*

"I told you to stop calling me Senator." Amanita crossed her arms. "Fine, we'll contact our ship from outside the compound then." She gathered up her handbag and swiped a pen from the desk for good measure, tucking it into the front pocket of her blazer.

The soldier shook his head silently and moved in front of the exit, and that knot of worry in Amanita's gut doubled in size. What was happening? She held it in. Held on to it. Channeled it into her most imperious stare. Isabella would be proud.

And prouder still of what she said next. "Soldier, I'm giving you three seconds to step away from that door."

The soldier—or guard, apparently—tensed his hands on his rifle, but did not raise it. "I can't do that, Ma'am."

"Two," she said. His eyes narrowed in confusion, but he held his ground. Amanita clenched and unclenched her hands, a stress control technique she learned at a young age. "Stand down now."

"With respect, ma'am, I have orders to keep you here."

She frowned. Orders from *whom?* This young man would not know, being about as far down the chain of command as one could be, but there could only be a single answer anyway. Just one person with that authority knew she was here, besides the admiral. And things were in very bad shape indeed if President Nadzieja had resorted to ordering the sequestration of a System Senator. Especially a powerless, forcibly retired one. "What is your name?" she said.

"Ensign Dugry Platt, ma'am."

"And how long are you instructed to keep me here, Ensign?"

"Until I am notified otherwise," Platt said, eyeing her nervously. "Now please, this doesn't have to be hard. I'm just doing my job."

"I understand," Amanita said. "But time's up."

Behind her, Willem bolted into action, crossing the distance at a full sprint. To his credit, Ensign Platt was not taken completely off guard, but still only had time to get his rifle half raised before Willem knocked it aside with one foot and spun to kick him in the chest with the other.

Platt slammed into the door, collapsing in a heap. He was still conscious but struggling to catch his breath. Willem knelt to retrieve the laser rifle, putting a hand on the guard's arm. "Just breathe," he said. "I didn't break any ribs. It will pass."

"Fuck you," Platt managed between wheezes.

Willem nodded and stood. He tossed the weapon over to Amanita. "What now?" he asked.

"Now?" Amanita pulled the rifle's strap over her shoulder and checked the power indicator. She fired a single bolt at Ensign Platt, stunning him. "We run."

Jolin had transitioned to the hammock by the time Grace arrived in the galley, so she was able to watch the gray-haired woman pouring a glass of water unobserved. Something tickled the back of her mind, something she knew about this woman, or had heard? Jolin balanced the mug on her belly and let the ship's inertia sway her back and forth. It was not much, but it was relaxing.

"I remembered where I knew you from," Grace said without looking up.

Jolin jumped, and almost fell out of the hammock. Again.

"You're wanted for something, aren't you?" Grace took a slow drink of water.

"And if I was? Maybe I did my time already."

"Did you?"

Jolin finished her coffee instead of answering.

"I can't figure you out," the admiral said, gesturing vaguely in her direction. "Colonel Ramos thinks you're dangerous, but I've known him about five minutes longer than I've known you, so I'll trust my gut."

"I thought he was your attaché or whatever."

Grace snorted. "Yeah, me too."

"He's not?"

The older woman ignored her. "What my gut tells me is you're hiding something, but I don't see danger when I look your way."

"Is that supposed to be an insult or a compliment?" Jolin used her foot to kick off the couch, giving her swing a nice arc.

"Honestly?" The admiral shrugged. "It's hard to be afraid of someone who looks at a person the way you look at the Captain's daughter."

Jolin sighed. *Way to play it cool.* "So everyone knows?"

The admiral smirked at her.

Swinging her feet to the side, Jolin climbed out of the hammock. "I used to be better at this," she said.

"At what?"

"Everything." She grinned, making her way into the kitchenette. Ajax had taken the last of the coffee, so she rinsed her mug and stacked it in the decontamination rack with the others.

"I tried searching the HDF databases and found nothing under the name Jolin Aster," Grace said, regarding her thoughtfully.

"Well there you have it." Jolin wiped her brow with a sleeve. "I'm innocent."

"That's a pretty flower." The admiral pointed at her jacket. "I thought about having the colonel run your IDENT, or your fingerprints. But seeing how I don't trust him any more than I trust you, I figured let's wait. See what happens." She refilled her glass from the tap and took a long, slow sip.

"And?"

"I'll say this: the Insurrection is large; far larger than any of us thought. So if you think you've stumbled on a winning lottery ticket by ending up on the same boat as the fleet admiral, maybe hoping to turn me in for a bounty..."

"I couldn't care less about that," Jolin said.

"I believe you."

"So, what, you're just making sure I know how much you think you know about me?" Jolin rummaged through several cabinets until she found the fruit, and grabbed a banana. "It's nice to see they keep more than nutrient mush on this one."

"So you *were* in the military."

Jolin rolled her eyes. At herself. *Ugh, of course...* Grace was trying to learn as much as she could, not spouting off what she already knew. Jolin had played right into her hands. *Rookie mistake.* She peeled the banana and took a gigantic bite. Her eyes nearly rolled back inside her head; it tasted so good. A little soft, but still.

"Then I saw that." Grace nodded toward her wrist.

"It's an old injury," Jolin said. "Flared up over on the station."

"It's a burned out ACIS node. And a wanted woman, ex-military, with one of those, well... that narrows the field of possibilities, doesn't it?"

"Ex-*para*-military." Jolin crammed the rest of her banana in her mouth, chewing aggressively at the admiral, who just watched her. Calmly. Patiently. Old instincts started to kick in as she withered underneath that authority-laden countenance. Her fingers itched to snap into a salute. She shoved her hand in a pocket instead. "I'm a fighter, not a patriot."

"I see. You can have your secrets, Miss Aster, until I suspect they'll stir up a wake at my dock."

"Nobody cares about me anymore, Admiral, I swear. Not for a long time."

"Now, I think we both know that isn't true," Grace said with half a smile. She glanced up at the entry, where Isabella was ducking into the galley. "I'm going to go check on my *attaché*," she added, and made her way out the aft hatch and down the back stair.

Frowning, Jolin rinsed the glass the admiral had left and stuffed it onto the rack.

"What did *she* want?" Isabella asked.

"To make sure I understood she knew things that weren't any of her business." Jolin sighed. Her stomach tied itself in knots worrying over this moment, and now here it was. She turned to face Isabella. "Listen, I—" she started.

"How are you—" Isabella said at the same time. She winced. "You go."

"I wanted to say I'm sorry for—" Jolin began again, but this time she was cut off by a ship-wide proximity alert.

"To your stations!" Ajax yelled over the intercom. "They're back."

17

Choices

"Evasive maneuvers!" Ajax bellowed as Isabella leapt into her chair. "Aster, on the guns."

Jolin was already on her way. She slid into the tactical station and pulled up the weapons and defensive subsystems. "Shields at maximum," she said. "But they won't be once that dreadnought starts firing."

"You think?" Ajax said. The Insurrection ship was vast, even at their current range. Too far for guns to be effective, thankfully. But not for long.

"At least we don't have to wait anymore," Grace said from the stairs as she approached. "Still no word from Europa?"

"Nothing, but I can't really do both." The captain's voice was strained.

"Set me up with communications then."

"You sure?" Ajax frowned.

"I've done damn near every job that exists on this bridge," the admiral replied. "I think I can manage parsing some radio chatter."

Jolin smirked despite herself. She had the defense algorithms panel open, and was trying to study them as quickly as she could. Basic stuff. *Amateur* stuff, really, not far off from out of the box. "Captain, permission to..." She hesitated, her fingers twitching with a sudden numbness. She made a fist.

"To what?" Ajax said as he sent communication control to one of the stations lining the back of the bridge. "Nevermind. Whatever it is, just do it if you think it'll keep us alive. That ship is closing fast. Izzie?"

"Working on it!" The ship shuddered as Isabella engaged the main engines. "I'm going to put the moon between us and them, but I have to bring us about." The images on the screens began to move as *Syracusia* pitched down. "I'm taking us deeper into Europa's gravity well to cheat some speed, but they're already accelerating."

"We're being hailed, Captain," Grace said.

Jolin would bet money the old lady had not sat in the cheap seats in decades. But she did it without hesitation. That was something. The target scanner indicated the *Syracusia*'s distance from the dreadnought was increasing. For now. If Jolin was going to do anything with the automated defenses, she would not get a better time.

Her hands shook as she held them over the controls. She grabbed her left wrist and squeezed it tight. *It's not just if-then statements*, Violet had taught her. *We're playing a game with them; target a subsystem, weaken their shields to draw their attention from your real objective. Cat and mouse.*

Of course, he was quoting manuals and formulating a synthesis of expert instruction back then; barely more than a holographic assistant. But with his help she was able to build on what she learned in the academy. And together they had developed elegant solutions for common scenarios.

The *Syracusia* had four guns. *Four.* Enough to fend off a short range fighter, but against a dreadnought? Nobody would call this a common scenario.

"Open the channel," Ajax said.

"Done," Grace replied, but only silence greeted them.

"Ahoy, unmarked dreadnought," Ajax began after a moment. "This is Captain Ajax Marquez of the free ship *Syracusia*. Can we assume your intentions are not hostile?"

Free ship? That was an old hauler designation, from pirate days in the early colonization of the solar system, when just setting out from space dock got you an automatic fifty-fifty shot at being killed out there. Cargo freighters still used it, rarely, to indicate they were not allied with the government, or any faction. Jolin shook her head. She needed to focus.

"Surrender Fleet Admiral Lewin, *Syracusia*." Something was familiar about that voice. Jolin's eyes narrowed, but now was not the time.

"To whom am I speaking?" Ajax replied.

"You have twenty minutes to comply."

"Surely you can—"

"They dropped the line," Grace interrupted.

"Shit," Ajax said.

"Twenty minutes?" Isabella said. "They'll overtake us in ten."

"That's the plan," Colonel Ramos said, stepping onto the bridge.

"What do you mean?" Grace asked, her face stuck midway between fear and anger.

"This group is ruthless; they're going to disable the ship, then board her and take you by force. Our only chance to avoid that is to send the admiral over in a shuttle immediately." Ramos tugged on a pair of flight gloves. "Which is *not* an option."

Nobody argued, which made Jolin smile. The lieutenant colonel had reminded her of Rolan Hector at first, but she saw a little bit of somebody else in him now. The set of his jaw, maybe. Her lip trembled as a wave of sadness threatened to drown her. *Concentrate on what you see,* she instructed. His words, his voice.

Ramos was out of his uniform, wearing a blue fitted shirt over dark slacks, and when he folded his coat over the back of a chair, his arms caught Jolin's attention. Bright metal reflected the myriad lights of the CIC. Cybernetic limbs were a deliberate choice these days. A voluntary upgrade. Like hers, with Violet.

"Scan for small vessels, Captain," Ramos continued. "Heat signatures. Whatever you can. They're out there, I can feel it."

"You're a pilot?" Isabella asked. She was staring at his arms too. That was only one application of such enhancements, but Isabella seemed to have picked up on something.

"I was." Ramos nodded. "A lifetime ago. Nguyen's ship is here. I'm going to see about keeping them off our hull as long as possible." He looked at Grace. "With your permission, Admiral."

"Captain?" she said, holding Ramos's gaze.

"I don't see anything on scanners yet," said Ajax, "but we're not exactly equipped for this kind of thing. Syracusia's size and pedigree is usually enough to scare."

"Permission granted, Colonel," Grace said. "And Colonel?" she added as he turned to go. "Don't blow up the sergeant's ship? I understand he's quite fond of it."

He offered her a brusque salute, then ducked into the corridor.

"I'm going too," said Isabella.

Jolin's heart froze.

"You got ammo loaded?" Ajax's voice was stoic, strained.

"No, but I've got twenty minutes."

"Eight," Grace corrected.

"Plenty of time." She grinned, giving Jolin a wink.

"But..." Jolin stammered. She had no rights in this conversation. *Starlight.* How was Ajax so calm?

"I'll be fine, Jolin," Isabella said. "Admiral, can you fly this boat for me?"

"I'll do what I can."

"I'll fly it," Ajax barked, transferring nav control to his console. "Just be careful out there."

Isabella put a hand on her father's shoulder, kissing his bald head. Then she was gone, and the bridge was darker without her. Despite the glow of Jupiter and the flames of Europa's atmosphere heating up the shields.

Jolin looked at Ajax. "How can you just let her do this?"

"I haven't been able to *let* her do anything for years, Aster," he replied. "Now, do I *want* her to go out there? Absolutely not." He adjusted their course. "But, then again, Isabella is safer in the cockpit of that fighter than anywhere else in the galaxy. And we'll be safer in here with her out there."

Jolin swallowed the lump in her throat.

"You'll see," he said, his face grim. "Now, about our defenses?"

"I have a few ideas," she said finally, gathering her courage. "I just... the last time..."

"You managed the defenses on your old ship, didn't you? The *Endless Star*." His brown eyes bored into her.

"I was in my bunk. When it happened," she said. The words resisted her, tried to crawl back into her throat. "We—*they*—didn't stand a chance."

"And where are you now?" His gaze was fierce.

She had no reply; they both knew the answer.

"Well then," he said. "Speaking of chances. Here's yours, First Lieutenant Gaster. Save my ship."

Jolin snorted a laugh, blinking away tears. Was it ridiculous to think she had a second opportunity here? Why would it be? She knew what to do and how to do it. And she would be on the bridge to make adjustments as needed, not in her bunk. She could take manual control when required.

She took a ragged breath and held it for a moment, closing her eyes. There was no way for her save the *Star*, no way to to bring back her family. But he was right. *Syracusia* was her ship now, even if just for these few hours. And she was done losing people.

The swell of emotion receded and the world clicked into place, solid and stable. "I can do this," she said, opening her eyes.

"Yes you can. Ready for a fight?" Ajax asked.

"What?" Jolin winked at him. "You think there might be trouble?"

Ajax chuckled, scratching at his beard. "All right then."

Isabella zipped up her flight suit and looked in the mirror. Her hair was a disaster, but her face was bright. *Syracusia*'s warm, ambient lighting had always been generous to her dark brown skin. She took a deep breath. "I can do this," she said.

Colonel Ramos was already climbing into *Prescient* when she arrived in the hangar. He gave her a little nod. "You know how to fly that thing?" he asked. He looked different. Excited.

Isabella glanced at her ship, her beautiful, wonderful ship. "How hard can it be?" she said, returning the nod.

Smirking, Ramos tapped his temple with two fingers in a brief salute. "All right then."

Willem choked out the final guard and beckoned for Amanita to enter the security office. She had hired him years ago, an ambitious kid looking to make a difference in the world after a failed stint in the private sector. His intelligence made him invaluable to her, as did his willingness to dirty his hands when necessary. Coupled with a skill set that made him extremely dangerous, those other qualities had made civilian tedium a poor fit.

She trusted him with her life.

As she hoped, there was a Gal-Net transmitter here, powerful enough to get a signal off-world. Stepping over an unconscious woman, Amanita tapped the console and entered the frequency she and Admiral Lewin had agreed on. She closed her eyes and inhaled slowly through her nose, exhaling through pursed lips. The implications of her suspicions were almost too dire to contemplate, and she could not escape a creeping fear that the whole system was on fire.

"I can do this," she whispered. Turning to Willem, she asked, "are we good?"

Willem held up one finger. He stood by the partially closed door, peering out into the hall. On a desk nearby, five stunner pistols sat in a neat row. A guard stirred at his feet, trying to get up, and Willem moved swiftly, firing off a single pulse with one of the guns that sent the man sprawling. He replaced the weapon, adjusting its position until it lined up in perfect precision with the others, then gave Amanita a nod.

She smiled, returning the gesture. "All right then."

Cannibal slid through the inky blackness like an assassin. Without her wayward passenger, Isabella was free to open him all the way up. She rolled the ship in a quick three-sixty, and her FSIC activated with a rush of fluid and grav waves. It always felt like sitting in a warm bath. Every sensor showed green, despite her skipping the pre-flight warm up a second time in twenty-four hours.

It would be fine, as long as she did not make it a habit. She owed *Cannibal* a comprehensive maintenance check, anyway. Leaving the ship alone in the hangar for so long was irresponsible. Her father always said a fighter is like a pet; you have to take care of it. And she usually did. Except lately, other things had taken priority. It did not matter. She would do it tonight.

The battery indicator flared yellow at her suddenly, and Isabella patted the dash. "I promise, buddy. A full diagnostic cycle. Just get me through this one quick thing, all right?" The light blinked and resumed a nominal green, as if in reply. Tuning her radio to the secure channel, she tapped the transmit button once to get Ramos's attention.

"I hear you, pilot," the colonel's voice crackled over the speaker in her helmet. "That's an old Army trick. You never served, did you?"

"Depends what you mean." Isabella adjusted the volume and disabled *Cannibal*'s exterior lights. "My uncle is who taught me to fly, and he and my dad both did. Plus, my mother served enough for both of us. I spent so much time waiting in the wings for her to finish speeches, or shake hands, it almost felt like a job."

"She's an important woman."

"To me, anyway. Not so much her constituents."

Ramos chuckled. "They're buckgravity bumpkins. She has a hell of a reputation, whatever they think."

"Thanks for saying that."

"Yeah." He paused. "Okay, I don't see anything yet, but keep an eye on your scanners, and don't fire unless you're ready to be fired upon."

"Mmhm," Isabella grunted into the radio, rolling her eyes. She switched off her mic and leaned back, scanning her surroundings with her own eyes before engaging the targeting computer. *Syracusia* loomed off her starboard side, but even at this distance it was a mouse compared to the dreadnought. What was its name, she wondered, squinting at the silent hulk bearing down on them.

"I see you, kiddo," her father's voice fuzzed in her ear. Isabella tipped her wings, and he laughed. "Good. Stay safe out there. No matter what happens, I believe in you."

"Daddy," she said, shaking her head. It was impossible to wipe tears out of her eyes in these gloves and in this helmet. "See you soon." She blinked, putting a hand against the canopy, and imagined she could see him at the helm, though *Syracusia*'s bridge was buried beneath layers of armour.

Movement caught her attention before a blip on the scanner confirmed it. Something was approaching. Fast. She set *Prescient* and *Syracusia* as friendly targets and maneuvered *Cannibal* to face the approaching ship. Her pulse pounded in her wrists as three more targets popped into range.

Then five more, scattered around the dreadnought and hurtling toward them. Abruptly it occurred to Isabella that maybe this had not been the best idea.

"Hit it," said Ajax, and Jolin gave her instructions a last look before tapping the execute button. The weapons subsystem would reboot and they would be as ready as they could be for, she hoped, whatever came next.

Syracusia would not long survive a sustained, direct assault, but she hoped they really wanted the Admiral as bad as Ramos seemed to think. That would be a stronger shield to them than anything.

"Thirty seconds," she said.

Ajax nodded. "Admiral?"

"Still nothing on comms." Grace had assumed Isabella's chair, and even though she had removed her jacket, she still looked every bit the admiral, calm and collected. As always. At some point she had even fixed her hair; not a strand was out of place. "We've negated their advantage for now, but if they don't follow us into Europa orbit it'll be a simple matter for them to just track us and wait until we emerge."

"They'll follow," Jolin said.

"How can you be so sure?" Grace asked.

"The longer they wait, the more likely it is we'll get an HDF response, right? I bet they bumped back here the moment they learned you weren't on board the *Dawn*."

"I wish I shared your optimism."

Jolin narrowed her eyes and scowled at her scanner. That could not be right. "I'm seeing... eighty fighters?"

"What?" Ajax and Grace spoke simultaneously.

"They're hanging back for now, but that's a lot right? I know I've been asleep for half a decade, but that seems excessive." AI drones, maybe?

Grace pursed her lips, eyeing her. Jolin grimaced. She had never been very good at keeping secrets.

Ajax tapped his personal communicator, which had a direct link to his daughter. "Izzie, don't be alarmed, but—"

"They have, like, a *hundred* fighters, Dad."

"Yeah."

"How is this Insurrection so big?" Jolin stared at her screens. "They just festered under everyone's noses?"

"We've known about them for a while," said Grace. "Well, a little bit. Nobody thought it was this bad."

"Gotta go, Daddy," Isabella said. "And hey, Jolin?"

"She can hear you," Ajax said.

"I'll try and save a few for you."

Jolin stood up, almost by instinct. She turned and... had nowhere to go. No way to help except sit back down and prepare for the onslaught. So, pushing up her sleeves, that is what she did. She could be useful here; make a difference even without Violet.

The two forward cannons were ballistic Gatlings, each with 10,000 rounds, which was not a lot, considering. They could be reloaded from the stores, but that would take time and personnel they did not have. So, guideline one: make each shot count.

The port and starboard cannons were plasma casters. Giant ones. She had inspected them last night, before she and Isabella had—Jolin cleared her throat. *Focus.* Giant meant slow. They ran on capacitors that fed off of the main reactor. But for max efficiency, without shutdowns, they could be fired about once every ten seconds. She had a workaround for that, but it was not pretty.

Even so, it was a grain of sand against eighty fighters. Casters were great at disabling shields on smaller ships, though, if it came to that. But these were single-pilot fighters, and small even for that. Harder to hit, easier to destroy.

"Don't fire until we have to," Ajax said.

Jolin flashed her best smile. "How about a warning shot over the bow? Maybe we can scare them off?"

"Yeah, that'll do it. We could throw water balloons at them while we're at it. Make a Field Day of it, like school kids."

Jolin's grin widened.

"What?" Ajax frowned.

"Nothing, you just reminded me of somebody I knew once."

"I hope he wasn't as dashing or as handsome as me."

"Oh, you don't hold a candle to her." Movement on the scanner. "A small detachment has broken off, heading this way.

"Call coming in," Grace said. "It's her."

"About damn time," Ajax replied. "Put her through."

"Go ahead."

"Amanita?" Ajax was gripping his chair arm tightly, but otherwise gave no sign he was nervous. *Syracusia* shuddered beneath their feet.

"Jax, the situation down here is worse than we thought."

"I know the feeling. But go on. As quick as you can."

"The President is talking to the press in about ten minutes. But she ordered us kept on lockdown here on the base. Supposedly to keep the information contained."

"Lockdown?"

"We're fine, Willem got us out, which will be a thing. But we'll deal with that later," the senator said.

Jolin heard noise in the background, like bricks crashing through a wall, and pulse rifle fire. Then silence.

"Amanita?" Ajax said.

"Willem's handling things. We're going to find Sergeant Nguyen and head for the port center. Can you send the shuttle?"

"Not for a little while," Ajax replied. "The Insurrection ship is back and spoiling for a fight. If you're able to get us some help, we'll be grateful."

"I'll try. I still have a few connections."

"Write this name down," Grace interrupted.

"Okay?" Amanita said.

"Salman Daniyah, Captain of the carrier *Idomeneus*. If you can get word to him, tell him I'm here. I hope he will come. They have to know I'm missing by now. It doesn't explain why nobody's showed, but..." Grace glanced at them, then nodded. "He'll come."

"You sure you want to give that intel away?" Jolin asked.

"No choice," said Grace. "Besides, it's not like these pirates don't already know where I am." She gestured at the view screen. "And if we survive this, I have an idea how to use their knowledge to our advantage."

"Got it," Amanita replied. "We'll do our best. In the meantime, try to stay alive. My daughter is on that ship." Amanita was silent for a moment. "Can I talk to her?"

Ajax winced. "She... took her fighter out."

More silence. "I see." The light winked off.

"Well, that could have gone worse," he said. "Okay, folks. Barring a last minute *deus ex machina*, it's just us out here."

On the view screens, bright cords of blue and white light erupted from the dreadnought. Plasma cannons. A dozen of them. Jolin set her jaw.

"We're all we've got," Ajax rumbled. "Let's make a stand."

18

Flight of the Syracusia

Isabella's eyes widened as the attack began. It took all her willpower not to turn *Cannibal* around and head home. But she was more useful out here. "Ramos, I'm engaging." She kicked the thrusters and the ship rumbled to life.

"Confirmed," the reply came. "Weapons—shit!"

Bright impacts cracked against Isabella's shields. She thrusted up and strafed starboard, pitching *Cannibal*'s nose down to face her attackers.

One target at a time.

Conserve ammo.

"And light 'em up," she whispered.

Up close, the fighters were smaller than she expected, almost too tiny for a pilot to fit inside. They popped so fast she was not able to get a good look at them. She maneuvered behind the shuttle and locked a missile on it. Four missiles were her contingent. Was this the right time to use one?

Isabella had never been in a fight against this many ships before. Not even a tenth this many. Typical hauler defense meant she was scaring off a couple poorly-armed pirates looking to make a few easy credits. At most she might face off with one other reasonably skilled pilot. Nothing like this. Skill made no difference in a swarm this size. Theirs or hers. Her ammo count was going to be more important than her skill or her kill count. Run out of shots, and that was the end. Guns, then. She would find a way for those missiles to have maximum impact on the coming fight.

She squeezed the trigger halfway, to engage the targeting laser, but just as it locked on, a wide beam of red light split the shuttle in half like a knife through bread. Colonel Ramos guffawed over the radio as he flew *Prescient* through the wreckage.

"This is some ship," he yelled, spinning past her. "It really moves.

You're welcome."

Isabella frowned. "I didn't need..." She was so worried about conserving ammo and he just—*Ugh*. "How many times can you do that?"

"It's got a pretty vague indicator, down to eighty percent," he said. "So, five, maybe six? This cockpit is a museum."

"Nice work, but this fight isn't going to be a sprint. Try and save a little something for the unknown, okay?"

"Roger that."

"And anyway, I'm still up by my count, three to one."

He laughed. "Oh, that's how it is?" It was like a different person was in that starfighter than the morose slab of beef she had met yesterday. Was this what Talon Ramos had been like when he was a brash young aviator?

"Well, weapons hot, pilot," he said, "because here they come."

Isabella's scanner bloomed to life as an entire squadron of fighters peeled off of the dreadnought, headed their way. She glanced at *Syracusia*. The barrage had nearly reached it. What was Jolin doing over there?

She did not have to wait long to find out. At the last possible moment, the light show started. Her cockpit window darkened automatically to shield her eyes as staccato blasts from *Syracusia*'s plasma casters impacted with the oncoming fire, transforming them into an expanding plume of coruscating gases. Laced with forks of lighting, the plasma-cloud hung in space behind *Syracusia* like a second shield. Not a single bolt made it through.

"Wow," she whispered.

"Say again?" Ramos said. "I didn't catch that."

"Nothing." She maneuvered to point her guns at the incoming ships, then slammed her main engine to one hundred percent for a two-count, sending herself careening toward them. The grav-force was a head rush, even with her flight suit compensators engaged.

She used *Cannibal*'s maneuvering thrusters to send herself up over the plane of their approach, keeping them in her sights. Interestingly, none of the fighters responded. They only had eyes for *Syracusia*. Apparently Isabella did not rate as much of a threat to them. Well, that was rude. And not very smart at all.

Her lips parted as she closed the distance, picking them off one by one. When the fourth ship exploded she was finally close enough to get a good look at the others in the light of the blast. No cockpits? Were they drones? She had never heard of a massive swarm like this.

Her shield flashed again, and the fighter shuddered. Like annoyed wasps, a small group had broken off from the swarm to intercept her. She rolled, cutting up thrust and strafing to port. Squeezing her trigger twice, she took down three of them. Five left.

Something impacted her, aft, ballistics-based, but the only thing on her aft scanner was *Prescient*. "Are you for real!" she yelled.

"Sorry," Talon said. "I was trying to save you. Your ship is pretty quick, huh?"

"He's got it where it counts." She took out two more drones mid-sentence.

"I can see that," he replied. He sounded... flirty?

Ugh. She rolled her eyes.

"You said your uncle taught you how to fly?" Ramos continued.

"Defend *Syracusia,* you can ask me questions later," she said. Bits of metal plinked off her shields. "Or, and here's an idea: never."

He laughed, and Isabella's cockpit lit up bright red as he fired that beam weapon again, slicing through half the squadron. He rolled *Prescient* through the debris at top speed, pitching until he was facing the drones, and fired it again. That laser was amazing.

"I want one of those," she said.

"Yeah. Me too. I think that puts my count at, let me see, triple yours?"

"It's not a competition," she growled.

Sweat dripped into Jolin's eyes as the firing subsided. She had barely managed that. And even now the Insurrection dreadnought was preparing to fire again. The plasma cloud would make it difficult to target them, but hardly impossible. Wiping her brow with a sleeve, she adjusted herself in the chair. Maybe she could get Ajax to transfer tactical to one of the standing stations in the back.

Her sensors lit up again as the dreadnought fired. The first barrage had taken two minutes to arrive, but now that *Syracusia* was plowing through Europa's atmosphere, the Insurrection ship was gaining again. She had been right, though; it was pursuing them lower into Europa orbit.

A ship that size would have to stay a couple thousand kilometers further away, but the range on those heavy cannons was a hundred times that. *Syracusia*'s scatter casters, on the other hand, launched spinning blobs of plasma that expanded and dissipated after about five thousand kilos, rendering them extremely powerful close-up, but shit at long range. Luckily that was not what she needed them for.

"Incoming," she said.

"I see it." Ajax was standing at the view screens now, hands clasped behind his back. He cut a broad, bold silhouette against the swift colors of Europa and Jupiter beyond it. "That was nice work, Aster," he said over his shoulder. "Can you do it again?"

"I'll certainly try."

The ship shuddered against a pocket of warmer air like a stone skipping across a pond. Try? What was it about Ajax that dissolved her confidence? Or was it even him at all? She centered her scanner on *Cannibal* as Isabella maneuvered through the swarm, twisting and spinning, abrupt changes of direction.

Jolin reprogrammed the angle of one of the view screen cameras, and an image of the fighter appeared on-screen. Tracer rounds from *Cannibal*'s Gatlings lit up the black as it maneuvered in hard turns and abrupt angles. Ship after ship fell to her cannons. The camera had trouble tracking her. It was a furious dance.

"Wow," she whispered.

"See?" Ajax said. "What'd I tell you?"

Jolin glanced at him. His wide face was beaming. She could not help but return the smile. "Yeah, all right, we get it," she said. "You're a proud father."

"Daddy, they're drones," Isabella's voice crackled over the comms.

Ajax hurried back to his chair. "Drones?"

Grace frowned. "They're using artificial intelligence? I suppose if you're trying to overthrow the government you don't much care what's legal or illegal anymore."

"Wait, drones are illegal?" asked Jolin. AI-controlled drones had been the cornerstone of conflict operations before she went into the ice. What had changed? Flashing lights caught her attention. "Hold that thought." The second barrage was almost in range.

She needed to wait until they passed through the remnants of the initial attack, because it would probably throw off their trajectories. Sure enough, five of the twelve ricocheted, and one was spinning now like a little galaxy, which added a pronounced wobble to its line of attack.

She fired her first round of ballistics, allowing for fifty rounds per bolt. That broke them up nicely. Then she initiated her caster algorithm, and the *brum brum brum* reverberated through her seat cushion like bass at a rock show.

The view screen lit up with fireworks. She looked for the wobbly one. There it was, spinning like a little galaxy, spewing super-heated particles in all directions.

"You missed one," Isabella reported over the radio.

The problem with her workaround—well, *one* problem with her work-around—was that it took the casters longer to recover. Staggering them helped, but there was still a good ten seconds when neither of them was ready to fire. Of course, Jolin had planned a contingency for this. Always be prepared for everything to go wrong, right? Ballistics ammo would pass right through with it broken up so much, but she did have access to another bit of tech.

The ship groaned as she rotated the mining laser into position. It was not powerful enough to break through molecular repulsor shields, even the lightweight versions on the drones, but it could disperse plasma that had already been destabilized.

Hopefully.

As Jolin brought the targeting reticule online, the dreadnought fired again. They were pushing those cannons past their limits. "They must really want you bad, Admiral," she said, engaging the laser. One quick burst should do it. The plasma evaporated into nothing as the red beam connected.

"Pretty," said Isabella. She added something else, but Jolin could not make it out over the interference. The growing field of plasma remnants was going to be a problem.

"It seems that way," Grace replied. She was controlling their flight manually now, and *Syracusia* protested loudly as they ground through more turbulence. "Don't they realize I'm not just playing hard to get?"

Jolin's scanner alarmed, distracting her from whatever it was she was about to say next. The dreadnought fired again. She stood. "Not possible!" On screen, twelve more cords of light spread out on different trajectories. "They're firing too fast," she said. How were they doing it?

"Daddzzzzz zzzt"

Ajax tapped on his panel. "Isabella?"

"Zzzzzt zzzzzzt zsszzt." Then nothing.

"Admiral can you boost our receivers?"

"With what?" Grace said. "I could siphon power from the shields, maybe. Or the weapons, but that would be extremely stupid."

"Dammit!" He punched a fist against the back of his chair.

"We're still at enough range that I can cycle the casters before they hit," Jolin said, "but that won't be the case for long." She could defend against seven more barrages like that. Which meant, if they kept firing at this rate, they had about five more minutes before the *Syracusia* had to start tanking those blasts with her shields.

"Now would be a great time for a sudden and unexpected arrival," Grace whispered, almost too low for Jolin to hear. The Admiral glowered at the comms. Equipped with a Galaxy-class Sigrid drive, a carrier like the *Idomeneus* could arrive at any moment. But they had no way to know whether Amanita had successfully contacted them, or if she had, if they were even coming at all.

"*Syracusia?* Do you copy?" Isabella checked to make sure her radio was transmitting. "I said I'm going to get in close and see if I can take out some of those guns." The only reply was static. More than half of the drones were destroyed, and the way they ignored her had made it surprisingly easy. Too easy, really.

She switched to Ramos's channel. "Can you contact the ship?"

"Too much interference from the plasma. The signal should clear up as we get away from it, right?"

"How should I know?" Isabella looked out her canopy at the massive pulsing sphere of color. "It doesn't matter. We have to take out those guns." The third bevy of bolts was passing through it now, and they spun wildly as Jolin's guns started firing. A few made it through this time, smashing against *Syracusia*'s shields.

"They do seem overpowered," Ramos said. "Then again, it's a dreadnought. You want to see how this beam weapon does against those cannons? I have two shots left."

"Yeah," Isabella said with a grin she could not suppress, "I really do."

"Well let's clean up the rest of these fighters and get in there, pilot."

Isabella pulled into a trajectory that shot her past *Syracusia*, and she waved her wings again. "It'll be okay, Dad," she whispered. She would need to take the long way around to ensure her shields were not vaporized by all that plasma. Ramos was already cockpit deep in the remaining drones, blasting away with his Gatlings, laughing like a berserker.

Bright orange light from the explosions bounced through the first ring of plasma as if giving it power. And then it splashed outward as the dreadnought's shields plowed through like it was not even there.

She tried her radio again. Nothing. Another volley exploded around them, echoed in her own shields as drone fire erupted behind her. They were finally taking notice. Isabella growled and rejoined the fight.

"We can't keep this up much longer," Jolin said as another round of bolts splashed against the shields. "Thirty percent." Her ammo was almost spent. She fired the mining laser a few more times to clear out some of the dross, but it was not enough. None of it would be enough.

Flames licked the dreadnought, its shields rippling with color as it carved a path through Europa's meager atmosphere. "I'll be honest, I never expected it to end like this," she said, steadying herself as the chair bucked beneath her.

"It won't." Ajax strapped himself into his chair. The turbulence was overwhelming. "You said it yourself, they need the admiral alive."

"So let's give her to them," Grace said. "I can't ask you to do more than you've done."

"Now you're being ridiculous," said Jolin. "All this effort to just give up? I'd *rather* die."

Grace smiled sadly at her, then turned back to the controls. "I had to offer," she said. "Or I couldn't live with myself."

Jolin rolled her eyes. "How magnanimous." Her fingers danced along the controls as she adjusted her algorithm.

"Nobody's giving anyone to anybody," Ajax declared.

The volleys were coming thirty seconds apart now, with no sign of stopping. She analyzed the dreadnought's heat signature. Its giant radiators were being pushed past max safety limits. Perhaps the crew did not mind a little sweat.

Isabella and the Colonel were mopping up the last of the drones, and somehow neither of them had been blown up in the process. Jolin assumed they would head back now, after a job well done.

"No!" Ajax yelled.

She looked up in time to see a sky blue streak sail past them, headed straight for the dreadnought, followed quickly by another. What was she thinking? What were *they* thinking?

Ajax used a hand gesture to zoom the cameras in, and Jolin saw *Cannibal* and *Prescient* weaving around the most recent bloom of plasma

Syracusia had left in her wake. It kind of resembled her chosen namesake; a giant blue flower in the sky. How did they plan to get past the dreadnought's shields?

And then, somehow timed so perfectly Jolin wanted to weep, the shield dropped as the cannons loosed their next barrage, and the two fighters sailed through unharmed.

"Starlight," Jolin whispered.

"What?" said Ajax.

"Nothing, I just... she's something else isn't she?"

"Yeah," Ajax replied, his jaw tightening. "She really is."

It was always a rush, even in combat; melding into her fighter, becoming part of a single mechanism. Was this how Jolin felt when she was connected to Violet? She had not said anything earlier, because she did not understand — and perhaps she could not — but *Cannibal* was an extension of her in these moments, as she twisted and yawed her way through the dreadnought's onslaught of defense fire.

A klaxon sounded, but she did not need to glance down to know her shields were at sixty percent. Plenty left for what she needed to do. Something rattled inside the hull behind her, a loose wire, perhaps? She gritted her teeth; nothing she could do about it now. The cockpit air pressure gauge blinked red once, then faded. *Hold yourself together, buddy; just a little longer.*

"Split up?" Ramos asked over the radio.

"Meet you in the middle." They had about twenty seconds until those cannons fired again, which meant they could take out at least half with his two and her four. "You hear that, hot rod?" she whispered to her ship. "Looks like we found a use for those missiles after all."

"They're going after the cannons," Jolin said.

Ajax grunted. His eyes were slits, his lips curled in a silent snarl.

Hold yourself together. Jolin glanced over at Grace, whose face told her she was thinking the same thing. If they tried to engage the dreadnought, it was all over. Then again, for Ajax, if his daughter died defending him... *Let's find a third option.* She looked around, muttering to herself. She needed a way to put some distance between the two ships. If she could just slow the dreadnought down, put them off course.

Jam their scanners? No, that was silly. They were near close enough now to reach out a hand and touch *Syracusia*, if they wanted. She watched as Isabella and Ramos weaved through the small ship defenses of the dreadnought. She had split the screens so they could watch both fighters, though the automated tracker was still having difficulty keeping up.

Isabella launched a missile, and a cannon exploded in a shower of blue and yellow. Scattered defensive fire prickled against her shields, but she evaded most of it. On the other screen, Ramos fired that impressive red beam of his, slicing another cannon in half.

Wait. Jolin tried to stand but was held in place by her seat straps. She unbuckled and vaulted over her console. "It's a mining laser," she said.

"That beam weapon?" Grace asked. "Maybe. It certainly isn't regulation."

Ajax grunted. His eyes were locked on Isabella's screen. Another missile away, another cannon gone in a shower of sparks.

"Mining laser tech, it has to be. See how the beam slices through the metal?" Jolin pointed at the screen. And it had gone through the drone shields like they were not even there. Nguyen must have built it himself, but how did he power it? And how much did it require? *Syracusia* might be able to charge up her own mining laser enough to do some actual damage to that thing. But where would she get that kind of juice?

Something Grace mentioned earlier came back to her. There was one conduit big enough to deliver such an enormous payload of energy. But she could only do it once, and would it even work? A lump of fear bubbled up in her belly. She would have to leave the bridge to set it up.

Her updated algorithms took over as the latest barrage of plasma bolts came into range. They got all but one that time. Shields were holding at twenty-eight percent. If she left, she would be gone a lot longer than thirty seconds. Did Isabella and Ramos have that much longer? Did any of them?

"I have to try," she whispered.

Grace's face was tight. "Try what?"

"Something stupid," Jolin said, unsure whether either of them heard. She was halfway out the door already.

Nestled inside the dreadnought's shields, Isabella had a front-row seat as the enormous capital ship plowed through the curling mist of another plasma debris field. She wondered how much that maneuver damaged the shields, and if the people on board were so intent on their objective that they just did not care. She rolled *Cannibal* so the dreadnought was above her and hit her main engine again.

"That's two down," Ramos called out over the radio.

"Four for me!" Isabella laughed as she loosed her final missile and dodged more gunfire. The world lit up around her as the remaining cannons fired. *Shit.* She had hoped to be fast enough to exit on this next barrage. They would have to wait another thirty seconds.

"Incoming," Ramos said.

A dozen blips lit up Isabella's scanners. More drones. She glanced down at her ammo levels. It was not enough. "I'm about empty."

"Yeah. Me too. It's been an honor, pilot."

"We're not done yet," Isabella replied. She spied him off her port side and tipped her wings. "Twenty-six seconds till the shields open. You can stay alive for twenty-six seconds, can't you?"

The Colonel laughed. "All right, Isabella. Tell you what, I'll stay alive for twenty-seven. Can't have you bea—" his radio cut off as blaster fire ripped through *Prescient.*

"No!" She pulled into a tight turn and spent the last of her ammo blasting away at the influx of drones swarming up from below him.

Prescient spun out of control, fire spewing from its engines. Isabella took down three of the four before her guns spun to a halt. Her trajectory took her straight through the fourth, and her shields exploded as she impacted it, both *Cannibal* and the destroyed drone careening in opposite directions. At least his tail was clear.

She regained control quickly, and Ramos seemed to be doing the same. Well, his spin had slowed. But *Prescient* was still angling down toward the dreadnought. With luck, he could crash it into one of the drone hangars. That was what she would do.

Her scanner beeped again and she lost sight of him. Another ten, twelve... *twenty* drones heading straight for her. Her shield indicator buzzed angrily; zero percent. She tried to cycle the power, but the switch was slack, like something behind it had come disconnected.

Fly by the seat of your pants long enough, and they end up around your ankles. Something her uncle used to say, emphasizing the importance of routine maintenance and yes... pre-flight checks.

She blinked away a tear. Well, she had done her best, given the circumstances. A brief hint of long black hair and smooth beige skin fluttered through her mind as she kicked the thrusters. Low laughter and whispered kisses. They could have been something, right? Her and Jolin? Yeah. Maybe.

Fifteen seconds. *You can live for fifteen seconds, pilot.*

All she ever wanted was to fly. Like this, or any other way. And as the blasters lit up her cockpit and the warm bath of her flight suit embraced her, Isabella grinned. Who needed shields, anyway? It was time to quit fucking around and fly.

Jolin spent countless hours on a ship just like *Syracusia*, crawling around in maintenance tunnels, fixing wiring, plugging in new components and replacing broken ones. She was elated the day she finally passed the officer's exam and got pulled out of the grease and tucked under a console.

Yet here she was, arms covered in synthetic lubricants and lugging a power hose across the deck to plug it in somewhere it did not go. *You always come full circle, if you live long enough.* Something Leannx Quin had said. Jolin was where she belonged. There was a metaphor in there somewhere, but she was too tired and anxious to find it.

She tripped on a cable, landing hard on her knee with a curse. The ship rumbled beneath her, as if willing her to stand back up. "Yeah," she said, struggling to her feet, "I know."

They would have a single shot at this, if she got it working at all. She tugged the hose with a groan and hefted it to the bypass she had rigged up.

One single shot, for everything.

Grace found herself standing, hands clutching the hem of her blouse as *Prescient* vanished from the view screen. Everything in her was screaming to pull the ship out of orbit and run, but atmospheric friction was the only thing keeping any distance between them. The *Syracusia* was far more maneuverable, but nowhere near fast enough to outrun a dreadnought. Those engines were bigger than the *Syracusia* herself.

"Isabella!" Ajax screamed as the drones swarmed around her. There was nothing he could do, standing half a meter away from the screens as if he could reach through and save her. Nothing to do except watch her die.

Only... she did not die. *Cannibal* wove like a dancer through a lightning squall of lasers and gunfire. Drones zipped past, dozens of them, but nothing touched her.

"Now!" Ajax said. His voice was raw. "Now, now!"

Ajax had transferred nav control to Grace not long after the fighting began, and the *Syracusia* was resisting her every move as if it knew the difference. The damn warship wanted to seize up on her. She hated flying these big ships this close to a planet, or a moon. Too much could go wrong. *Should* go wrong. They were not built for atmospheric flight.

Risking a glance, she saw what Ajax was yelling about. Isabella had disengaged from the drones and was making a beeline away from the dreadnought, spiraling into a complex barrel roll to avoid fire. Several shots hit, blasting bits of the fighter into space. But still she flew.

"Two," Ajax whispered. "One."

Cannibal passed through the shields again just as the remaining plasma cannons fired. Ajax fell to his knees. But she was not out of trouble yet. The drones stayed on her.

"Here we go!" Jolin yelled as she careened onto the bridge. She tripped and fell, banging her head on the tactical console. "Shit," she mumbled, pulling herself up and into her chair. Blood dripped down her face. "We can—Ow." She held a hand to her temple. "Okay, we can only do this once."

"Do what?" Grace asked. What trick did this woman have up her sleeve? It had better be something.

Jolin tapped away at her controls, hunched beneath those impressively broad shoulders. "I need you to get our trajectory headed away from the planet and into open space, Admiral."

"They'll close the distance in seconds if we do that," Grace said. What was she thinking?

"If this works, that won't matter."

"I hope you have something figured out," Isabella's voice sputtered in over the radio. "If you can even hear me."

"Just do it," Ajax said. He ran to his chair and smashed the comm with his fist. "I hear you, Izzie," he said, tears on his face.

Grace nodded, and adjusted course. The ship groaned in protest, but obeyed.

Ajax turned to look at Jolin, and Grace was suddenly aware of the immense weight of his desperate, unearned faith in this woman. "We got you, baby girl," he said like he believed it. She supposed he had to.

"Pull hard to port on my mark," instructed Jolin.

"Are you sure?" Isabella said.

"Mark!" Jolin shouted, yanking on the mining laser controls.

Cannibal veered out of the way, deeper into Europa's atmosphere, drawing the drones after her. But a microsecond later, a beam of red light four meters wide rippled out from under the *Syracusia*.

Alarms sounded as the bridge went dark, then silent.

"What did you do?" Grace yelled. Her navigation was gone. *Everything* was gone. The lights flickered as emergency batteries stuttered online.

Autopilot took over as the navigation system rebooted, and the *Syracusia* began an automated ascent. Grace stared at the view screens as they came back online. Explosions rocked the face of the dreadnought along the edges of a hundred meter long gouge across its surface. At least a hundred. The drones were gone. Vaporized.

"Zzzbter your shields so I can land," Isabella was saying.

Ajax's voice cracked, "Aster."

"Shields? We don't have any of those," Jolin said with a shrug.

"What?" Grace stomped over. "What in hell do you think you're doing?"

Ajax was right behind her. "You blew out our shields?"

"I saved your daughter." The girl had the temerity to look self-satisfied, even.

"It was a hell of a thing," Isabella said. "I didn't know a mining laser could do that."

"Me either," Jolin whispered low enough that Grace only heard it because she was standing so close. "I recommend we boost out of here, pronto," Jolin said. "After Isabella lands, of course." She tapped her controls. "Yeah, that won't stop them for long, but we do have a window."

Grace closed her mouth. The girl had a point. Recriminations could wait. She hurried back to nav and began to chart a course. To where? Well, anywhere but here. She feared all Jolin's stunt had done was buy them a few more seconds to hope someone would arrive to protect them.

Ajax stood there, staring at her. Almost as if he was caught between wanting to choke her and hug her. He settled on neither, instead putting a hand on the young woman's shoulder. "I don't know what the hell you thought you were doing, but it seems to have worked out. For now. Thank you."

Jolin looked up at him, a kind of sheepish guilt playing across her face.

"Admiral," Isabella squawked. "I'm sorry about your friend. He was a hell of a pilot."

"Thank you, Miss Marquez." Grace found herself nodding, and stopped. As much as she appreciated the sentiment, she would have thrown Isabella and the Colonel in the brig for a week if they had pulled a stunt like that under her command.

"I saw the ship's name finally," the girl added. Her radio crackled. "It's painted across the bow. *Chooser of the Slain.* Super cool. I like it."

Jolin frowned. "*Chooser of the Slain?*"

"That's old Norse mythology." Ajax collapsed into his chair. A thousand years had melted off his face as soon as he heard Isabella's voice. "Valkyries, Odin, Valhalla. Thor. That stuff."

"Wait." Jolin looked at him sharply. "Did you say Valkyries?"

19

Fighter, Pilot

Sergeant Nguyen was in the hotel lobby when Amanita found him, sitting at the bar and staring at the video display amid an assortment of empty beer bottles and a tall glass of something fruity. She climbed onto the stool next to him and ordered one of whatever he was having, determined neither to worry about her daughter nor stew angrily at the girl's father, whose name she refused to say, or even think.

Isabella would be okay. She was the finest fighter pilot in the system, and that was not just parental pride. The girl was almost preternaturally gifted. She had sprung forth from the womb in full flight gear. *Quite painfully I might add*, Amanita smirked. It was a joke she repeated often, but it still got her.

A few meters away, Willem stood silently, eyeing the crowd with his usual wariness.

"It's called a sea breeze," Nguyen offered.

She watched the bartender pour her drink; a casual mix of cranberry and grapefruit over a double shot of vodka, with a twist of lime. "It looks delightful."

"Reminds me of home."

"And where's that?"

"Honolulu."

"You're from Earth!"

The sergeant stirred his straw in a slow circle. "Technically, I'm from space. Born in a battlecruiser med bay."

"So all this is in your blood."

He nodded.

"How's your wound?" she asked as the bartender set her drink in front of her. It tasted as good as it looked.

He rolled his shoulder. "It's tight, but I'll recover." There had only been time for him to do a cursory stint in the recovery pod to staunch the bleeding. "Maybe I'll start doing yoga."

"I didn't thank you for what you did back there, on the station."

He laughed. "You mean when I thoughtlessly charged the guy who stole my gun?"

"Yeah." She smiled. "That."

"I'm drunk enough to admit I almost wanted him to kill me in that moment." He stared into the mirror behind the bar. "Not anymore, of course, but after I stupidly ordered the kids in my command to…" He shook his head and took a long sip of his cocktail. "It doesn't matter. The only thing two lefts get you is headed back the way you came."

Nguyen did not look old enough to be calling anyone a kid, but Amanita respected the feeling. Empathized with it. And she also knew he would appreciate a change of subject.

She nodded at the video screen. "Anything interesting on?"

The sergeant shrugged, then winced and massaged his injured shoulder. "Judging from the scrapes on your man's knuckles, I'm guessing your meeting didn't go well?"

Amanita glanced at Willem. He frowned, glancing down at his hands before stuffing them in his pockets. "Yeah," she said, "that's an understatement. I don't know what they're hiding, but it isn't good."

"They didn't loop you in? That's a little concerning."

"Yeah." Catching the bartender's attention, she pointed at the hologram. "Can you turn up the sound?" The President's head and shoulders appeared, the SSA flag hanging behind her. "She looks tired."

"She looks old."

Amanita frowned at him, but she could not disagree.

"My fellow citizens," the President began. "Over the past twenty-four hours the entirety of the Sol System has been under siege by terrorist forces intent on spreading fear, uncertainty, and doubt throughout our peaceful union of worlds. In short, chaos."

A hush fell over the bar.

"Yesterday, six colonies across the system were attacked, and in some cases entirely destroyed, with massive loss of life and infrastructure."

Amanita stood, her drink forgotten.

"As I speak, carrier groups are being dispatched to each location, to secure them and help with search and rescue. Have no doubt, this is a declaration of war, and neither I nor anyone in my administration will rest until those responsible, this so-called Insurrection, have been d—" A gunshot rang out and the president's head vanished from sight amid screams.

One voice in particular was loudest, crying, "No!"

The holofeed blinked and swirled, resolving first into the image of a young girl reaching out towards… *something*, but it quickly reformed into a symbol Amanita did not recognize, like three interlocked triangles. She tried to relax her fingers, which were clutching her blouse, but they did not obey.

"Thank you for your service, Madam President," a heavily obscured voice said as the symbol spun slowly in space. "Please allow *me* to enumerate the destruction for you." As they spoke, listing each location that had been attacked, video of the destruction played. Mars Two. Venus Five. Lunar One. *Artemis*.

Amanita could not breathe. The footage played in slow motion, captured from orbit. Her home was on fire, half destroyed. Her constituents—her *people*. She fell to her knees. Willem was at her side in an instant. She could not speak, or see. Blood pounded against the inside of her skull like timpani echoing through an empty orchestra hall.

"You know," the voice continued, "she was right about one thing. Chaos is coming."

When the *Idomeneus* finally arrived, the *Chooser of the Slain* was listing to starboard above Europa, belching black smoke into space, and *Syracusia* was booking it toward the far side of the moon. Although the damage to the tactical power array was more extensive than she expected, a quick scan showed Jolin's mining laser hack sliced through two of the dreadnought's main radiators, almost exactly as she planned.

With its reactor pushed past the limits of safety, it was a simple matter of applying the right pressure to the right point. The gambit turned out to be enough to fry a lot of circuitry on her end, too, unfortunately. The coppery stench of crisp wiring and charred semiconductors wafted throughout the ship.

A minor victory, but there was no time to celebrate. Isabella volunteered to pilot *Nosferatu* down to pick up her mother as soon as *Cannibal*'s engines were powered down, though they had not yet heard from Amanita. And as a reward for her quick thinking and ingenuity Jolin was banished to Engineering by Ajax to clean up the mess she had made.

Grace was speaking to Captain Daniyah privately as Jolin stepped down off the bridge. The Admiral's face was grave. Large events were ripping the system apart, and after what Jester had said, Jolin could not help but feel responsible. She rubbed her wrist as she hiked down the corridor toward the battery.

Captain Quin would tell her to lay that blame at Rolan Hector's feet, or on the shoulders of the ambitious woman who took over for him and, for whatever reason, decided to take on the SSA. What had her name been? Phyllis? Penelope?

Mira would admonish her for thinking the murder of a freighter full of pirates would do anything to tip the scales toward justice; the fierce vegan chef would be mortified to hear of blood shed on her behalf.

Freeman would shrug and say he would have done the same. Gus would ask her why she did not bring back Rolan's head as a trophy. She snorted, imagining him fashioning a plaque to mount it on. He had been a hunter as well as an engineer, which had been Leannx's reasoning for putting him in charge of weapons.

But he was more a doofus than anything, and they were lucky Jolin had come along... she stopped, putting up a hand to steady herself. Bitter sorrow settled in her chest and she sagged against the bulkhead, knocking a fire extinguisher off its hook with her shoulder. It landed with a clang, and she sunk to the deck beside it, tears stinging her eyes.

"It's a burden," Jennifer said, sitting down across the table as Jolin stared into a half-empty daiquiri. "For years I struggled with it, having to decide who lived and died. Knowing it was within my power to save them if only I had more time." She lit a cigarette and leaned back in her chair, exhaling into the cool evening air. "This is the same spot as our date, isn't it?"

Jolin looked around. "Maybe." Not that it mattered. Jennifer would not have asked if she did not already know the answer. "So?"

"So? So momentous things happened here, Jolin Aster!"

"Yeah, real world-shakers. I pulled a *coin* out of your ear."

"Oh my god, I had forgotten about that!" Her tone said she had in no way forgotten about it. Especially since she brought it up at least once a week for seven years. "And you with the real magic inside your wrist all along."

"ACIS? He's a parlor trick at best."

The hologram flashed. "I resent that and will hold it against you for ten thousand cycles."

Jolin rolled her eyes. "And how long is that?"

"Zero point zero five four seconds. I forgive you."

Smirking, the Doctor continued. "Anyways, I was saying I didn't know how to handle it. How to deal. How do you *choose*? They teach you triage, objectivity. Logic." She sucked deeply on the cigarette, then closed her eyes and puffed out the smoke in chubby rings. "But how well do you think that plays when you're telling somebody their best friend died when you could have saved them, because some other asshole had a slightly better chance to recover? It's why I went into private practice. Well, *part* of why."

"And now look at us," Jolin said, "on the raggedy edge." She raised her drink in a mock salute, then tipped the rest of it down her throat. The harsh chill in her stomach was a welcome change to the numbness threatening to overwhelm her. "But I'm not in the mood to talk."

"Those boys made their choice today, same as you and me. That's my point."

Jolin shook her head. "The bounty was dead or *alive*, Doc. You wanna talk choice, I could have put them down a dozen different ways that didn't involve killing."

"And the risk to the rest of us? If they put a gun to my head and pull the trigger because of your uncertainty, how does that balance out?"

"I should have found a way." *Esmerelda*. The memory glitched in

Jolin's mind, threatened to shatter.

"Maybe you're not cut out for this," Jennifer whispered, watching the end of her cigarette burn. A drink was delivered by a tall waiter in a smart suit. "I didn't order that," she said without looking up.

"Of course, Madam. It was sent over by the gentleman at the bar." He smiled and set it in front of her.

She ignored the waiter until he walked away. "Jolin, if you can't weigh the lives of your crew and your family against strangers intent on doing them harm, maybe it's time to rethink your priorities."

"I did it, didn't I?" Jolin snarled. "Ugh, whatever." She got to her feet in a huff. "It's your turn to pay." She glared at the dunes as they stretched annoyingly away toward infinity. It had been a relaxing evening until Jennifer sat down. She fumed, wrapping her hands around the waist-high wrought iron bars fencing the patio.

"I'm just telling you what I learned years ago. Logic, or what's right and wrong, or easy or hard, can't enter into it. There's just no room for it. No choice when it's family." Jennifer deposited her cigarette into the untouched drink. "The scales *don't* balance against that, my love. And you're a liar if you say they should..."

The memory faded, and *Syracusia*'s emergency lights flickered through the corridor as Jolin sobbed into her hands. Everywhere she looked, she saw their faces. It was getting harder to ignore. Taking vengeance on the man who killed them had left her hollow. And it was not how any of them would choose to be remembered, if she was honest with herself.

The wound was so fresh, so brutal. Six years passed in a frozen heart-beat. Jolin could have folded, should have, and nobody would blame her. Just like Isabella had not blamed her for what she had done on *Valkyrie*. Esmerelda. Rolan Hector. Those and other names flickered through her mind like leaves in a hurricane. Some choices she had made. Some, instinct.

But the Stars were her throughline; her constant. Without them, she was just another heartless merc taking up space in the system. A petulant daughter hiding from a past she was too afraid to revisit. A thief on the run. Nobody.

Today, though? She stood on a bridge again, put faith in a crew. Believed in something; in herself.

It was an instinct... no, a *choice* she could be proud of.

Maybe that was the piece she was missing, the way to honor them—to avenge them—was to keep moving forward; to not give up or give in to the despair within her or the rage she had buried deep, that she had been fleeing since she was a child. Stepping forward into this new future willingly.

She wiped her nose on her sleeve and it came away gross. A rueful laugh escaped her lips as she squeezed her eyes shut.

"We're always with you," Jennifer said, wrapping her arms around Jolin from behind and hugging her tightly. "That's the difference between family and strangers." She pressed her chin into Jolin's shoulder. "I'd let a hundred strangers die," she whispered, "before I let anything happen to any of you."

"Why is that, exactly?" Jolin asked, leaning into the embrace. "I don't know if I deserve that kind of love."

Jennifer kissed her on the cheek. "Well, maybe not you. But the rest of 'em, sure."

Jolin laughed, fighting off a full body shiver. "Don't start something you don't want to finish, old woman."

The doctor pushed her away. "And you've ruined it. Are you ever *not* horny?"

"Hey! You kissed me!"

"I'm going back to the ship." Jennifer poked her in the kidney. "Captain'll be back with the bounty soon and we're off to the next thing. With or without you."

"Please, you'd all be dead five times over without me."

"Now you understand why we keep you around..."

The words echoed softly as Jolin opened her eyes and struggled to her feet in the corridor. She replaced the fire extinguisher on its hook with a grunt. The Stars could come with her, to whatever was next. Whether she stayed aboard *Syracusia* or went off on her own. As long as their flower bloomed in her memory, they were never truly gone.

She put a hand to her breast and traced the embroidery with a fingertip. She closed her eyes and filled her lungs, ignoring the scent of burned wiring. The weight was not gone, but maybe she could carry it a little longer.

For them.

Smiling, and even feeling a little bit of joy, she promptly tripped on one of the cables she had strewn around the place, landing hard on her knee—the *same* knee—with a curse.

"Aster, what's the hold up?" Ajax's voice blared over the ship's speaker.

"Yeah, yeah," she said, reaching for the toolbox. "Can't a girl have a moment of clarity without some man yelling at her to go faster?"

"What?" he said.

"I'm working on it!"

Her mother was waiting with Nguyen and Willem when Isabella landed the shuttle, and none of them were happy.

"What is it?" she asked as the doors opened and they clambered somberly aboard.

Before answering, Amanita hugged her, deflating in her arms so that Isabella had to struggle to keep her upright. Her eye makeup had run down her face in streaks. She looked awful.

"The President has been attacked," Nguyen said, strapping into one of the passenger seats. "Or killed. We don't know."

Ice poured down Isabella's spine. "What?"

Willem nodded. "It's worse than we thought," he said. He had a couple scrapes and contusions on his face Isabella was certain had not been there when she dropped them off.

She assisted her mother into a seat and fastened the safety harness around her. "Mom?"

"I'm okay, sweetie," she whispered. "I just... my home."

Isabella kissed her on the forehead, and then smashed the door controls with a fist. Willem filled her in on the details as she piloted *Nosferatu* back to *Syracusia*. Her mother sat quietly, staring off to nowhere. And by the time the old warship came into view, Isabella's face was smeared with eyeliner too.

"So many people," Amanita said as Ajax folded her into a hug. She did not resist, which was not a good sign based on what Jolin knew about that relationship. The senator's home colony attacked; multiple other worlds targeted. The Insurrection had dealt a killing blow to the system's status quo. And for what? Chaos? It had to be something else. Something she was missing.

Sergeant Nguyen stood at the view screens, glaring at the moon below. He had taken the news about his fighter in stride, or what could be taken as stride with the entire universe falling apart around them. Or maybe his regret at losing his soldiers presented the bigger upset. Jolin certainly understood that.

"Isabella, can you plot us a course to rendezvous with the *Idomeneus*?" Ajax said.

Isabella glanced around. Her calm demeanor had shattered, and for the first time since Jolin met her, she seemed afraid. Their eyes met, and Jolin looked away in shame. She had tried twice to speak to Isabella, to apologize for her behavior last night, but circumstances had—No, she had *let* circumstances stand in the way.

And now? Her body ached, and all she wanted to do was wrap her arms around Isabella and cover her in kisses. She had learned nothing.

The admiral leaned against the aft bulkhead, holding an empty wine glass. "The enemy dreadnought jumped away soon after the *Idomeneus* arrived, and I have it on good authority that a significant portion of my fleet has been destroyed or captured. Some kind of rampant AI virus brought down our defenses."

Jolin's breath caught. "Valkyrie," she said. It could not be, could it? Her eyes sought Isabella out instinctively, but the younger woman was focused on her console; had turned her back to Jolin, even. *Starlight. She must be furious with me.*

Grace glanced Jolin's way, but continued. "They've disabled public communications networks and are broadcasting the same propaganda message on a loop. Captain Daniyah and I agree that for now it's best I stay somewhere safe."

"This is hardly a safe place for you, Admiral," Ajax interrupted. "We won't survive another—"

"Agreed. We'll be affecting a transfer, so the fleet computers will think I'm aboard the *Idomeneus*. It's the only way I can think of to throw them off the trail."

"It's sounding less and less like they even need you at all," Jolin said. "If their AI is as powerful as you're saying."

"Why they want me is up for debate, but ultimately unimportant. Short of flying down to the moon here and digging myself a cave to hide in, this is our best option. But your Captain is correct. I won't be hiding here," she said. "The *Firmament of Heaven* will be picking me up in a few days."

Ajax stepped around his console. "And then what?"

"I left someone aboard the *Rosy-Fingered Dawn* I can't live without, and I intend to get her back. That's all you need to know. But I plan to figure out the extent of this virus, and this insurrection, on the way."

Jolin frowned. She knew that ship, had even been contracted there for a year. The *Firmament* was an Off-Grid Interceptor; no connection to the HDF sub-net. Laser comms only. Smart. Grace obviously knew more than she was telling.

Then again, she was not the only one.

"I should say this," Jolin said, holding her wrist protectively. "Violet, my ACIS node... he encountered something six years ago. Aboard a ship called the *Valkyrie Centerfold*." She related her story as quickly as she could, including her cryo-sleep, leaving out the part where she killed Rolan Hector. Enough people knew about that already.

Amanita watched her closely, dabbing her eyes with a handkerchief occasionally. Those who had been on *Europa Two* knew some of the details, of course, from what Jester had revealed, but there was no reason to get too graphic.

When she was finished, the bridge was silent.

"There was a pirate freighter called *Valkyrie Centerfold*, a scavenger ship, around that time," the admiral said. "They disabled two SSA Patrol Corvettes with some kind of virus, then vanished out into the lawless space beyond Neptune. Took months to get control of it, the thing spread through the entire military sub-net in seconds. That event was the catalyst for AI controlled ships being phased out. Are you saying those pirates are the Insurrection?"

Jolin nodded. "I don't know for sure. I know a few of their names, but—"

"But you've been asleep for six years," said Grace.

"Yeah."

"And before that you were wanted by the System Authority for stealing this... Violet."

Jolin met her gaze with all the stubbornness she could muster.

The admiral laughed.

Sergeant Nguyen rounded on them. "None of this is funny. With all due respect, Admiral, you're in hiding, the government is falling apart around us, and what, we're just supposed to slink away in this heap of trash?"

"Watch it," Isabella said.

"And what do you propose?" Grace asked. "Want to join me?"

"I've known Talon Ramos for twenty years." Nguyen shook his head. "If anyone could have landed *Prescient* and walked away from it..." he trailed off.

"I saw the ship going down," said Isabella. "Nobody could walk away from that."

Nguyen was insistent. "You lost sight of it, right? All I'm asking is that we make the attempt."

Ajax cleared his throat. "The attempt to... what, find the dreadnought we just barely escaped? Son, that's an awfully big risk—"

"To rescue him," Nguyen said. He tapped his wristband and a sixteen digit number appeared in the air above it. "This is the encryption key to the tracker I installed on my ship."

Isabella gasped.

"No, no. We can't just bring the Admiral to them," Jolin said. "What is the point of all this if we do that?"

"The Admiral goes to find the *Dawn*, as she planned." Nguyen stepped forward, twisting the wristband anxiously. "And we recover Talon."

"You're talking about a journey that could take months, if not years," said Ajax.

Nguyen shook his head. "Not if we install a Sigrid drive in the *Syracusia*."

For some reason, the bottom dropped out of Jolin's stomach. She steadied herself on her console.

The captain scoffed. "And where do you propose we find one of those; they're not exactly listed for auction."

"I have contacts," the sergeant replied. "You saw my ship. I can find one."

"It's not a bad plan," Grace mused.

"He..." Isabella hesitated. "I didn't know him well, or for long, but he seemed like the sort who would do the same for one of us."

"Isabella," Ajax started.

"I owe him my life," the admiral spoke over him. "And if I get the chance to repay him, I will, and maybe that's how we do it. But this organization is larger and more powerful than we ever suspected. We need to know more before we can even contemplate just storming their castle."

"What if there's a way?" Isabella offered.

"A way to what?" Grace said.

"To know more. Jolin, she... Violet is a special program, and we think he's still here somewhere, on the shuttle maybe. He might have learned something from Jester?"

Jolin slumped into her chair. It was possible. Violet was very fast. She had seen inside his mind somehow, seen inside his programming? However that worked. He would have learned everything Jester's ACIS node knew about the Insurrection. "She's right."

"So how do we get it out of the shuttle and back into your wrist?" Nguyen asked.

"We were going to Ganymede," Isabella replied. "To see if somebody there might know enough about AI to help us."

"Ganymede?" Grace interjected. She set her wine glass down on Jolin's console. "There's an old robotics research base outside Galileo. Closed down a few years ago, after the virus business. Someone in the city might know about AI, or know somebody who does.."

"Sounds like we have a plan," Ajax said. "Any objections?"

Isabella looked over and grinned, and Jolin melted.

"I need to talk to you," Jolin said.

"I need to talk to *you*."

Jolin hesitated, stepping toward her. "I just... I didn't mean to..."

"Do you want us to leave?" Ajax said.

Amanita laughed, a loud bark that echoed through the corridors. After sitting there dumbfounded for an hour, was she finally coming around? Isabella grabbed her mother's hand.

Everything was going to be okay, Jolin realized, her queasiness forgotten. She felt it in her stomach, in her bones. The seven of them, standing here on this bridge. The admiral. The senator and her assistant; the captain, the sergeant.

The pilot.

The fighter.

Syracusia rumbled her protests as Isabella turned them slowly toward the *Idomeneus*, and Jolin let herself smile again. They had a plan. It was not much, but it was enough. The tension flowed out of her shoulders. The Stars were still with her; they always would be. And her new crew was with her, too.

That realization widened her eyes. When had that happened? Her crew. Her ship. She ran her hands along the console. But first, before any of that... Jolin stood and motioned for Isabella to follow.

"It's okay," she said to the rest of them. "We'll step out."

After setting the rendezvous course, Isabella followed Jolin back to her cabin, heart fluttering, stomach churning. She had been thinking about this moment all morning, despite the galaxy-altering events erupting around them, despite almost dying a dozen times, it was all she could focus on.

"I understand if you—" she started, but Jolin interrupted.

"Let me go first." She pulled her beautiful hair into a ponytail and tied it off with a band she pulled out of one of those charming vest pockets. Was it the same one Isabella had given her? Regardless, as she snapped the band into place, Jolin had the demeanor of somebody preparing for a battle.

Isabella swallowed. "All right."

"I don't expect you to forgive me," Jolin said, meeting her gaze, "but I need to say I'm sorry."

Isabella took a step back. "For what?"

"Last night, I took advantage of your kindness. Forced myself on you."

"Jolin!" Isabella could not contain herself, not to listen to that nonsense. "You did no such thing, oh my god. It was me, I made you do it. *I'm* the one who took advantage, of your emotional state, your confusion."

"You think I didn't know what I was doing?" Jolin frowned.

"No, I... you were crying, and—"

"And you comforted me. And I pulled you into something you weren't prepared for. I'll never forgive myself for it."

Isabella felt her mouth working. *Of course.* How could she have been so stupid? "You have no idea, do you?"

Jolin winced.

"Listen to me," Isabella blurted. "The first time I saw you my heart exploded. Standing there looking like death warmed over, but still smiling. Are you listening?"

Confusion played across Jolin's face. "I'm listening."

"Your smile, your laugh, your confidence, I can't handle it. I want to throw you on the bed and kiss your stupid lips right this instant."

It was Jolin's turn to gape. "I—"

"You did nothing wrong. You asked me to touch you, and I touched you. You asked me to kiss you and I kissed you. Those are choices we made together." Isabella met her eyes. *Ridiculous.* Had they both really thought... She grinned, and at the same time the churning in her belly took on a new edge, spreading like a fire into her thighs.

"I took advant—"

"Shut up," Isabella said, stepping closer. "Please. *I* need this. Kiss *me.* Touch *me.*"

Then Jolin's warm arms were around her, lips pressed to hers, tongue insistent and invasive. Isabella squealed as Jolin lifted her off the deck and laid her gently on the bed, kissed her neck, tugged at the buttons on her blouse.

"I thought I hurt you," Isabella whispered.

"All I've wanted from the moment I saw you walking down those stairs," Jolin said, sliding her hand between Isabella's legs. Her brown eyes glistened. "Is this."

Isabella writhed at the touch, at knowing they felt the same thing, the same longing. Squeezing her thighs around Jolin's hand, she pressed her lips to the other woman's ear. "So take it, then."

* * *

Ajax stared at the *Idomeneus*. He had not been on board an HDF carrier in decades. Long enough that he forgot how big they were. Easily the size of two dreadnoughts. A city in the sky.

The admiral was at the comms station, talking with Captain Daniyah—or someone over there—in hushed tones. The looks Isabella and Jolin had been giving each other all day had worried him. He could not make his mind up about this person they had defrosted, who had somehow gotten into a position... he cleared his throat, trying to banish unwelcome images from his mind.

Isabella was capable of making her own decisions, a fact he reminded himself of daily. But he had never quite managed the ability to let her get hurt without wanting to pound his fist into whatever, or whoever, had done the hurting. No matter how old she got, she was still his little girl.

As if reading his mind, Amanita walked over to stand beside his chair. "She's fine."

"I know," he said, trying to hide his concern. He had never been very good at that, not with her.

"We raised a fantastic daughter, didn't we?" she asked. The harrowed gleam in her eyes had faded, but her voice was far away, like she was lost in thought.

He glanced up at her. "We?"

"That's not fair."

Ajax frowned. Amanita had been basically absent for the last twenty years of Isabella's life. Since she was *twelve*. What would have been fair, to Isabella at least, was for her mother to be more than some unknowable figure off caring about everybody but her own child.

His anger surprised him, and he shook his head. He had been her most ardent supporter all those years. It was an important job, and she was good at it. Besides, this was not the time to pick at old wounds. "You're right," he said. "I'm sorry."

She regarded him for a long moment, as if deciding whether he was going to pop off. "This Jolin is a good person, I think," she said eventually.

"I hope so," Ajax said. "There have been moments I wondered what trouble I brought onto my boat by chasing down that damn distress signal."

"I suspect it's the kind of trouble you're going to regret and appreciate in equal measure," Grace interjected. "Sorry to eavesdrop, but it's not that big of a bridge."

Amanita smiled at her. "Are we good?"

"We're all set. I'm now officially on board *Idomeneus*. The *Firmament of Heaven* will meet us at Ganymede in five days."

"This Captain Daniyah is a friend?" Amanita asked.

Grace shrugged. "Something like that."

He looked up at Amanita. "I know how that goes."

Amanita sniffed loudly. "But you trust him."

"I do," said Grace.

"Jax, I need to see about my home." Amanita's voice was steady, but strained.

He nodded. "Admiral, can you ask your friend?"

"It's the least I can do." Grace nodded. "But for now, call me Katherine. Just in case." That was her sister's name, if Ajax remembered correctly.

The bridge was bathed in multicoloured light as two smaller ships appeared off *Idomeneus*'s bow, riding their rainbow waves out of oblivion. "And these are friends of yours, too?"

The admiral adjusted her hair clip, her face flat. "Cleanup operations. They'll be trying to track the *Dawn*'s Sigrid wake, too, though that's not likely to lead anywhere."

"I never get tired of seeing that," Isabella said from the stairs. She was glowing. Whatever she and Jolin had discussed—for an *hour*—it must have gone well.

"It's something all right," Grace said. She made as if to offer Isabella back her seat, but Isabella waved her off.

"Go ahead. I'm never quite comfortable in that chair."

Ajax looked around. Sergeant Nguyen and Willem were discussing something in the corner. "All right, everyone else," he said. "If you're going to be on my boat for a few days, you'll need something to do. What are you good at?"

"I'm good with engines," Sergeant Nguyen offered. "And I can cook."

"You can cook? Well, welcome aboard, Chef. That will be a welcome change."

Isabella scoffed. "If you hate my cooking so much, Daddy, we can always go back to Nut Mush."

"Gross!" He laughed. "You know I hate when you call it that!"

Jolin lay on the bed for a while after Isabella left, naked and covered in sweat, quivering with the occasional shudder. That had been special. She felt silly for thinking Isabella would be upset with her, but she could not exactly blame cryo-sleep for that awkwardness. No, that was a birthright passed down in her biological family for generations, made worse by… well, made worse over the years by a lot of things.

Her entire body was loose. Relaxed. Even the pain in her leg was gone. She had a bad habit of storing anxiety and stress in her muscles, and it manifested in uncomfortable ways sometimes. But right now, she felt healthy and strong for the first time since her last night aboard the *Endless Star*.

Hoisting herself off the bed, she wiped her face and upper body with the towel she had left on the floor yesterday. She smirked; both times they had made love, it had been in her shitty room instead of Isabella's magnificently plush suite. At least they had the pillows this time.

Jolin pulled on her clothes and made an effort to get her hair presentable in the lav, but whatever. Everybody knew, right? She adjusted her vest and stuffed her arms into her jacket. "All right, beautiful," she said to her reflection. "You can do this." And, surprisingly, the smile on that woman's face seemed genuinely optimistic, despite the black eye and abrasions. And the bruise around her neck. She sighed, but the smile did not fade.

"I have some experience with tactical and security," Willem was saying as Jolin stepped onto the bridge, tugging at the sleeves of her jacket. She really needed to get it tailored.

"That position is already filled," Jolin said, sliding into her chair and pulling up her algorithms. She risked a glance at Isabella, who was staring at her with a dopey look on her face. She laughed. Yeah, everybody knew. She blew her a kiss. Isabella seemed startled, as if she had not even realized she was staring, then she grinned.

"Comms and logistics it is, then," Ajax pointed to the dedicated communications console Grace had been stationed at during the attack, along the aft bulkhead. Willem nodded, ignoring Jolin's glare as he passed by her tactical station.

"Look at us," Ajax said. "I don't remember the last time *Syracusia* had a real crew."

Jolin followed his gaze, taking in this so-called crew. They were the very definition of a rag tag bunch. She rubbed her wrist absently.

"The *Idomeneus* has agreed to the transfer," said Grace.

Ajax nodded, turning to Jolin. "Good. Then to Ganymede. We'll find out about this AI specialist, with luck, and get your... get Violet back."

"Thank you, Captain," Jolin said. He was a good man. She had known it from the first moment, of course. Even wary, he was unable to hide his kindness. And now? She wondered if they had earned each other's trust yet. "I guess we'll see," she whispered.

"We'll see what?" Grace asked without looking up from her console. That woman was going to be monitoring her like a hawk.

"Whatever comes next?" Jolin shrugged.

"Whatever comes next," Isabella echoed, coming to stand behind her chair. She gave Jolin's ponytail a little tug.

Starlight.

THE END

Acknowledgements

I owe an immeasurable debt to the *#WritingCommunity* on Twitter (RIP). Every time I thought about giving up or procrastinating myself into unproductiveness, I found welcoming, encouraging solace in (and among) the thousands of others just like me, trying to drag words out of their hearts and slather them onto a page. Editing, revising, and polishing this book is one of the hardest things I've ever done. You made it not only bearable, but actually kind of fun.

Adam, this book absolutely would not exist without your wonderful art, insight, and your foolhardy willingness to endure the first drafts of awkward, steamy love scenes. You changed my life, bestie.

Elaine Marie Carnegie-Padgett, whose edits and patient suggestions were beyond invaluable. Winter Willoughby-Finn, whose helpful critique and extreme generosity lifted me out of a difficult place and onto the right path.

Dorothy. Your relentless enthusiasm and thoughtful feedback buoyed me through a maelstrom of self-doubt; a gift I can never repay. *Avenge the Stars* would still be just a first draft on my Google Drive without your support.

Eldrene's Veil, this novel was completed *despite* your best effort (and failure) to make me accidentally roll over your beautiful soft ears with my office chair. I will miss you forever.

Finally, Gentle Reader... 97,815 words aren't enough, so here's eleven more: This story was written for you; I hope you love it.

Glossary

A note on dates in this glossary: known colloquially as H.E. or the Human Era, the Holocene Calendar, initially proposed by Cesare Emilani in 11993, added ten thousand years to the old A.D. / B.C. or C.E. / B.C.E. calendars, estimating "year zero" around the start of the Holocene Geological Epoch (approximately 10,000 B.C.E.), when humans first began the transition from nomadic tribes to settlements. The Holocene Calendar was adopted by the United Nations of Earth in 2545 A.D. (12545 H.E.).

ACIS - Alam Communications Infrastructure Satellite network. Pronounced like *Access*. Established by behemoth technology corporation E-Squared Industries using a proprietary implementation of their faster than light Sigrid technology. ACIS powers Gal-Net, a solar system-wide web. A differentiation exists between the ACIS "nebula" which is the hyperluminal conduit for all galnet traffic, and an ACIS interface node such as the one carried by Jolin Aster, which acts as an intelligent human interface to the nebula. Other ACIS interfaces do exist, including those made by third parties. The E^2 logo is a multicolored river turning through a dense forest.

Artemis - Lunar One Moon colony, on Earth's moon.

Aster, Jolin, 34 - She / Her - Tactical Officer, *Endless Star*. Born Gao Ju Ling to parents of Chinese ancestry, Jolin was raised on freighters running cargo from the Outer Rim to Earth and back. She left that behind at a young age to try the fit of a few other worlds. Military, security, gardening. Eventually she settled down for good with a rag-tag crew of bounty hunters called The Stars.

Beneg Research - Weapons manufacturer specializing in affordable personal defense; handguns, shields, small explosives. Beneg's logo is a diamond inlaid with a *B*.

Blitz Fighting - A hand-to-hand combat sport held in caged arenas.

Callisto - One of the Galilean moons of Jupiter.

Cannibal - Isabella's two-seat starfighter, a Sultan Spitfire 6250.

Carolyn Porco Harbor - Also known as Portco. Capital City of Jupiter's moon, Europa. A thousand-year-old colony, reinforced and expanded over the centuries. Military designation: Europa One.

Cedalion - The Headquarters of ORION, on Callisto.

CIC (Combat Information Center) - On a warship, a room that functions as a tactical center of operations. Usually the bridge.

Redhorn, M.D., Sharice, 69 - She / Her - Chief Surgeon, *Rosy-Fingered Dawn*. Vice Admiral, retired, HDF. Former Surgeon General of the SSA.

Daniyah, Salman, 62 - He / Him - Captain, *Idomeneus*.

Dillan, Amanita, 61 - She / Her – SSA Senator representing the Moon colony Artemis.

DSFV (Department of Space-Faring Vehicles) - The Sol System DSFV is responsible for licensing and taxation of personal and commercial ships and satellites.

EMB (Electromagnetic Barrier) - A form of traversable shielding used to seal hangars and cargo bays against the vacuum of space using argon plasma.

Endless Star, The - A refurbished Cantonese Fengru-class Light freighter. Shaped like a half-moon and measuring seventy meters wingspan, the Endless Star has four main engines along its wide stern. The middle of the three-deck interior contains ten crew cabins (five in each wing) for a max of twenty passengers and crew, and a large captain's quarters at the forecastle with deck to overhead graphalon windows along the bow. The galley is midships on the first deck. The bridge is situated directly above the galley, and engineering is aft of the bridge. The cargo bay and engineering take up most of the lower deck.

Europa - One of the Galilean moons of Jupiter. Terraformed. Home to a significant community of fishing villages.

Faraday Shielding - A type of passive sensor shielding that uses an electromagnetic resistant mesh weave throughout the hull of a ship or container to block signals and scans. Named for scientist Michael Faraday who invented the technique in 11836 H.E.

Firmament of Heaven - Long range HDF scout ship. Built to move fast and in secret, scout ships are purposefully not connected to the ACIS communications nebula.

Freeman, David, 49 - He / Him - First Officer, *Endless Star*.

FSIC (Flight Suit Inertia Compensators) - Pronounced like *Fessik*. Artificial gravity-based protection against excessive g-forces for fighter pilots. Flight suits fitted with FSIC have dozens of tiny gravity generators built into them, providing variable counter force.

Gal-Net - The system-wide information network.

Galileo - Capital city of Ganymede. Known for its white, knifelike skyscrapers and a perpetually seedy, neon-drenched market district known unaffectionately as the Undertunnels.

Ganymede - One of the Galilean moons of Jupiter. Terraformed.

Gonzales, Andreas, 66 - He / Him - Engineer, *Endless Star*.

Graphalon - An extremely durable compound of graphene and transparent aluminum. Used for starship windows and blast doors, among many other things, with applications in holographic technology due to its variable electromagnetic resonance.

Greinning Astrofacturing - Based on Mars, Greinning is the largest designer and builder of inter-system transport, freight, and salvage vessels in the Sol System and beyond. Initial ship designs all included a massive grinning smile across the bow, though this is no longer the practice. Aficionados and nostalgists will still often add or restore this detail. Greinning's logo is a half-moon turned on its side like a bowl.

Hardlight - A form of holographic projection that exploits the resonance of ionized air particles to conduct electricity and form a semi-solid surface.

Harriman 650 - An antique arc energy pistol.

Haul-Ace Load Lifter - Forklift designed to maneuver through freighters.

HDF (Homeland Defense Force) - The military arm of the SSA. While the HDF is purportedly concerned with providing security for government officials, the bulk of its force are leased to private security corporations via the Outbound program, by presidential mandate. To discourage any one faction from becoming too self-sufficient, all security corps are bound by law to lease a minimum of 51% of their agents from the HDF.

Hector, Rolan, 59 - He / Him - Captain, *Valkyrie Centerfold*.

Himeran Corps - An elite, autonomous unit tasked with proactive defense of the SSA. If they exist. Which they don't.

Holoserial - A weekly television program... but in the future!

Huygens Base - A moon base on Titan; a resort town.

HydroCorp - One of several corporations fighting over resource rights on Lunar, and other places.

Hydrocycle - A two-wheeled ground vehicle used for transportation and as part of terraforming maintenance on Saturn's moon Titan. Its engine converts nitrogen and methane from the atmosphere to hydrogen for power, and exhausts water and breathable air.

Idomeneus - Capital carrier. The largest ships built for the HDF, carriers are military bases in space, often home to tens of thousands of permanent residents.

Jupiter One - A space station in orbit around the gas giant.

Lewin, Grace, 65 - She / Her - Fleet Admiral, HDF.

Marquez, Ajax, 57 - He / Him - Captain, *Syracusia*.

Marquez, Isabella, 32 - She / Her - Communications, *Syracusia*.

MRS (Molecular Repulsor Shielding) - Advanced shields for starships, intended to repel physical threats such as ballistics or atmospheric friction, while still providing adequate defense against energy weapons like lasers and plasma cannons.

Nadzieja, Adrianna, 70 - She / Her - President of the Sol System Authority, duly elected, serving her first term.

Nguyen Vinh Quan, 30 - He / Him - Federal Incursion Agent, Sergeant. Black hair. Serious brown eyes. Tall and fit. Stationed aboard the *Rosy-Fingered Dawn*.

Ooblek — A non-Newtonian fluid made from a mixture of water and cornstarch. Named after an old Earth children's story.

O'Reardon, Penny, 62 - She / Her - Second in Command, *Valkyrie Centerfold*.

ORION - One of several Guilds of Bounty Hunters in the system. The name is written in all caps, but is not an acronym. Or, if it is, the meaning is not public knowledge.

Pollyanna Light - An electronics corporation based on Earth. Named for its founder.

Prescient - Starfighter piloted and built by Sgt. Nguyen Vinh Quan. Cobbled together from parts of other fighters over the years, it looks less like a functioning ship than the wreckage of one.

Quin, Leannx, 52 - They / Them - Captain, *Endless Star*.

Ramos, Talon, 35 - He / Him - Federal Incursion Agent, Lt. Colonel. Stationed aboard the *Rosy-Fingered Dawn*. Assigned as temporary attaché to Admiral Lewin.

Rosy-Fingered Dawn - HDF Battle-class Heavy Cruiser.

Rousseau, Mira, 30 - She / Her - Chef, *Endless Star*.

Sigrid drive - Able to induce instantaneous travel between vast distances, the Sigrid drive was invented by Elizabeth Jeane Sigrid in 13340 HE. This method of space traversal is prohibitively expensive for most civilian users, both in fuel and maintenance costs. Also known as a "Bump Drive" due to the unique sudden weightless feeling on activation, and immediate recovery. Or, more colloquially, a "Flush Jump" due to it also feeling rather like being flushed down a toilet... one assumes.

Sitayana Marines - A subset of the official government military apparatus, the HDF, that leases out personnel and equipment to private security forces. Ostensibly an establishment to ensure peace among the various corporate factions, they are nevertheless highly trained warriors. You know, just in case. Their sigil is a falcon with an Amritsari hood over its eyes.

Smithcut - A weapons manufacturer. Ancient Earth corporation.

SP-1K Interceptor - The "Spike" Interceptor is a single-seat space fighter, known for its nail-like shape and a distinct, howling squeal as it accelerates in atmosphere. Originally developed for the old UNE Navy, the design was released to the public domain and now many private manufacturers build and sell their own versions of this reliable fighter.

SSA (Sol System Authority) - Governing body of the solar system, based on Earth. Structure: President & Senate / House & Judicial.

Stone, M.D., Jennifer, 49 - She / Her - Medical Officer, *Endless Star*.

Syracusia - A hundred-year-old, decommissioned HDF Leonidas-class Destroyer, currently captained by Ajax Marquez.

Tennesin, Oliver, 61 - He / Him - Captain, *Rosy-Fingered Dawn*.

Titan - Moon of Saturn, known for resorts.

Trade Winds Report - An hourly freight hauler news and job listing broadcast.

UNE (United Nations of Earth) - Worldwide government between 12256 and 12600 H.E. Focused on early space faring and exploration.

Valkyrie Centerfold, The - A refurbished Greinning Comet-class Heavy freighter. Decorated with a giant grin that features risque depictions of Norse warriors on several of its teeth.

Willem - He/Him - Personal attaché for Amanita Dillan. Trans man and perhaps the only hand-to-hand combatant in the galaxy capable of kicking Jolin's ass in a fair fight.

Thank You!

Thanks for buying the Deluxe Print Edition of Avenge the Stars. The short post-script chapter on the next page is a bonus just for you; exclusive to this physical release. It's sort of the novel equivalent of an after credits scene, and as such isn't necessarily a promise of more to come.

That said, I do have more stories to tell in this universe. Drop a comment card in the box on your way out if you'd like to read them:

contact@jayeephen.com

Alone on a Dying Planet

The forcefield protecting *Syracusia*'s hangar sputtered fitfully across the twenty meter opening, tinting the bay—and the two women lying on a blanket near the edge—a muted blue. Jolin waved a hand in front of the electromagnetic barrier. Her fingers multiplied, strobe-like.

"Are you sure this thing will hold?" she asked.

Isabella shrugged, reaching up to entwine her fingers through Jolin's. "It's looking good so far," she said.

Jolin snorted, resting her head on the other woman's shoulder. "I've always been respectably adequate at the first forty-eight hours of a relationship," she said.

"Is that what we're calling this?"

"A relationship?" Jolin got up on one elbow, instinctively letting go of Isabella's hand. She grimaced at her own awkward cowardice. "I will if you will."

Isabella smiled, arching her back. She was a goddess, fitted into that old, loose-fitting tee like it was poured on, dripping down every subtle curve. "I'm thinking of dying my hair pink," she said before relaxing with a contented grunt.

Jolin reached out to touch her but stopped short, fingertips hovering. It felt like sacrilege, or at least inappropriate. Isabella bit her lip, grabbing Jolin's hand and pressing it against her belly.

"I like it when you touch me," she said.

Jolin shivered, sliding her fingers under Isabella's shirt. "Pink, huh?" Her smooth, dark skin was almost hot. Her brown eyes made black by the cyan hue.

"No?" She twisted a lock of Jolin's hair in her fingers; moaned as

Jolin's thumb found a nipple and teased it gently.

"Sure, it'll look amazing," said Jolin. "*Everything* looks amazing on you."

Isabella laughed. "Please, I'm a string bean. I have *no* boob—"

Jolin kissed her. She had heard enough of Isabella's self-deprecating humility. The woman was gorgeous, built like one of the statues they kept in museums. Not that Jolin had been to very many museums, but she had read about them. Well, seen pictures of them. And videos.

Isabella's tongue traced the grooves of her teeth; her hands gripped the back of Jolin's head, pulling her closer.

"You're beautiful," Jolin whispered, kissing her cheek, her neck, pressing herself against her. "You're perfect."

Isabella pushed her away, frowning. "I'm really, really not. You know that, right?"

"No, I know. I just..."

"Don't lay the weight of your expectations on me, Jolin."

Jolin sighed and rolled onto her back. "It's just an expression."

"Oh, so you didn't mean it?"

"No, I did. I *do*." Jolin eyed her suspiciously. "You're confusing me on purpose."

"Not on purpose," Isabella said, her playful smile fading. She turned on her side and put a hand on Jolin's shoulder. "I'm sorry, I... haven't been with someone in a while."

"I can relate."

"It's been so long I almost forgot what it feels like," Isabella whispered. "To be wanted."

"Well I want you." Jolin surprised herself, saying the words out loud. It was true, though. "Since the moment I saw you walking down the stairs."

"You're sweet."

"I've been saddled with a lot of very... *colorful* adjectives over the years, but that ain't one," said Jolin.

"Please, I'd say you're one of those 'gruff on the outside and soft inside' types," Isabella said. "Except you aren't, are you?"

"If I am, I don't mean to be."

"That's what I'm saying. You aren't that. You have the look, like you'd be somebody I should be scared of meeting in a dimly lit corridor."

"Oh...kay?"

"Shit. I never say anything right." Isabella sat up. "You're a mushy beefcake."

Jolin laughed. "That's another new one." She traced a circle pattern on Isabella's back, then tapped the center of it.

"I'm trying to say I felt safe with you," Isabella said. "That I wanted you the first moment I saw you, too."

"Was that before or after I stabbed your dad?"

"No, okay. I guess not the *first* first time. You were quite terrifying, covered in blood and raving about... well..." She trailed off.

"About my family," said Jolin. "It's fine. I feel like I made some peace with that, here with you. And, you know, everyone," she added quickly.

"You found a community," Isabella offered.

"Kinda, yeah. I don't do well on my own."

Isabella nodded thoughtfully, rubbing the back of her neck. "But what's that mean? What are we doing?"

"Do we have to be doing anything?" Jolin heaved herself up from the deck to join her, crossing her legs. She swayed a little as her vertigo confronted the mind-blowing emptiness of the universe, and scootched around to face away from the opening. "Can't we just be here, like this, for a little while, and not worry about what it means or what it's for?"

"Just..." Isabella closed her eyes. "I dunno. There's times when I feel like I'm alone on a dying planet. I love my parents; I'm proud to be on this ship. Daddy and I make a good life here, you know?" She sighed. "But that's the thing. What *is* it for?"

Jolin frowned. That was one question she had never known how to answer. Never much wanted to, either.

"And now *you're* here," Isabella added. "Mucking up the works. And I wanna leave, and stay, and do a dozen other things at once."

"There's time," Jolin said.

"But we're stuck here, Jolin!"

"For now. We'll be at Ganymede soon. And after that..."

"What? We figure it out?"

"I guess so." That was how Jolin lived. Figuring things out one day at a time. "It's worked so far," she muttered, only half lying. It *had* worked that way for a good long while, just floating from experience to experience; job to job. But what do you do with yourself when the fragile world you've built shatters, and the air you breathe is sucked into the void?

"I can't live like that. I need a plan, which is what I've been missing the last year. The last several years." Isabella hugged her knees with those long arms and stared pensively out into space. Wistfully, even.

Jolin's stomach fluttered. "How do you do that? Just... look at it like that."

Isabella glanced at her. "Look at what?"

"Nothing. The universe. It's all out there... just big and empty and forever."

"It's not empty, Jolin. It's full of life and planets. And stars." She ran a finger over the flower embroidered on Jolin's coat, over her heart. "I know it is."

"Science has proved you wrong so far."

"Infinite time and infinite space." Isabella stood gracefully, stretching her back. "We're just in the preamble."

Blue lightning crackled as a meteoroid or space particulate skidded across *Syracusia*'s shields. The preamble, huh? Jolin forced herself to turn, to gaze out into the black absence of everything.

Isabella offered a hand and hoisted her to her feet, sliding her arm through Jolin's. "Something big is waiting out there. I really believe that."

"Waiting for who? Us?"

"Humanity. Everyone. Maybe not now, or a thousand years from now, but sometime. Before it's all over and the world turns to dust. We won't be alone anymore. Same as you and me."

"That's a fine sentiment, but it's awfully unlikely."

"Like a girl frozen in a capsule for six years somehow finding herself exactly where she needed to be?" Isabella squeezed her hand.

Since she put it that way... Jolin shrugged. "What, like destiny?"

"Don't be so full of yourself."

"You brought it up!"

"I just meant, if something like that can happen, can bring you and me together over so grand a distance of time and space..." Isabella's voice cracked, in the manner of someone facing an extraordinary sadness. But her simple smile had not faded. "Well, you know, maybe anything's possible."

"Maybe. But I don't believe in fate."

"Doesn't have to be destiny *or* fate. You being here gives me hope that it all isn't just random chance. That is what I'm saying."

"Yeah, sure. Maybe." Jolin's thumb pressed the sore spot on her wrist. It made sense, though not in the way Isabella intended. Was it really happenstance, her ending up here, now, and not floating alone in a pod until the heat death of the universe?

Isabella reached out a hand as if she would press it flat against the forcefield, only centimeters away from it. It would not shock her or anything, not if it was working properly, but the feeling was not exactly pleasant either. Like a punching bag full of ooblek. One of many unorthodox training methods she was taught by David Freeman during her years aboard the *Endless Star*.

Punch it hard enough, it becomes steel. Soft enough, it gives way like water. Learn to do both. Fond memories aside, Jolin had certainly never felt like touching the forcefield a second time. She flexed her fingers absently.

"Yeah, maybe," Isabella echoed. "All that stuff has been on my mind the last couple days."

"I'm glad you can share it with me," said Jolin, looking up at Isabella's face. How was she so tall?

"Me too." The younger woman's eyes searched Jolin's face.

"This reminds me of our first.... you know." Jolin fought the self-conscious urge to turn away. Her entire head was a bruised apple.

"On the station?" Isabella asked. She did not seem to notice those glaring imperfections.

"Nothing between us and the edge of forever but a flimsy little forcefield." Jolin wrapped her arms around Isabella's waist.

"I think I recall it," Isabella said. "Remind me?" Her lips curved into a mischievous smirk.

And then they kissed. Long and slow and absent eagerness or youthful expectation. Jolin's eyelids closed as Isabella cupped warm hands around her face, the touch pulling her in with effortless strength.

Is this what love feels like? thought Jolin, as if she did not already know the answer. She folded herself into the moment, her spirit bound by a golden thread lifting her up past darkness, past the fear and doubt she had only begun to overcome—despite her words. Eyes tight, Jolin relaxed her grip on idle worries and emptied herself into Isabella like a drink offering to the old gods.

There was only this warmth, forever.

"Holy shit," she managed when they finally separated.

"You're good at that," said Isabella, a bit breathless herself.

"I, uh..." Jolin stammered. The curve of her cheekbones. Those radiant eyes and glistening lips. Time seemed to shimmer and stretch.

"You know," Isabella said at last, breaking the spell. "I've never been to Ganymede before."

"Wow," Jolin murmured as the warmth receded. Not fully, though; as if something in her chest had been irrevocably changed. Uncertainty replaced with... "Wait, really?"

"Well, to the stations obviously. A few times. But down on the planet? To Galileo? I'm excited to see it."

"It's a hell of a town," Jolin said. "Like it's built of ice knives, but deep down beneath all that is a neon bum rush of things to do. Concerts, bars, comedy shows, illegal fight clubs, legal fight clubs, chess bazaars, sex dungeons, dung sections."

Isabella grinned. "Mostly I'm hoping they've got what we're looking for. A way to find Violet."

Jolin extricated her arm and took Isabella's hand. Beneath her feet, the deck trembled as *Syracusia*'s engines rumbled to life. One final burn to set their trajectory toward Ganymede orbit.

"They will," she whispered. The stars wheeled soberly, almost imperceptibly, and the discomfort in Jolin's stomach melted away. She had what she needed for once. Maybe. Pulling the other woman close, Jolin nestled herself into Isabella's embrace. "They have everything."

About the Author

Jaye Ephen writes from Kansas City, accompanied and supported by a patient spouse and one very old dog. Thanks for reading.

www.AvengeTheStars.com

Content Warning

This is a safe space. And as such, I want to list a few things to be aware of if you prefer to avoid stories about or containing certain themes, situations, or anything else.

This book contains...

Spoiler Free Version
Moderate violence, foul language, depictions of grief and trauma, and mild sensuality.

FULL SPOILER VERSION
Violence including: Stabbing, choking, shooting, neck snapping, and tendon slicing. Consensual romance and physical intimacy between queer women, non-explicit. One inferred threat of sexual violence. Extensive thematic exploration of grief, loss of family, and death. And no, the love interest does *not* die, even though it looks at one point like she might.

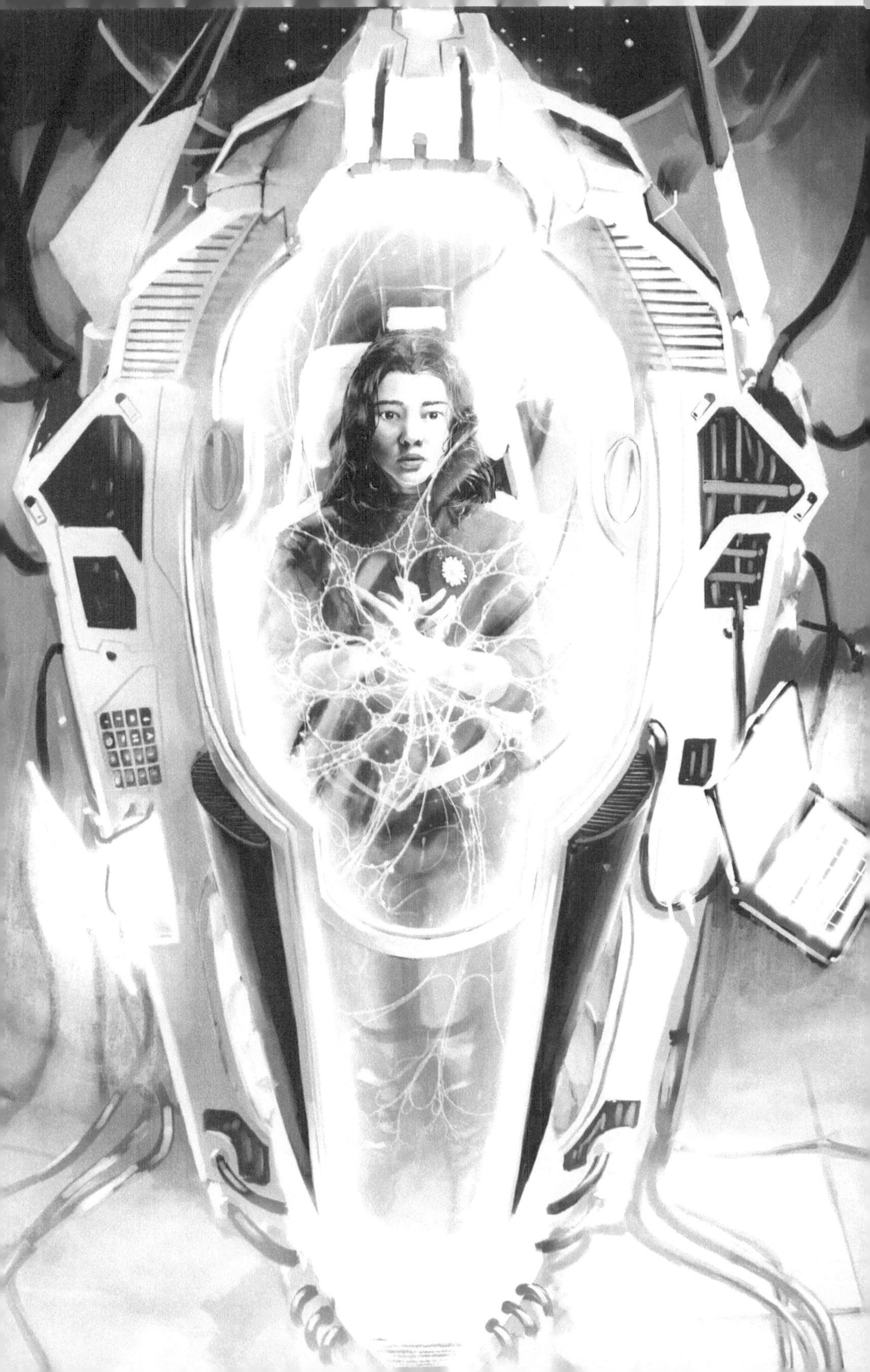

ODETTE.A.BACH

SEE YOU SPACE LESBIANS...

www.ingramcontent.com/pod-product-compliance
Lightning Source LLC
Chambersburg PA
CBHW051223130726
47988CB00001B/198